KU-224-910

'A fascinating autobiography which has also gained a new topicality ... highly gripping and entertaining.' *Birmingham Post*

'The story of a young girl's courage and perseverance against adversity ... warm-hearted and excellent.' *Manchester Evening News*

By the same author

HELEN FORRESTER

A CUPPA TEA AND AN ASPIRIN

HarperCollins*Publishers*

HarperCollins*Publishers*
77–85 Fulham Palace Road,
Hammersmith, London W6 8JB

www.harpercollins.co.uk

This paperback edition 2004
1

First published in Great Britain by
HarperCollins*Publishers* 2003

A catalogue record for this book
is available from the British Library

ISBN 978-0-00-777077-9

Typeset in New Baskerville by
Palimpsest Book Production Limited, Polmont, Stirlingshire

Printed and bound in Great Britain by Clays Ltd, St Ives plc

For Vivien Green,
with much gratitude

AUTHOR'S NOTE

The author would like to thank sincerely her editors, Nick Sayers, Jane Barringer and Jennifer Parr for their support and sound advice while she was writing this book.

The book is a novel, not a history. Though the dreadful slums of Liverpool did exist, the care Home was a figment of the author's imagination, as were the characters who lived or worked in these places; whatever similarity there may be of name, no reference is made or intended to any person living or dead, except for the well-known historical figure of Lee Jones and his wonderful work on behalf of the poor of the city which form a small part of the background of the book.

When the going gets tough,
the tough make tea

Anon

PROLOGUE

'I Look Proper Awful Without Me Gnashers'

1965

'Angie! You mean you don't know what a court is?' In disapproval, the old woman's lips pursed over toothless gums. She stared in genuine shock at the uniformed nursing aide who was slowly tucking in the sheets at the bottom of her bed. 'Really, nowadays, you young folk don't know nothing about nothing.'

'It's true, I really don't know, Martha, unless you mean a magistrates' court?'

'Tush, I don't mean a court up steps like that,' retorted Martha irritably. 'I mean a place where you live. Like a house.'

The aide smiled absently, her black face not unkind. She did not answer. Working in a crowded old folk's Home, she was used to being scolded

1

by the fifty-eight elderly, bedridden women and five equally incapacitated men, for whose daily care she was largely responsible; that is, being scolded by those who could speak. Some of them were the impotent victims of stroke, supposed to be turned every two hours and have their dirty nappies changed; and what a hopeless instruction that was: there simply wasn't time. Its frequent omission accounted for the strong smell of old urine in the room and for the cries of misery from patients because of bedsores.

Opposite Martha's bed, two women suffering from dementia were tethered to their beds. They chattered inconsequentially to themselves most of the day, their minds wandering – and God help me, thought Angie as she shook up Martha's pillow, if they ever get loose: I'd be fired by Matron, sure as fate. Between the door and the dementia patients lay a victim of stroke, able only to grunt when she wanted anything.

In the bed next to Martha lay poor Pat, another bundle of helpless skin and bone. To Angie, the look of impending death was clear on her face, and she had already anxiously reported this to Matron. With a grim smile, Matron had assured the nervous aide that she was overreacting, as a result of her inexperience in nursing: the woman had seemed normal for her condition, when she had toured the ward two days before.

Angie had made no reply – she needed to keep her job. In her native Jamaica, rent by civil strife and surrounded by hunger and disease, she had seen so much of death. She certainly did not lack experience, she thought angrily.

For ten hours out of the twenty-four, all the patients were largely dependent upon Angie. Two other nursing aides, Dorothy and Freda, also from Jamaica, covered respectively the early morning and evening hours. A retired Irish nurse, Mrs Kelly, also working alone, cared for them from midnight to four in the morning, and there were many ignored complaints from patients at her inability to cope with their needs for bedpans or glasses of water.

The patients were either without family, or they were aged relatives of poverty-stricken local families who could not care for an invalid. Once they arrived in the nursing Home, Matron assumed that they were all uniformly permanently incapacitated. Some, like Martha Connolly, however, had suffered a broken hip or similar and might have hopes of being restored to health, if appropriately treated.

Matron was keen to retain patients like Martha, who, after the first few weeks, needed little care.

Because they could do many things for themselves, they enabled her to keep her staffing costs low.

Uncouth, coarse Martha Connolly, Bed 3, Room 5, daughter of the Liverpool dockside, knew that she was not totally disabled. But she had had to agree with Matron's sharp assessment that, if she tried to walk, she was liable to falls. She must, therefore, remain in bed unless an attendant was in the room to escort her.

Without any visitors, who might have spoken up on her behalf, unable to read or write, she knew herself to be stranded, just a numbered bed, her humanity forgotten.

Since all the aides were grossly overworked, she did not get much exercise. Her chart said that she was sixty, which was no great age. But her thin wispy hair was white, her back was humped and, at times, her mended hip hurt sharply. On the rare occasions when she was allowed out of bed, she had, until recently, used a stick. Her empty days dragged on from meal to meal, with nothing to alleviate their dreadful monotony.

'Sometimes, I want to scream and scream,' she once told Angie.

Angie smiled. 'Well, don't,' she advised. 'Matron might hear you. And she'd make you take a pill to quiet you.'

Fear crept up Martha's back like pins and needles. The warning was justified. She had seen other patients drugged into silence.

One day, boiling with rage at Matron's studied disregard of anything patients said to her, she had furiously brandished her walking stick at her. Matron hastily snatched it from her, and took it away to be safely stowed in her office. Since then, Martha had not had any exercise.

Better for her to be here, Martha had decided gloomily, rather than being left, as she had been found, hungry and with a broken hip, lying in the unheated hallway of an old house by the Herculaneum Dock.

She had been lucky that the rent collector had found her. When there was no answer to his pounding on the door, he had decided that she might be in but hiding from him, in the hope that he would go away: she was already behind with her rent.

He had knelt down to lift the flap of her letter box and peer through it. When he saw her curled up at the bottom of the narrow staircase, he had immediately run to find the policeman on the beat.

With his own key to the house, the rent collector opened the door for the constable, an ambulance was called from the corner telephone box, and an exhausted, moaning Martha was taken to hospital.

After a spell in hospital, she had been discharged to this old folk's nursing home, she had told Angie, because she had no one to care for her.

As Martha scolded Angie for her ignorance of the infamous Liverpool court system, she became quite animated, and heaved herself painfully into a sitting position, to better lecture her.

'You see, Angie, I were born in a court and so was me hubby; we lived in one till the war, so I know how dreadful they were.' She paused for a moment, and then said thoughtfully, 'It's funny, though, I never thought of them as dreadful in them days – they was just normal life.

'People what had never seen one usually denied they existed – 'cos they didn't want to know. We was a family of eleven living in one room.

'There's people, even now, as don't believe any-body's starving or living with at least half a dozen other people in one room – 'cos nice people don't want to know.'

From her own experience, Angie knew about people who ignored the misery of others, and she nodded agreement, while Martha paused to instruct her fretfully, 'Don't tuck me feet in so tight. I get cramp, you know that.'

'OK,' Angie replied easily, in her strong Jamaican accent.

Martha repeated vehemently, 'People don't want to know anything as makes them feel uncomfortable, 'cos then they might have to do something about it.' She went on to explain how men like her husband, employed on the docks, had to live within walking distance of them.

''Cos, they was casual labour and had to sign on for work twice a day, wet or fine, you see. So houses was built in courts, to cram as many into one acre as they could – and to cram as many people into each house as you could find a piece of floor for them to sleep on. As close to the docks as they could, like, so they could walk to work in a few minutes.

'All you could see from the main street was an archway, and, if you went through that, you come into a little paved yard. It had eight or ten houses in it.

'There was two privies at the far end, against the back wall of the next court, and they had to do for all of us.'

She chuckled suddenly, and then added, 'There was often a proper rush on them, specially in the mornings.

'For years, there was near thirty people in our

house alone. That were nothing like as bad compared to them that lived there fifty years ago, when I were a little girl.

'There was a pump in the middle of the court, so as we could get water – and you often had to queue for that, too.'

She sighed at the recollection of carrying water for eleven people into her family's room.

Then, as Angie, astonished at such a lack of lavatories, paused in her tidying of the room, Martha continued, 'Each house had three storeys and a cellar, two rooms on each floor. And at the top there was an attic.

'Back rooms had no windows, of course – because their back wall was the back wall for another court's houses behind ours, you see.

'Because the houses was in two rows facing each other, with the two lavatories across one end, it meant that we was walled in. Only the front rooms had windows – looking onto the court.

'The main catch about living in our court was that there was a family in every room,' Martha went on, the words dragging out of her, as she realised that Angie was beginning to lose interest.

'You was never alone, Angie, and it was so cold in winter. The back rooms, as well as not having windows, didn't have no fireplaces either. So even if you could buy coal it wasn't no good.'

'It sounds awful,' replied Angie politely. She did not mention that her own current accommodation was not much better. Instead, she sighed wearily, as she took a quick peek behind the curtain which surrounded Pat's bed. The curtain had been drawn round her because the doctor was expected to come later in the week to see her, thank goodness; Matron had, at last, taken notice of the aides' reports on her.

'It was hell!' went on Martha forcefully. 'And yet, you know, I was often happy then. The neighbours was wonderful – good, solid friends.'

Angie could not think of a suitable reply to this confession. She did her best, however, to provide an understanding smile. She knew she would miss her tea if the old bird didn't stop talking soon.

Martha sighed. She felt that she was as good as in prison. She was never taken out. She had never even been into the garden surrounding the old Victorian house, a garden which she was allowed to look out on only when she was moved into a chair by the window, while Angie changed her sheets each week.

Matron seemed to imagine that clean sheets were the most important thing you could want, and that if something to eat was brought to you three times a day and you had a bath and a shampoo once a week, that was all you needed in life.

Martha grimaced. A fat lot she knew; the frantic aides often skipped both bath and shampoo.

But where had real life gone to? Where were the family, the visiting priests, the well-meant visits of amateur social workers, the busy streets, the cars, trams and lorries making pandemonium, the cries of the stallholders in the market, the children all pestering her at once, the family rows, the trips to New Brighton, the colossal fights after the football finals, when everyone got drunk down to their last penny, the interesting gossip with friends she had known all her life, the comfort of a Saturday night pint at the local, the weddings and wakes, the processions on holy days, the men tipsy and longing for you of a Saturday night?

All gone, slowly slipping away through two generations in the turmoil of the war and its aftermath – and no hope of their return, she decided mournfully. Instead, only a clamour of angry young people who did not know what suffering was, all of them wanting things – tellies and phones and expensive blue jeans and fancy kitchens and bands what made a racket like you'd never believe. I wants, she called them.

'Bring us a cuppa tea, Angie – when you've had yours?' she whined.

The aide nodded conspiratorially, and fled: the patients were supposed to wait for tea until it was served with the last meal of the day. Martha always received a clandestine mugful from Angie, however, because no other patient in the room had a clear enough understanding to demand a cup of tea for herself.

Angie, thanks be, was proper kind to her, Martha decided; she risked Matron being real mad at her if she found out about the illicit cup of tea: she was certain that Matron would consider it to be a wilful waste of tea.

Most of the time, Angie was the only person Martha had to talk to, and now, as the girl went for her meal, an anguished sense of loneliness, of desertion, crept slowly over her. She began to cry hopelessly, allowing the tears to run down her face unchecked.

'Jaysus, how can I bear it?' she muttered.

Absently, she took her rosary out from under her pillow. Other than her artificial teeth sitting in a glass of water beside her bed, which she always referred to as 'me gnashers', it was the only personal possession she still had: she did not feel that the teeth, provided through the National

11

Health Plan, were really hers, though the dentist had assured her that they were.

Except for the rustling movements and mutterings of the other patients in the small room, and a distant tinkle of china and teaspoons, there was no sound.

'Dear God Almighty, how do I get out of this place?' she prayed without hope. 'I might as well be dead.'

Then she asked herself in despair, 'And, come to that, if I ever get out, where can I go?'

She could not answer her own questions.

While she waited for her cup of tea, she lay with the rosary in her hand. Then she ran her fingers along the familiar beads.

'Hail, Mary, full of grace,' she began. At least, in your loneliness, you could talk to the Holy Mother, she sobbed to herself. Even if she never replied, her silence did not mean that she hadn't heard you.

ONE

'He Were an 'Ero That Day, He Were.'

April 1937

Mrs Martha Connolly, wife of Patrick and purveyor of clean rags in the city market, sometimes remarked that she did have one lucky strike in her life, although she was not too sure even about that – in the end, she felt, it just seemed to mean more worry and more work for herself. The lucky strike was that her husband Patrick, though only a casual dock labourer at the time, was a good swimmer.

'Anyways, he were an 'ero that day,' she would boast proudly to her friends.

In explanation to less well-informed friends, she would say reflectively, 'He were a lively lad. He swum in the canal ever since he were a kid, and won a few races in his time. It isn't his fault that he never had a trade. He had to start earning a living the day

13

he were twelve – or he'd have starved. So he took what there was – he went down to the docks with his dad and he's been there ever since, poor lad.'

After she married him, she ruminated, he had kept up his skill by swimming in the nearby Wapping dock, if there were no ships tied up in it.

Both of them knew that such trespassing was illegal, but she never said a word to anyone about it, because it was such a welcome relief to him after working in claustrophobic warehouses or ships' holds, or from the fetid confinement of their over-crowded, noisy court dwelling: from her point of view, it was much better than his getting drunk with his pals in the Baltic or the Coburg.

The dock master and the other men working the dock knew his face. They never attempted to stop him unless there was a boat coming in to berth, in which case, they would warn him for his own safety. But in the depth of the Depression of the 1930s boats were few and far between.

One fine Tuesday morning in April, however, instead of trying for work or swimming in the dock, he was hanging around the Pier Head for another reason, while at the same time watching the ferries come and go across the river. On Sundays, during good weather, watching the river traffic was a popular after-church occupation for Liverpool people.

On this weekday, however, there was an unusually large crowd, because HMS *Ark Royal* was being launched from the other side of the river: the Pier Head was a perfect place from which to view it. Chances of getting any work, he had decided, were remote, and his Sundays off would never offer such a good spectacle as the launch of a big ship. Better, by far, to be present at this historic occasion.

He made the excuse to himself that his back hurt abominably from a particularly heavy job he had done the previous day: working today would only make the pain worse. He hoped that Martha would never find out that he had failed to go to the stand, as usual, in hope of getting work.

On Sundays, if he did not go down to the Pier Head, he preferred to lie on the old mattress on the floor of the family's single room. There, he rested and enjoyed the rare quiet, while Martha herded six of their nine children to the nearby church. As a live-in servant, Lizzie usually attended the church closest to her employer's home; Colleen, aged ten, lay fighting tuberculosis of the hip in Leasowe Children's Hospital, far away on the other side of the River Mersey; and James, little Number Nine, was babysat by their neighbour, Mary Margaret, who lived in the back room upstairs.

Nowadays, Mary Margaret always said she coughed

too much to be welcome at Mass – the noise disturbed the praying. But, in truth, though she loved the glittering little church with its theatrical service, she no longer had the energy to walk that far.

This particular Tuesday, amongst the many others strolling up and down or waiting for the launch, Patrick recognised a well-known city councillor. Most Merseysiders had seen his ruddy, moustached visage more than once in either the *Evening Express* or the *Liverpool Echo*. He was a man much given to noisy controversy on any subject which might give him publicity and convince Liverpudlians of his care of their city.

Outstanding in a crowd of mostly thin people, the councillor's well-padded frame, encased in a three-piece suit, with a bowler hat rammed firmly on his head and a walking stick beneath his arm, suggested a successful man well content with himself.

His dirty macintosh flapping in the wind, Patrick watched him with the lazy indifference of the unemployed and hungry, as the floating landing stage heaved gently beneath their feet.

He was standing near the end of the stage, where a small private yacht with a broken mast had been temporarily moored: he had wandered over to look at the little craft. The councillor reached the end of his stroll at the same point, but, before turning back, paused beside him to peer down at the stricken boat.

'Must've got caught in last night's storm,' he remarked to Patrick, as he turned to view him with friendly condescension.

'Oh, aye,' replied Patrick. 'Real bad, it was.' He was not interested enough to continue the conversation, or to warn the stupid man when he unwisely stepped over the guarding chain to look more closely at the little yacht.

While docking, a ferry bumped into the floating stage. The stage gave an unexpectedly big heave. The councillor staggered, failed to regain his balance, stumbled over a mooring rope and with a mighty plop fell into the river.

Patrick stared dumbly as the water settled again. Then the councillor, his bowler hat bobbing slowly downstream, came spluttering to the surface.

It became obvious to Patrick as the man floundered that the councillor could not swim. The current began to push the struggling man away from the stage, and, before going under again, he screamed for help.

Patrick swore to Martha, afterwards, that he did not plunge in to save him because he was a councillor and therefore important.

'Might've left the silly bugger to fend for hisself, if I'd remembered,' he told Martha scornfully. 'What use is he to folk like us? And him a Prottie, too.'

But Protestant or not, he did instinctively plunge in to rescue the drowning man. A few powerful strokes and he caught him by the collar of his jacket. He shouted to him to stop struggling, but it took a second or two for the instruction to penetrate. Then, to Patrick's relief, the councillor obeyed.

Swimming on his back, Patrick began to tow him towards the landing stage.

The current was against them and it took all Patrick's strength to make headway towards the stage, where, as the accident was noticed, there was sudden activity.

With one hand Patrick finally managed to grab a hold on the gunwale of the little yacht.

As a crowd of helpers rushed to the edge of the stage, all shouting advice at once, the yacht threatened to turn over. One would-be rescuer with more sense threw a life buoy with a rope attached to it.

The current pushed the buoy away. A swift jerk brought it closer, and Patrick and the terrified councillor thankfully grasped its looped ropes.

In addition, a small rowing boat nudged at

18

Patrick's back, as its owner shipped his oars. Breathless after his quick row towards them, the rower gasped encouragement to both men to ''Old on, there, na. Seen you dive in, I did. Soon get you out.'

With the aid of an assortment of idlers, the city councillor was roughly heaved back onto the landing stage, while a panting Patrick hauled himself out.

Sitting on the edge of the stage, Patrick wiped the water from his face with his hands. Then he took his boots off and emptied the water out of them. He examined them ruefully. 'Should have took them off,' he muttered to himself. 'Nobody should try swimming in boots.'

Reclining on the stage, supported by two friendly ferrymen, it seemed as if the councillor spat up half the Mersey River before both he and Patrick were escorted into the nearest warm place, the Pier Head teashop.

The sopping wet councillor was soon seated in the tiny café. A mug of hot tea was immediately proffered him by the startled woman in charge; she kept asking no one in particular, 'Whatever happened to him, poor bugger?'

Near him stood the owner of the little rowing boat, who had helped to push the pair of them up out of the water. He was nearly as wet as the other two.

In the opinion of the boat owner, this chap in a three-piece suit was obviously a Somebody. Though he did not recollect who he was, it seemed likely that he might receive a decent tip for taking care of a Somebody. So he paid the penny for tea for him, in addition to a mugful for himself.

All attention was focused on the councillor and on the boat owner standing close behind him. It did not occur to anybody in the small crowd of interested onlookers, amongst whom stood the penniless Patrick, boots in hand, that he, also, might be glad of a hot cup of tea; or might even like the chance to mop the water out of his hair with the dish towel quickly produced for the councillor's use.

While his ruined suit still dripped mournfully over the bare wooden floor, the councillor, aware of who had really rescued him, groggily thanked Patrick. Then, after a moment's silence, he asked what he could do for him in recompense for his remarkably quick deliverance from drowning.

'You could have lost your own life – that current is deadly,' he added, with a hint of respect in his voice.

Looking like a sewer rat newly removed from a

drain, Patrick stared at him, nonplussed. He had lost his cap and scarf to the river, and his ill-cut hair draggled over his eyes and down the sides of a gaunt face blackened from years of dust from a multitude of ships' cargoes.

With an effort, he tried to clear his mind. He wondered if the councillor would consider the replacement of his cap and scarf. Then, as he trembled with exhaustion, the very basic desire of his life swelled up in his mind and expelled any other consideration.

Why not ask? he thought. Why not?

He took a long chance, and whispered almost without hope, 'If you could get me a regular job, sir . . . if you could, sir?' His exhaustion made it difficult to speak.

It was like asking for gold, in a city with thirty-three per cent unemployment. But bearing in mind that this was probably his only chance to talk to a man who might be the equivalent of Father Christmas, he added hastily, 'And a decent place to live.'

The equally exhausted councillor blew through his lips, and his moustache dripped its last drip.

He turned to the woman behind the counter. 'Ask this man his name and address and write it down for me,' he ordered, in a voice still rather weaker than his usual stentorian tone. He turned to the boat owner, and added, 'And this man's, too.'

The boat owner smirked with satisfaction.

While the woman hunted in the pocket of her grubby apron for a nub of pencil and then in a drawer for a piece of paper, the councillor turned back to his rescuer and, with a wry smile, said to Patrick, 'Aye, that's an 'ard one, lad!' He chewed his lower lip for a moment and scratched his wet grey hair, while Patrick waited in almost unbearable suspense. Then he asked, ''Ave you got a trade?'

As a member of the City Council, he enjoyed, occasionally, being able to show a little munificence, and here he was, now, seated in front of a small crowd: a good moment. He'd be sure to get his picture in the paper; he had noted that a holidaymaker had leaned over the side of the tied-up ferry to take a snap of him, as he sat on the landing stage. Just now, he had seen the same man at the back of the crowd raise his camera to take another one. He would probably sell the pictures to the *Post*. Not exactly dignified, he considered, but to have it on the front page of a local newspaper would be useful publicity. And he might, at least, be able to get his rescuer a medal.

Because he had had no breakfast and felt faint, Pat badly wanted to sit down on a nearby stool. He feared to do so, however, because he might offend, by his disrespect, a man who was rich enough to own a gold pocket watch, which still dangled on a chain, secured to a button of his waistcoat.

'I'm a dock porter, sir,' he replied, shame-facedly.

'Humph. Casual? Unskilled, eh?'

'Yes, sir,' Patrick muttered. 'It's all I could get, ever since I were a kid.' Then, gaining courage, he added, 'But I'm strong, sir. I'm a hard worker.'

The councillor nodded, accepted a second mug of tea from the fawning boat owner, and drained it.

'That's a real problem,' he sighed. He was suddenly very tired. He wanted to go home. He glanced again at the forlorn wreck in front of him, and said with compassion, 'I'll do what I can, I promise you.'

'Thank you, sir.'

The councillor knew only too well what being a dock labourer entailed. Casual work was the curse of any port, a nightmare not only to dockers, but also to lorry drivers, warehousemen, victualling firms, anybody who served shipping. Owners wanted a quick turnaround for their ships, whether they were freighters, liners or humble barges; loading

23

and unloading must be done immediately by a readily available workforce, regardless of time of day or night: time and tides waited for no man – and demurrage was expensive. Once the job was done men were immediately dismissed.

For the dock labourers, it meant standing twice a day near a dock, hoping to be chosen for half a day's employment. Patrick stood at 7 AM and again at 1 PM in pouring rain, in broiling sun or on icy January days, waiting, just waiting to be called for about four hours of arduous work.

To draw attention to himself, he would call out his name from amid the jostling crowd. With occasional gifts of tins of tobacco or a packet of cigarettes, he greased the palm of a buttyman, who all too often ignored him and ran his own gang of favourites.

He tried also to be at least recognisable to the shipping companies' stevedores. When a ship needed a few more hands, over and above those gangs already chosen, this employee of the shipping company would go through the struggling, desperate mob of men, and, with supreme indifference, pick out the extra labourers as if they were cattle being chosen for market. When Patrick was lucky enough to be chosen, he worked steadily and mechanically, hoping that his face might be noted by the stevedore and that he would be chosen again.

His speed of movement did not make him popular amongst his mates. Some of them had a system whereby half of them took an hour off to rest while the other half worked, then vice versa. This doubled the hours of work to be paid for by the shipowner but, to the labourers, it was much less exhausting than doing the heavy work without breaks.

Sometimes, a few men would find an obscure spot in the ship or at the back of a warehouse, and settle down to play cards for half the day, their absence unnoticed amid the general mêlée of dozens of identical-looking labourers unloading a large ship. On paydays, they turned up fast enough to collect their unearned wages.

Even if the shipowners disapproved of it, Patrick was thankful for the rest system, which he felt was fair when doing such an arduous job. He never joined the card players, however, partly because it was blatantly dishonest, and, more precisely, because he was not good at such games and would probably lose most of what he was earning.

He preferred, if he had a few pennies, to play the football pools, where he stood a faint chance of winning thousands of pounds.

In addition, Martha never made a fuss about his playing the pools; like almost everybody else in the court, regardless of the pressing need to pay the grocery bill at the corner shop, she played them herself. Rather than confess this dereliction to the priest, she added an extra Hail Mary to the small penances he usually gave her for any other sins to which she owned up.

Even if he was given work, Patrick collected at the end of the week what could only be described as starvation wages. Or even worse, on mornings when he was not chosen, he would have to go home and admit his bad luck to a hungry wife and children, only to set out again to repeat the whole performance that afternoon.

And thanks to a huge birthrate in the city, thought the councillor as he drank his tea, and a constant migration of even more desperate men from Ireland, there was a great surplus of casual, and, consequently, most satisfactorily cheap, unskilled labour on Merseyside. This fact was not conducive to persuading many of the powerful business interests of Liverpool, or even its City Council, to study methods by which the system could be made more humane. The councillor had himself brought the matter up in council, but the dreadful Depression lying over the whole country made impractical his request for a committee to plan a better system in collaboration with reluctant employers.

Even after two mugs of tea, the councillor was still shivering with cold and delayed shock, so when the waitress handed him the paper on which she had written the addresses, he asked her to get him a taxi. She called a barefoot lad lurking nearby and sent him to find one.

Anxious to earn a quick penny for going to fetch the taxi, the child shot out of the little café and scudded up the incline to the street to hail one.

As they waited uneasily for the vehicle to arrive, Patrick felt that he could no longer stand around in his drenched state. Balancing shakily, first on one leg and then on the other, he put on his sodden boots. He forgot all about the *Ark Royal*, but the date of its launching reminded him for the rest of his life of the day he met a city councillor.

In an effort to be polite, he now said diffidently to the councillor, 'I think you'll be all right now, sir. I'll be getting home.'

TWO

''Aving a Good Natter with Mary Margaret'

May to September 1937

'And he missed the *Ark Royal*, he did; and nobody, except the councillor, give no thought to him at all, they didn't,' sighed Patrick's wife, Martha, to her friend and neighbour, Mary Margaret, while they sat on the doorstep of their court house.

They were warmed by a few rays of welcome spring sunshine, sneaking into the tiny court from between the chimney pots. It lit up Martha's dark visage and birdlike black eyes, and Mary Margaret's skeletal thinness, which was apparent even when she was wrapped in her shawl.

As they gossiped, Mary Margaret steadily hemmed a pocket handkerchief: on a protective piece of white cloth on her lap, she held a little pile of them, already finished. Beside her, Martha methodically tore up old sheets and folded them into small, neat squares; she would sell the squares to garage hands or to stallholders in the market, so that, from time to time, they could wipe their oily or bloody or fish-scale-encrusted hands.

A month after the rescue, they were once again mulling over Patrick's unexpected adventure with the city councillor – and, in more detail, his promise to help Patrick get a better job. Help had not as yet materialised.

'I suppose he must've forgot,' offered Mary Margaret.

Martha smiled wryly. 'Right,' she agreed, and then shrugged as if to shake off any wishful thoughts she might have about it.

Mary Margaret Flanagan and her family lived in the back room on the first floor of the crowded court house, in which the Connollys had the front room on the ground floor. She suffered from tuberculosis of the lungs.

Crammed in with Mary Margaret were her widowed mother, Theresa, her four children still at home, and her husband, an unemployed ship's trimmer.

Because of the lack of a window, her family lived, without much complaint, much of their lives in semi-darkness, relieved in part by a penny candle, when available, and the daily kindness of the two elderly women in the front room of her floor: Sheila Latimer and Phoebe Ferguson left their intervening door open, day and night, so that light from their front window could percolate through to Mary Margaret's room.

Sheila and Phoebe had been mates ever since they were tiny children. They had shared their sorrows through childhood beatings and sexual misuse, through marriages that were not much better, and, finally, when their husbands had been drowned at sea and their children were either dead or gone, the old chums had decided to live together.

From other inhabitants of the court, they endured a lot of jokes as to their sexual preferences, but they had been through so much together that they did not care. They were thankful for the luxury of a room to themselves, after their earlier experiences of being packed in with children, elderly relations and bullying husbands.

As paupers, they lived on Public Assistance, outdoor relief provided by the City. This, they both thankfully agreed, was a great improvement over the old days, when they could have been consigned to the bitter hardships and tight confinement of the workhouse. Now, as long as no one told the

Public Assistance officer about their working, they were able to earn illicitly a little more on the side, by picking oakum, which was used for caulking ships. The oakum picking meant they could buy a trifle more food, and it took them out of the packed house for most of the day. They considered themselves lucky.

Up in the attic, in a single, fairly large room under the roof, lived Alice and Mike Flynn, both of whom enjoyed a certain popularity in the court as a whole, Alice because she was easy-going and Mike because he had a radio.

Mike Flynn was a wounded veteran of the First World War. He had been paralysed by shrapnel in his back and had not been out of their room for years. He lay by the front dormer window, which looked out directly at the window of a similar house across the court. That was all he saw of the world, except for a few visiting birds. He occasionally put crumbs out on his tiny windowsill, which encouraged pigeons and seagulls to land and perch there unsteadily, as they jostled for position.

Mike had been given a radio by a kindly social worker, an ex-army officer. He said it kept him sane. The Flynns' greatest expense out of their tiny army pension was getting its batteries recharged.

The clumsy-looking box radio, however, brought

him unexpected friends. If he was feeling well enough, all the children in the house were welcome to come into the room to sit cross-legged on the bare wooden floor to listen, in fascinated silence, to the *Children's Hour*. It might have been broadcast from outer space for all the connection it had with their own lives, but they loved the voice which actually said 'Hello, children' and 'Happy Birthday' to them.

In addition, their fathers could, sometimes, get early information from Mike regarding the outcome of a football match or a horse race, on which they had bet. Mary Margaret loved nothing better than to listen to the distant music which drifted down the stairs into her room, though her husband, Thomas, grumbled incessantly about it.

Determined to see the bright side, patient Mary Margaret said frequently that it could be worse. The house was not nearly as crowded as it used to be, and, just think, they could be without a roof at all! Or she could be like the old fellow, who lived in the dirt-floored cellar, a cellar which had been boarded up by the City Health Authority as unfit for human habitation.

Martha's husband Patrick had helped the desperate old Irishman who now lived there to prise the door open.

'But it's an awful place to live,' Martha had protested. 'Every time it rains real hard, it gets flooded with the you-know-what from the lavatories, and then he's got to sleep on the steps.'

'He's better off in the court than in the street,' Patrick had argued, and Mary Margaret agreed with him. So Martha shrugged and accepted that you had to help people who were worse off than yourself.

On days when it did not rain, Martha Connolly, Alice Flynn, Mary Margaret Flanagan and her wizened mother, Theresa Gallagher, spent much of their time sitting on the front step, their black woollen shawls hunched round them, as they watched life proceed in the court. As the court was entirely enclosed by houses similar to the one they lived in, all equally crowded, there were plenty of comings and goings on which to speculate.

Until recently, they could have contemplated the midden in the centre of the court and the rubbish which was thrown into it, but the City had had it removed and replaced by lidded rubbish bins outside each house, which were not nearly so interesting to the many rats which infested the dockside.

The almost perpetual queue for the two choked lavatories at the far end of the court was a regular source of amusement. Each person stood impatiently, with a piece of newspaper in his hand, moaning constantly and with increasing urgency at the delay. On the filthy, paved floor of the court, the usually barefoot children of the Connollys and Flanagans relieved themselves in corners, and fought and played. The women intervened only when juvenile fights threatened to become lethal.

'If you don't stop that, I'll tell your dad,' the women would shriek. This awful threat implied a whipping with their father's belt on a bare bottom, so it was usually effective.

Ownerless cats and, occasionally, a stray dog stalked rats and mice; and the children found big, dead rats endlessly engrossing.

By the narrow entry from the main street, men stood and smoked and argued. They read a single copy of the *Evening Express* between them, in order to keep up with the racing news, and also to work on the football pools. Like a ship's crew, they tried not to quarrel, though not infrequently fist fights did break out. These scuffles, however, were more likely to occur outside the nearby pubs, when, drunk at closing time on a Saturday night, they were emptied out into the street, to be dealt with by the pair of constables on patrol.

Although it was remarkable how a rough kind of

order prevailed amid such a hopelessly deprived little community, the younger men enjoyed nothing more than a Saturday night fight, particularly if the two unarmed police constables got involved. It formed a great subject of conversation on a Sunday morning, as they nursed their aching heads and black eyes.

Within the court itself, a family row was high theatre, which brought almost every inhabitant out to watch. When a woman being beaten hit back, the female onlookers frequently cheered her on. 'Give it 'im, Annie – or Dolly – or May – love,' they would shriek, joyously adding fuel to male rage.

As the four women sat together on their step, they did not seem to notice the general stench of the airless court or the rarity of a single beam of sunlight. Only when it rained or was too bitterly cold outside, did they seek the lesser cold of Martha's room, which at least had a window – and a range which sometimes held a fire.

Martha was extremely protective of her frail friend, Mary Margaret. If she had a fire in the range, she would sit her close by it on the Connollys' solitary wooden chair. She would then boil up old tea leaves to make a hot drink for her, which she laced with condensed milk from a tin. To add to her warmth, she would, sometimes, wrap round her knees the piece of blanket in which her youngest child, Number Nine, slept at night; or she would pat and rub her back when she was struck with a particularly violent bout of coughing.

As they gathered on the step, after the rescue of the councillor, Martha continued her doubts about him.

'When we never heard nothing, Pat gave up hope, he did, 'specially when he saw the pitcher in the papers of the councillor and the boatman, and nothin' about himself. And us havin' to find him a new cap and scarf, an' all. He lost his old ones when he dive in. And his boots was finished.'

Mary Margaret sighed: the loss of a cap and scarf was indeed serious, the lack of strong boots dreadful.

'Never mind, love, he were a brave man to do what he done,' she soothed. She was one of those blessed people who travel without hope, and could not, therefore, ever be disappointed. 'You have to make the best of it,' she advised, as she always did. 'At least, neither of them got dragged under the landing stage by the current.'

'Oh, aye. If they had, they would have both been drowneded – and without our Pat, it would be the workhouse for us, no doubt about it.'

For a moment, both were silenced by their permanent dread of this fate, despite the recent provision of outdoor relief by the City's Public Assistance Committee. It was a traditional fear, which ranked close behind their horror of a pauper's funeral.

Summer turned to foggy autumn and still they heard no more of the councillor.

Patrick grinned cynically, when Martha brought up the subject. 'It's to be expected,' he told her. 'Why should he remember? Folk like us never waste our time voting.' He laughed. 'We don't mean nothin' to nobody.'

He continued his usual dockside waits for work; he knew no other world.

THREE

'We Buried Him With Ham'

October 1937 to March 1938

Influenza swept through the courts, and suddenly it was winter, that deadly bitter winter of 1937–1938, a time when lack of coal, lack of light, lack of medical attention and lack of food tested the courage of every man, woman and child: some of them simply gave up; as uninteresting statistics, they quietly died. They left behind them, however, consternation amid their myriad of dependants.

The stalls in the market were practically deserted, and Martha and the inhabitants of Court No. 5 were so desperate that they barely noticed, floating in the background, the black storm clouds of threatening war. All they cared about was how to stay alive each day, and, somehow, keep their big families going. In particular, if their husbands had survived the flu, the women sought desperately to find enough food to keep them fit for any work that might be available.

Two mothers in the next court died, leaving widowers with young children, some of whom also had the flu. This caused a flurried effort, even in Court No. 5, as a little food was collected to be taken in to the stricken families, to help until they could contact relations to come to their aid.

Local charities were besieged, their limited resources stretched. Women begged for coal to heat their freezing rooms, for a blanket in which to wrap a grandfather, for boots for their children's bare feet, even for pairs of woollen socks, anything woollen.

They especially needed more food, any kind of food. Rubbish bins behind restaurants were climbed into by men, more agile than women and accustomed to the awkwardness of ships' interiors. The contents of the bins were quickly picked through in the hopes of salvaging table scraps or unfinished cigarette ends. Street rubbish bins were, likewise, anxiously inspected.

Unemployment insurance, Public Assistance or the wages for casual labour all failed to yield more than bare existence, particularly in winters like this remorseless one, where coal was a grim necessity.

In Court No. 5, Mary Margaret's five-year-old younger son, Sean, died of the flu, and a number of others very nearly did. A Sister of Charity came to help the broken-hearted woman prepare the skinny little body for the ultimate insult, a pauper's burial: few in the court could afford to pay the Man-from-the-Pru sixpence a week for burial insurance.

Tear-stained Mary Margaret had not the strength to follow the little body to the cemetery: his grim, silent father, Thomas Flanagan, did, however, and watched it being thrown into a common grave.

Mary Margaret's tears overflowed again, when a neighbour remarked cruelly that the child's death was not all bad – it was one less to feed.

A week later, her eldest son, Daniel, a ship's boy, came home after a long voyage. She greeted him with both relief and joy. He had put on a little weight, though his face was pasty, and his voice had broken.

'You're my real big lad now,' she told him as she hugged him to her.

Best of all, he had a bit of money in his pocket. As a result, a good wake for his little brother was unexpectedly enjoyed by the whole building.

'At least we buried him with ham,' a weepy Mary Margaret announced with pride to her patient, oakum-picking friends, Sheila and Phoebe, in the adjoining room. With a sigh and a gentle pat of the hand, they agreed with her. Sometimes, kids just died and there was nothing you could do about it.

When all Daniel's funds had been spent on canned ham, fish and chips, and toddy made from smuggled rum, the songs and rueful jokes exhausted, Mary Margaret relapsed into an apathy broken only by her occasional fits of coughing.

Martha Connolly wished very much that she had a lad at sea. A boy at sea earned little, but you did not have to feed him while he was away. You'd be paying for his kit every week, of course, on the never-never system. But he would still make a few shillings to give to his mother, which she could spend on canvas plimsolls for some of her other children. She could even, perhaps, buy some black wool to crochet herself a new shawl – that would be nice, she considered wistfully – her current one was threadbare and there was no warmth in it. But her own needs were at the bottom of the list.

After Patrick's unexpected swim at the Pier Head in the milder days of the previous spring, when charities had not been quite so hard-pressed, it had taken her several days to prise out of one of them another pair of boots for Patrick. She had plodded through the narrow streets from charity to charity, begging for boots, so that he could once more stand at the docks, morning and afternoon, waiting for work.

She had endured long interviews in no less than three offices, during her quest, as she was redirected from one charitable organisation to another. Visits by voluntary social workers ensued, to make sure that she belonged to the clean, deserving poor and that her husband was not simply a lazy good-for-nothing. When the first visitor refused to recommend help for such a shiftless-looking household, Martha swallowed her rage as best she could: it was unwise to lose one's temper with Them.

It was clear to Martha that the second lady visitor, also, was completely overwhelmed by the sight of one small room filled with the impedimenta of daily life. It was cluttered with wooden boxes on which to sit, a pile of rags in a corner, presumably on which to sleep, and an old mattress leaning against a wall; even the mantelpiece was heaped with grubby rags. In the middle of the floor sat five children, shouting and arguing as they played with pebbles.

As she viewed the room, one small girl got up, hitched up her skirt to exhibit a bare bottom and peed into a bucket. Unconcerned at a visitor being present, she returned to the game. The outraged visitor turned and walked out. Her written report was damning about a mother who would so neglect a child's manners.

As she had walked through the court itself, the third visitor had heaved at the odour of the lavatories. Before knocking at the open door of the house, she wrapped her scarf across her nose and hoped she would not be sick. She gave the name of her charity and Martha asked her to come in.

She spent about one minute at the door, surveying nervously a room in which a number of children were quarrelling violently, striking out at each other with fists and bare feet.

Martha shouted angrily to her warring offspring, 'You kids get out – now! Or I'll tell your dad.'

The noise stopped. The children stared at the visitor. One of them sniggered. Martha belted her across the head and pushed her towards the door. The visitor hastily got out of the way.

Protesting and snivelling, the children shoved each other through the narrow doorway into the courtyard, where their original altercation recommenced.

The visitor swallowed. She took a notebook and pencil out of her side pocket. 'Now,' she said with false brightness through the thickness of her scarf, 'how many bedrooms do you have?'

Though used to the idiosyncrasies of visitors

from Them, Martha looked at the woman in amazement and wondered what relation bedrooms had to boots.

'We haven't got none,' she said slowly. 'We sleep here.'

'Where is your kitchen?'

Martha began to lose patience. 'This is our everything,' she said dully through gritted teeth.

'My God!' muttered the lady. She had read the Connollys' file before the visit. It had not registered with her that the room, described by an earlier visitor a few years previously, was the only room which the family rented. She was shocked by Martha's remark. The file had also given details of the family's financial circumstances and included some unkind remarks on the incompetence of the parents.

Martha passed wind, and the visitor looked round her a little wildly; the stench was unbearable.

She took a small breath, and then said, her voice faint, 'Tell Mr – er – um – Connolly to come to the office on Monday and we'll try to find a pair of boots which will fit him.'

She pushed past Martha and fled down the steps. As she passed the overflowing rubbish bins, her neat black shoes skidded on the ordure-covered paving stones. A couple of men idling at the entrance hastily made way for her, and she ran out onto the crowded pavement of the main street.

Gasping for breath, she wondered, as she turned to walk back to her office, how she could ever report such awful conditions and filthy people as suitable for aid; there was nothing to recommend them at all: they were neither clean nor respectable – nor trustworthy. She had feared that her pockets might be picked while in the court: she had not brought a handbag lest it be stolen.

But she pitied them. In a way, she understood their dilemmas. How could you get washed in a room full of people? With, at the back of it, another room opening into it, which housed another family?

If the Connolly man was to get boots on his feet, she must state, without even seeing the man himself, that he was worthy of them and was not likely to sell them.

In a wash of compassion and against her better judgement, that is what she did. And Patrick got his boots.

Martha breathed a prayer of thankfulness to St Jude, patron saint of lost causes.

At the first charity to which Martha had applied for boots, the volunteer who interviewed her and checked the Connollys' file had scared Martha nearly to death. She had remarked sharply, 'Your eldest son Brian is working, I see. That should be of help to you.'

Full of dread that the worker would tell the Public Assistance Committee that Brian was indeed working, Martha admitted that he was a butcher's errand boy. This fact had not been revealed by Patrick to the relieving officer. If he had done so, the officer would have deducted most of the boy's wages from the allowance or from the food vouchers they had sometimes to beg from him.

'He earns five shillings a week, but I've got to feed him and see he looks clean, like – it takes all he earns,' Martha explained patiently.

The interviewer looked at her with undisguised disgust; her toothless mouth, her face mahogany in colour from never having been washed, the vile stench of clothes never taken off and, under them, a body never bathed since birth.

It did not occur to the untried volunteer that cleanliness cost money: in her world, there were always towels, soap and hot water in the bathroom. She had yet to see a court.

'She asked me if I thought I was deserving of help,' Martha had wailed to Mary Margaret. 'Deserving? And me trying to make one egg stretch round six kids this morning, and little Colleen still sick in Leasowe Hospital and I can't even get to go and see her.

'And I didn't have much luck selling me rags in the market, this week, neither.'

She cleared her throat and spat onto the paving stones.

'As if it's our fault if there's no work and the men get drunk when they draw their unemployment or their Public Assistance or their wages. Wouldn't they need a little bit of somethin' to cheer them up if they was workless? Or a glass or two to ease their thirst, after all the sweat they lose when they do work?'

She glanced miserably round the darkening court. 'Do they think we enjoy it?'

Mary Margaret laughed weakly. 'Oh, aye. I think they do. They think that if we didn't like it, we'd leave it. Or if we weren't lazy, we'd clean it up.'

Martha looked at her aghast. 'And how do they think we'd do it with no water to speak of and the lavs spilling over all the time? And me broom is worn out. And if we leave, where are we going to go? I'd like to know that. We've got to be close to the docks for Pat and Thomas's sake.'

'Martha, love, they don't know nothin'. You have to go and tell them and hope for the best.'

'Well, I got the boots in the end,' Martha

responded, a hint of triumph in her voice. 'They're second-hand, and they're too big for him – he's got a wad of newspaper in them, so he don't trip up and have a fall. It's so easy to fall in a ship.'

Amongst the hapless community strode, occasionally, an elderly Catholic priest, his biretta crushed down on his bald head, his long black robes nearly brushing the filthy ground. Women were afraid of him, as were some of their husbands, because behind him stood the wrath of God, who did not like sinners who drank at the Baltic Fleet or the Coburg, or who had suspiciously small families which might indicate a form of birth control in use.

Yet, the priest and his assistant, Father James, were sorely grieved by the suffering they saw daily in their crowded parish, already famous as a surviving remnant of the worst slums in Britain. All they could do was to preach obedience to God's will, acceptance of the circumstances to which men were born, and the glories of the life to come.

Many of their male parishioners spoke disparagingly of them. But none of the women would hear a word against them. In their hearts, they rarely doubted the Church's teachings and they clung to them as the only ray of hope in their lives.

They dearly loved the younger priest, Father James, who was so gentle that some of the women thought he was a saint; and they loved and respected him as they would a saint.

Like most of her female neighbours, Martha often wept as she considered all the problems of her life, particularly in winter. Her feverish prayer, addressed to the Virgin Mary, was that she should not become pregnant again. It was surely sinful to beg such help from a Holy Virgin. But if She did not understand the affairs of women and how hard life was, who else was there?

Having her latest baby, little James, named after the priest, had left her feeling very exhausted. He was a sweet-tempered child and was known affectionately throughout the courts as Martha Connolly's Number Nine.

How Number Nine was surviving his infancy was a mystery to Martha. She had not been able to feed him herself, and he never really thrived on tinned milk; even now, with his second birthday coming up, he was nought but skin and bone and protruding stomach. But, then, life was like that. You couldn't do much about it: God sent children. But, sometimes, He also took them away again.

The Church said that nobody was supposed to love anyone more than God himself – and Martha felt uneasily that God might be jealous of her beloved Number Nine. In quiet moments in her busy life, she prayed almost daily that He would never take him.

FOUR

'I'll Take a Whack at the Lee Jones'

January to March 1938

In January of 1938 it was so cold that small boys and girls were able to make slides on the pavements. Frozen puddles were used as a base, and each child took a short run and then slid the length of the puddle, and gradually the slide lengthened to five or six feet. Though sometimes they fell, nobody seemed to get hurt and it was a marvellous way in which to have unexpected fun without skates.

Of course, adults whose balance was not nearly so good swore at them roundly as, hurrying along the pavement, they sometimes skidded and fell. Children who did not often laugh would shriek with merriment, as huge black skirts suddenly ballooned on the pavement or men ruefully rubbed their bruised behinds.

Men and boys who were able to obtain a pair of skates, no matter how ancient, skated on frozen ponds, and, as the exercise warmed them up, they temporarily forgot their hunger.

Though Martha's school-age children were usually kept home from school during such bitter weather, they could not play on the slide created outside the court's entry: they had only tattered canvas plimsolls or were barefoot. All of them were suffering from itchy chilblains on their heels and toes; some of these had burst open and had become infected. To wear any kind of shoe over them caused considerable pain.

They screamed when Martha boiled up one of the cleaner rags from her stock prepared for the market, wrung it out and slapped the resultant hot poultice onto an offending chilblain, to cleanse it by drawing out the pus.

Instead of being out in the street, therefore, the children were daily crouched together on the floor, in front of the small fire in the range in the Connollys' room.

It seemed to weary Mary Margaret that one of them, at least, would be grizzling miserably after Martha's poulticing efforts, and be told sharply by their mother, 'Shut up, or I'll give you something to cry for.'

This threat would reduce the whining for a little while, unless another child, in the confined space, accidentally knocked the treated foot. Then there would be howls of pain and an immediate exchange of blows between offender and offended. Martha would slap both, and further wails of woe would ensue.

During this winter, Martha unfailingly invited Mary Margaret, her mother, Theresa, and her children to share the warmth of the Connollys' fire, and Mary Margaret was extremely grateful for this. She dreamed, however, of having a room of her own with a fireplace or a paraffin heater; it would be so much quieter; and the more sickly she grew, the more she longed for peace.

She sat on the Connolly family's only chair, her sewing on her lap, as she hemstitched men's white handkerchiefs. Her daughter, Connie, was also kept out of school because she, too, had no shoes; nor had she a jacket to wear over her cotton dress.

Too young to go to school, Minnie tended to wander up to the attic to visit Mike and Alice. She was a welcome small diversion to the childless couple.

Pugnacious Dollie, her eldest, rarely joined them: she had plimsolls to wear and was hurried, protesting, off to school, just to get rid of such a quarrelsome child. But even she could not always face the cold outside without a jacket: she would dig her heels in, like a stubborn cat refusing to be put in a cage, and would sit sullenly on the house's staircase, until finally Martha would have pity on her and let her into her room.

If Martha did not seek the steamy warmth of the public wash house, in order to launder her rags ready for market, she usually sat on an orange box near the fire, with Number Nine on her knee.

By special arrangement as to which day it was to be, her rags were hung out to dry on the clothesline outside. The line belonged to the Flanagans' Auntie Ellen. It was stretched across the court from her house and was anchored to the wall of the Connollys' house. The cloths dried quite well even on a really cold day, but were a problem when it rained; at such times they were piled over a piece of string stretched across the range in Martha's room. Patrick always grumbled that their bulk took up far too much space.

As Mary Margaret chatted with Martha, she sewed with feverish speed, barely looking at her work as the needle flashed in and out.

When Dollie was present, she received, very reluctantly, a lesson in how to hemstitch: Mary

Margaret hoped that, soon, she would be adept enough to earn a penny or two by helping her. Connie, her second daughter, aged six and a half, was quite proud that she, too, could already thread a needle and do clumsy running stitches.

Even if they had boots or shoes, coats or shawls, few women or older girls ever joined in the sliding games; at best, they had babies to look after, food to find, rags to sell in the market or flowers or chewing gum to hawk at the street corners.

Looking like a series of waddling black turtles in their shawls, some older girls and women, like Sheila and Phoebe who lived in the front room on Mary Margaret's floor, trooped off to work at picking cotton or oakum. Others, like Mary Margaret, took in sewing to do as sweated labour in their homes: sewing men's cotton handkerchiefs yielded threepence a dozen; finishing buttonholes or decorative embroidery which needed more skill yielded a fraction more per piece.

The greatest problems of a woman who sewed white material was that she had to keep her hands clean and, also, own an iron in order to press the finished work: it had to be returned in a reasonable state to the man who employed her.

All the women in the court were acutely aware that, each day, pennies for food had to be found somewhere. In too many families, men smoked and drank regularly and women not infrequently: it was the only relief they had from the misery of their lives, lives which they regarded as absolutely normal, fixed and inevitable.

According to any one of them, the best you could do was to squeeze what you could out of the far distant world of Them. Unable to explain very coherently to Them the pressure of their days, they would sit meekly in front of a nurse or a nun or a social worker and accept the interviewer's assessment.

Behind the social workers' backs, Martha and Mary Margaret would laugh at their suggestions that, if they did not drink or smoke, they might save a little money to improve their lot. If their requests for specific help were refused, they simply begged somewhere else. In truth, the problems the women faced were so huge that it was beyond the scope of any individual to do much to right them.

Men put their small hopes on choosing a winning horse in the day's races or winning a game of pitch-and-toss – or the football pools. Unfortunately for their families, in the majority of cases they lost.

Martha thanked the Virgin Mary and the saints

regularly that Patrick did not drink his way through all the Public Assistance he received when out of work; he gave her at least half and shared his cigarettes with her. She screamed at him regularly for more. But in her heart she loved him and understood his need to get something for himself out of his thankless existence, even if he was at home on Public Assistance.

As a result of being kept out of school as a girl, to look after her siblings, Martha herself could neither read nor write. This put a severe limitation on how she could earn a living or understand what was going on in the world outside the confines of the waterfront. She trusted to the constant gossip in her little community to keep her informed on the latest news.

She would say determinedly to Mary Margaret or Alice Flynn or anyone else who would listen, 'You gotta get on with life.' And, with constant hefty sighs, she did.

She did her best to keep the family alive from day to day, and Patrick did his best to control his urge to hit her when she yelled at him.

It grieved her that this very morning, despite the bitter wind bringing warning icy blasts of cold into the court, Patrick had gone out, as usual, with only bread and a cup of tea in his stomach, to stand around in the open at 7 AM, waiting at a dock gate amid a crowd of others.

Amongst the rags for sale which she collected from better homes, from dustbins, or from the local pawnbroker as unsaleable junk, she had found a badly worn man's woollen pullover. Patrick had thankfully put it on under his shirt so that its disrepair did not show.

A little smile had broken the deep lines of his chapped face, as she had stood watching him pull it down and tuck it into his trousers. He sadly inspected the holes in the elbows and the ragged cuffs.

'It'll keep your chest a bit warm,' she assured him.

'Ta, ever so,' he said unexpectedly with a sly grin, as he reached for his grey collarless shirt.

As he tucked in his shirt, she saw for a moment the young man she had married. She thought how lucky she had been to marry a man who was often kind and rarely beat her, despite her own merciless nagging of him.

When he had picked up his docker's hook and had gone, she had sat by the fire on the orange box, nursing Number Nine for a few minutes. He had been fussing much of the morning, despite the piece of crust she had given him to chew. The boil he had on his bottom must be troubling him, she decided: he would feel better when it burst.

She wrapped her shawl round him, and he snuggled into her breast, but she was dry and could not feed him.

Finally, when he seemed a little comforted she let him slip down from her knee to join the other children.

Despite the cold, Kathleen had opted to escape to school, so Martha instructed Bridie, aged twelve, 'Now you mind him, and don't let him bother Auntie Mary Margaret. I'm going up to the Lee Jones.'

Bridie was deeply involved in a game of I Spy with Mary Margaret's girls. She looked up sourly through straggling rat tails of hair, cunning brown eyes gleaming as if she were about to say something vicious. But, after a moment, she silently shifted herself to make space for the child to sit by her; she then raucously rejoined the game.

Delighted to be included in a big girl's game, Number Nine joyfully tried to chant, 'Spy! Spy!'

Martha got up. Bridie was a real tartar. She wished, with a sigh, that her daughters were as passive as those of Mary Margaret – except for Dollie, of course. Dollie was like Bridie, a proper cross for any mother to bear.

She took a large metal ewer from a corner and screwed its lid on tighter to make sure it still fitted. Then she said to Mary Margaret, 'I'm going to have a whack at the Lee Jones. See if I can get some soup. Where's your jar? I'll try to get some for you.'

Mary Margaret nodded and ordered, 'Our Connie, you go and get it – it's in the wooden box.'

After several wails from the upstairs room of 'I can't find it, Mam,' and shouts of further direction from Mary Margaret, Connie came pounding down the stairs, and handed to Martha a big, old-fashioned sweet jar with a screw-on lid. Its exterior was still grubby from its previous visits to various soup kitchens.

'Soup?' she inquired hopefully, pale-blue eyes wide.

'Can't promise, love. They may run out.'

Connie was not yet seven years old, but she already understood the power of Them. They were people who decided how your life would be lived. They themselves lived in faraway parts of Liverpool called Princes Park or Orrell or even further away in places called Southport and Blundellsands. Sometimes they lived across the river, and you could watch them coming off the ferries each morning, to work in the big buildings by the Pier Head. One of the buildings there always seemed special to her;

it had two huge dicky birds perched on the top of it, and she dreamed that, one day, she might travel on the ferry and have fancy clothes and a fancy job in that very building.

As she quietly handed the jar to Martha, she reflected that They did sometimes give you bits and pieces to help you out – but not always.

At Martha's remark, her face fell, and Martha chucked her under the chin. 'Cheer up, chick. Auntie Martha'll do her best for you.'

But Connie did not smile. With the back of her hand, she simply rubbed the mucus off the end of her nose and turned back to the fireplace, to rejoin the game of I Spy. Connie was learning, slowly and reluctantly, the deadly acceptance of life that her mother had.

To facilitate transporting the ewer and the big jar, Martha stowed them in an old perambulator, kept in a recess behind the building's front door. It was very difficult to get the pram in or out of the recess without opening the door of her own room to make enough space, so it was fairly safe from theft.

The pram was the most useful possession she had; it not only carried Number Nine, Ellie and Joseph whenever she had to take them out, but it could hold a hundredweight of coal or a pile of old bedding bought for tearing into rags. Without it, she knew she would find it difficult to function.

She bumped the pram down the front steps, lifted her shawl over her head and went out to face the elements and the world of Them.

FIVE

'Me Pore Feet'

January 1938

The water in the freezing puddles squished through the cracks in her boots, as she trudged slowly up to Limekiln Lane, the site of the office of Lee Jones' League of Welldoers. She had not recently approached the League for help and she hoped that she would not be noticed as a regular beggar: she had learned from experience that one should not go too often to the same place; they got tired of you.

If the League's premises had been closer to her home, she would have sent the younger children themselves to beg a meal; they would almost certainly have been fed. But there was food for Patrick, Brian and Number Nine to think about, too; the weather was so bad that she feared that they might become ill if they did not get something hot to eat:

Tommy and Joseph were already coughing badly, and all the children were snuffling with colds.

Like Patrick and the children, she had chilblains on her heels; they seemed more than usually painful today, and she muttered, 'Christ, me pore feet!' as she trod on a cobblestone and the frayed lining of her boot caught the sore spot. She would give a lot, she thought, to have a thick pair of socks to cushion them.

As she plodded along, she sighed one of her gustier sighs. If she did not count little Colleen in hospital in Leasowe, there were eight people ahead of her in the family, all of whom could do with socks. Patrick was always the first to get them, also the first to be fed – because he was the breadwinner, or was supposed to be, thought Martha with sudden asperity, as she considered her own ceaseless efforts.

Woollen socks wore out so quickly, she would moan to Mary Margaret, and, though she could darn, she did not always have wool to do so.

As she approached the Lee Jones' League of Welldoers' shabby brick building and saw the length of the queue, she quailed. Despite a cup of tea for breakfast and eating up a piece of crust that Number Nine had abandoned, she felt faint.

So great was the number of people lined up

patiently alongside the building's wall that a police-man stood there to keep order. It would be a long wait.

She went to the end of the queue and leaned against the wall for support, while she mechanically wheeled her pram backwards and forwards at her side, as if she were rocking Number Nine to sleep in it.

There were many charities in Liverpool which tried, each in its inefficient way, to ease the city's horrifyingly intense poverty. Unlike some other cities, the deprivation of its poorer citizens was blatantly obvious to the ladies who came in from the suburbs to shop and to the menfolk who had offices in the centre of the town.

In the heart of the city, the interfusion of the two streams of inhabitants, the poverty-stricken and the fairly well-to-do, was impossible to escape; it flowed through the shopping areas and then the business districts, flooded along the dock roads and the Pier Head. And many a kind soul tried to do something about it.

Amongst some of the upper classes, there was still, also, the latent folk memory that, if something was not done about the suffering, there might be a revolution – like the French one, with its nasty guillotine and baskets of bleeding heads.

Amongst the dreadfully poor, Lee Jones was, perhaps, the most beloved benefactor. It was said that he squandered nearly all his fortune in order to help, but hardly made a dent in the need. As few others did, he understood, also, that not only was food for the body needed, but also some happy times to lighten the burden of misery.

As she leaned against the wall, eyes closed, and tried not to faint, Martha remembered a day when he had brought into the court, on a wheelbarrow, a gramophone accompanied by records of popular songs. She smiled slightly, as she recalled with what enthusiasm she and her neighbours had poured out of the houses and nearly burst their lungs as they sang old Victorian music-hall songs along with the scratchy gramophone records. It had been a really good afternoon, with rays of summer sun creeping their way in between the close-packed housetops to light up the jolly faces.

Her Brian, now pedalling his way round delivering meat for the butcher, would still whistle the same songs as he went. The boy had been thankful, also, to join the boxing club which Mr Jones had started, to give the lads something to do of a Saturday morning. Now, though Brian had to work Saturdays, he still went to practise on a

Wednesday night. Patrick had said that Brian was good at it, Martha mused.

Real nice lad, our Brian, she thought. When delivering to houses which did not have distrustful cooks, who weighed in his presence everything he delivered to them, he would sometimes take a sausage or a chop from one of the white, loosely wrapped parcels, and secrete it inside his shirt.

When Martha made a half-hearted protest at its being theft, he would say stoutly that if she saw the pounds and pounds of meat which he delivered, she would know that it would never be missed. She would thankfully drop the rather black-looking offering into the soup pot.

Sometimes, on a Saturday night, when a bit of tripe or shin of beef did not look good enough even to go into sausages, Mr Beamish, his employer, would give it to him, with the strict admonition that it should be cooked immediately he got home. The two assistant butchers whom Mr Beamish employed would snigger as Brian wrapped the gift up, but the lad did not care – food was food.

The queue, mostly women, but with a few flat caps interspersed, shuffled along slowly. She moved with it, keeping her back to the wall for support, pushing the pram alongside her.

'Atternoon, Mrs Connolly,' said a cracked voice at her side.

Martha blinked in surprise, and made an effort to straighten up. The voice of the local illegal moneylender in a charity queue?

'Atternoon, Mrs O'Dwyer,' she responded cautiously.

She looked fearfully at the four-foot-high ancient crone, who was, equally, the bane and the person of last resort of all the housewives in the courts. She herself owed her a shilling from last Saturday. She had borrowed it in desperation. Patrick had had only two days' work that week, and she had not even bread in the house. She had agreed to repay one shilling and threepence for the loan by next Saturday.

Though the repayment was not yet due, a fearsome apprehension went through her. If she failed to pay this woman, her threats of disclosure to the relieving officer of undeclared earnings, or a hint to a husband that his wife was being unfaithful, whether true or not, or a whisper to an employer of a small theft, like Brian and his chops, could play havoc with a family.

There seemed to be nothing that she did not know, nothing that she could not use to coerce money out of petrified borrowers. What was she doing here?

Thoroughly enjoying her client's obvious fear, Mrs O'Dwyer grinned toothlessly. Martha's shocked expression was very satisfying to her: fear was part of her stock in trade.

She was actually hunting for a debtor who had vanished mysteriously while still owing her five shillings, a very big debt. It had occurred to her that the woman might, on such a bad day, surface at the one place where she was likely to get food, the Lee Jones. She had not had any luck, but had decided, since she was there, she would beg a meal for herself.

'Mr Connolly not doing so well, eh?' she inquired of the paralysed Martha.

Martha's hands under the ends of her shawl were like ice, and her feet in her sopping wet boots felt that they would never move again.

Holy Mary, help me, she prayed.

It did not occur to her that she need not answer the moneylender's question, that her polite salutation was sufficient. Her mouth opened and shut soundlessly as she groped for words.

She was saved by a sudden ripple of shuffling down the line. The policeman on duty shouted, 'Move along there, now.'

Like well-trained dogs on leashes, the patient queue wended its way slowly through a doorway and into a narrow passageway, where they were, at least, out of the wind and sleet. Martha quickly pulled the pram in behind her.

She glanced back and saw, with relief, that she was the last to be let into the passage. The money-lender was looking up sourly at the policeman, who was holding her back. Mrs O'Dwyer could not command any particular respect in a charitable organisation; she was merely another old woman who would be let in from the cold as soon as there was room.

Martha was greeted by a superb smell of cooking, and a smiling young woman who kept the applicants in single file as they surged down the passage. She then passed them to an older lady seated at a table. Their names and addresses, with brief reasons for their being there and the number in the family, were noted.

When Martha explained that she was trying to get something to eat for two big families, there was a pause, and she realised with a sinking heart that anybody could make that excuse in order to get a double ration.

'Me friend has the TB, Miss. It would be the death of her to come out on a day like this,' she pleaded.

'Is she a widow?'

The implication that Mary Margaret's husband could have come on her behalf silenced Martha.

She reluctantly muttered, 'No.'

She watched the lips of her interlocutor tighten, and wondered frantically if there was anybody among these charming-looking ladies who would understand that married men rarely came to such charities, unless they wanted something for themselves; it was the wife who scrounged, begged, borrowed or stole to cope with the needs of their huge families.

Yet another lady was called and a whispered conversation ensued. The new lady, elderly, dressed in black, ran her fingers through a card index as she checked on Mary Margaret's name. The card evidently told her something more than the name. She looked hesitantly at Martha. Then, with genuine pity at the sparrowlike creature before her, she said, 'We'll make an exception today – the weather is terrible.'

Martha's eyes filled with tears. She said with genuine feeling, 'God's blessing on yez, Miss.'

The lady smiled at the weeping woman, and said, 'I hope times get better for you soon.'

In relief, Martha cried quietly to herself most of the long way home. In the pram, she had the huge bath-water ewer and Mary Margaret's jar, both full of soup right up to their lids, and almost too heavy to lift. In addition, in big brown paper bags lay three two-pound loaves of bread, two for her own family and one for Mary Margaret's, and a pile of potatoes baked in their jackets.

The fact that the potatoes had been cooked told her that They understood the predicament of those who often had nothing with which to cook: no coal, no gas, no wood, no fireplace, no nothing.

Some of Them was real nice, she snivelled to herself. In her gratitude, she even forgot the excruciating pain of her chilblains.

SIX

'Stop It, or I'll Put the Boot to Yez!'

January 1938

As she carefully pulled the old pram up the front steps so as not to spill the soup, she could hear the ruckus in the house.

She quickly loosened her wet shawl from her head, and, with one elbow, pushed open her own door. She bumped into little Number Nine who was apparently bent on escaping into the court.

He looked up at her with a tear-stained face, and said thankfully, 'Mam!' as he hid himself in her skirts.

She pushed him off and shoved the pram over the sill. She hastily backed it through her own doorway and then heaved it forward to slot it into the hall recess. As the raucous racket within rose in intensity, her expression became grim. With great care she picked up the containers of soup; their comforting warmth penetrated her blouse.

Out of the corner of her eye, through the open door of her room, she could see that a full-scale fight was in progress between her daughter Bridie and Mary Margaret's Dollie.

'Jaysus! What's up?' she exclaimed, as she paused to get a better picture of what was happening.

Tommy, Martha's eleven-year-old, had hold of Dollie round the waist and was trying to pull her off a recumbent Bridie, to make her loose a chunk of Bridie's hair and stop punching her in the face. Joseph and little Ellie, behind Mary Margaret's chair, were clutching each other and screaming in unison. The two younger Flanagan girls cowered behind them, apparently paralysed at the sight of their bigger sister's ferocity.

Martha's eyes narrowed as she slowly slid the soup containers to the floor by the door.

Mary Margaret, grey-faced, stood holding onto Martha's only chair with one hand, while with the other she clutched her sewing to her. She was shrieking, 'Dollie, let go of her!'

'She cheated,' screamed Dollie, and hit Bridie squarely on the nose.

As her nose began to bleed, Bridie roared in fury.

Martha flung off her shawl, and waded in. With all the weight of her thin, muscular body behind it, she gave Dollie a resounding slap across her face. She swung her other hand and gave an equally heavy slap to Bridie's bloodied face.

'Stop it,' she snarled, 'or I'll put the boot to yez.'

Dollie let go of her antagonist and clapped her hands to her stinging mouth. She reared up and tumbled backwards over Tommy and brought him to the floor. He let out a curse which would have done credit to his father, and kicked her in the bottom. Beside herself with rage, Dollie turned on him.

Martha leaned over her and grasped her round the waist. She lifted her bodily off the boy, turned round and shoved her out of the open front door of the house, into which the sleet was blowing steadily. She slammed the door shut on her and turned the key, in the comfortable belief that the shock of the cold would sober her. Her father's sister, Auntie Ellen, who lived on the other side of the court, would probably take her in, listen to her and send her back home when she had sobered up.

Bridie began to splutter to her mother a defensive explanation of the quarrel. Mary Margaret sat down suddenly on the chair and reeled in a faint.

Impeded by all the smaller children hurling themselves towards her for comfort, Martha ignored Bridie.

'Catch her, Tommy,' she shrieked, pointing to Mary Margaret as the angry boy got up off the floor.

She pushed roughly through the panic-stricken children towards her friend.

'Now then, shut up, the lot of yez,' she roared. 'There's your poor mam in a faint, now. And where's our Kathleen in all this? Isn't she home from school yet?'

A muffled, scared voice from the top of the staircase outside said, 'I'm here, Mam. I'm doing me homework.'

'Well, forget it and get a cup of water for your auntie. Quick. Make yourself useful for once.'

Quaking because she was certain that, as Martha's eldest daughter at home, she would be blamed for the uproar, Kathleen tucked her exercise book and pencil into a corner of a stair. She scrambled down and hastily did as she was bidden: the water pail with a cloth over it was kept close against the staircase wall, so that it would not be knocked over. She dipped a grubby enamelled mug into it and handed it, dripping, to her mother over the heads of the whimpering younger children.

Except with regard to Bridie, who was using the front of her frock to wipe her bloody nose and whose anger was reduced to a wail for attention, order was being restored. Even Dollie's hammering on the outside door was easing off.

Tommy had half lifted Mary Margaret so that she was leaning back in her chair. He was now doing his best to keep her from sliding down off it. He was so afraid that she would die that his face was nearly as colourless as that of the woman herself.

He thankfully gave way to his mother, and retreated to sit on the stairs out of her way. He ignored Dollie's slowly lessening pounding on the locked front door. Let her rot.

Martha cooed gently to her friend, as she proffered the water, 'It's all right, Mary, love. Take a sip of water. I got lots of soup for you.' She glanced at the fire which was low, but still glowed. 'I'll heat it for you and you'll be all right, love.'

She snatched a rag out of a basketful already neatly folded for the market, and dipped it into the water. Gently she dabbed Mary Margaret's face.

She yelled to Tommy over her friend's head. 'Come back and pull the mattress down from the wall. We'll lay her on it, near the fire here.'

Tommy slid back into the room. He called, 'Mind out, everybody!' and the children scattered, as he heaved the sagging mattress onto the bare floor.

Mary Margaret showed signs of coming round, and, with Tommy, Kathleen and Martha's help, she was gently laid down.

Martha knelt by her and tucked her skirts and shawl around her, while she hissed in Kathleen's ear, 'How could you let them get into a fight like that? You're the eldest, you should know better; and you know your auntie's ill.'

Kathleen, thirteen, emaciated, with a death's-head face out of which peered huge, red-rimmed pale-blue eyes, looked back at her mother sullenly. She knew she could not win. Since her fourteen-year-old sister Lizzie had gone to be a kitchen maid in a house in Princes Road, she had not enjoyed being promoted to eldest and, therefore, responsible for all her siblings' misdoings.

Resentment in every line of her, she started to cry. 'Sister Elizabeth was angry with me and says I must do me homework and she give me a pencil and book to do it in.' Her voice faltered, as she remembered the biting remarks of her teacher. 'The kids was all right. They were playing "I went to the market and I bought . . ."'

Her mother grunted and her mouth closed in a tight line. 'Doesn't Sister know you're the eldest and you got other things to do besides homework?' she snarled, as she again dipped the rag into the mug of water and absently continued to wipe Mary Margaret's face with it.

Kathleen swallowed a sob. 'It's only happened just now. I heard Dollie say Bridie had missed one item – and I think Bridie had – I heard her – but she wouldn't admit it. And in no time at all they were at it.' She looked imploringly at Martha, as she added, 'I thought Auntie Mary Margaret would stop them.'

'Don't you start,' Martha ordered through gritted teeth, as the tears ran down the child's white cheeks. 'Your auntie needs all the help she can get.'

She looked towards the fireplace, and asked, 'Is there any tea in the pot?'

Kathleen got up off her knees and reached for the teapot keeping hot on the hob by the fire. She weighed it in her hand. 'There's some,' she said doubtfully, and sniffed back her tears.

On the mattress, Connie and Minnie, their grubby faces greyer than usual, knelt near their mother's head. They whimpered hopelessly, 'Mam, Mam.'

Exhausted, Mary Margaret ignored them. She had, however, heard Kathleen being scolded. She slowly raised herself on her elbow, as she whispered

79

to Martha, 'I'll be all right in a minute. It's not Kathleen's fault.'

'You stay right there, love. Kathleen's going to get you a cup of tea. Then I'll feed everybody.' She turned to look for another daughter.

When Martha had knelt down by the mattress, her younger son, Joseph, had picked up Number Nine and was now trying to make him laugh. He was promptly instructed, 'Joe, you give Number Nine to Tommy – he looks as if he wants to pee. Then bring a few bits of coal over from the box there, to get the fire going.'

Since the room was so crowded, Tommy had retreated again to the bottom stair, and was listening to the scene without much interest; he was, however, relieved that Mary Margaret was apparently showing signs of life.

He obediently came in and took Number Nine to show him, yet again, how to do pee-pee in a bucket without spraying the floor.

When the child had finished, Martha told Tommy to bring in the rest of the food from the pram, 'Before anybody from upstairs gets ideas about it!' she added savagely: petty theft was always a problem which had to be guarded against.

Feeding everybody was going to be a loaves and fishes job, she worried. Patrick had not returned at midday so she hoped that he was working. She must keep something in reserve for him and for Brian. Mary Margaret would want to do the same for her Thomas.

SEVEN

'Suffering Christ! Norris Green?'

January 1938

Supported by Martha's arm round her back, Mary Margaret sipped the promised tea. From long being kept warm on the hob, it was a bitter brew, its flavour unrelieved by either tinned milk or sugar: but it was at least hot.

As she regained her senses, Mary Margaret glanced vaguely round the room crowded with children, some of them still whimpering, and asked, 'Where's Dollie?'

Martha explained Dollie's temporary banishment and that, by now, she was probably safe with her Auntie Ellen. 'She knows how to look after herself, she does,' she said with a wry grin.

Mary Margaret sighed. 'Oh, aye, she does. I wasn't quick enough to separate them – I didn't want to drop me sewing on the floor – the ould fella gets mad if the hankies aren't clean when he comes to collect them.' She paused, and then went on more firmly, 'But Bridie did cheat.' She took another sip of tea.

'Oh, aye, she probably did,' responded Martha, eager not to start a quarrel. She looked up at blood-spattered Bridie, whose nose was still running red. 'I'll deal with her later.'

At the implied threat, Bridie rubbed her dribbling nose on her sleeve and broke into a fresh howl.

'Shut up,' shouted her harassed mother, 'or I'll really give you something to cry for.'

Bridie feared another slap, so the howl was reduced to a whimper. She considered joining Dollie outside. Then reluctantly decided against it: Dollie had probably cooled off, but she might still be resentful enough to hit her again, a harder blow than her own mother would give her. Though the sight and smell of her own blood was scary, she rubbed her nose with the back of her hand, and held back her sobs.

Tommy had been to see what was in the pram. The situation eased as the children's attention was diverted when he brought in the brown bags.

Now, he inquired eagerly, 'What you got in the bags, Mam?'

His mother actually smiled. 'Something to eat,' she replied. 'And don't you touch it – any of you,' she added, as her smile turned to a glare.

She poked Kathleen, standing uneasily beside her. 'You and Tommy line up all the mugs – and your dad's bowl. And there's Mr Flanagan's bowl by the hob. Put that by your Auntie Mary Margaret.'

She turned back to the sick woman. 'I got your jar filled with soup for you and a loaf of bread – and some spuds, ready-baked. Do you want to have it now – or will I put it up in your room for when your hubby comes home? It's cold already – from the walk home.'

There was an audible gasp of hope from her two little girls, as Mary Margaret hesitated. 'Maybe we could make a fresh cup of tea, now – I've got a quarter of tea upstairs – and we could have some bread with it – and a bit of potato.' She looked at her expectant children, still kneeling by her on the mattress, and promised, 'We'll get Auntie Martha to heat the soup when your dad comes home – and we mustn't forget Dollie, must we? And Mr Connolly and Brian.' She turned back to Martha. 'I'll share the tea with you.'

Martha nodded agreement. 'I got a tin of milk I was keeping for Number Nine,' she offered. 'Instead, he can have some soup at teatime like the others. Then we can use some of the conny-onny in our tea.' She got up off her knees, and was suddenly aware of how wet she was.

She kicked off her boots into the hearth and shook out her skirts, to which a nervous Number Nine was again trying to attach himself. Mother of God, how cold her feet felt. She smiled down at her baby, as she picked up her shawl from the floor and hung it on the oven door to dry. The coal added by a quietened little Joseph was beginning to catch, praise be, so she paused for a moment to warm her hands over the fire and let her feet be eased by the warmth of the hearth.

Still rubbing her swollen red hands, she turned to Kathleen and ordered her to fill the kettle and put it on the fire.

Mary Margaret asked Connie to get her precious quarter-of-a-pound packet of tea from underneath her camp bed upstairs.

'And, love, take the jar of soup up for me,' she instructed. 'Be very careful, ever so careful not to drop it!' There was a hint of laughter in her voice at this latter instruction.

The children caught her lighter tone and began to giggle. Even Bridie grinned slyly. Though she was sick hungry herself, she thought what fun it would be if Connie did drop the jar and break it;

then, surely, she would be slapped for clumsiness.

Bridie thought sourly that she had had it up to there with the Flanagans: Connie had backed up her sister Dollie in her accusation of cheating. She'd learn them, she promised herself.

As she watched in savage hope, she began to pick the drying blood out of her nose.

While the younger children watched pop-eyed, Tommy eased the loaves of bread out of their brown paper bags and, on Martha's instructions, laid each family's share on top of its bag on the floor.

He watched Connie climb the stairs, with her mother's glass sweet jar clutched against her stomach. Despite the shuffling about in Martha's room, they heard the thud as it was slowly lowered to the floor above, and in a moment a triumphant Connie came whizzing down the stairs with the packet of tea in her hand: unlike Kathleen, she was enjoying being treated as a big girl, while Bridie, who was older, was in disgrace.

The kettle boiled, tea was made. One of the loaves was handed to Mary Margaret to divide as she thought fit for her own family, the slices laid out in a neat row on the bag. Then the knife was returned to Martha, who also had to divide her two two-pound loaves very carefully.

The mothers gave each child a slice. Some of them sat on the stairs, the little ones on the floor near the mattress. Then tea was poured, carefully diluted for the children with more hot water from the kettle and a little tinned milk. The mothers then allowed the pot to simmer on the hob for a while so that they could obtain a stronger cup.

The children wolfed down their share of bread; even little Number Nine came out from his mother's skirts and was fed piece by piece by her so that he did not abandon any of it on the floor. He ate with gusto, pushing the bits into his mouth with grubby fingers.

The older children looked longingly at what remained of the loaves, but knew better than to ask for more. Their mothers carefully wrapped the remains in sheets of newspaper and put the bundles inside the brown bags again, to be kept for the members of the family who were absent.

For the first time since arriving home, Martha relaxed in the chair she owned, while her friend continued to recline on the mattress. The night was drawing in and the only light was from the fire; the little room was cosy.

After eating their bread, the children had decided that the stairs were a bus; Bridie forgot her blood-stains and appointed herself bus conductor and

Tommy became the driver. Their noisy altercations over unpaid imaginary fares were a contented background, broken occasionally by muttered curses, as tenants from the upper floors pushed resignedly by them to get to their rooms.

'Hisself didn't come home at dinnertime?' Mary Margaret inquired of Martha.

'Patrick? No.'

'Maybe there's another boat in?'

'Could be.' Martha nodded.

'If he is working, it'll be his third day this week, won't it?'

Martha agreed doubtfully. Then she said, with a wistful sigh as she remembered that she had to pay the moneylender on Saturday, 'I hope he is working, not just hanging around somewhere. But he did tell me that there's been more ships this last two months than there's been for a long time.'

'Now, why would that be?' asked Mary Margaret.

'He thinks there's a war coming – and the warehouses is being filled up – in case. A lot of grain went into the terminal last week, he said. And maybe it's true – you could hear the trains shunting all night, as they moved out.' She made a wry mouth. 'It'd take a lot more stuff coming in, it would, to give him a chance at a full week. There's so many men fighting for work.' She shrugged. 'I don't need to tell you – there's half a dozen in these very courts.'

'There'll be fewer men soon, Martha. Did you hear They've closed off Court No. 2?' asked Mary Margaret. 'I suppose they'll pull it down one of these days, like they done the other courts.'

'They've closed it? Jaysus Mary!'

'Oh, aye, They have. Thomas says there's more kids in that court than in any other one, and he said they're dead set to get them out of it. It's going to be all boarded up, and everybody's to be moved out come Friday.

'You must have noticed they've been emptying houses there for a while, and boarding them up.' Mary Margaret hitched her shawl closer round herself, and then went on, 'I remember your sister saying. And they were real hard on a family which opened up one room again and camped in it – the rent man told on them, and they got marching orders real quick. Alice Flynn upstairs told me.'

'Where are they all going to live?' asked Martha in a shocked whisper, as the implications of this piece of news sank in. 'Me sister Maria's lived there all her married life, as you know. She must have known. She never told me.'

'Well, you had that fight with her not too long back – and I've not noticed her visiting us much lately,' Mary Margaret replied with a sly grin, and then continued, 'Most of them is going to Norris Green. Some is going into Corporation flats in the city. They decided to do it quick. Don't ask me why. Maybe the kids was getting sick.'

Martha did not have Mary Margaret's calm acceptance regarding the deeds of Them. She exclaimed in horror, shaking her head in disbelief.

'Suffering Christ! Norris Green – or one of them flats? All stairs, they are. But Norris Green, that's awful; it's miles away. How's George going to get hisself down here to work? How's Maria going to manage, even in a flat, with only City housing round her? In Norris Green, there's no factories, no markets, no shops, no schools, they tell me; not even letter boxes out there. I'm told there isn't even a pub!'

Mary Margaret shrugged. She truly could not imagine the bleakness of a new housing estate; neither Martha nor she had lived anywhere else but in a court.

She did not seem to realise, however, as Martha immediately did, that the almighty They could descend, next, on their own Court No. 5. Then both their unskilled husbands would probably be out of work for the rest of their lives – simply because of the problems of travel.

Thomas was probably right – They usually pounced on the biggest families first when clearing out a court.

And, Mother of God, her own family would likely be the biggest remaining hereabouts. Martha, not easily scared, was, at that moment of revelation, terrified.

How could any dock labourer living out in a desert like Norris Green get down to the docks twice a day to stand in the calling centre and wait for work – even if he could afford a bike – and few could? How could a ship's fireman, like Mary Margaret's hubby, sign on, if he was miles from ships or the Mercantile Marine Office, or anywhere a merchant seaman was supposed to be?

Martha was more afraid than she had ever been in her life. If her family were marooned in a council house on the far outskirts of Liverpool, it would take away from them any hope they ever had of obtaining regular work. Even the pennies she brought in by her dealing in rags would not be possible in a soulless Corporation estate consisting only of houses. No docks, no factories, no market, no nothing; not even rich people who had rags to dispose of. Not even schools for the kids.

And what would young Brian do? And he with every hope at present of being taught how to be a butcher, and really improving himself one day.

'Holy Mother, help us!' she muttered in a moment of white terror.

'What did you say?' asked Mary Margaret lazily.

Martha swallowed. She did not want to frighten her sick friend. 'Ach, nothing,' she gasped. 'I was only muttering to meself.'

EIGHT

'He'll Have to Sling his Hook'

January 1938

When Patrick came home, it was late evening. He was wet and exhausted. All day long, he had worked, through rain and sleet, wheeling trolleys of sacks of wool from dockside to warehouse and stacking them neatly into ever higher piles, as a biting wind blew remorselessly up the river. He had then walked back through ill-lit, almost deserted streets where thin rain still whirled in the wind.

Although he had bought himself a quick lunch at a tiny café during a brief break, he was very hungry: the thick cheese sandwich, made from white bread, had been decently large and the mug of tea welcome; nevertheless, it had cost him his last twopence. He hoped that Martha would have something better waiting for him.

She had, of course, put aside Patrick's share of soup, potatoes and bread. Like most other women, it was the fundamental tenet of her life that he was the wage earner and had to be fed first; the fact that she also earned rarely occurred to her.

Nearly half the ewer of thick soup lay warming in the hearth in front of the fire; and a quarter of a loaf of bread, together with two big potatoes, had been rewrapped in one of her cleaner rags and placed in the oven, where she could watch that the children did not attempt to steal it. She longed to have some soup herself; but she refrained for fear that the food she had kept for Patrick was not enough for a labouring man.

The only light in the room was from the embers in the range and it was comparatively quiet.

Bridie had had her face wiped and a clean cotton frock found for her. Still complaining that the garment was too small for her, she and her sister Kathleen had gone upstairs to be reunited with a Dollie now in a much better temper and full of bread and jam given her by a wise and sympathetic Auntie Ellen.

They were going to play cards, by the light of a candle, and had been warned by Martha that they must do it quietly because 'Your Auntie Mary Margaret is resting.' She was glad to be rid of them for a while; it made more space in the room for her husband.

Joseph, Ellie and Number Nine slumbered on the mattress at her feet.

Tommy had gone to visit one of his pals in the court house nearest the street entrance. Brian worked late on Thursdays, Fridays and Saturdays. Martha's eyes drooped and she, also, had nodded off to sleep.

As the door opened to admit Patrick, she awoke with a start. He paused to allow his eyes to adjust to the dim red glow of the fire. Then, with a mere nod towards his wife, a vague shadow in the gloom, he picked his way past the mattress on the floor, and sat down with a thud on the old wooden fruit box opposite her to heave off his donated boots. He rubbed his freezing toes in front of the dying embers of the fire, and then looked ruefully at a blister on his heel.

Martha stood up and stretched herself. She gestured to the vacated chair, and said, 'Come and sit here – it's comfier, and give me your mac; I'll hang it on the line over the fire – it'll be dry by morning.'

Still silent, he stood up in his bare feet and padded across the mattress on the floor towards the chair, being careful not to tread on his sleeping children. He took off his mac and handed it to her. His jacket underneath was also damp, so he divested himself of it and silently passed it to her. Then he sat slowly down on the chair and leaned his head back. He longed for a pint of ale.

After hanging up his clothes and loosening the laces in his boots, so that the heat got to their interior, Martha briskly moved the hob with the kettle on it over the fire. It began to sing almost immediately.

She opened the oven door and first took out a large empty white pudding basin put there to warm. She silently handed it to Patrick to hold. Then she lifted the tin ewer out of the hearth.

'Hold the basin steady,' she instructed, and when he had it firmly on his knee, she slowly slopped the soup into it. Finally, she turned the jug upside down and shook out a few recalcitrant bits of carrot. She straightened up, smiled, and said, 'There you are.'

She fetched another box from the other side of the room and placed it beside Patrick. Then she unlatched the oven door, took out the bundle of bread and potatoes and laid it on the box.

From the mantel shelf, she took down a ladle, which she had earlier used to measure out soup for the children, and handed it to him. It had not been washed, but he took it from her without comment. He opened up the bundle, broke some of the bread into the soup, and began to slurp the food into his mouth.

Though he knew he had had to leave her without money that morning, he did not ask where the soup had come from: Martha always found food somehow. She sold her rags in the market, didn't she? Tommy brought in pennies and, occasionally, a silver threepenny piece, which he earned, according to him, from holding the bridles of carthorses while the drivers went into a pub for a quick pee and a drink. Brian gave her his five-shilling wage each week, and Lizzie, his girl in service, sometimes sent her mother a one-shilling postal order from her tiny wages. And, when he himself earned, he always gave her enough for the rent and a bit over for coal and candles, didn't he?

As food and warmth began to put life into him again, he admitted idly to himself that he drank too much and it took money – but she herself could get through several half-pints while sitting in the passageway of the Coburg with the other women, while he drank in the bar with his friends. The brightly lit pub was the only warm refuge they had, the only consolation which kept him going from day to day, week to week.

He grinned. Most of the children had been conceived in the narrow, fairly sheltered alleyway behind the pub, while they were a little drunk and still sufficiently warm to enjoy the encounter.

While he ate, Martha poked the fire, and then made a fresh pot of tea, courtesy of Mary Margaret, who had given her a couple of spoonfuls of tea leaves in thanks for bringing her the soup and bread. She laid two mugs on the floor beside the range, where they could be visible in the firelight. She then sat down close to Patrick on yet another sturdy fruit box, used for storing coal.

Inside the box were a few lumps of coal, which Mary Margaret had also given her. Since Mary Margaret's room did not have a fireplace, she cooked what little she had to cook on a primus stove. When she did not have paraffin for her stove, she would put a stew pot beside Martha's on Martha's fire.

Mary Margaret's Dollie thought it was a great game to follow a coal cart round the local streets and pick up any lumps that the coalman dropped. When he lifted the one-hundredweight sacks from his cart and carried them across the pavement to pour the contents down the coalhole in front of each terraced house, she would listen for the clang of the lid being put back onto the hole, and for the weary man to shuffle away. Then she would race over and pounce on any small bits she could find. Sometimes, when the horse moved with a jerk to the next house, a few pieces would roll off the back of the cart. Quick as a cat after a mouse, she would garner these, too, before any other child could beat her to it. She would bring it all back to her mother in an old cloth bag.

Her mother promptly gave the coal to Martha in thanks for being allowed to share her fire. She would tell Dollie, 'Without your Auntie Martha, I don't know what I'd do, I don't.'

As Patrick finished the last ladleful, he gave a small sigh of relief, and handed the bowl back to his wife. She put it with the ladle on the mantel shelf: if it had stopped raining by tomorrow, she would take out anything to be washed to the pump in the court and rinse it there.

She picked up a potato from the box top and, with a little smile, handed it to him. He tore it into pieces and ate all of it, including the skin.

After he had finished eating, he belched and then sat for a while staring silently at the glowing embers.

When Martha felt he was rested enough, she broached the subject which was worrying her most. She asked, 'Did you know that Court No. 2 is to be emptied? That means that our Maria and George has got to move.'

Patrick belched again, and then said, 'Oh, aye. George told me. They're getting a new house in Norris Green.'

'What's he going to do out there?'

Patrick gave a grim laugh. 'Go on Public Assistance. He'll have to sling his hook.'

Martha nodded. George would, indeed, have to hang up his docker's hook for ever, if he was to live so many miles away in a suburb with no places to work and no transport. Even if there were a bus to take him down to the docks, how could he afford bus fares on a docker's wage? It was ridiculous.

'Can't they find a Corpy flat nearer here for them?'

'Na, Corporation flats is all filled up. All the court houses is being cleared, as you well know.'

He stirred uneasily. 'I heard some more today, though. They're going to build air-raid shelters outside in the street all along here, right across the pavement from the front entry.'

'Holy Mary! What for?'

'They reckon there's going to be a war. And what's more, they're going to pull down the wall of our court, so we're open to the street.'

'Humph, and where are they going to put the rubbish bins? They're fixed in the wall.'

'Don't ask me. Maybe the council will give us a bin or two. They must reckon that if there's no wall, we can run into the shelter real quick.'

It did not strike either of them that the Public Health Department had viewed the statistics of the recent influenza epidemic with anxiety. Unable to bulldoze the remaining unhealthy courts until more City housing was built, they were using a cheap remedy, the removal of the enclosing wall, to get some cleaner air to circulate in the crowded court.

Martha gave a little laugh of relief as her fear of being moved receded. 'They must be expecting that this court won't be moved for a while, if they're building us a shelter.' She chuckled. 'We'd have a right job all of us getting through the entry at the same time, that's for sure – Alice Flynn upstairs is that fat she has to edge through it sideways already. Why aren't they moving us to Norris Green?'

'Dunno. I suppose they haven't built the houses yet.'

'It's real funny that they've found a way to make room for an air-raid shelter, but they can't build new houses for us right here.'

'Maybe they've stopped building houses everywhere and are doing air-raid shelters instead?' suggested Patrick.

Martha leaned forward to put her empty mug on top of the oven. 'Is there really going to be a war, Pat?'

'Oh, aye. I believe so.'

'But Thomas said as Mr Chamberlain was talking with Adolf Hitler, and thought Germany was being reasonable.'

Patrick shrugged, and then said shrewdly, 'Na. All he's doing is get us a bit of time to build tanks and guns. He'll sell the Czechs down the river to do it, you'll see.'

'Will you have to go for a soldier, Pat?'

Pat laughed. 'Me? Na, I'm too old.'

'Well, praise all the saints for that. And our Brian is too young?'

'Oh, aye.' He glanced round the dark room. 'Where is the lad?'

'He's working late – it's Thursday. And Tommy's gone down to see his pal. They'll be back just now.'

Their father heaved himself up from the chair. 'Well, I'm going to turn in. I'll be working tomorrow.'

He knelt down and moved little Joseph further

across the mattress. He winced as he laid himself down, turned on his side and closed his eyes. He was asleep in seconds.

Martha sighed, got up, took an old coat from a hook on the front door and laid it over him. She then rearranged Number Nine's blanket to cover his sister Ellie as well. She would not lie down herself until she had decided what to do about breakfast – she would have to go out again into the cold, that was for sure.

She stood uncertainly, her toothless mouth tightly clenched as she looked down on the sleeping children and her snoring husband. She had not a crumb left to give them for breakfast, and, as she had sat patiently waiting for Patrick, this fact had been gnawing at her, almost outweighing her fear of being whisked off to Norris Green.

After the children's fighting that afternoon she had not wanted to leave home until Patrick returned. She reckoned that Mary Margaret alone could not reasonably be expected to watch them all tonight; she really was not well, and this knowledge added to the painful ache of Martha's own hunger and to her other worries – Kathleen, for example. She'd have to give the girl a good talking to: she must be taught to take care of the kids better.

She turned, and quietly padded up the stairs and

through Sheila and Phoebe's room to reach Mary Margaret.

Her friend was asleep on her narrow camp bed in the far corner, her head pillowed on a roll of rags, her shawl wrapped tightly round her.

By the light of a candle, the girls were playing very quietly close to the entrance to Sheila and Phoebe's empty room. Martha hissed at her daughters to come down and settle for the night.

In chorus, they hissed back that they weren't making any trouble and why couldn't they play longer.

'Because your dad's home, and he wants you downstairs and sleeping – now! Meself, I got to go down to the corner shop for a few minutes. You come on right now – or do I have to get your father to you?'

At this awful threat to tell Mr Connolly, Dollie Flanagan picked up the grubby cards and shuffled them neatly together. If Mr Connolly was home, probably her father soon would be from the pub. He could deliver a slap a good deal harder than the one Mrs Connolly had given her – and suppose Mrs C told her father about her behaviour that afternoon?

'You'd better get going,' she told her guests with a sigh, and got up off the floor.

With Martha's brood safely wrapped in bits of blanket, they were each allotted in irritable whispers a piece of floor on which to sleep.

Finally, Martha warned, 'Now, our Kathleen, you're in charge, remember? Brian and Tommy will be in just now.'

'Oh, Mam!' protested Kathleen, as she reluctantly spread herself as close to the fireplace as she could get without her mother noticing that she was hogging most of the heat.

'Shut up and go to sleep. You're the eldest. And mind you don't wake your father.'

Martha picked up her shawl from the back of the chair and wrapped it tightly round her. When she opened the outer door, she flinched at the cold. Her long walk up to the Lee Jones had tired her, but desperation drove her out again.

She quickly shut the door behind her and looked up at the tiny patch of sky visible between the enclosing court housetops. It had stopped sleeting, and, far above her between dark shadows of cloud, she glimpsed a single star.

Despite her despair, she thought, 'Perhaps it's my lucky star. At least They won't turn us out come tomorrow.'

NINE

'Old Folk's Home? Feels More Like a Bleeding Gaol'

1965

'You know, Angie, when I had to go down to the corner shop that night, I was more worried than I'd been in years.'

Angie acknowledged the remark with an absent-minded nod. She was attending to Pat, the comatose patient in the next bed who had to be turned every two hours. She impatiently whipped back the curtain drawn round her and pulled the bedclothes off her.

Martha was sitting up in her bed watching her, while she gratefully sipped the illicit mug of tea which Angie had brought up for her. Nowadays, every time the grossly overworked nursing aide came into the bedroom, which held five invalids, Martha would remorselessly continue the story of her life: it was as if, by doing so, she gave some meaning to her current existence.

Today was no different.

'For one thing, Angie, I was real worried about Them pulling down the wall between us and the main road. It meant that any stranger could walk in on the court. We'd always been safe in that court 'cos you knew everybody. You knew who to warn the kids about, who'd steal, even which women was giving the men the eye. And all the women watched out for the kids.

'And that was the evening I realised that me Number Nine – that's James – was the last kid born there: no new tenant had come in for years. It would only take two empty houses in Norris Green or Dovecot or some other place to rehouse Mary Margaret's and my families. Then all the single people living there would be told – legal, like – that they must find themselves places to live, and, bingo, They could empty the whole court and pull it down.

'I didn't feel safe at all, I didn't. Not about nothing.'

She paused to take another slurp of tea, while Angie braced herself, heaved and successfully turned over the hapless Pat. Despite her coma, Pat screeched with pain.

Martha winced. She carefully put her empty mug down on the smelly Victorian commode next to her bed.

Then she went on more vaguely, as if anxious to justify the growth of old fears, 'They'd been closing off the courts in the north end of the town for years: them houses in the north end was only ten feet by ten feet, one room to a floor. They was much more crowded than us – and they was a long way off from us.

'But when George and Maria in the very next court to us was to be moved, it suddenly seemed as if me hour had come.'

She flung her arm across her heart, as if to indicate her shock. 'And I knew I'd have to go and see Maria, poor dear, fight or no fight. Couldn't leave a sister to face eviction alone. In the end, I didn't have time, I were that harassed. Weeks later, I walked all the way to Norris Green to see her in her new house.'

Angie did not respond. She looked down at Pat, and hesitated: her undersheet was soaked; the bed should be stripped. Then she pulled the woman's blankets over her. Leave the bedding to the night nurse, Mrs Kelly, to change. Let her do something for once, other than sleep on the visitor's settee in the hallway – ignoring the cries of the patients, according to the sufferers themselves.

Martha watched Angie with the same fascination as a rabbit might exhibit if faced with a snake about to eat it; she dreaded becoming entirely helpless, as were the rest of the women in her room. How would she bear the pain?

She eased herself down into her bed, as if to evade the issue.

Angie turned to Martha.

Ignoring her monologue, she warned her, 'Bath before breakfast for everybody tomorrow.'

Over the edge of her top sheet, Martha stared at Angie with disgust. 'Do I have to?' she asked irritably.

'Yes, doctor's coming round.'

'Strewth! Who cares? I don't need no doctor. All the bloody fuss, just because the fucking doctor's coming.' She turned her face to the wall, and growled, 'What with not being allowed out of bed, being here's like being in a bleeding gaol, it is.'

'Come on, Martha. No bad language, please.' A weary Angie's voice sounded cold and mechanical.

'Fuck you,' muttered Martha, and pulled the bedding over her head. Suddenly, silently, she began to cry.

She remembered the liveliness of the court compared with her current desolation. Full of kind folk, it had been. Helped you out. Made you laugh. Even she herself had managed to make Maria and George laugh at their predicament, when eventually she went to commiserate with them over their move. Both George and Maria in their almost empty new dwelling had welcomed her with open arms.

Now there was nobody, not even Jamie, her beloved Number Nine.

TEN

'Them Protties'

January 1938

Before stepping into the street on her way to the corner shop, Martha hesitated in the arched doorway of the court to allow her eyes to adjust to the single gaslight above her head. There were few people about on such a dank night.

In the distance, she could see the lights from the pub windows making a welcoming pool of warmth on the wet pavement. She stared at it wistfully, and then turned the other way and proceeded past the barber's, now closed but with a body tightly crouched for shelter in the doorway, past the Chinese restaurant, haunt of numerous prostitutes in search of of an ever-shrinking number of seamen with money to spend.

She turned the corner that flanked the entrance

to the sail maker's loft, where Mary Margaret, dearest friend, had once worked when she was young and strong – a place where, normally, canvas awnings, tents and other needs of modern seagoing ships and yachts were still patiently stitched. Mary Margaret had been taught the trade by her father as she was his only surviving child – she must have been one of the few women who had undertaken such heavy work, thought Martha. There was, however, at present no light in any of its tall windows, because there was little reason to work late, nowadays.

In the darkness, Martha clicked her tongue at the hollow sound of her own heavy footsteps as she passed the shut door. Anyway, Mary Margaret, poor dear, was too sick now to do anything so arduous.

Two men eyed Martha and then eased past her on the narrow pavement. She increased her speed.

As she opened the spring door to the corner shop at the end of the street, Mr O'Reilly was edging his way between three customers being served at the counter by his wife. Thin, bald, garbed in a fairly clean white apron, he was sweeping the wooden floor of his grocery shop.

Martha stood shivering directly in the path of his broom, unsure how to approach him amongst so many chattering customers.

He stopped his broom in mid-sweep and stared at the small, black bundle of womanhood. Martha Connolly!

Trouble, he knew it. And she still owed him two shillings from last week. Play it carefully, he adjured himself.

The courts, with their tight knot of casual labourers and merchant seamen, were the main problem of his life. Yet, if, on the day the men got their Public Assistance or even a bit of a wage, he could squeeze out of them what they owed him, they were a very profitable part of his business.

For example, their wives bought single ounces of lard or margarine: a fourpenny pound of margarine, cut into sixteen one-ounce pieces at a penny a piece, or a sixpenny pot of jam, sold by tablespoonfuls at a penny a spoonful, represented a wonderful profit; it helped to cover inevitable bad debts. At the same time, this splitting up of jars, packets and bags for his clients' benefit, gave him an enviable reputation for kindly helpfulness.

'Evening, Mrs Connolly,' he greeted her carefully, as he leaned on his broom.

Martha gulped. 'Evenin', Mr O'Reilly,' she replied, as two of the customers picked up their baskets and turned to depart. They knew her, and, as they edged past to get to the door, they greeted her quite cheerfully.

She smiled faintly at them, jealous that they had full shopping baskets. She did not even own a shopping basket, only a laundry one in which she carried her rags for sale in the market.

When they had gone and the third customer seemed safely involved with Mrs O'Reilly at the counter, she muttered, 'Could I have a word with you, John?'

Resignedly, Mr O'Reilly turned and led her to the far end of the little counter, beside the bacon slicer.

'I was wondering,' she began cautiously, as he leaned his broom against a pile of boxes of Sunlight soap stacked against the wall, and turned towards her. 'I was wondering if you could let me have a loaf of bread and some bacon bits – on the slate, till tomorrow night?'

He looked down at her without expression. Then he said firmly, 'You still owe us two bob from last week.'

'I know, John – but I always do pay . . .' she whined.

'Not always. I've had to write it off more than once.'

'Come on. Not that often.'

'Too often.'

She tried again patiently. 'Including tomorrow – that's Friday – me hubby'll have four days' work this week. But he won't get paid till Saturday, of course. Meanwhile, on Friday night I'll get Brian's wages. I'll be able to pay for sure by Saturday night, at latest.'

'Oh, aye, if Patrick don't spend it all down at the Baltic.' As a Wesleyan – a Protestant – he was a firm teetotaller. He felt for his broom, as if to start sweeping again.

At his remark about Patrick, Martha looked deeply hurt. 'John O'Reilly, that's not fair. He don't drink that much. He's got a heavy, sweaty job and he needs to drink lots, and you know it.'

She was trembling now, with weakness from lack of food. She thought, If I can't get a loaf of bread out of him, I'm buggered. Despair filled her.

As the faintness which had threatened all day finally overcame her, she began to reel. She clutched the counter, and then slipped to the floor.

Shaken, Mr O'Reilly called to his wife, 'Oh, my goodness! Mam!' as he bent over his would-be customer.

'Dear me!' exclaimed the lady, as she looked up from folding a small blue bag of sugar for the

115

customer she was tending. 'That'll be fourpence,' she told the man.

He laid down the pennies and picked up his sugar, as she ran around the other side of the counter, lifted part of it and carefully stepped through the opening, past the boxes of soap.

She knelt down by Martha, and laid her hand on her forehead. It was icy. No influenza to infect her, thank goodness. Must be a faint.

As the customer opened the shop door to depart, he stared at the two women. He shrugged and said good night to no one in particular. Women were always fainting.

Mr O'Reilly glanced up as the door slammed. He hoped the unknown man had not shoplifted anything in the few seconds during which both his and his wife's attention had been diverted. You really couldn't be too careful.

In an effort to waken her, Mrs O'Reilly patted Martha's cheeks, but an exhausted Martha was well out. The shopkeeper bent over and felt her hands. They also were ice-cold.

Mrs O'Reilly looked at her husband.

'I think it's the cold,' she said doubtfully. 'We'd better get her by the fire.'

'She's almost certain to be lousy,' Mr O'Reilly warned her.

The last thing Mrs O'Reilly wanted was lice or bugs in her furniture. But she knew Martha, and she had used her children to run messages for her. Anyway, the woman had to be revived somehow. She could not lie on the shop floor as other customers came and went – her own reputation as a very understanding person would be irrevocably lowered.

She stood up. 'We'll put her on a wooden chair,' she said. 'Ted's doing his homework on the table. Ask him to come and mind the shop while we move her inside.'

So twelve-year-old Ted was shouted for, and came reluctantly out of the back room. He was surprised to see Tommy Connolly's mam lying on the floor, and he asked, 'What's up?'

'She's fainted from the cold,' his mother replied. 'We'll put her by the fire for a bit, and I'll make her a cup of tea. You mind the shop.'

He opened the swinging lid of a biscuit box and nonchalantly helped himself to a digestive. 'OK,' he agreed and wandered down behind the counter.

Martha slowly returned from a deep blackness to find herself in a very strange place. She was in a wooden rocking chair and in front of her glowed what looked like a big fire. She was bathed in its blissful warmth. She closed her eyes again.

Something cold was pressed to her forehead and trickles of water ran down her face and neck.

She blinked and turned her face away from the cold. The fire was still there and, strangely, a big black kettle which certainly did not belong to her was steaming on it.

A relieved voice said, 'Ah, she's coming round now.'

Annie O'Reilly? Memory suddenly flooded back to her. She tried to sit up straight.

'Now, hold still, love,' urged the voice. 'Give yourself time. John's making you a cuppa tea.'

She thankfully relaxed. She was so very tired and the room was so blessedly warm. And what a room! She smiled slightly at the idea of an invisible Annie standing behind her, wet teacloth in hand, as she herself looked at the good brass clock on the mantelpiece and the equally well-polished brass fire irons in the whitened hearth, not to speak of the worn green velvet chair on the other side of the hearth. It was a room beautiful enough to dream about.

She must, she realised, be in the O'Reillys' living room, which she knew lay behind the windowed door at the back of the counter. The window was always discreetly lace-curtained so that people in the shop could not see into the living room, but the O'Reillys could see if anyone had entered the shop.

Suddenly she wanted to cry. Two big tears slid slowly down her face to join the cold water already there.

John O'Reilly slipped between her and the hearth. He had a big brown teapot in one hand which he filled from the boiling kettle.

'There now,' he said, and she heard the plunking sound of his putting the teapot down somewhere behind her.

The wet cloth was removed from her forehead, and Annie said in an anxious hiss, 'John, take this out and throw it in the yard – lice.'

The humiliation of the remark made Martha's tears run a little faster. Who didn't have lice? No matter how much you used Mary Margaret's lice comb, the wretched insects were there again in a day or two. And who could afford to waste paraffin by rubbing it in your hair, to really kill them?

Annie O'Reilly came into focus. She held a mug of tea in one hand and a couple of biscuits in the other. Martha looked at her through tear-filled eyes.

'There, there, Mrs Connolly. Don't take on so. You just fainted, that's all. You'll be all right in a minute. Now, have a sip of tea. I'll hold the cup for you.' Careful not to touch her guest's shawl, Annie O'Reilly tipped the mug gently against Martha's lips.

Martha dutifully sipped.

It was marvellous tea. Strong, with plenty of milk and lots of sugar. She tried to steady the mug herself, as she drank eagerly. When it was emptied, she said, 'Thank you, Annie. It were lovely.'

Annie's shrewd little blue eyes weighed up her patient, and she said with real kindness, 'Take these bickies, while I pour you another.'

While Martha smiled slightly and then stuffed both biscuits into her mouth, her hostess went to get the promised second cup of tea.

Martha leaned back in the chair. Her own unadmitted hunger welled up in a tremendous pain inside her. For the moment, it outweighed her fear at having nothing for Patrick's or Brian's breakfast, and her awful apprehension that little Number Nine could die very easily if he did not have, at least, some more milk. He and the other children must be fed somehow, even if she had to steal from the very people who were being so good to her.

When Mrs O'Reilly returned with another cup of tea and a plate holding two big slabs of stale bread and margarine, Martha felt very guilty at her sinful thought of theft.

Annie O'Reilly said to Martha, almost apologetically, 'I thought you ought to eat something solid before you face the cold again.'

Martha looked at the offering on the plate. Her first instinct was to say with pride that she really did not need it.

But I do, I do, she cried inwardly. I can't bear it any more – and, somehow, Annie has sensed it.

Humbly she mumbled thanks and took the plate from her.

Annie watched, fascinated, as Martha broke the slices of bread and crammed them into her mouth with both hands. The woman must be starving.

As, with her toothless gums, she ground up the last piece, Martha said apologetically, 'Ta ever so. I was fair clemmed. It's been a long day.'

Annie smiled slightly. Hunger and cold at the same time was something she remembered suffering in her own childhood, after her father had been called up for the Great War: it had been a while before her mother could find a job with a living wage. But she had never been physically filthy as the women in Court No. 5 were, and her pity for her unwelcome guest was tempered by her disgust at the sheer smell of her – at present, her nice clean living room had the strong odour of humanity, which her shop sometimes had on a busy day. She could endure that stench outside the lace-curtained door, but not in her home.

'How are you feeling now?' she asked Martha.

Martha did not know whether to laugh or to cry. Despite her best efforts, the tears began to run down her face once more. She had not been so beautifully warm for months, and the pain in her stomach had been assuaged; yet she still had no breakfast or lunch for Patrick and the children.

She sniffed and swallowed hard. 'I'm feeling steady now, Annie. You've been so kind.' She stood up and immediately felt woozy again.

She grinned at Annie. 'Oh!' she exclaimed. 'I'm wobbly – feel as if I've had too much to drink!'

What am I going to do? she wondered desperately. I can't ask these people to let me have bread on tick, after they've been so good. Maybe, if I walked round to see Maria, she'd give me a loaf.

Not likely, she decided. I told her weeks ago in my stupid temper to go to blazes. Tonight, she'll be all packed up ready to move to Norris Green first thing tomorrow morning. I should have gone to see her about her eviction and made it up with her, and now it's really too late. And, Jaysus, I'm so tired.

She sighed, and her shoulders sagged. Sisters were a quarrelsome lot at best.

Annie made a determined effort to be hospitable once more. 'Sit down again and rest for a few minutes. There's no hurry; we're not that busy in the shop. And I'll get our Ted to walk you back home.'

Martha sat down rather quickly, because she had no option. For the moment, she realised, she could not walk home.

Ted, who had been relieved from his shop duties by the return of his father to the counter, was again struggling with his geography homework. He was partly trying to remember the tributaries of the Mersey River and partly listening to the two women.

When his mother committed him to escort duty, he muttered 'Blast!' and chewed his pen savagely. The last thing he wanted to do was to walk a dark and, to him, rather threatening street with a woman from the courts. Though he knew Martha's Tommy, he did not play with him – Tommy was a Catholic.

Both the O'Reillys had been born in the district. His parents' attitude, however, was that they were socially far above court people, except when dealing with them as customers. This petty snobbery had rubbed off onto their only child, making him, occasionally, even more vulnerable to attack by the Roman Catholic urchins round him. He was scholarship material, his father would tell him; they hoped he would win one to a grammar school and do really well for himself; his teacher said he could. Perhaps he could hope to be a teacher himself, one day.

So Ted was sometimes a little hard-pressed to find enough boys to put together a game of footer or cricket in the side street onto which the living-room window looked, and he was prone to being bullied.

'You don't have to bother Ted, Annie. I'll be all right in a few minutes.'

'Are you sure?'

Martha fought back her tears. 'Oh, aye,' she said.

Ted sighed with relief, and wondered if the Leeds–Liverpool Canal counted as a tributary.

ELEVEN

'You Can't Do Nothing about Consumption'

January 1938

Martha sat for a few minutes more in front of the O'Reillys' fire, and talked desultorily with Annie. She mentioned the likelihood of the removal of the wall which shielded her court from the main road.

'Aye, I heard that,' replied Annie, as she straightened up after adding some pieces of coal to the fire with a pair of tongs. 'It'll give you more fresh air.'

'I'm afraid of strangers from the street getting in,' responded Martha, her mind temporarily diverted from her current woes. 'I mean, you know everybody in the court. You can sit on the step in the dark, and know all who pass, even if they're drunk – a strange seaman walking through the street entry shows up like a sore thumb – and you can watch the kids – makes them more careful, because they know you'll tell their dad if they steal or are real naughty.'

'You're probably right,' agreed Annie amiably; she was nothing if not diplomatic. She silently thanked God that she had married a widower, who already had decent living quarters behind his busy corner shop.

Finally, with a shaky sigh, Martha rose from the high-backed wooden rocking chair. This time she felt reasonably steady. She wanted urgently to be engulfed in the darkness of the street so that she could have a good cry.

She leaned towards Annie to kiss her in thanks. Annie hastily stepped back. Then to cover her horror of picking up vermin, she took Martha's hand and squeezed it hard, as the disconcerted woman, in stumbling fashion, expressed her gratitude.

Annie turned and opened the door into the shop, and Martha walked through it. There were a number of customers, standing around chatting to each other. When Mr O'Reilly heard the door open, he glanced back over his shoulder and said, with forced cheerfulness, 'Ah, Mrs Connolly. Feeling OK now?'

As all the customers turned in surprise to view her entrance, she hitched her shawl over her head, and said, with an embarrassed smile, that yes, she was. Annie followed her and lifted the counter lid for her so that she could move to the customer side of it and thence to the street door.

Martha noticed Alice Flynn, her neighbour from the attic, among the interested customers and nodded politely to her. Thanks to her crippled war-veteran husband, she, at least, had a regular small pension coming in, thought Martha enviously – and he couldn't get out of bed to spend it.

She jumped, when John O'Reilly called to her, 'Hey, don't forget your groceries. I've got them under the counter here.'

He bent down and fished out a brown paper bag, lifted it over the counter and put it into her arms. 'See you tomorrow night,' he said with a wink.

She wrapped her shawl round the bag, as she gasped. 'Why – why – thank you, Mr O'Reilly. I'm much obliged.' She stood looking at him, her mouth agape, not believing her luck. She could smell the bread in the bag and she salivated.

Since she had her hands full, a man waiting at the back of the little knot of customers opened the door for her.

With a huge sob, she turned and ran down the two steps to the pavement, while the customers, in surprise, turned to Mr O'Reilly for an explanation.

He said, in unexpected defence of Martha's obvious distress, 'She's a bit upset. She fainted in the shop. So we took her into the house, and the wife's been taking care of her.'

All the customers grinned and resumed their chatter; the story confirmed their high opinion of the O'Reillys, even if they had the misfortune of being Protestants. Always got a smile for you, they had, and would let you have a bit on the slate – most of the time.

Annie O'Reilly let out an audible sigh of relief. She ignored the need of her help in the shop, and went to wash down with pine disinfectant the chair in which Martha had sat.

It was not that she disliked Martha, she told herself, as she scrubbed the cleanser thoroughly into every joint in the chair and her living room was flooded with the strong odour of disinfectant. Martha was a good woman and kept her kids in order. It was that the very thought of lice made her crawl all over.

She was not sure if it had been wise to give the woman a bag full of groceries – if other customers spotted it, it might make them too ambitious about obtaining credit. But John had carried it off very well, she realised, in simply handing it to Martha as if she had already paid for it.

Martha cried all the way home. She opened the door as quietly as she could and was greeted by Patrick's steady snoring. She glanced quickly round the room, to check that everybody had returned home.

Despite the darkness, she managed to account for all the children, who seemed sound asleep.

A hoarse, newly broken voice from one corner greeted her, however. ''Ello, la, Mam.' In the dimness, a shape unfolded itself.

'Hello, Brian, love.' Martha was thankful that the darkness hid her tears.

It did not deceive Brian. He sensed from her voice that something was wrong, and he asked, 'You OK?'

'Oh, aye. I just went down to O'Reilly's to get something for breakfast. Did Kathleen tell you about the bowl of soup in the oven for you?'

'Oh, aye. Thanks, Mam. I'll light the candle for you.'

He reached over to the mantelpiece and accidentally kicked Bridie. She muttered crossly and slept on. He cussed her, as he found the matches. Then he struck one and revealed a room which, with its crowded bodies, resembled one of Hogarth's engravings.

'That's enough, lad. No swearing.' Martha stepped

cautiously into the room, carefully avoiding the pee bucket and the water bucket. She dumped her parcel on the floor.

She turned towards her son and, for a second, the dying match showed the boy a shiny wet face and weary puffed-up eyes.

'Mam,' he whispered. 'What's up?'

In the darkness, he dropped the dead match and moved towards her. He put his arms around her.

Broken, she sobbed out her humiliation at the great kindness of the O'Reillys, who had been so diplomatic when giving her the groceries.

A skinny, clumsy youth, Brian did not say anything much. He simply held her tightly, and stroked her tangled hair. He knew all about humiliation, the sniggers of the other butchers because his employer sometimes gave him leftovers; even the very mention of where he lived was enough to tell anyone that he was scum.

Thanks to the efforts of the League of Welldoers to provide diversions for boys in the slums, he was learning to box. It gave him unexpected hope that, one day, he would not be simply a trained butcher's assistant living in a court; he would be a champion boxer, like Joe Louis, and be able to beat the daylights out of anybody in the whole world;

the magical stories he had seen at the cinema had confirmed this hope.

Finally, as Martha began to apologise in a whisper about her weakness, he tried to comfort her. 'Never mind, Mam. It won't always be this bad. I've a feelin' there's a bit more work around – there's more people coming in to buy meat, you know. Maybe Dad'll have a bit of luck.'

Martha sniffed, untangled herself from his long arms, and wiped her nose on the end of her shawl. Brian's observation was a shrewd one; meat was not high on the shopping list of the unemployed. If the butcher was doing better, so were his customers. His remark confirmed Patrick's observations.

'Don't you worry, love. I'm all right,' she assured the boy. 'I'm just tired – that's all.' She gave a shivering sigh. 'Now, you lie down and sleep. I'm going to settle down meself. I got to go to the market tomorrow.'

Uneasily, he did as he was told. One day, he promised himself, I'll earn enough to rent a decent house and she can have a good fire all day and a bed to sleep in, like they had in films.

Martha took off her boots and laid them in the hearth. Then she arranged herself carefully on the edge of the mattress, watching that she did not disturb the other sleepers. She eased her feet down until they touched Bridie sleeping across the foot of the mattress. Then she tucked the ends of her skirts round her own feet and slept immediately, the sleep of the completely exhausted.

It seemed almost no time at all before she heard the tap-tap of the wand of the knocker-up on the window and his subsequent call. As the whole family stirred uneasily at the sharp noise, she rolled off the mattress, got to her feet, opened the front door and assured a crabby elderly man mumbling to himself outside that she was indeed up. Because she did not own a clock, she paid twopence a week for this service from a neighbour who did own one; he had, in consequence, been persuaded to become the court's daily knocker-up.

Before closing the door against the clammy chill, she looked up at the narrow patch of dark sky above the rooftops. The sky looked clear, though it was cold enough to make one want to stay close to a fire. And that would be her next problem – some more coal, she thought glumly; little Dollie Flanagan could not supply it all.

She went quickly to the mantelpiece and lit the candle, and then opened the bag of groceries. Two good two-pound loaves of slightly stale bread and a whole wrap of bacon bits! She stumbled to the fireplace to rake out the ashes, put a few twigs and some paper on top of the cinders. She felt in the back of the coal box for her last pieces of coal.

She woke Patrick, while the rest of the family settled down again for another precious half-hour.

After splashing his face in the freezing water of the pump in the courtyard, Patrick went to work replete from a heap of fried bread and took with him a hefty sandwich full of bacon bits.

He paused to kiss his wife on leaving, which was unusual. Martha sensed his desire for her, but, despite her own longings, she was thankful he had to go to work: she dreaded another child.

'Go on with you,' she said with a grin, and pushed him playfully through the door.

Brian was scolded into washing his hands and face at the pump, and had his hair combed with the nit comb, which must, Martha reminded herself, be returned to Mary Margaret one of these days. He was packed off to walk to work in an old tweed jacket too big for him, with a piece of bread in one pocket. His delivery bicycle was kept, with his white apron, at the shop under the close eye of the butcher, who lived above the premises.

His brothers, Tommy and little Joseph, and his sisters, Kathleen and Bridie, were given a slice of fried bread and a cup of weak tea each and were hustled off to school, protesting about the cold.

'It's not wet out there, the sun's out. You won't hurt,' Martha assured them, as she wiped each face with a damp cloth as they went down the steps. 'Now, Bridie, button up your cardigan, and hold Joseph's hand all the way.'

Kathleen wailed that she could not find her jacket, and it was eventually discovered in a crumpled heap in one corner, having been used as a pillow by Bridie.

Now that Kathleen was thirteen, she was beginning vaguely to wish to look pretty, so she spent the walk to school shouting at Bridie for spoiling the threadbare coat that Martha had originally found for her in Paddy's market.

Having got rid of everyone, except Number Nine and four-year-old Ellie, who were crouched sleepily by the fire, both of them fretful, Martha realised that Mary Margaret's Dollie and Connie had not joined her daughters for the walk to school. Thomas had not come down either, but then he did not get up early unless he believed that he had a chance of getting a ship.

She hesitated. Should she go upstairs to inquire if all was well? Mary Margaret usually babysat Ellie and Number Nine for her on market days, not that she had to do anything for them, only watch that they did not stray beyond the pavement outside the court entry.

Sheila and Phoebe from the room in front of Mary Margaret's had gone off to their oakum-picking less than five minutes after Patrick's departure.

Fear haunted Martha every time it was quiet in the upper room. Nowadays, Mary Margaret looked like a ghost, she did.

'But you can't do nothin' about consumption,' she would say to a silent Patrick, who simply shrugged. In his opinion, death amongst women was so common that it was normal.

Today, however, was Martha's day for the market, and she must go soon or miss the best time to sell her rags. What should she do about Ellie and Number Nine?

She went uncertainly into the tiny hall and glanced upstairs.

Fat Alice Flynn was just plodding downwards, slightly sideways, so as to accommodate her girth to the narrowness of the stairwell. She was carrying the bucket of slops from the night, to empty them into a drain in the yard. Upon being asked, she agreed to watch both children until Mary Margaret woke up and could take over.

They agreed that Mary Margaret needed all the sleep she could get, poor dear. Today, her kids must be getting a good sleep: it wouldn't hurt them. They took it for granted that her husband would sleep as long as he could – he had little else to do, unless he got a ship.

TWELVE

The Fent Woman

January 1938

With her left hand, Martha arranged her shawl
over her head and across her chest for maximum
warmth. She then hoisted her laundry basket full
of neatly folded rags onto the top of her head and,
with her right hand, picked up another bundle
of them. Straight-backed, she swayed off down
the court, her tiny figure almost overwhelmed by
her cargo of fents. She was followed by mournful
wails from Ellie and Number Nine and Alice's
reassurances to them that Mam would be back
soon.

As usual, she was walking to her regular spot in
Elliot Street, outside the market, where she stood
amongst women selling dishes of various kinds.
There she would call her wares, watching all the

time for the police, because she had no pedlar's licence.

It would be so much easier for her, she often thought, if she could wheel the bundles of fents down to the market in the pram. But there was nowhere safe to put the pram while she dealt with her customers: if she turned her back on it, it could, in a flash, be stolen. Furthermore, if an interfering flattie did show up and ask to see her licence, she could abandon the rags and run for it; an anonymous woman dressed exactly like half a hundred other women around the market could soon get lost. But, encumbered by a pram, she could not move fast – and the pram was too precious to be abandoned.

She had considered keeping Kathleen out of school on market days, to come with her and watch the pram. But not only would the school attendance officer be after her, so would formidable Sister Elizabeth, who taught the kid. Sister seemed overly keen on Kathleen staying in school.

Martha was the only woman to sell clean cotton rags in this particular market, which would suggest that there was not much demand for them in a place where the majority of the shoppers were women. A surprising number of women, however, bought them for their husbands' use: their menfolk worked at skilled jobs involving grease, paint, blood, sewage, etc, and needed to wipe their hands or their engines frequently, with material cheap enough to be discarded afterwards.

She also delivered regularly to several garages employing oil-soaked mechanics who served the increasing number of private cars in the city. The butchers, poulterers and fishmongers in the market itself were also often glad to see her, to buy a rag with which to wipe off fishscales or blood from icy-cold hands.

Her biggest problem was to assemble the basket of suitable rags in the first place, and, furthermore, to accumulate them without having to pay for them.

She begged for rags from door to door in the various neighbourhoods of Toxteth, offering, in return, a coloured balloon for the children in the house.

She also had contacts amongst the Jewish community in the wholesale dress trade along London Road, where she sometimes got very tiny pieces of new material, which she occasionally had to pay for. She sorted the scraps into big bunches of varied colours that she thought might go together, for sale to one or two women customers who did old-fashioned quilting. They would pay as much as sixpence for an assortment of pretty new patches.

Occasionally, pawnbrokers had torn, grubby sheets hanging up outside their shops. These had been used as the outer covering for bundles of clothing which had been pawned and not redeemed, and she would bargain a penny or twopence for any that were hopelessly worn. She would then take them to the public wash house and launder them. When they had been dried on the clothesline slung across the court, she would tear them into one-foot or eighteen-inch squares and sell the smaller ones at three squares for a penny, the larger ones at two for a penny. If any were strong enough to stand being washed after use, she charged more.

Once, when canvassing in Princes Road, she stumbled on an estate auction being held on a front lawn. She watched, fascinated by the pantomime being enacted, and discovered that, towards the end of the sale, much-used cotton sheets, pillowcases, tea towels and everyday tablecloths and bath towels were almost given away.

She mentioned this to her neighbour, Alice Flynn.

'I don't know why they let the stuff go so cheap, Alice, but if I had had a bit more cash, I could've bought a great boxful from just that one sale.'

Alice considered this information at length. She had, in her youth, been in service, and finally she said a little doubtfully, 'I'm thinking that it's stuff from the servants' quarters, and kitchen stuff. The family wouldn't want to use it themselves. They was really throwing it away, no doubt – just put it out on the lawn to get a few pence for it, more to clear the house than anything.'

'But there aren't that many servants nowadays, are there, Alice? We had a right job to find our Lizzie a place.'

Alice laughed. 'Well, if they're moving out of one of them big houses, maybe they've got rid of the servants as well. But you was telling me that Lizzie isn't the only girl working for her mistress?'

'True. There's a cook. Proper bitch she is to our Lizzie.' Martha was silent for a minute, and then she said grimly, 'And a proper pest to her is the sons of the house.'

'Oh, aye. And I bet the mistress don't want to know about that, even if you dares to tell her. Lizzie must watch it.'

Martha sighed. 'I told her that.'

'Some of them'll put a little rubber cap on their you-know-what, to avoid a bun in the oven.'

'I did tell her. 'Cos they can afford it. Wish we could.' She laughed ruefully.

Alice Flynn laughed with her, though she would herself have loved a child. But the war had 'fixed' her husband as certainly as a gelded horse was fixed. So that was that.

Martha could not read. She had a habit, however, of picking up any discarded newspapers she could find. Newspapers were extremely useful. You could kindle the fire in the range with them; you could stuff one between a child's jersey and his vest to keep his chest warm; if you could collect enough to fill a sack, it made a good mattress to sleep on, not nearly so cold as the bare floor.

Now, very thoughtfully, she first took the papers to Mary Margaret, who could read, and asked her if estate sales were advertised. Together they discovered that they were, and Mary Margaret read the advertisements to her.

Sometimes, Martha, looking very out of place in her black skirt and shawl, would put on her faded flowered pinafore, washed for the occasion, and go to such sales. She was viewed with suspicion by the auctioneers, as she edged through the crowd, to look at piles of old kitchenware, some of which a woman of her social station might manage to buy.

She did not draw attention to her real quarry, the bedding. No one else at the sale came near her because she stank. She ignored them and simply watched the auctioneer. She did not bid.

Better quality blankets, eiderdowns and bedding usually went in large lots. She waited until the sale drew to a close, only to find, sometimes, that the stuff was taken indoors again, perhaps to be given to a charity.

Where a likely pile remained on the lawn, she caught the eye of the auctioneer's assistant or someone who seemed to be a member of the family tidying up, and asked if she could look through the stuff. She always told him flatly that she was looking for rags.

Sufficiently often to make it worth her while she got a pile of aged linen for a few pence, or sometimes it was even given to her carelessly, as to a beggar.

She would tie her purchases into a bundle in one sheet and hoist it onto her head to carry home.

'Aye, Mary Margaret, love,' she said wistfully one day to her friend, 'I wish I'd got a bit more money. I could get a lot of fents what would sell well in the market.'

Mary Margaret smiled and said placidly, 'Wait till the kids get a bit older and can bring in something. You might start a business yet.'

'Oh, aye. What a hope!' Martha replied scornfully and laughed at the very idea – after all, Number Nine was not yet two. What money she had was for spending – there were always so many immediate, pressing needs – and you had to have a bit of fun, didn't you? – a visit to the pictures or a drink with your hubby at the Baltic Fleet or the Coburg. One day's worries were more than enough to bear.

Of course, you could dream of having a living room like Mrs O'Reilly's, with a good coal fire constantly roaring up the chimney. But dreams were just that; you did not waste your time on them.

Nor did you normally worry too much about horrors like having to go to live in Norris Green: you only worried when it seemed suddenly that such a fate was right on top of you. And that was such an enormous worry, anyway, that she felt helpless. Sometimes all you could do was to let a thing happen to you and hope that you would live through it.

THIRTEEN

'Me Own World'

January 1938

As Martha tramped steadily down to the market, the cold wind whipped round her skirts and made her wish that she had not sent her inadequately clad children to school quite so early. Her intention had been to make sure that they did, indeed, set off to school, instead of loafing round the court all day, which would mean yet another visit from the school attendance officer. The children would, however, have to hang around in the playground for at least an hour, she fretted, until the teacher on playground duty arrived.

As she struggled to keep her heavy basket steady on her head despite the wind, she finally consoled herself with the thought that the pavements were now drying, so their feet would not be very wet, and the sun was coming out. They would probably run all the way there, and that would warm them. And, at worst, they could stand under the rain shelter.

She refused to consider that the shelter had no walls to break the chilly wind.

She forgot, also, that, even when the teacher had arrived, they would not be allowed into the school until all the pupils had been arranged in neat lines in front of her, class by class, and the nine o'clock bell had rung. Then they would be marched into the school in numerical order, beginning with the Babies. By the time Class Eight had entered, the teacher herself, well wrapped up, would be complaining, as she usually did, that her hands were frozen, despite her gloves.

The colder Martha became, however, as she walked down to the market, the more she worried. But as she approached the building's exterior and was hailed by beshawled acquaintances, also shivering, as they crouched on the pavement amid cheap crockery for sale, she shrugged. It was no good: she could not do anything about the kids. They must learn to endure cold. They would face plenty of it when they grew up.

She always felt, with relief, that the market was her own place, totally apart from family worries.

Once she stepped over the threshold, she was in a world of her own.

Today, she made a joke with her friends about first going into the market itself to get warm and to see if she could sell some rags to her men friends, the butchers and fishmongers. The women were ribald about who her favourite stallholders were.

Inside, she was at least out of the wind, but she continued to shiver as she edged swiftly through the milling crowd like a skinny weasel seeking dinner down a rabbit hole.

Many of the early swarm of people were small shopkeepers, like John O'Reilly, who used the stallholders as middlemen from whom to buy modest quantities of fresh stock for their own tiny corner stores.

The baskets of produce on their arms were a menace to Martha, as they scraped by her, catching her crocheted shawl on the wickerwork and leaving her forearms scratched or bruised by its sharp points.

When her own basket was nearly knocked off her head by the jostling crew, she would snarl resentfully, 'Aye, be careful, can't you?'

But the offender, heaved along by the crowd behind him, would stumble blindly past her, and Martha was left to curse him unnoticed.

She coasted to a near stop amongst the fish-mongers, and called, 'Want to buy some fents – best clean cotton, George? Hugh? Joe, there?'

Today, wet hands were even colder than usual, so she immediately sold a pennyworth of rags to each of two fishmongers. As they thankfully rubbed dry their scarlet, scale-bedewed hands, they teased her absently.

She grinned, and moved quickly out of the crowd, to a stall against a wall: the stallholder sold hot tea from a huge Russian samovar.

She thankfully put down her basket in a niche in the wall. With the twopence she had just earned, she bought herself a cup of tea and a bun. She was served by a woman whom she did not recollect having seen before.

She put the bun in her apron pocket, and, holding the cup between her hands to warm them, she cautiously sipped the scalding tea. Gradually, her shivering ceased, and she stood staring into the empty cup.

I should've bought a second cup instead of the bun, she thought regretfully. I'd have got more heat out of it.

She sighed, and put the empty cup down on the grubby counter. As she did so, she again caught the eye of the stout woman who had served her.

'Want another cup?' the woman asked.

Martha looked wryly at her. 'I don't have another penny to spare,' she said.

The woman clicked her tongue. 'Here, give me your cup: I'm going to empty the samovar anyway. There's at least another cup in it. It may be bitter, but at least it's hot.' She grinned as she took the cup from Martha and held it under the little tap. As she handed back the filled cup, she said hospitably, 'Help yourself to sugar and milk.'

Martha's face lost some of its fatigue. 'Ta, ever so,' she said with sudden warmth, and she smiled.

She drank the hot, very bitter tea slowly, while the vendor carefully lifted the samovar up off the tube of charcoal which heated it. She added a lump or two of the fuel to the tube and then threw the tea leaves from the samovar into a bucket. She rinsed it and carefully set it back on its heater. She then filled a ewer with water from an adjacent tap and lifted it to refill the samovar.

As she lifted the heavy ewer, it caught on the edge of the counter and she spilled water down her flowered apron.

'Blast!' she exclaimed, as the cold water penetrated her clothes.

Glad to show that she also had some grace of

manner, Martha turned and snatched a nice white rag out of her basket.

'Here you are,' she offered. 'Wipe yourself down.'

The woman thankfully did so. Afterwards, she held it uncertainly in her hands until Martha said grandly, 'Keep it – for the cuppa tea, love.'

As the tea lady laid the damp cloth on the counter, she smiled her thanks, and then said, 'I'm OK today, because you give me one, but I could use a rag or two next time you come by. To mop up, like.'

She looked Martha up and down, and then inquired, 'I seen you around before, haven't I? Do you sell here every week?'

Martha brightened further, and replied, 'Sure I do. I don't remember seeing you before: it's usually an older woman what serves here.'

The tea lady replied that she had only very recently taken over the stall from her mother and that she was not yet well acquainted with all her customers. 'I used to come in sometimes when she weren't well,' she explained.

'Oh, aye. You must be Lilly's girl? What's your name?'

'I'm Tara. I've taken over the stall now that Mam's rheumatism is so bad. Pleased to meet you.'

Martha smiled and nodded. 'Likewise,' she said. 'I'm Martha – Martha Connolly.'

As she swung her basket back onto her head, she added, with a knowing grin, 'You must be Irish – with your name? Your mam was always so busy, I didn't talk to her much, so I didn't notice.'

The woman laughed. 'You'd better believe it. Me folks came from County Cork. But me mam never was one for talking much.'

'I'm sorry she's sick.'

'Well, she's getting on. As far as she knows, she's fifty-one now.'

Martha nodded agreement that fifty-one was a ripe old age. 'See you next week,' she said amiably.

And thus began a friendship which, through years of penny cups of tea, Martha learned to treasure.

Steadying her basket on her head, Martha rescued the bun from her pocket. She ate it as she made for the outside of the market.

At the exit, the sun seemed a little warmer, and she began to shout her wares with gusto. About noon, she decided to walk across to the big bus depot nearby, where the mechanics were usually glad to see her and her cargo of fents. If she had any left after dealing with them, she decided, she would go down to the Pier Head where there was another large garage.

This week, because she had soft, heavy white cotton, which could be washed and re-used, she got a better price than usual and sold all of them within a few minutes.

On the way home, as she swung the empty basket with one hand, she promised herself, 'I'll get some meat pies for the kids' tea, from the chippy.'

She turned into the next fish and chip shop she came to, and put the heavy brown paper bag into her laundry basket and carried it home on her head.

The warmth of the hot pies penetrated her tangled black hair, and the heat set the lice scuttling round her scalp. Unfortunately, laundry baskets do not have a big handle with which to carry them when filled, so she had to defer a good scratch until she got home.

She wearily climbed the steps to the front door. It was inordinately quiet, she thought, as she turned the handle. She was not sure of the time: perhaps Kathleen had already fed the children the bit of bread she had put aside for their midday meal, and they had gone back to school.

When she opened the door to her room, she was surprised to see sitting in her single chair not Mary

152

Margaret or Alice Flynn but Auntie Ellen from across the court. In addition to Martha's children standing silently round her, she had, sitting on her knee, Mary Margaret's youngest girl, Minnie.

Martha smelled trouble. She slowly lowered her basket down onto the floor, as she stared at the little tableau.

Auntie Ellen O'Hara, Mary Margaret's sister-in-law, was not usually asked to babysit, because it interfered with the washing which she took in to augment her husband Desi's uncertain wages as a sandwich-board man. In the corner of the boarded-up condemned cellar beneath their room, Desi had, unknown to the rent man, built a brick copper in which to boil clothes. It was lined with clay and equipped with a tap at its base so that it could be emptied. It had a wooden lid. Beneath it was a little grate for a coal fire to heat the water.

Her flat irons could be hooked onto the front of the grate to heat; and Desi had ingeniously connected appropriate flues to the house's main chimney.

Desi collected the dirty washing from her clients and returned it clean, by humping it on his back in a canvas kitbag.

She owned the outdoor clothesline which, by careful arrangement, Martha also used for her rags. Outside Ellen's door, in the court, stood an old-fashioned wooden mangle.

On wet days, she had lines on which she dried the washing spread across the cellar and across her living room.

The last thing Auntie Ellen needed was children running in and out of her clean, flapping washing.

'Ellen, what's up?'

Ellen turned a troubled face towards her.

'It's Mary Margaret,' she said, as she shifted Minnie on her knee. 'She come down here, when the kids come home, and she had a coughing fit. She spat blood on the floor, and it frightened Kathleen and she run across to find me.'

Kathleen stood silently behind Ellen, her head drooped and her tangled hair covering her face, as she waited for her mother to shout at her for not having enough wit, herself, to deal with such a situation.

Her mother ignored her. She was suddenly engulfed by fear for her friend. Had she leaned on her too much for babysitting?

Her voice trembled, as she asked carefully, 'And where might she be now?'

'She's in her room, with Alice Flynn.'

'Mother of God!'

Martha hitched up her skirts and turned to run upstairs. As she ran, she was followed by Ellen's cry, 'I sent one of the lads for the nurse!'

Martha paused in mid-flight. 'Ta, ever so, Ellen,' she shouted back, and tore up the remainder of the steep staircase.

The district nurse might be able to do something to help, she thought, though she was well aware that there was nothing much that could be done for people who spat blood. Coughing up blood meant deadly consumption in your lungs; and that was that, like Martha's own little lass, Colleen, in Leasowe Hospital.

Through the open door of Mary Margaret's windlowless room, candlelight gleamed.

Before entering, Martha stopped to catch her breath.

With her mother, Theresa, standing grimly at the foot of it, Mary Margaret lay on the narrow camp bed which her husband Thomas had bought her, when her illness had become obvious.

Her daughter, Connie, home for lunch, was cuddled in her arms. Above her frightened daughter's head she wheezed laboriously.

Beside the bed, Alice Flynn knelt, one arm flung over both of them to comfort them.

Martha crept in.

'How is she, Alice?'

Alice looked up. 'She's breathing easier now.'

'Praise God.' Martha knelt down beside Alice, to peer into Mary Margaret's face.

'Can you hear me, love?'

'Better not talk to her,' interjected Alice.

The wheezing eased for a moment, and Mary Margaret whispered, before taking another laboured breath, 'I can hear you. And you can stop that nurse coming. She'll want me in the hospital – and I'm not going there.'

She managed a weak laugh. Then she gasped, 'You only go there to die.'

Theresa croaked agreement. 'I'm not having my daughter in no bloody hospital,' she said. 'She'll be better with us.' She stared defiantly at Martha, as if Martha might, without further thought, try to whisk her daughter away.

FOURTEEN

'You Only Goes to Hospital to Die'

January 1938
Despite Theresa's and Mary Margaret's protestations, her neighbours affirmed that it was too late to stop the nurse coming.

'Ellen's lad'll be at her house by now and she'll be on her way on her bike,' Martha said with a knowing look at Alice; they weren't taking any chances. Mary Margaret seemed real ill this time.

Alice wondered if they should call the priest, too. She did not mention this thought, however, for fear of frightening the sick woman to death.

Shaun O'Hara trotted back into the court, shouted to Kathleen, watching anxiously from her doorstep, that the nurse was coming. He then vanished into Auntie Ellen's house.

The arrival of Miss MacPherson, district nurse,

was not immediately noticed by the tenants of the other houses: the shadowed court was chilly and most of the womenfolk were huddled indoors, so they missed this interesting event.

Observing the emptiness of the court, Miss MacPherson assumed correctly that the menfolk were probably hanging round the docks, gossiping in sheltering warehouse doorways after trying for a morning's work – feminine illness would not be unusual enough to bring them home. Those who had a few pennies to spend were likely to be keeping warm in the many stuffy cocoa rooms which lined the dock road.

She nodded to Kathleen, standing with her arms crossed tightly over her chest to help make up for the inadequacies of her precious jacket. The girl's greasy hair hung across her dark, sullen face; but, at the sight of the nurse, her eyes lit up with relief.

She shouted, 'This way, Miss.'

Because she had been told by Shaun O'Hara that the need was urgent, the nurse had hurried. She had pedalled with all speed in and out of the heavy dockside traffic. Huge drays, pulled by horses as large as elephants, were, as usual, frightening to her; and really, she would never get used to the foul-mouthed lorry drivers leaning out of their vehicles' windows to curse the slowness of the animals – and of her bicycle.

She now paused to pant for a moment, before wheeling her bicycle over the paving stones towards the expectant girl.

She had, at first, suggested quite strongly to a breathless Shaun that Mary Margaret should be taken straight to hospital. She pointed out that she was a nurse, not a doctor, and she was in the middle of a long list of visits to bedridden patients. It was pure luck, she told him, that he had found her at home: she had forgotten her bottle of iodine and had had to return for it.

As Shaun continued to plead for help for his aunt, however, she finally agreed to a quick visit: she knew only too well the dread these ignorant, feckless people had of all hospitals – and of most doctors who sent you there. On the other hand, a nurse, she reminded herself with a wry smile, was on the same comfortable level as a nun, someone to whom you could confide all your fears, except anything to do with sex.

On checking her notes, she found that she had, once, already visited Mary Margaret, to instruct her family on how to nurse a tubercular patient. She noted that she had ordered a plentiful diet of milk, fresh fruit and vegetables, and lots of fresh air and

159

sunshine. At that time, she knew she was wasting her breath. But she had done her best.

With a sigh, she now bent to lock her bicycle to the railing guarding the entry to the house's condemned cellar, took her shiny black bag from the basket on the front of the machine, and marched up the steps.

'Where's the patient?' she snapped irritably to Kathleen, as she realised that she had not only missed her morning coffee but would probably have to forgo lunch as well, thanks to this unexpected call.

Kathleen gulped nervously, hugged her jacket tighter to her, and said, 'Upstairs, Miss.' She turned into the house.

Miss MacPherson grunted and followed her in.

At the bottom of the stairs, which were to her right, she stopped as the full effluvium of the house hit her. A particularly nauseous wave of the odour of infant excrement rolled over her from the open door of the Connolly room. A woman with a child on her knee was sitting there surrounded by children of all ages. They were unnaturally silent.

They should be back in school was her first thought, as she glanced at her watch.

The children stared at the nurse in her navy uniform, and she stared back at them.

They looked so scared, so wide-eyed. Had the woman died? she wondered suddenly.

Kathleen was waiting for her halfway up the stairs, so she squared her shoulders and plodded silently upwards.

Near the top, Kathleen edged round a very old man, a wraith of a man, sitting on a step. He was the cadaverous, illicit inhabitant of the condemned cellar, and he had taken refuge on the staircase in the hope that it would be a little dryer and warmer than his usual shelter. He was of appalling thinness, with a face like a skull, out of which stared pale-grey eyes bereft of hope.

Used as Miss MacPherson was to the suffering of slum dwellers, she winced. He should be in a warm bed, she thought despairingly: he's near to death.

Despite weakness, he did, however, manage to shuffle himself to one side so that she could pass him. He continued to stare upwards at her face, as, without a word, she squeezed her plump body past him.

His odour was so intense that, seasoned as she was, she held her breath. She knew that there was nothing she could do for him, except advise him to go to the workhouse, where at least he would be fed. She doubted that he would have the strength to get there, so she said nothing.

161

They had now reached the first landing, and Kathleen preceded her through a door.

'Mam,' the girl called. 'She's come.'

Miss MacPherson ran a finger round her starched white collar, and entered.

By the light of an undraped window, she saw an empty, unmade double bed; an old tablecloth, hanging on a clothesline across the room, partially shielded it from the gaze of people walking past.

Much of the room was occupied by a Victorian wardrobe, its double doors closed by a big iron hasp, a huge padlock hanging from it. In it, the oakum pickers, Sheila and Phoebe, kept what little food and valuables they had: the lock was to keep children away from their food and men away from anything else they owned; it was doubtful if the female inhabitants would chance the terrible beating they would get if they stole from each other, and were caught. Furthermore, they trusted Mary Margaret, and she was there most of the time.

Miss MacPherson took all this in, and paused for a moment, puzzled. Then she realised that Kathleen had gone round the bed to another doorway, and was beckoning her. She suddenly recollected that Mary Margaret's rear room was one of the few she had seen that was windowless:

most such rooms had been condemned and closed down.

Martha came forward to greet her, relief clear on her face. She hastily informed the visitor in a loud whisper, 'She had a proper awful bout of coughing. Then she spat blood, Nurse.' She paused for dramatic effect, and then burst out, 'And she fainted!'

Miss MacPherson nodded. Faints were common-place amid a population of inadequately nourished women, but, in this case, loss of consciousness might spell deeper trouble.

In the dim light of a guttering candle on a high shelf, she approached the narrow camp bed through a muddle of cardboard boxes, stools, a mattress littered with discarded bits of clothing, and a small table laden with dirty white crockery and a primus stove. On a solitary chair lay a pile of neatly folded, clean white cotton pieces, sur-mounted by a reel of thread and a pair of rusty nail scissors.

Alice Flynn still knelt by the bed, one arm flung protectively over her friend.

At the approach of the nurse, she looked up, frowned and climbed stiffly to her feet.

The nurse was shocked to see Connie curled up by her mother. Over her shoulder, the child viewed the visitor with scowling distrust. Above her blonde head her even more distrustful mother tried to smile.

The shaken nurse said sharply to Martha, who appeared to be in charge of operations, 'The child should not lie with her mother. She could be infected by the tuberculosis. Surely her father knows that. Do you know?'

Martha knew, but thought that mother love was more important. She answered defensively, 'I wouldn't know, Miss. I'm just her friend what lives downstairs.' Then in an effort to exonerate Thomas from the implied accusation, she went on, 'Her hubby goes to sea and he don't see much of his kids.'

'Humph,' Miss MacPherson snorted. Would these people never learn?

She looked down at Mary Margaret, and said in a far gentler tone, 'Mrs Flanagan, let your friend take your little girl so that I can get a better look at you.'

Mary Margaret obediently whispered to the child.

Connie woodenly said, 'No.'

She pushed herself closer to her mother.

The nurse tapped her on the shoulder, and said in a playful way, 'Come on, young woman. I must help your mother.'

Connie snarled, 'Go away.'

Martha silently bent down and wrenched the child away.

Connie screamed and tried to fight her way out of the firm grip.

Martha bared her teeth, and said, 'You do as you're told for once, or I'll smack your bottom so hard, it'll be the death of you!'

The nurse looked shocked. The tantrum was shut off immediately, however, because Connie believed that Martha would do what she threatened. She managed, however, to kick Martha in the stomach, before being handed over to a woman standing behind her.

'Take her for a minute, Kitty,' Martha ordered, and turned back to the nurse.

Silent, elderly Kitty Callaghan had stolen down from the second floor to see what was up. Very lonely, because her husband was in gaol and her son at sea, she tended to get passed over by everyone in the house, except for the unwelcome attentions of Joseph, the elderly pickpocket, who lived in the windowless room behind hers.

Not knowing what to do, Kitty simply held Connie firmly by her hand and told her to be quiet. Unexpectedly, Connie obeyed; she was diverted by the nurse opening a most interesting-looking bag.

The nurse took out a thermometer, shook it hard

and popped it into her mother's mouth. To Connie it looked just like a glass cigarette, and she half expected smoke to come out of it.

Alice Flynn dragged a stool forward so that the nurse could sit down.

Miss MacPherson seated herself, and smiled reassuringly at the invalid. After a minute or two of complete silence, she removed the thermometer. Temperature normal. She inquired, 'Tell me what happened. Are you in pain?'

'Not very much, Miss, now,' Mary Margaret whispered. 'It happens like this sometimes. Only after I coughed up, I were out for a while – and that frightened Kathleen. And she didn't know what to do, and she thought of you. And it's real kind of you to come.'

With an effort, she lifted herself onto one elbow in order to face her visitor. 'But I'll be all right now.'

The nurse glanced again at the thermometer, wiped it with a cloth, moistened with a smelly disinfectant, and then put it away.

She was frequently amazed at this patient acceptance of suffering and death as being inevitable, part of existence, and that you couldn't do much about it except dull the pain – if possible. Mary Margaret's calmness saddened her.

Without hope of her advice being taken, she said gently, 'You know, Mrs Flanagan, you should be in a sanatorium having proper treatment. I can arrange for you to be seen by a doctor at the dispensary, perhaps a specialist, who could arrange it.'

'Oh, aye,' replied Mary Margaret hoarsely, 'I seen doctors before and they know there's not much they can do. They thought I wasn't listening – and they said TB is "terminal" – and that means, dying, doesn't it? That's God's will, isn't it?'

Miss Macpherson opened her mouth to doubt this statement, but Mary Margaret had not finished. Her voice strengthened, as she continued, 'So I says I wasn't going nowhere. And I come home to be with me kids and me hubby, till it happens. Sanatoriums is like hospitals; you die in them.'

She paused to catch her breath, and then added defiantly, 'And the doctors is wrong up to now. I'm not dead yet!'

While the nurse took her pulse, she lay exhausted with the effort of such a long reply, her heart fluttering with fear that the nurse might have the power to order her into a sanatorium.

Miss MacPherson was not really surprised at her patient's reply. With sudden insight, she tried another tack.

'Did you faint before or after breakfast?' she inquired.

A little surprised at the question, Mary Margaret replied cautiously, 'Well, you see, I usually has a cup of tea at breakfast. But by the time I'd given our Thomas his bread and tea, the pot was empty – and I was out of tea and milk – and sugar.' She stopped for a moment, and then, in case she should be accused of child neglect, said, 'I give the kids some bread to eat.'

'So, if you had had your tea and some bread, you might not have fainted?'

Mary Margaret thought this over and then agreed.

'Have you had anything to eat since?'

Mary Margaret, eyes, half closed, stirred uneasily. It was hard to admit that, once she had fed the children, she had had nothing edible in the room.

'I didn't feel like nothing when I began to cough,' she hedged. 'Martha here brought me some tea just now. But I only took a sip or two.' She gestured towards a grubby white mug on the table.

'I understand. You probably would not feel like it until you had washed your mouth out, would you? But to keep well you must eat well.'

At this, Mary Margaret wanted to laugh. Life was not like that – you ate when you got the chance. She did not respond to the nurse's remark: she considered it stupid. If she had enough food, of course she would eat it.

The nurse observed a shiver go through her emaciated patient, and her expression became grim. In her daily struggle to alleviate the suffering of the sick and housebound, she could do nothing about malnutrition, that polite, political word which covered the fact of starvation. So many of her patients would be a lot better if, each day, they simply had enough to eat.

She consoled herself with the usual argument against more welfare: the dire situation of many of her patients was not helped by their own hopeless improvidence and their huge birthrate. They must themselves, therefore, shoulder some of the responsibilty for their woes.

As she took Mary Margaret's wrist once again to feel her lagging pulse, she longed, for the umpteenth time, to teach birth control to such women – another child would certainly kill this woman. Yet, she would lose her job if she did so.

Not only would there be outraged complaints at such teaching from the Roman Catholic Church, but there was in Liverpool, she felt, an unexpressed opinion that the maintenance of a mass of cheap casual labour was not totally a bad idea: labour should not be discouraged from breeding; it could be bad for the economy. One thing was certain: any charity that did encourage birth control was liable to find that donations to their funds would shrink.

'Are you on the housing list?' the nurse asked.

'Been on it for five years or more. But we want to be close to here. We're in no hurry to move.'

'Your health would improve in an airy house with windows and sunshine.'

Mary Margaret wanted to explain her husband's and her own paramount fear of being moved out to one of the new public housing suburbs, far away from the docks which were their source of work.

But her strength was fading, as she tried to cope with this unwanted interrogation. She was afraid she might faint again – in front of the nurse – and then find herself whisked away to some God-awful sanatorium, like Martha's poor little Colleen, miles and miles away from family or friends.

Martha sensed some of Mary Margaret's fear and intervened. 'I can bring something for her to eat, right now. And the tea's still on the hob – she could try another cup – but I haven't got no milk.'

'I got plenty of milk,' a voice from the rear interrupted. 'You can have some now, if you want it.'

The offer came from a bleary-eyed Helen O'Brien,

the prostitute. She was flanked by her yawning sister, Ann, who nodded agreement.

At this time of day, Helen and Ann O'Brien, who lived in the room behind the Connollys', were usually in bed, resting before mincing along Canning Place in search of lonely seamen, their long skirts swishing, their blouses unbuttoned. They had had, however, a very busy late morning and early afternoon.

Warned that a whaler would dock that morning, letting loose a large number of desperate crew, womanless for six months, they had gone out early. Money for jam, they had giggled. Now, exhausted from the hard work they had done and slightly drunk from the gin they had consumed, their skirt pockets jingled with a myriad of silver half-crowns.

'I'll bring up a pint bottle right now,' promised Ann magnanimously. She turned and tottered unsteadily downstairs to their room.

Nurse MacPherson smiled at the woman's immediate offer. It would at least stir up for this poor invalid the very lively tribal instinct that existed between such hard-pressed neighbours; from almost empty purses and larders, help would be found for her.

Such care would be far more humane than if the whole family was sent to the workhouse, which could well happen to them: Mary Margaret to the workhouse hospital; the husband to the men's ward, so that he would never see his wife; the children to a children's department, where they would rarely see their parents.

Like the vestiges of Victorian slums in which the poor dwelt, the Victorian belief still endured among the more conservative that such families were not much better than animals: Miss MacPherson knew them to be otherwise.

The tired, overworked district nurse was determined not to push Mary Margaret unfairly into accepting anything which would make her more scared than she already was. The patient was right: her death was inevitable. Let her die at home – and let's hope the children don't get the same disease, she prayed.

She determined to emphasise to the group of neighbours, as well as to Mary Margaret, the need for the children to sleep elsewhere and not to be kissed by their mother.

As gently as possible she would suggest to her patient that her husband should be examined by a doctor. Being a seaman he might be the source of her infection: too many sailors suffered from the same deadly disease.

She would also have a word with Father James, when next she saw him. Though he was a Catholic priest, he seemed to understand his people better than most did. She felt that the Church could rustle up a bit of practical help from the multitude of charities in the city, as well as the spiritual help they usually purveyed.

As she rose from the painfully small stool, she said kindly to Mary Margaret, 'Have a good rest today – and keep the little girl away from you. Remember!'

Mary Margaret smiled weakly. Rest? When she had a whole new pile of hankies to hem?

As an anxious Martha led Miss MacPherson downstairs again, the nurse explained about the need to keep the children separate from their mother as much as possible. Then she suggested, 'Try to persuade Mrs Flanagan and her husband to go to the dispensary. They can see a doctor there who might be able to suggest some treatment for her. Meanwhile, she will be much better if she has good food – and drinks plenty of milk.'

'Oh, aye,' agreed Martha. 'But I'll have to watch her eat; otherwise, she'll give it to her kids.'

And how are we supposed to even get her to the dispensary, she wondered resentfully. She can barely climb the stairs.

The nurse paused uneasily on the doorstep.

'You know the family would be better fed in the workhouse?'

Martha glanced up at her in horror. 'Oh, no, Miss! Separated from her kids, she'd die in no time.'

Mentally, she said goodbye to the pie and chips awaiting her in her own room – Mary Margaret had to be fed, that was certain, and Martha would give her share to her; perhaps Number Nine would not eat all of his and she could make do with what he left.

'I can find a bit for her,' she assured the nurse.

Resignedly, the nurse looked down at the scrawny bundle of skin and bone wrapped in a shawl which was Martha – and admired her generosity.

She couched her report on the family in the vaguest terms and hoped that she had made the best decision for them.

FIFTEEN

'Bevvied'

February to October, 1938

Frail but determined, Mary Margaret got up from her bed and, shakily, resumed her normal life. She was aided by the thought that, if she could survive the winter, she would strengthen in the warmer weather of spring and summer, which she did.

One starlit night in October, when the only other light was the dim rays from the street-lamp near the arched entry and the only sound was the rustle of rats in the dustbins, a raucous voice rolled through the court and echoed on its enclosing walls.

' "It's a long way to Tipperary, it's a long way to go. Goodbye, Piccadilly, farewell, Leicester Square," ' roared the voice. Then it faltered, as a rat leaped across the path of the singer, followed immediately by a suddenly awakened stray mongrel. The dog's teeth glinted threateningly in the faint light.

The singer wobbled on his feet, watched the pursuit for a moment, cussed both animals and then proceeded across the yard. He had forgotten the next verse, so he went back to the beginning and recommenced the song.

Inside the houses, sleepy heads were raised in surprise. Since it was Friday, most of the men were, of necessity, home and fairly sober: if they had earned anything, most of them did not draw their wages until Saturday.

Saturday, now that was different. That was the night when you got as drunk as possible and then enjoyed a lively street fight, mostly one on one, where, despite bumps and bruises, nobody got kicked to death – there were definite unwritten rules about that.

But it was only Friday, and somebody out there was bevvied, for sure. Perhaps there had been a party, thought some of the listeners, of which they themselves had missed word, a happy occasion when neighbours helped a bewildered sailor to spend his pay on them as fast as possible. Whatever the cause, the singer must have struck lucky.

When the voice was recognised, awakened children

were ordered to stop whingeing, ragged coverings were rearranged and weary eyes were closed again. It was too bloody cold to stir out in the middle of the night; the story could wait till morning.

Except for Mary Margaret. Kept going by sporadic gifts of extra food and enough donated tea to float a rowing boat, if not a battleship, she lay, most nights, wide-eyed and fearful. She feared Thomas giving her another child and dreaded the implications of her death.

She did not care about herself – she would be in the arms of Lord Jesus; she worried for her children.

What would happen to Dollie, Connie and Minnie? Dollie already knew that life was not fair and was pugnacious enough to fight anyone who tried to crush her; she might survive. But Connie and little Minnie were still so small, mostly silent and very helpless – though quick enough to steal food if they got the chance.

And then there was Danny. In February, he had celebrated his sixteenth birthday at sea, but he was really still only a kid. Where would he go when he came home from sea?

She ran her fingers along the wall by her bed. It was covered with postcards from Danny and from his dad, posted to her from ports all over the world; on the back of each of them were real nice messages to her.

Thomas could find another wife, but she might not like her stepchildren; and, during the next few years, while he was still young and most needed his mam to come home to, Danny would be alone.

Tears filled her eyes. Would Thomas manage to keep the family together? Or would the little ones be condemned to an orphanage, like Olive Mount or the Kirkdale Homes? Or a stepmother who beat them? Though he had wept over the death of Sean and had gone to his funeral, she thought feverishly, Thomas did not take much interest in his children.

There was always her mother, Theresa, of course, old and stiff as she was. She would help him; she'd have to.

When distantly in her windowless home she heard Thomas's drunken voice, she was bewildered. She heaved herself up on one elbow, and listened. He was obviously gloriously and happily drunk.

Where had he got the money from?

She had not been surprised that he had been absent all day – she had assumed that he was holed up with a friend in a cocoa room, talking, as usual, about football matches or racehorses and the bets he had laid on them, and, occasionally, without much hope, of ships in need of crew.

In the dead dark, Dollie turned over and inquired sleepily, 'Is that Dad?'

Mary Margaret sighed. 'Yes. Now, you be quiet – you know his temper.'

She turned laboriously and said, 'Light the candle by my bed, love. Ann O'Brien give me two, so as I could have a light for most of the night. And then you can help me over to the pee bucket.'

Rather than stand up and chance falling over her siblings, Dollie untangled herself from the grey army blanket in which she was wrapped and slid on her bottom unerringly across the floor towards her mother's bed. She found the matches and lit a candle stuck in a saucer. Minnie stirred at the sudden flare, but did not wake.

When the nurse had come to see their mother earlier in the year, neither Dollie nor Connie had understood clearly what the fuss was about. Mothers, when they weren't scolding you, were always coughing up or complaining of chest pains or their aching feet, and Dollie had seen a number of women faint: to her, it was normal.

Bridie Connolly had told her that if they threw up in the mornings, you knew mothers had another baby inside them, and that, somehow, your dad had put it there. You'd always know it was his fault, she said, because there was always a bloody row in which he was accused of it. She had heard her father say that it must belong to someone else.

At such times, Bridie had advised her, you should keep away from both of them, because they were liable to hit out, not only at each other, but at anyone else who happened to be near.

But her mam had not thrown up in the ordinary way; she had coughed a lot and then spat out some blood. So it wasn't a baby.

The priest said babies were the will of God and should be welcomed: Dollie herself had heard the priest with white hair say it. She had noticed vaguely that there seemed to be a fearsome and threatening amount of His will about, because there were babies everywhere – dozens more than those in the court – you could see them playing in the gutters in the streets, or wrapped in their mams' black shawls against their mothers' chests. Heaps and heaps of them.

While Mary Margaret, her skirts hitched up, stood unsteadily over the bucket, Thomas ceased to sing; he was absorbed in slowly pulling his bulky duffle bag up the dark stairway and then carefully through Sheila and Phoebe's room, which was not quite so dark.

At the sound of flowing water near her, Mary Margaret's mother, Theresa, awoke.

She sat up, her eyes dazzled by the flickering candle flame. 'You all right, Maggie?' she asked anxiously.

'Oh, aye. Dollie's giving me a hand.'

Holding onto Dollie's bony shoulder, Mary Margaret picked her way unsteadily across the littered room back to her bed.

'Thought I heard somebody singing,' the old lady muttered, as she lay down again.

'It's Tom coming in.' Mary Margaret sank thankfully back onto her bed: at least, she was able to get up and pee, without Martha having to hold her.

When Thomas got entangled in the old tablecloth the sisters had draped on a clothesline across their room, both Theresa and Mary Margaret heard Phoebe inquire blearily who was there.

Thomas mumbled, 'It's only me, Miss,' and stumbled to his own door, which was shut. He dumped his duffle bag down on the floor. In the darkness, he could not find the knob, so he hammered impatiently to be let in.

'Dollie, let him in, love. And don't open it too sudden; he might fall over. Quietly, now.'

'Bugger him,' muttered Dollie, as she stopped rearranging her blanket over herself and, this time, got to her feet. Savagely, she longed to swing the door open really fast, to see if he would, indeed, fall down.

'You'll get punched if you do,' she warned herself under her breath. She opened it with exaggerated slowness, inch by inch. It was she who stumbled and hit her knee painfully on the corner of a wooden box when her father forcibly pushed the door open.

He kicked his kitbag through the doorway and then stood staring bewilderedly around the crowded room, as if he were having difficulty in recognising his own home.

Mary Margaret eased herself up on her elbow. Her angular, bony face looked thinner than ever as she peered at him through long greasy tresses.

'Where you been?' she asked.

'None of your business. Where's me dinner?'

Though already thoroughly well fed, he asked the question simply to annoy his wife.

Conflict appeared imminent, so Dollie slid silently under her blanket.

'On the table,' replied Mary Margaret wearily, and yawned. 'It'll be cold by now.'

Thomas shut the door behind him and picked his way unsteadily round Dollie and the box on which she had knocked herself. He stretched out one hand and used the end of the table, under which the girls were sleeping, to steady himself until he reached their only chair.

In front of him, on the table, was something wrapped in a newspaper. A faint odour of food still emanated from it.

Alice Flynn had wrapped up for him a bowl of soup provided by Auntie Ellen.

'Watch you don't spill it when you open it up,' advised Mary Margaret. 'And mind you don't knock the paraffin stove off the table.'

His drunkenness was beginning to fade and he felt nauseated. Filled with self-pity, he began to cry.

Mary Margaret was familiar with this reaction. She asked, however, 'What happened?' She felt weak and resentful, unable to comfort.

'I got a ship.'

She was truly surprised. 'What?'

'A ship. Report tomorrow. Sail on Sunday.'

'What about your kit?'

'Got it out of pop this afternoon – it's here.' He pointed to the dark lump lying in a corner by the door. 'You know I always carry the pawn tickets in me discharge book, so you don't lose them.'

He paused, hoping that his head would clear. It did not, so he continued weepily, 'Signed on, and all.'

'Holy Mother!' his wife breathed in genuine amazement. Thomas had not had a ship for over eighteen months, and, most of the time, they had scrimped along on Public Assistance food tickets, her own hand sewing, Theresa's old age pension and the tiny allotment Daniel made to her.

Her wonderment grew into apprehension, as she remembered her own helplessness.

'Where you going? How long will you be away?'

'Dunno. She's a tramp, the *Belinda*, with a cargo for Lagos.' He wiped his dripping nose with his hand and sniffed hugely. 'With a bit of luck, we'll pick up something else there. Could be away for months.'

'Strewth! Lagos is far enough. What'll I do?'

'You've nothing to worry about,' he sneered. 'You'll get your allotment.'

'I've got to live eight weeks before they start to pay it,' Mary Margaret retorted. 'Even then, how will I collect it? I can hardly walk down to the shop, never mind to the shipping office. I would never have got Danny's last one if Martha hadn't lent me a penny for the tram.'

'Ach! Stop being such a natterbag. Ask the clerk at the counter: he'll fix it,' Thomas replied irascibly. 'Or Theresa'll fetch it for you.'

How thankful he would be to sail out of all this, to

leave on land a nagging wife and three pestiferous brats, and not have to think of anything. Even rotten food and crowded space on board was, at least, fairly worry free – you did what you were told, laid low and held your tongue, and you were OK. Then, in foreign ports, you could find a woman and get drunk and have a fine time; with a mixed cargo, the *Belinda* might dock in several places before she hit Lagos.

He began to feel sleepy and laid his head on his arms on the table. He barely heard his wife's sarcastic remarks which now poured out of her.

'It's great for you. You'll be fed daily, starting Sunday, but the kids won't be. I suppose old Grossi in Paradise Street gave you part of your ticket from the shipping company in cash – and you've spent it?'

The ticket represented an advance on Thomas's first month's wages. It was supposed to enable him to get his kit together for the voyage.

Thomas grinned slightly as he replied, 'He give me twenty-five per cent, like usual.'

He fully expected his wife to explode at the thought of the money being spent before she got a share of it. But she was silent. How had he got a ship? she wondered. She eyed him suspiciously. Was he telling the truth? Had he stolen something and sold it? Maybe there was no ship to account for his unexpected affluence?

Finally she asked him. 'How come you got a ship so sudden, like?'

He rubbed his red face hard, massaging his eyes to keep them open. Since it showed him in an excellent light, he told her quite honestly.

'I walked up to the registry office this morning and hung around – to see if I could find anyone who might know a ship short of crew.

'And going up the steps, damned if I didn't run into Sam Molloy what I went to school with, Catholic, like us. I've sailed with him before, but I hadn't seen him for months.' He paused to yawn. 'He's done well for himself. Done three trips on the *Belinda* as second mate.

'And, you know, he had orders to find a trimmer, pronto, 'cos one of theirs has got a real bad fever – from Africa, they think – he hadn't been well, like, though he kept on working – and it finally burst out when they was coming into port.

'He's in the Isolation Hospital and there's hell to play with the medical officer – and the ship was quarantined, until the Health Authorities was sure nobody else had it. The crew had to be vaccinated, and, just in case, I had a needle this afternoon – and I feel rotten with it.

'Sam was one of the first crew members ashore. So I got the job. Pure luck – and the ship's still delayed till Sunday.'

He did not tell Mary Margaret that he had had to practically go down on his knees to Sam to get the job for him, a fellow Catholic. He had produced his precious discharge book with its years of columns of 'Very Good', entered by a legion of ship's masters. It was pitifully blank for the last eighteen months. Pinned in the back of it were the pawn tickets which represented his seaman's kit.

They had gone immediately back to the boat. Sam had been persuaded to vouch for him not by any cogent argument, but by the despair of an old friend. Thomas was a decent man and a good worker, who was prepared to chance a ship which had carried a bad fever – a job which many would turn down for fear of infection. Added to that was the fact that a trimmer or fireman's job was itself mercilessly hard: at best, only the really desperate would want it.

The ship's master, anxious to sail, was quite thankful to have his crew completed so quickly. The ship's agents, to whom they had hastened next, were even more so; the demurrage bill was mounting up.

With a sly grin, Thomas reflected that Sam had

earned the grand evening they had had together on the twenty-five per cent in cash advanced by old Grossi.

Mary Margaret lay flat on her bed and considered resentfully how the money left over from getting the kit out of pawn and buying any extra necessities from old Grossi would have helped to feed the kids for the eight weeks before Thomas could earn another month's wages.

At the end of eight weeks, she herself would receive part of his wages from the shipping company as an allotment. At best, when a man was at sea, you delayed the rent payment and lived on credit. You also scratted around for any job you could get yourself – because the allotment was never enough: you were dependent upon your man reaching home again with the balance of his earnings nearly intact, so that you could face the rent man and the corner store and pay your debts.

She gave no consideration to the sickness there had been aboard ship. Sickness was as common in ships as it was ashore – as Martha had reminded her after the nurse's visit, when she had been talking about how tuberculosis could be spread by a seaman.

'What time you got to show up tomorrow?' Her voice was dull and listless.

'Seven o'clock.'

Thomas laid his head on the table and suddenly succumbed to sleep. He dreamed a frightening dream of the hell of heat he would work in for the next few months. As a trimmer, he would shovel the coal to the firemen, who would feed it into the huge furnace in the bowels of the ship. In up to 140 degrees of heat, he would work to exhaustion.

It was an Australian ship working its way back to Sydney, he comforted himself as he half awoke in a panic, something he had not told Mary Margaret. It belonged to a small company which tramped between Australia and England. It was known to be fair to its crew and, according to Sam, the food was not bad either.

He dozed again and the dream continued. In it, he realised that he was too old to stand the stress of the job. He saw himself die and then fly through the sky to Australia, where, unexpectedly resurrected, he stayed and picked apples for a peaceful, cool living amid a myriad of trees in full leaf.

As loud snores erupted from her husband, Mary Margaret knew that he would never, if left to himself, wake up in time to join his ship in the morning.

It was too late in the evening to ask Martha to give him a call when the knocker-up roused her.

Since her own alarm clock, though it still ticked, had long since given up on its alarm settings, she dared not sleep.

She must dispatch him in time; a seaman who missed his boat could be in real deep trouble, no matter what his excuse: it was the law.

Despite a night which stretched her endurance to the limit, she finally surrendered to slumber; it was Dollie and Connie fighting over their blanket who actually woke Thomas in time.

SIXTEEN

'Me Allotment'

October 1938

By half past five, in response to the knocker-up, Martha was shaking Patrick and the children awake. She wanted time to go down to the garage near the Pier Head to peddle her rags and, perhaps, if she had enough stock, do a bit more at the market. Since it was Saturday, Patrick, also, must collect his week's earnings.

Patrick met Thomas by the water pump in the court, as they went to splash their faces in its icy water. The seaman had a blinding headache as a result of his spree with Sam Molloy the previous evening.

As they roughly shaved themselves with their long-bladed, cutthroat razors, both complained that their razors needed stropping and wished that they had some soap. Pat told his neighbour that his strop was still useable and that Thomas could come in, any time, to sharpen his razor; he said he had forgotten to sharpen his own the previous night.

As he rinsed and folded his razor, Thomas mentioned that he had a ship.

'Oh, aye? That's good.' Patrick took off his flat cap, and ran his hands through his unruly curly hair in the hope of arranging it to cover his bald patch. Before replacing his cap, he thoughtfully twisted the ends of his droopy moustache. 'There's a right collection of boats in this week. More than I seen for years.'

'You're right, Pat.'

'War's coming.'

Thomas nodded. 'Heard from the old woman, months ago, that they was going to build an air-raid shelter on the street. They haven't got round to it yet, though.'

Other men and women were appearing on their doorsteps to peer up at the leaden sky, before going to the latrines. Patrick and Thomas hastened to these filthy conveniences, before a queue should form.

Then, still together, they clumped back to their home, two comparatively young men already bent and greying, and, as usual, hungry.

Thomas slipped his razor into his kitbag and tightened the rope that held it closed. He ate the cold soup for breakfast.

With a stub of pencil stolen by Dollie from school and by the light of the last candle, he wrote down in large print on the margin of an old sheet of newspaper the name of his ship and that of its agents with their address.

He repeated this aloud for Theresa, who, like Martha, could not read.

'I'll try to fix it so you can collect the allotment instead of Mary Margaret,' he told his mother-in-law with a yawn. 'I don't know for sure, with a foreign company, how to fix it – but Sam Molloy will know.'

Lying on her bed, absolutely exhausted from her broken night's sleep, Mary Margaret missed the significance of her husband's boat being a foreign tramp.

Though it was obvious from Thomas's remarks that Sam Molloy, a Liverpool man, had served for some time on it, it did not mean that the boat would necessarily return to Liverpool. It could wander from port to port, picking up and delivering cargoes wherever they could be found: Thomas could be away for six months or even a year.

At her husband's promise about the allotment, Mary Margaret relaxed slightly. Her mother was the only person in the world she would trust with her allotment money. Furthermore, she was sure that, if need be, Theresa was capable of standing up to some irate clerk in the shipping company's office who might query her being there instead of Mary Margaret herself.

Facing up to shipping clerks was no joy to the barely literate, smelly wives of some of the crews. At best, the clerks were patronising; at worst, they were quite ill-tempered.

Mary Margaret smirked as she remembered how the wives, shuffling along in the queue, occasionally retaliated by making snide, disparaging remarks about the manhood of the men on the other side of the mahogany counter.

The innuendos did not endear them to the shipping company staff, still less did the stench which rolled across the counter.

Thomas kissed Dollie goodbye on the top of her head, because her mouth was full of bread. The bread had been donated the previous evening by the O'Brien sisters: with more ships coming into port there were more seamen, so they were doing very well, and could afford to be generous.

Dollie stopped munching and stared balefully up at her father before she turned her back on him. He picked up Minnie, who was still clutching her morning crust, and kissed her on her cheek. He dealt similarly with Connie, who was thankful he was going away.

Sensing that something unusual was happening, Minnie broke into frightened howls.

'Be quiet, can't you?' hissed Theresa. She stood in the background, hands folded under her black shawl, looking resentfully at her three grand-children, aware of the responsibilities likely to be thrust upon her.

Thomas ignored the wailing. He hesitated by the bed and said heavily to his wife, 'You'll be all right with Theresa here.'

'I suppose so.' Didn't the fool understand that she might not be here when he came back? Didn't he realise that she didn't know whether she was going to be able to keep the family fed for the next eight weeks – without the strength to work herself or get help from Them? She was not like Martha, who could take things day by day. Martha had the strength to do it. She had not.

She thought wearily that he was a typical seaman, shaking off the responsibilities of home the minute he had a ship. He'd never be any different. She closed her eyes. Afraid of infection, he did not kiss her.

Guilt-ridden, not knowing what else to do, he turned, hoisted up his kitbag, and left her.

'Goodbye, everybody,' he shouted towards Theresa, as he opened the door to the oakum pickers' room.

Awakened by Minnie's howls, Phoebe and Sheila were not yet up. They muttered a malediction at Thomas's passing through and at the noise coming from both the Connolly and Flanagan families. Then they groaned as they turned over and tried to sleep again for another half-hour.

En route out of the front door of the house, Thomas shouted goodbye to Martha and Patrick.

The Connolly door was hastily opened and the whole family surged out to shout farewell and good wishes. Getting a ship at last was stupendous luck for Thomas, they agreed.

The noise caused further havoc to the hopes of sleep for everybody in the house. This cheerful sendoff, however, raised Thomas's spirits considerably.

Patrick turned back to deal with the chaos in his own home. 'Lucky devil,' he muttered.

Mary Margaret listened to the noise, trembling with weakness.

'What am I going to do, Mam?' she asked Theresa frantically. 'Eight weeks before I see a penny from him!'

In the failing light of the guttering candle Theresa looked down at her daughter, her lips folded in over toothless gums. Her forty-nine years weighed upon her. She had outlived most of her friends, and she was tired of the constant struggle to stay alive. She said dully, 'I'll get a job, and you can sew your hankies – you could get Dollie on them, too. She can hem.'

'She won't like that – and neither will the old goat from the school.'

'Ach, we'll think of something to tell him. And she's got to learn to like it. It's time she worked.'

At these words, Dollie paused, a piece of bread halfway to her mouth. Stay at home all day in Martha's room, stitching and stitching? Not bloody likely. Unless she was paid, which was unlikely.

She glanced up at her stony-faced grandmother, her mouth open to protest. Then she had second thoughts; Gran was a real tartar. She could still deliver a cutting blow to girls who queried what was said.

If she had to stay at home, she would bargain later with her mother about getting some money for her work.

She finished her piece of bread, and then sidled out to visit Bridie Connolly and go out to play in the street, before her grandmother or her mother could order her to do anything else.

SEVENTEEN

'What Do You Think Girls Is For?'

October 1938

On the Saturday on which Thomas told him about his finding a berth, Patrick collected half a week's pay. Despite a huge row, Martha had been unable to squeeze all his wages out of him. She decided, therefore, to accompany him to the Coburg that evening to help him spend the portion he had withheld.

First, however, it was vital that she go down the street to pay John O'Reilly at the shop, out of the money her husband had given her. She knew that she must do this; otherwise she might never get credit again.

Then she had to wait for Jock, the rent collector, popularly known as Satan Hisself, to come bicycling into the yard to do his round. She was already paying off arrears at the rate of a shilling a week and dared not miss another week.

If rent remained unpaid, Satan Hisself's employer had the power to call in the bailiffs to sell the contents of their room, and put the family out of the court: they would be left sitting on the pavement, with little hope of finding local accommodation.

It would be worse than being condemned to Norris Green; at least, if she was moved there by the City, a roof would be provided for them.

Contentedly aware of his threatening nickname, Jock arrived in the late afternoon at Court No. 5.

Martha paid him unsmilingly. She was very weary from the fight she had had with Patrick. The sound of her screams of rage demanding money for plimsolls for Tommy and Joseph had been heard throughout the house, as Patrick woodenly refused. He had a fixed idea that she could conjure up other essentials from her own earnings or from charities.

'I give you the rent and O'Reilly's bill, plus a bit. You do the rest,' he had snarled.

Fearing that he might beat her if she insisted further, Martha was silenced. She was seething with quiet rage, however, as she turned to Kathleen. The girl had finished gulping down her bread and cold tea, and she ordered her to take Martha's own share upstairs and deliver it to Mary Margaret.

'With me love, don't forget,' Martha instructed her, as she gathered up Number Nine's leftovers, some of them strewn on the floor, and stuffed them into her own mouth.

Later, Kathleen came slowly back downstairs. Auntie Mary Margaret had accepted the little newspaper-wrapped bundle with suitable thanks.

Martha's room was nearly dark now, lit only by the distant rays of the lamp at the court's entry. It was also cold. Her mother seemed to have forgotten that they had no coal and that, consequently, the fire was out.

'And, being Saturday, they'll go out tonight,' the girl lamented to herself. 'Then they'll come back home, the pair of them, so drunk they'll hardly be able to stand on their feet.'

She wondered what it would be like to sit a whole evening in a really warm place like a pub, and get drunk. When she had asked Helen O'Brien whether pubs were warm inside, she had been assured that, indeed, they were. It had sounded most enjoyable.

One night, Helen O'Brien had given her a sip of her evening glass of gin, before the sisters set out on their evening amble in search of seamen just paid off. As usual, they both had their hair done up in neat buns and their faces garishly painted.

To Kathleen, they seemed ghostly in their floured whiteness.

The gin had been bitter beyond words, and, on an empty stomach, it had made her feel a little light-headed.

Helen had said, 'We always has a glass of gin afore we starts.' She did not say why they always went out in the evenings: she did not have to because Kathleen, though lacking exact details, already knew what some grown-up women did for a living. According to hints from the nuns at school, they would burn in hell for it.

She did not, however, understand the significance of the glasses of gin, which were only the first of many, judging by their drunkenness when they returned; gin was supposed to protect them from pregnancy.

Kathleen had hardly groped with her toe for the bottom stair, when Martha ordered her to look after the five younger children while her parents were out during the evening.

'I'll be going down the road with your dad for a glass of Guinness,' her mother told her.

'Why can our Brian take off for his boxing and it's always me what stays with the kids?' Kathleen yelled in sudden revolt.

Martha jumped at the unexpected objection. She

turned and pushed her face into the face of the angry girl, who was nearly as tall as she was. All the wrath subdued by Patrick's stubborn denial spurted forth.

'Brian's got to work and you know it. You stay 'cos you're a girl – and don't you forget it. What do you think girls is for?'

Kathleen was silenced, partly by her mother's ferocity and partly because of the surprising question. She did not know precisely what girls were for. In dumb acceptance of life, she always shifted through her days as best she could, propelled by circumstances over which she had no control: she had never considered what her future might be.

Girls became mams and had babies, didn't they? But, in the meantime, why couldn't they have fun like boys did? She hadn't had even a game of hopscotch since Lizzie went into service; and Lizzie didn't think service as a kitchen dogsbody to a grand lady in Upper Canning Street was much fun either.

She turned, and flounced out of the room to sit on the front step to consider the question. It was nearly dark and the cold of the step struck through her faded cotton dress to her naked bottom. As she burned inwardly with resentment, she pulled her knees up to her chin to keep herself a bit warmer and tucked her dress tightly round her to cover her nakedness.

Her unhappiness was added to when, in the half-dark, a young man paused to grin knowingly at her. He was the son of a neighbour in the next court, just home from sea, and, judging by his unsteady stance, was already fairly drunk.

Suddenly engulfed by another fear, she started up and whipped inside. Acutely aware of her budding womanhood, she had seen that grin on other male faces, and sensed uneasily that it meant trouble; other girls had told her that men put their you-know-what inside them, and it hurt.

She believed that this might mean babies: the nuns at school had said as much in their muddled, vague warnings about the dangers of men.

What did they really know about babies? the girl wondered, as she stood shivering in the tiny hall of the house. Wrapped in their black habits, nuns were safe from such threats, weren't they? But Kathleen had once seen a baby born in the courts and dreaded going through such an ordeal herself. And what would the Sisters have said if she had turned up at school with a big round tummy?

She knew. They would have verbally torn her to ribbons and called in the priest, and what a to-do that would have caused. Even now that she was older and working, her father would beat her if she ever became pregnant, if only to show the priest that he was a caring father. She might even be sent to a home. It would be hell on earth, never mind hell in the hereafter.

In the house in which she lived, she felt fairly safe. There were enough women around most of the time, watching with interest every move of their neighbours, ready to tell your mam – or even the priest – what they had observed. Men knew this and it acted as a brake on them; except for her father, who, when at home, made her very uneasy these days by touching her in a way which made her tingle strangely. It frightened her, and she was keeping out of his sight as much as possible.

She wondered if she dared tell her mother, and decided that Mam would not believe her and that she might be beaten for trying to cause trouble.

She continued to stand in the tiny hall and shiver for a few minutes, even when the young man had staggered on up the court to the latrines. Then she re-entered the Connolly room to face her mother again.

Martha said immediately, 'Here, take Number Nine,' and thrust the little boy into her arms. 'I got to cut the bread and cheese for tea.'

His bare bottom was icy on Kathleen's arms, but he gurgled with laughter at the sudden transfer, and stuck his finger in his mouth.

Instinctively, she grinned back at him. Aye, he was a little pet: not like Joey and Ellie, who were forever whining, or Tommy who always seemed to be out, even when she herself was supposed to be looking after him; or Bridie who was a little bitch.

Her grin turned to a glare as, over the baby's head, she caught her mother's eye.

Martha felt the need to reinforce her earlier remarks. 'And don't forget to watch Ellie,' she warned. 'She's gone in a flash these days.'

Kathleen did not reply. Except for Number Nine, she did not care if all her siblings fell through a grating and down a drain, followed closely by her mother.

She dropped her eyes, lest Martha see the vicious rage she was in, and then she turned away, still holding the baby close to her.

Patrick clumped down the stairs from seeing Mike Flynn in the attic. He accepted a thick hunk of bread with a lump of cheese on it thrust at him by his wife, and stood eating it while Martha doled out bread and jam to the children. Then he went to the latrine.

On his return, he put his head through the doorway; he felt it judicious to inquire, 'Are you coming, Martha?' He did not want another row. He was still feeling resentful about the previous shouting match. She had screamed something about plimsolls for Tommy, blast her: maybe he'd give her something for them. But he'd make her wait: and she could bloody well pay for her own drinks tonight, seated separately with the other women, as she would be, on a bench in the hallway.

Paying for her own drinks did not really bother Martha: on her weekly trip to town she had sold every white rag she had, some at the Pier Head garage and the rest in the market. Even after buying bread, cheese and jam for the family, together with a pint of milk for Number Nine, she still had a whole shilling left.

She flung her black shawl over her shoulders, and signalled to Patrick over the heads of her quarrelling toddlers that she was coming.

She left a forlorn Kathleen who was still hungry: in her fast-growing years, the girl yearned for food, lots and lots of it. She had spent most of her time in school thinking of it – and of having pretty clothes and her hair curled, like the young women she saw on her rare visits to the city centre.

Sometimes, oblivious to Sister Elizabeth's notes on the blackboard, which she was supposed to copy into her exercise book, only a slap across her ear would bring her back to the dreary routine of the classroom.

Then she would once again pick up her nub end of pencil and laboriously form the letters for words which she barely knew; yet Sister Elizabeth was the only person who ever gave her a word of encouragement, telling her that she had brains and should use them. 'If you can read, girl, you can learn anything.'

Learn anything? For what? To have babies? To do what you're told by your parents? The priest called the latter 'honouring them'. And he was another one who had to be obeyed. Reading seemed a useless skill: her mother never seemed to need it.

As she stood cuddling Number Nine, Tommy pushed past her and, without a word, went out. She really envied Tommy his freedom. Mam didn't seem to care what he did. It was as if he was free to do anything, she considered enviously.

He was an amiable boy and she rarely quarrelled with him. Nice-looking, he was, fair-haired with bright blue eyes. And what's more, she considered, as she absently separated Joseph and Ellie, whose quarrel was rapidly becoming a fight, he earned a lot of pennies, more than he ever told their mam about. She had seen him buy himself a bun at Mr O'Reilly's on more than one occasion.

When she asked him, he always said he got his money from the carters who thronged the dock roads with their drays drawn by huge Belgian horses. If an animal was not particularly well trained or the drayman expected to be absent for some time while doing a delivery – or went into a pub for a drink or a pee, a boy would, for a penny, hold the horse's bridle and keep the animal calm. He would also raise the alarm if a thief tried to steal part of the load.

She had in the past wondered, idly, if Tommy ever dared to drop his shorts for the many paedophiles who haunted the narrow alleys across the street, alleys which were playgrounds for Hide and Seek or Cowboys and Indians. Boys did sell themselves on the streets: she knew that from friends at school; but boys didn't have babies, the girls always pointed out with sheepish giggles. If boys could endure whatever it was they did to them, men would give them a silver threepenny bit or some sweeties.

She did not envy Brian: she felt that, now he

was at work, he was no longer really part of the family. He had pocket money. Also, he took his boxing seriously and that took up his free time; when he was full grown, he wanted to be a professional boxer. Lucky him. In contrast, she had to babysit, in addition to going to work. And had all her wages taken by their mother, she thought resentfully.

Mams were much more suspicious of what girls got up to, she considered, with a sigh. Mechanically, she ordered Bridie to stop going through the food box to see what was left.

'Mam'll kill you if anything's missing,' she threatened. 'Just you keep your hands out of there. You've had your tea.'

'I'll do what I like,' came the muffled reply, as the younger girl stuffed the heel of a loaf into her mouth.

Kathleen slipped Number Nine to the floor, and sprang like an angry Alsatian over Ellie and Joseph, who were locked in friendly combat.

She seized a handful of Bridie's hair and forced her head back, while she grabbed the bread protruding from her mouth.

Bridie grinned, let the bread go and bit her sister's wrist.

Kathleen cried out, let go of the hunk of bread

and clutched the girl by the throat. She pressed hard until Bridie choked. As she fought for breath, Bridie fell backwards.

Kathleen let go of her throat and, with one bare foot, kicked her hard in the stomach.

Bridie screamed.

Kathleen ignored her, while she rescued the half-chewed piece, which had fallen to the floor, and threw it back into the box.

'If you go near that box again, I'll kick you till you have to go to hospital. Mam'll give you what for, anyway, when I tell her.'

A furious Bridie was saved from further threats, because Helen and Ann, on their way to their own room at the back, unexpectedly walked into the candlelit Connolly room. They had been to the corner store and were laden with bursting cotton shopping bags.

The children immediately ceased their noise at the sight of the friendly faces.

The women were taking a respite after a very busy week, and they paused to smile at Kathleen with easy good humour.

'Now, there, what's to do?' Helen asked the younger children. 'It sounds like Lime Street Station on Cup Final day, it does.'

Bridie immediately pointed an accusing finger

at Kathleen. 'She kicked me!' she shrieked, and clutched her stomach. Keeping one eye on the two prostitutes to see the results of her dramatic presentation, she continued, as if in terrible pain.

For a moment, Kathleen wished that her big sister Lizzie was there to help her. Lizzie was big-built and a full year older than she was, with the same commanding voice that Martha had. When she had been in charge, all the children had quailed before her.

Kathleen stared helplessly at her neighbours. She did not want to explain how the racket had come about. All she wanted to do was to walk out of the door and leave the children to rot.

While the newcomers laughed at Bridie's histrionics, Ellie and Joey caught at the prostitutes' skirts, their playful altercation forgotten. Fearing that they might be blamed for the noise, they began a steady frightened whimper.

Number Nine got up off the floor, and clutched at Ann's flowered apron. He raised his eyes to her, and asked, 'Butties?'

He often received tiny bits to eat from the women, and, since he had not eaten much dinner or tea, he, like Kathleen, was now hungry.

Unwilling to open up her shopping bags to such an avaricious collection of children, Ann answered

him, 'I don't have no butties, but I got a toffee –
I think.'

Smiling at the child, she dug into her deep
skirt pocket and a wrapped toffee was produced.
Number Nine laughed and toddled away with it,
while Ellie and Joey stopped whining and looked
expectantly up at the giver.

'I don't have no more,' Ann told them regretfully. 'Maybe next time?'

Her sister produced a box of matches, and then
unlocked their door. A match was struck, a candle
lit to illuminate their windowless room. Then the
door was shut, and only a dim line of light at the
bottom of it and soft murmuring voices indicated
that they were home.

Joey was already trying to get Number Nine to
give him a lick of his toffee. More trouble.

Kathleen snatched up Number Nine, so that he
could happily dribble toffee without interference.
Afraid of her venting her obvious frustration on
them, Joey and Ellie fled to the hallway and climbed
halfway up the stairs. There they sat close together
in the dark, two little bundles of nerves.

When her audience vanished into their room,
Bridie stopped shrieking. She got up from the
floor, and announced sulkily that she would go
to play hopscotch with Dollie and Connie in the

street outside the court. There the paving stones were more even and offered ready-made squares; she did not need chalk to mark them out.

'No,' retorted Kathleen firmly. 'It's too dark.'

'Dollie and Connie's out there already.'

Bridie moved towards the door. 'You're not Mam. You can't stop me.' Her lower lip protruded menacingly.

Kathleen smirked. 'No, I'm not Mam, but I'm bigger than you. And I can tell our dad when he come home – and you know what he'll be like. And what's more, it's raining.'

'I don't care. I want to.' Bridie stamped her foot and clenched her fists.

The threat of further violence was suddenly extinguished by the return of Tommy at the open doorway. He absently pushed Bridie to one side and shut the door slowly behind him. He stared emptily past Kathleen and Bridie into the jungle of a room. His hair was plastered down by the rain. Drops of moisture clung to his guernsey and shone faintly.

Joey opened the door behind him and he and Ellie crept in.

Tommy suddenly woke up from his lethargy and shook himself playfully like a dog. ''Lo, la. Ack, it's wet out there,' he greeted Kathleen.

Kathleen pointed at the wet boy, and said tartly, to Bridie, 'See. I told you!'

'What?' responded Bridie without interest. She was watching Tommy.

'Guess what I've got,' said Tommy and rattled something behind his back.

In the shadowy darkness, Ellie could not see what he was holding behind him. She toddled round him. 'Let's see,' she commanded.

Tommy danced away from her. 'No. You got to guess.'

Remembering the toffee, Ellie suggested hopefully, 'A sweetie.'

Tommy stopped his little dance. In mock astonishment, he replied, 'You're right, love. You pick the first one.'

He brought forward a half-pound box of liquorice all-sorts. He opened the lid and exposed their lurid pink, black and white glory.

Ellie swallowed and then plunged her tiny, clawlike hand into the gaily decorated box to scoop up a handful.

'Ah, ah,' Tommy warned. 'One at a time.'

Very carefully, she selected a large one covered with brilliant pink speckles, while Joey jostled her in his haste to be next.

Little Number Nine, in Kathleen's arms, stared

down at the box. He had never seen a whole box of sweets before and did not know quite what he was looking at. He was still sucking his toffee and was fairly content with that. He did, however, demand to be put down, so that he could get a share of whatever it was that was on offer.

Her eyes on the box, Kathleen slid him slowly down onto the floor.

Who would give you a whole box of sweets? And for what?

As the delicious odour of liquorice and coconut reached her, a burst of saliva ran down her chin. Then she looked at Tommy. His expression was so strained, far beyond normal, and his cheerfulness so forced. Was she correct in the uneasy suspicions at his long absences which had haunted her for some time?

Real pain shot through her. Not Tommy, surely?

Tommy hastily lifted the box high so that the contents should not be spilled by Number Nine's groping hands.

'One at a time,' he ordered, and chose a big black and white one for the baby. While the others clamoured for more, Number Nine looked doubtfully at the sweet.

Kathleen slowly and thoughtfully squatted down by him to encourage him to take a little bite. He hastily swallowed the remains of his toffee, and obeyed her. Then he immediately grabbed the all-sort and stuffed it into his mouth.

She did not know whether to laugh at the child, or cry for Tommy. Would he burn in hell?

As she rose, Tommy thrust the box under her nose, and grinned. She took a sweet and tried to smile back at him. With his ill-gotten gains, Tommy was being as generous as a seaman just returned to port.

'How did you get them? Pinch them from Lewis's?' she inquired hopefully.

He swallowed, and then responded quite surlily, his expression defiant. 'Them what doesn't ask questions, doesn't hear no lies.'

'Ma'll ask you quick enough if she hears about it.'

'She won't care.'

'Tom, you know that there are things that she won't stand for. Lewis's is a big store, and she's often took socks and such herself. Lewis's or Blackler's is fair game. But some other things – you know what I mean – she'll raise hell about.'

He stood like a small statue for a moment, while his face began to flush and his defiance faded.

He looked wretched, as he mumbled, 'I don't

know what you mean.' Then realising the kindness of her concern for him, he said, 'Kath, don't bother your head about me. The kids'll eat the sweets before she gets home.' He shrugged wearily. 'All Mam will hear, if she's sober enough to listen, is that I brought a few sweets home – and it made a treat for the kids.'

She was silent. She did not know how to cope with the situation.

He continued to plead. 'You know that anybody'll give you a sweetie or two just for going a message for them.'

'But they didn't, did they? That's a half-pound box.'

Improvising quickly, he replied, 'I mucked out Mr Murphy's cow shed on Wesley Street.'

The milkman did indeed keep several cows in his shed, considered Kathleen. But was he that generous? She doubted if he could afford to be.

She absently took another sweet out of the box he was still holding. What could she say? Come to that, what could she do?

If she told her suspicions to either Mam or Dad, Tommy might get a real beating and run away from home and go to sea. Boys did that regularly. Paedophiles were a common enough danger; but even at sea, if what was whispered was true, he would almost certainly be similarly misused. In a ship, there would be no escape.

Perhaps he had been hurt enough already; he certainly didn't look too good.

'OK,' she agreed reluctantly. 'That's what we'll say, if she asks.' She paused, and then pleaded, 'Don't be angry with me. I'm worried about you. You don't have to do it.'

He slowly screwed up the empty box, and then smiled grimly. 'Don't worry,' he replied. 'I can look after meself. I'm not going to go hungry, when I can earn a bit.'

Bridie had been watching the pair of them. Now she lost interest, and turned away, thoughtfully picking pieces of liquorice out of her front teeth. She knew very well what Kathleen was referring to. Freer to roam than Kathleen, she had observed other boys do it.

She stored the incident of the big box of sweets in her memory, to be used as a threat to tell their dad and thus squeeze pennies out of both Kathleen and Tommy.

Kathleen turned sadly back to the subject of babies. Her mother had instructed her never to let a man touch her, 'Because you can get terrible diseases from them. You can rot to death – lose your nose, like African Mary did.' Did her warning include fathers, she wondered fearfully?

This threat of disease was, to Kathleen, far worse than the nuns' vague warnings about babies. Sickened, she wondered if Tommy would lose his nose – or did it only happen to girls?

In her desperate ignorance, the more Kathleen pondered over the situation, the more muddled and frightened she became.

EIGHTEEN

'Soap Makes You Smell Real Funny'

1965

Martha was seated in a few inches of lukewarm water in the Home's original Victorian bath. Angie was bent over her, hastily scrubbing her back with a soapy face flannel.

'Done your underneaths?' asked Angie, as she sloshed water over her patient's bony shoulder blades.

'Yes,' replied Martha reluctantly. Ever since her arrival in the home Matron's obsession with soaping all over the body, especially 'underneaths', had been beyond her. With a faint wisp of humour, she wondered what Patrick would have had to say if his wife had smelled of Sunlight soap instead of like a proper woman.

After such a soaping, she always feared that she

would come out in spots or that she would peel. She was certain that her skin would never be the same again.

In the latter idea she was correct. For a woman of sixty, except for her red hands a remarkably fine skin had been revealed once the dirt had been removed. It now had a peerless, almost unwrinkled whiteness which had been protected all her life by its natural oils, and Angie had made her laugh by telling her that she had a skin like a pearl.

Martha's proud boast had always been, like many women of her ilk, 'I never had a bath in me life, not since I were born.' Now she could not even be proud of that after the bath Angie had given her, she cursed inwardly. Pearl, indeed.

Angie wrung out the face flannel. 'Right. Now I'm going to help you onto the chair and you can dry yourself and put on your nightie. I got five bed baths to do yet.'

As she straightened up, Angie paused for a second and winced. God, how her back hurt nowadays. She blamed the pain on having to lift and turn too many patients. She wished the home had a proper invalid's bath, where you sat the patient in a kind of spoon which lifted her in and out of a tub. Things like that would certainly ease matters for nursing aides, she thought wistfully.

Not that Mrs Connolly was particularly helpless. Angie felt that, with exercise to strengthen her muscles, Martha could manage for herself. But she dared not suggest any such thing to Matron. Matron had the fixed idea that the only way to make sure no patient had a fall was to keep her charges in bed: and Martha had certainly been sent to the home because she had broken her hip in a fall, and, in consequence, could not look after herself.

It was Angie's private opinion, based on experience, that the underlying cause of Martha's fall had been weakness caused by malnutrition. During the time she had been in the home, despite being unsteady on her legs, the woman had begun to bloom on the boring, mushy food provided.

It was, however, not her business to tell Matron how to care for her patients. Nor did she dare tell the doctor, who came in from time to time, that, rather than take for granted Matron's reports to him on her charges, a thorough examination of the patients might show that some of them could be discharged. They would first need proper physiotherapy and, of course, good advice on their own care, thought Angie, and help to buy walkers or sticks.

But empty beds did not bring in any money, she concluded cynically, and beds filled with really sick people, who needed proper nursing, would cost Matron more to run: she would have to employ more aides.

She placed her arms under Martha's and clasped her firmly. Then she lifted her to her feet and steadied her, while Martha raised one foot carefully over the side of the bath and onto the rumpled mat; then, after a little hesitation, she swung the injured leg over.

Angie seated her on a chair draped in a towel.

'She's still not much weight,' considered the aide, as she compassionately viewed her tiny naked patient. 'But she does look better.' She put another towel in Martha's lap, and said aloud, 'Your nightie's on the rail there, love. Must run. Back in a few minutes.'

She fled to assemble what she needed for the first bed bath. For fear she would increase her work by having to run back to the storeroom for something forgotten, she enumerated her needs as she ran: hot water, towels, soap, face flannel, clean nightie, bedpan, toilet roll.

Meanwhile, Martha sat naked and depressed by the bath of dirty water. Until she had been taken to the hospital, she had rarely looked at herself. Now, she gloomily examined her stomach. It had never looked rounder, except when she had been expecting. When she leaned forward, her waistline bulged slightly, and all of her looked exceedingly white; even her legs, with their blue varicose veins, shiny pink skin and the scar left by the surgeon when setting the broken hip, seemed to her very different from normal.

The hurt leg seemed to have shrunk, she noted nervously.

She wondered what her face looked like: all mirrors had been taken down off the walls before she came to the Home. Dementia patients were, she understood, liable to get very upset if they saw a reflection in a mirror.

She picked up the towel and rubbed her wet hair. She then decided that she had dried off well enough, and took the nightgown off the rail. She hated it because it was open at the back and was held together by a tape at the nape of her neck. How was a woman supposed to look respectable in a garment like that?

She reluctantly pushed her arms through the appropriate holes and clumsily tied the tapes. Then she sat looking at the scratched woodwork of the half-open door.

She had meant to chat with Angie about the nice time she and Patrick had enjoyed at the Coburg on the Saturday night after Thomas got a ship. She felt it had been a turning point in their lives, because, the following week, Patrick had, for the first time for months, worked the full week. He had finally coughed up money for two pairs of plimsolls, a pair for Tommy and another for Joseph.

And when Father James had asked him, he had actually found a shilling for him towards the building of the new cathedral. Of course, it wasn't anything like the ten per cent of whatever you had that you were supposed to give to the Church. But it had pleased the respected priest very much.

And then there had been the Letter which had changed their lives.

Now, the preparations for the impending visit of the doctor to the Home had spoiled her plan to continue telling her story to Angie. She was sorely disappointed. Talking to Angie kept her sane, it did.

Angie did not return to take her back to her bed. Matron had waylaid her. She had ordered her to help another aide, coming in to relieve Angie herself, to get a wandering dementia patient back into bed and strapped down until the doctor arrived.

Finally, Martha pushed her feet into her bedroom slippers and decided that she would go back to her bed alone. 'As if I can't do it,' she muttered scornfully.

Very carefully, she used the edge of the bath to raise herself to her feet. Then, to steady herself, she caught the brass handle of the door. It wobbled slightly, but she managed to keep her balance.

She sighed wistfully.

'Reckon I could walk down the stairs if I still had a stick. And out of the front door and down the steps and into the garden – and away from this bloody gaol.' She opened the door wide, and sighed again. 'But you don't have a stick – and you don't have no money neither.'

Balancing herself cautiously with her fingers against the dark, panelled walls of the house's upper hallway, she edged along the passage. When she came to an open bedroom door, she had, for a second, to walk without support. She paused and then warily took a quick couple of steps across the aperture and caught the doorframe on the other side. She whimpered. Then, though her damaged leg still hurt, she grinned. Not bad, she decided.

At the next doorway, she paused again and glanced inside the room.

It looked similar to her own room. Five beds crowded it. Each patient lay on her back, staring at the ceiling, her bedding tucked tightly under the mattress. They looked exactly like dolls in boxes in a toy shop.

'Mother of God,' she whispered, as a cold, creepy feeling went up her back. 'Are they all paralysed? Does anybody know who they are? Do any of them know where they are?'

She was getting cold in her backless nightie, and she shivered. Where were their families?

And, come to that, where was her own family when she needed them? Like now? Tears, never far away, welled up in her sharp, birdlike eyes and the dolls in their boxes blurred. She turned her head to rest her forehead on the wooden panelling.

A harassed, scolding Angie suddenly caught up with her and made her jump.

'Scared me to death, you did – when I went into the bathroom and you wasn't there. Come on, now. Put your arm round me waist – and we'll get you into bed before you catch your death.'

'Oh, Angie,' wailed Martha.

'Come on now. Stop crying. You'll be all right once you're all warm again in bed.'

Martha sniffed, and allowed herself to be hustled into her room and into bed.

'Wish I had a stick – and a proper dressing gown,' she said to Angie, as the aide tucked the sides of her bedding in.

'You're not going anywhere, love. What would you be wanting a dressing gown for? Eh? And

Matron won't allow sticks, as you very well know, 'cos they can be used as a weapon. That's why yours was taken away from you, remember?'

And how I'd love to use it on Matron, the old nit, thought Martha savagely, as she wiped her tears away with the edge of her sheet.

Angie turned and ran to the door.

'Where you going now?' Martha called. 'I want to tell you something.'

'Bed baths. Then, when I've finished that, I'm going home,' snapped Angie, and slammed the door after herself.

'Humph,' grunted Martha, and glanced towards Pat's bed. The curtains were still drawn round it.

As she lay propped up by her pillow and contemplated a future like Pat's, she began to rebel against such certainty.

'I'll ask the doctor if I can have a stick to walk up and down the bedroom,' she determined. 'I'll make meself better if it kills me, I will.'

But Matron will be with him and you'll never get a chance to talk to him yourself, common sense warned. And you can't shout over her voice – you might be sent to a mental place. They'd say you'd gone crackers.

Her determination wilted. She began to cry

again, quietly so as not to disturb the other women in the room.

'I thought I'd seen it all,' she wept. 'But I never dreamed of a place like this.

'Dear Holy Mary, Mother of God, get me out of this hellhole. Intercede for me dear Mother, I beg you!'

NINETEEN

'It's Clouding Up, I Tell Yez'

January to June 1939

The sleet of January and rain of February 1939 gave way to the penetrating winds of March and longer daylight hours. April followed with a mixture of heavy showers alternating with fleecy clouds chased by the sun's rays. Though an improvement on the spring of 1938, these changes in weather passed almost unnoticed over the roofs of Court No. 5.

No crocuses poked their heads up between the paving stones. In the surrounding streets, no trees existed to put out soft green buds. In Church Street in the city centre, a girl peddled small bunches of violets for ladies to pin into the fox furs draped round their necks. Martha noted these. Of all the inhabitants of Court No. 5, only Martha, searching for sources of rags and then selling them in the market, ever saw daffodils or any other flowers, and these were usually in the gardens of homes holding auction sales.

As 1939 progressed, the international political situation became increasingly threatening. In far-away London a worried Ministry of Health, which knew barely anything about the real suffering of the north of England, quietly ordered one million burial forms to be dispatched to the local authorities of the larger cities. In their turn, in May 1939 the local authorities had discussed piling up a store of cardboard coffins; and subsequently the City of Liverpool, much to the irritation of the occupants of Court No. 5, finally pulled down the wall which blocked it off from the main street.

'It lets all the wind in from the river,' fretted frail Mary Margaret, as she sat on the step to get a breath of air before going back to her sewing. She pulled her shawl tightly round her, her hands too cold to hem a handkerchief outdoors.

One morning, at Martha's suggestion, Mary Margaret asked Joseph Duggan, the old pickpocket who lived in the second-floor back room in which he had been born, to carry her chair downstairs to Martha's room and set it by her window so that she could sew her handkerchiefs as long as the daylight lasted. Sheila and Phoebe had recently become rather short with her, because, if she was sewing by their window on the few days they had off, their privacy while the daylight lasted was invaded.

Because Patrick was subsequently so cross about *his* privacy being intruded upon, Martha was thankful that she had not asked him to move the chair.

Previously, if Patrick was at home and Mary Margaret was visiting Martha, she thoughtfully removed herself to her own room or to that of Sheila and Phoebe.

Now, as the price of food climbed steadily, the necessity for Mary Margaret to continue to sew far into the evenings in order to help to provide for her little family meant that the presence of his wife's friend in his room infuriated Patrick. On days when he had no work, or money to spend at the races or in a pub, he liked to lie on the mattress and snooze in the afternoon.

Martha pleaded, 'She's so desperate to do her sewing – and so ill – I couldn't refuse her, could I now?'

Reluctantly, Patrick grunted agreement. The woman would not last long.

Mary Margaret's eldest daughter, Dollie, was even more outraged when she was frequently kept away from school and made to sit cross-legged on the floor beside her mother and put her rather imperfect knowledge of hemming to work. It was not that she liked going to school; it was rather that she would be made to work at home – and would not receive a penny for it.

Grandma Theresa had made sure she did as she was told. She had assured her that unless she worked she could not be fed, would not be fed.

A frightened Dollie knew that Grandma Theresa never issued an idle threat. Furthermore, whenever she got the chance, she loved to eat.

Muttering many rude verbal protests under her breath, she took up her needle. Because she was angry, her first handkerchief had to be painstakingly unpicked and rehemmed and, despite her mother's gentle protests to Theresa, she did not share the other children's meagre lunch.

When the school attendance officer, his own handkerchief at his nose, came to see why Dollie was not at school, Mary Margaret snatched a piece of linen out of Dollie's hand and, in the nick of time, pushed it under herself. She made her own illness the excuse for the child's absence.

'Me hubby's at sea,' she whined. 'And me so sick – it's TB, you see. And I've nobody else to turn to.' She was careful not to mention the existence of Grandma Theresa, busy mending sacks in a local warehouse.

During the previous winter, as the little family fought its way through the dreadful eight weeks before Mary Margaret's allotment came through, Theresa had contributed to the family the whole of her ten-shillings-a-week old age pension, and, in addition, had found a job that nobody else was desperate enough to want to do; it brought in a few extra shillings.

'I see,' the school attendance officer had responded through the thickness of his handkerchief. He was used to this kind of excuse regarding absences of eldest daughters. As long as it was a girl who was kept at home, attendance was rarely enforced, except after very prolonged absence; lots of girls missed school every Monday: they looked after their siblings, while their mother took the washing to the public wash house. It was a different matter if it was a boy who was absent.

Full of resentment, her eyes cast down, Dollie stood silently beside her mother during this exchange, not daring to say a word.

The officer retreated, with the admonition that Mary Margaret should make some other arrangement as soon as possible.

Out in the street, he took a huge breath of air polluted merely by factories, trucks and horse manure. As he scribbled a report in his notebook, he wondered how the court inhabitants survived at all.

Even when Thomas's allotments came through, Mr O'Reilly at the corner shop refused Mary Margaret any further credit; he said he could not risk it: she owed too much already. She must first pay off her existing bill.

Jock, Satan Hisself, was occasionally persuaded by Theresa to let the payment of rent slide: he had many seamen amongst his tenants and understood this hiatus when seamen's families were sometimes reduced from abject poverty to almost destitution. Once the man's allotment of about half his wages began to be paid by his shipping company, he could sometimes squeeze some of the rent out of their enterprising wives. Arrears, however, continued to accumulate and would not be made up completely until the happy return of the seaman with, it was sincerely hoped, almost half his wages still in his pocket. As far as Satan Hisself was concerned, the secret was to find out the expected date of the man's return and then pounce on him before the entire population of the court retired to the local pubs or cafés to help him spend his money.

As he resignedly made a note that Thomas Flanagan was on a tramp steamer, date of return, therefore, unknown, the London authorities took notice of the loss of civilian lives during the Spanish Civil War and increased their request for burial forms. They theorised that, if war broke out and London and other big cities were bombed as Bilbao had been, casualties would be even greater than they had first estimated.

During 1939's lovely summer and after the rubble of the broken wall had been shovelled into lorries by a gang of labourers and had been driven away, Alice Flynn went out one morning to buy some milk. She was puzzled to find another gang of men marking the edge of the pavement with white paint.

Mystified, she asked, 'What on earth are you doing that for?'

One man slowly eased himself upright and winced at the pain in his back. He grinned. 'What do you think?'

'I dunno.' Alice smiled back at him; he was a nice-looking youngster.

'It's for the war.'

Alice burst out laughing. 'You don't fight wars with paint, you silly bugger.'

'It's so as you can see the pavement.'

Alice continued to chuckle. 'There isn't no war.'

'There's going to be, Missus. It's clouding up, I

tell yez.' He bent to smooth a drip of paint off the end of his brush into the pot. He then gestured at her with the brush. 'You can see it coming. And you know what they'll do first?'

'No.' Alice was suddenly sobered.

'They'll turn all the lights off – and you won't be able to see nothing. White paint'll help you find your footing.'

'You're kidding me. Streets is dark enough already.'

'No, I'm not kidding, Missus. Lights on – and the Jerries'll see us from above and be able to aim straight, when they come in the night to bomb us.' He pointed heavenwards. 'Lights off, they won't be able to find us in the night.'

A pang of real fear went through Alice, not for herself but for her invalid husband, Mike, bedridden in the attic.

She stood stupefied in front of the workman who had bent once more to his task, stolidly dipping his brush into his tin of paint.

She watched him slosh further rough oblongs along the pavement edge.

Not another war? She felt an overwhelming sense of helplessness. In the background of her busy life, she had heard Mike's wireless babble about someone called Adolf Hitler, but she had dismissed it as a lot of male political drivel. Was it all true? It couldn't be, could it?

Since nothing warlike happened during the next few days, and, after she had discussed the strange conversation with Martha, both women decided that the workman had been teasing her and she had been frightened by a pot of paint.

She forgot her fears. Martha had said with a laugh, 'Whoever heard of turning the streetlights off or painting the pavement white to fight a war? Soldiers with their legs wound round with puttees fight wars.' Even the rumour of the building of an air-raid shelter out in the street made more sense than turning lights off or painting kerbs; and there was, as yet, no sign of the shelter.

Alice returned to her usual problem of making an army pension stretch to cover a slow, but remorseless, increase in the price of food that summer. Loath as she was to leave Mike to manage by himself, she found a part-time job cleaning the floors of a ship chandler's store: the previous cleaner, a younger woman, had volunteered for the Auxiliary Territorial Service.

Meanwhile, Theresa continued to mend sacks, despite the steady payment of the allotment.

Theresa would never forget walking down to the shipping office to collect Mary Margaret's first allotment payment during the previous winter. As the widow of a sail maker, she had had no direct experience of shipping offices or the kind of officialdom she might face: she feared she might not receive the allotment if, at any point, she made a mistake.

Found wandering in a huge Edwardian office building, she had been directed to a mahogany counter over which she could just peep. She had explained to a clerk on the other side of the counter that her name was Theresa Gallagher and she had come to collect her daughter's allotment. 'Mrs Flanagan, that is.'

The clerk checked a list. In an accusing voice, he queried her name.

She was scared as he leaned over the counter to see her properly, but she faced him without flinching; she was inured to being treated like muck.

'Me son-in-law arranged for me to collect it for her because she's proper sick with TB.'

'I have no record of it. What is her husband's first name.'

'Thomas.'

'Mrs Flanagan must come herself.'

'I tell you, she's sick.'

'Many people with tuberculosis are quite mobile.'

Theresa stared at him stonily. 'Mary Margaret can't barely walk.'

She made no movement to slink away. Instead, she suggested, 'Ask your boss.'

Pinch-mouthed, the irate clerk went in search of his manager, while the queue behind Theresa became restive. They muttered as the delay lengthened, and shuffled their boots on the wooden floor. The muttering slowly became loud remarks on the inhumanity of shipping agents. Other clerks, though safely defended by the high mahogany counter, became short-tempered, as they dealt with other queues of black-shawled women, some of whom could neither read nor write: they signed with a cross, witnessed by the clerk, for the cash handed to them.

Theresa steadied herself by clinging to the counter, so that the clerks on the other side were faced with two rheumy blue eyes, a greasy, yellowy-white tumble of hair over a dark forehead and ten dirty claws.

When she glanced hastily back at the increasing queue, the woman behind her saw a dark visage which had never had more than a cursory wipe since she was born, a figure thin and frail, a tattered black shawl drooping over a tiny body. Her only sign of cleanliness was a large white pinafore, carefully washed for this important occasion.

It was a familiar sight, and the woman behind her, who was younger but did not look much better, smiled sympathetically at her plight.

The clerk returned with a bald-headed, bustling man who ignored Theresa, as he riffled through papers on the counter. Then he looked up, and asked the name of Thomas's ship.

She told him in a very loud, though quavery voice, as if he were deaf.

'She's in the wrong office. She should be downstairs.' The man turned and hurried away.

Since the women who came to the office usually sorted themselves out quite successfully, the clerk had assumed that Theresa's seaman relative was in the same ship as the husbands of the two women who had preceded her. He was annoyed with himself, and spoke sharply to Theresa.

'You heard,' he said and turned to the woman behind her. 'Next, please.'

Theresa had had only a cup of weak tea for breakfast, and her knees were beginning to give under her. She gripped the counter more firmly and did not reply.

Another great staircase to struggle down, another huge tiled hall to cross, probably another queue in which to wait. She could not do it. Even with the woman behind her trying to push her to one side, she could not move.

A younger woman, further back, who had been idly watching the wraith at the top of the line, saw that Theresa was shaking. She left her place in the queue, and went to the old woman. She tapped her on the shoulder.

Theresa jumped in surprise, and half turned her head.

The woman said kindly, 'You sit on that bench over there till I been done, and I'll take you down.'

Theresa nodded. She slowly let go of the counter, crept over to the beautifully polished bench which had been indicated, and thankfully sat down. For a minute, the office whirled around her and then settled back into place.

A number of women smiled quite benignly upon her, as they flowed slowly along in the queue: it was unusual for any of them to take a seat in such a sumptuous place, and they were pleased to see that there had been no objection to Theresa's doing so.

The young stranger was as good as her word. After a slow and careful descent of the stairs, her hand under Theresa's elbow to steady her, she even made sure that the old lady was at the right counter; and she remained with her until her request for the allotment had been checked against the company's records and had been carefully counted into Theresa's clawlike hand and she had equally carefully signed for it: she was proud of being able to write her name.

'Put the money in your skirt pocket, love, afore you goes outside,' the young woman advised Theresa.

Theresa saw the point and stuffed the cash well down into the deep pocket in the folds of her black skirt; no pickpocket could extract it from there.

'Be all right now, love?'

'Oh, aye. Ta ever so.' Theresa smiled toothlessly.

With a great sense of unexpected opulence, she treated herself to a twopenny tram ride from the Pier Head. It dropped her near home and, through a sudden shower of sleet, she then dragged herself up a short slope to the court.

Ever since then, as long as the allotment was available, she had taken two hours' leave of absence from her sack-mending to collect it. She was always proud that she had been able to cope successfully with the staff of such a big office.

TWENTY

'Men Are a Real Cross'

July to September 1939

Patrick Connolly found himself surprisingly busy during that lovely cloudless summer; there were many more ships in port. Occasionally, he ached so much from the long consecutive hours of physical labour that he did not go to the stand: he would argue that he had earned enough that week for the family to get by on.

Instead, he sometimes took the tram out to Aintree to watch the races.

More often, he could be found in Meg's cocoa room or in a pub. In either of these places there would be a bookie's runner to take his bets, whether on horses or on greyhounds. If he lost a bet, a comforting mug of cocoa or a glass of ale was immediately available: its cost would be recorded on a slate hanging behind the counter, to be paid when he drew his wages at the end of the week.

He did not, of course, tell Martha about these expeditions. She did, however, nag at him for more cash, because she knew from the general gossip .in the court that the docks were much busier, and she felt that he must be earning more than usual.

When he was at home, her nagging tended to send him, in fast retreat, upstairs to visit Mike in the attic, on the irreproachable excuse that he had promised old Mike; exactly what he had promised, he never told her. Sometimes, it was to deliver to the invalid winnings he had made from bets Patrick had laid on his behalf; some-times it was merely to escape from her shrieks of rage.

To most of the men who lived in the court, Mike was a good friend. Many of them could not read very well, and Mike had far more up-to-date sports reports than did the newspapers, thanks to his radio.

The radio was itself a subject of respectful conver-sation, and every family longed to have one. Mike's ran on a wet battery and a dry battery.

Getting the wet battery periodically recharged was one of Alice's regular chores, and Mike would lie and fret until it was safely set up again by his bed.

No matter how carefully she carried the battery down the steep, narrow staircase, the acid always slopped onto her black serge skirt and sometimes onto her swollen, bare ankles. It burned badly both skirt and skin, so that her garments were much more darned than those of her neighbours. There was, also, the fear that the leg burns would go septic, which they occasionally did.

The infection necessitated hot poultices made from rags, so a piece of cleanish linen was begged from Martha and boiled in a pan of water on Alice's primus stove. The water was squeezed out, with much wincing because of the heat. Then the steaming poultice was slapped onto the sore. The recipient invariably shrieked with pain as her tender skin was scalded.

This treatment was repeated until the sore was declared clean, a matter of several days.

During this miserable period, Mike often consoled his suffering wife with tots of smuggled rum given him by seagoing relatives.

In Martha's opinion, a casualty of the Battle of Mons was entitled to male company and plenty of rum. Furthermore, he was married to kindly Alice: so, when Patrick vanished up the stairs, Martha would content herself with a final furious threat from the bottom step. She swore that there would be further mayhem if he didn't get up betimes in the morning and get himself to work.

Seated by the invalid on one of the family's two chairs, a Woodbine dangling from one corner of his mouth, Patrick, too, was sometimes given a small tot of rum. Glasses in hands, both men were at their happiest when they could hum along with the radio to old wartime songs. It did not matter whether the songs belonged to the Boer War or to the Great War. Occasionally cigarettes were removed from lips, while they belted out a particular favourite, like 'Goodbye, Dolly, I must leave you'.

Alice did not always share their enthusiasm and sometimes sought temporary refuge from the noise on the front doorstep. There, she would hear from a fuming Martha about Patrick's failure to do all the days of work offered to him. They decided that men, on the whole, were a real cross to bear.

Alice had reason to know this. From time to time, she wept over poor Mike, who often became irascible because of his enforced confinement and his sexual impotence.

Though she was now at work and did not hear the news so often, she sometimes picked up bits of information from it. She was able to tell the other women about the impending distribution of gas masks and the instruction which would be given on how to use them. This information struck fear in the hearts of all who heard it.

Nobody had forgotten about the use of gas in the last war, and most people knew a man who had died as a result of it or who was still struggling from its effects.

'Maybe the man what was painting the kerb was right,' Alice added nervously.

When Bridie overheard the conversation, she interrupted it. 'We was shown in school. I can put on a gas mask.'

Her mother rounded on her. 'Why didn't you tell me?'

Bridie shrugged. 'You never asked me.'

It was Alice, on her way to work at the ship chandler's, who, a few days later, met the postman on the doorstep. He inquired if Patrick was at home.

'He's at work, and his wife's at the market,' Alice replied.

The postman hesitated. The front door had an opening through which letters could be dropped onto the floor of the hall. But he knew, from experience, that they could be easily lost in such a house – and that could cause an inquiry to be made. He preferred to hand the missive, if possible, to the addressee.

As a wounded veteran, Mike received more letters, official or charitable, than most of his neighbours, so the postman was acquainted with Alice. He asked if she would take the letter in.

She liked the trim little man in his neat navy-blue and red uniform, popularly known in the court as His Nibs. She cheerfully agreed, took the missive from him and tucked it down the neck of her blouse to rest safely between her breasts.

As he made a note of her name so that, if necessary, the letter could be traced, he said, 'Be sure to give it to Mr Connolly himself. It's got the City coat of arms on the back of it – it could be important.'

'Oh, aye,' she promised. Inside, she felt suddenly sick. A letter from the town hall? What could that mean, other than an eviction notice preceding slum clearance?

After she returned home from work, she retrieved the letter from between her breasts, and, with a heavy heart, turned it over and over in her hand. She did not show it to Mike: no need to worry him yet, she decided, and laid it on a shelf beside her mugs.

As she prepared tea for Mike, she listened anxiously for the return of Martha or Patrick.

While she was sitting by Mike's bed, sharing bread and jam and tea with him, she finally heard Martha open the door of her room and greet Mary Margaret.

On the excuse of getting some more water from the pump, she picked up the kettle and ran downstairs.

Martha was standing swinging her empty basket and talking to her friend, who, as usual, was hemming in the light of Martha's window. At Mary Margaret's feet, Number Nine was curled up on an old coat sound asleep, unaware of the struggles of his babysitter.

Seated cross-legged on the floor was Dollie, also hemming, though rather slowly.

Even after the allotment had come through, she had continued to be kept at home sporadically, to sew.

'Because your mam is sick and you got to help her a bit,' her relentless grandma had told her, despite her mother's gentle protests.

Mary Margaret was slowly realising, however, that she could not work as fast as she used to. She had decided that it would be as well if Dollie became adept at sewing as soon as possible; if her mother died, she might, with such a skill, manage to maintain herself and thus keep out of the hands of Them.

At Alice's unheralded entrance, Martha swung round.

Alice smiled at Mary Margaret, and then said to Martha, a little breathlessly, 'I've got a letter for your Patrick. The postman left it with me to give him. Will you tell him when he comes in? It's from the town hall.'

'Mother of God!' exclaimed Martha. 'And what would that be meaning?' She reached out to take the letter from Alice, shades of Norris Green running through her head.

Alice immediately said, 'It's on me shelf upstairs.'

Martha looked surprised that she had not brought the letter down with her, so Alice added apologetically, 'I got to give it to Patrick only. His Nibs has got me name down in his notebook, seeing as I took it in.'

'Tosh! I'm as good as Patrick. You can give it to me.'

'I'd better not, Martha. I don't want no trouble with the Post Office. And you might open it.'

That was exactly what Martha wanted to do. 'I wouldn't do nothing like that, I wouldn't,' she wheedled.

'No,' said Alice again. 'His Nibs trusted me.'

Martha's face darkened, so Alice hastened to add, 'I'm sorry, Martha.'

Martha crossly threw her basket into a corner and went over to the range. She picked up the poker and attacked a few smouldering embers. Then she took some small lumps of coal from the box and laid them very carefully on top.

'I don't see why not,' she snarled at Alice.

Mary Margaret dropped her sewing into her lap. The last thing she wanted was a quarrel between two of her friends; she could not bear the stress of it.

Anxious to placate, she said, 'Martha, love, it won't be long till Pat comes in – and the kids will come back from school any minute now. Let's have a cuppa tea and enjoy it while we got a bit of peace. Never mind the letter.'

Martha swung the hob with the kettle on it over the fire. Her lower lip stuck out belligerently, as she said, 'I want to know what's in it.'

Mary Margaret laughed gently. 'We all want to know. But Alice is right, you know. His Nibs did trust her – if Pat complained that you opened it, you never know what might happen.

'There's Theresa now. She sometimes gets letters about her pension; if she wasn't home, rather than chance leaving letters with someone, His Nibs might send them back. He'd say he couldn't find her. Her pension would stop, sure as fate, while They checked that she was still alive.'

The kettle began to sing. 'Well, he's stupid. He can trust anybody in this house,' Martha responded sharply, knowing full well that she was lying through her teeth.

'Love,' Mary Margaret pleaded. 'You might get it from Patrick if you open his letter. And I couldn't bear for you to get a black eye. You couldn't read it, anyway; I'd have to – and if he were angry enough, he might hit me.'

Martha paused, teapot in hand. Mary Margaret was right – and a blow might kill her friend.

She said with a wry grin to Alice, 'Aye, none of us wants a beating. Would you like a cup of tea before you go back up?'

'No, ta. I left Mike eating his tea. I'd better go.' And she thankfully ran back upstairs.

'Where you bin?' asked Mike.

'Oh, I just got caught by a bit of gossip from Mary Margaret. The school attendance man's after her to send Dollie to school.'

'Humph.'

Downstairs, apart from Martha being rather short in her responses to Mary Margaret's efforts at placating gossip, they did have a peaceful cup of tea.

The rattle of cups woke Number Nine. He stretched and exposed his bare bottom. Then he turned over, arched his back, and unexpectedly produced a spray of water over the women's skirts.

'Jamie,' screamed his mother, giving him his correct name to show her displeasure.

Unable to do anything else to stop the tide, he hastily turned onto his stomach again and soaked the coat under him.

Mary Margaret began to laugh, and soon both women and Dollie were laughing.

Number Nine giggled.

Assured that he would not be scolded further, he finished his peeing and scrambled to his feet. His distended stomach glistened with wet.

He caught his mother's damp skirt. 'Butties?' he asked innocently.

The women were convulsed with merriment.

TWENTY-ONE

'Think About It? My Foot!'

July to September 1939

When the daylight failed, Mary Margaret and Dollie packed up their sewing and went upstairs to their room, where, by the light of a candle, Mary Margaret gave her children some bread to eat. Then she and Dollie, crouched together by the candle, began again to sew.

Soon after Mary Margaret had left, Martha's children ate their tea of bread and margarine, and went out to play in the court.

'Now you, Kathleen, get out there and watch they don't go out of the court – it's getting dark.'

'Oh, Mam!' wailed Kathleen. She always felt tired these days.

'Shut up and get going.'

Kathleen went.

A few minutes later, a weary and irate Patrick came home. He passed his children without a word; Kathleen shuffled to one side of the step to allow him to pass her, but kept her head down.

Feeling the benefit of more money in the house, Martha had fed both the children and herself more generously, and she was in a better mood.

For Patrick, she had stewed some minced beef and baked two potatoes: this repast had been intended for his midday dinner. But he had done a full day's work and, at midday, he had not returned; instead, he had bought a sandwich at Meg's cocoa room. She now produced his plate from the oven, where it had been warming up for the past hour.

As usual, he did not greet her. He merely sat down on the chair and slowly took off his boots and tossed them into the hearth. His bare feet looked red and swollen.

As she sat on a box and watched him eat, his wife did not say a word about the letter. After the hubbub of the dockside, the silence was welcome to him.

When he had finished, he handed her the empty plate. Then he leaned back in his chair and closed his eyes. In the warmth of the fire, he was about to drift off to sleep, when Martha remarked casually,

'Alice has got a letter for you. The postman asked her to take it in, 'cos I was out.'

Patrick's eyes opened slowly, but when the import of the remark sank in, he jerked upright, his fatigue forgotten. 'A letter? You don't say?'

Martha smiled a little grimly. 'She has, and – you'll never believe it – she wouldn't give it to me. The postman wrote down her name and she was afraid he wouldn't trust her again, if she give it to anybody else.'

'Humph.' He rose slowly to his feet, and leaned down to retrieve his boots from the hearth. 'Who's it from? Do you know?'

'Town hall,' she replied. 'Hope it's not an eviction.' She kept her voice calm, though she was on tenterhooks.

He shrugged, and slipped his feet into his boots. Anything was possible: you never knew what They would hit you with next. Without another word, he went slowly through to the hall and then she heard him clumping up the stairs.

She was frantic to know what the letter portended and she felt that, just to be awkward, he might keep the information from her, so she let him get to the foot of the second flight and then quietly followed him.

He knocked on Alice's door, and on hearing her

response, he opened it and walked in. The room was dimly lit by a candle.

Mike raised a hand in lazy salute, and said, 'I just heard you got an invite from the Mayor asking you to tea!'

A vastly interested Alice smiled and hastily took the letter down from the shelf. She handed it to him. Patrick grinned slowly, and said 'Ta' to her. As he walked past her towards Mike and the candle, he tore open the envelope.

Martha slipped in through the open door. She winked at Alice. In perfect silence all three watched, as Patrick unfolded a single sheet of paper and began slowly to spell it out to himself.

Alice could read well and she longed to snatch it off him and run through it more quickly; nevertheless, wanting to be polite, she remained quiet.

'Well, I'll be buggered!' he finally exclaimed.

'What is it?' hissed Martha.

'It's a job – for a fireman. It's not from the town hall, it's from the municipal offices.'

'Temporary?' queried Mike promptly.

Patrick agreed, and continued to stare at his letter.

Alice noticed that Martha was puzzled by the emphasis on the job's being temporary, so she explained. 'The City's near stony broke, love. So they won't want to pay for, say, a pension scheme for you.' She paused, and then said thoughtfully, 'They don't have to pay nothing but the wages, if they make all new workers into temporary, even if they're not. I read it in the paper a long time back.'

Patrick sank down on the corner of Mike's bed. He looked at Alice and handed her the letter. 'Could you read it to me, Missus, to make sure I got it right?' he asked quite humbly.

Delighted to have her superior abilities acknowledged, Alice took it from him, while Mike remarked with a nod towards her, 'She's a real good reader, she is. Loves a love letter.'

Alice laughed, as she perused the short epistle. 'This isn't no love letter – my bad luck! But you're right, Pat. The job's yours, if you can do the training and pass the physical exam. Three pounds a week to start, and all.'

Martha looked at Pat, stupefied. 'Three pound a week? Every week?'

'Yes,' confirmed Alice.

'It's like winning the pools!' burst out Martha.

Alice laughed again, and went on, 'It says that a councillor who knows him has been kind enough to recommend him.'

Mike snorted with amusement. 'No names, no

pack drill! Since when has you been hobnobbing with 'igh society, Patrick, me lad?'

'Must be the councillor I hauled out of the river. I thought he'd forgotten me.'

'When've you got to go?' asked Martha, her mind already running over the question of a new shirt and some socks.

'Next Thursday,' replied a bewildered Pat. 'I got to think about it, though.' His main thought was that Martha would, if he took the job, know exactly what he earned – and that could make life difficult.

'Who signed it?' asked Mike.

Alice peered at the signature. 'It says Per pro J. Brown, Civil Defence Service. Never heard that name before, have you?'

'Nope,' replied Mike. 'Except Civil Defence Service is a set-up to make ready for a war, I know that: BBC said so. Extra police an' all that, and firemen and air-raid wardens and rescue service. It'll be shift work, sure to be.'

Patrick continued to sit quietly on Mike's bed, while the rest of them discussed his future. He saw himself toiling for eight hours a day, with no hope of going to the races when he felt worn out; he wasn't sure that he wanted that. He glanced apprehensively at his wife. He knew what she was thinking: he'll be a walking bank!

He got up slowly, and said, 'Ta, ever so,' to Alice, who handed his letter back to him. Then he looked down at Mike. 'See you later, maybe.' He sighed heavily. 'It's a big change. I got to think about it.'

'Think about it, my foot!' muttered Martha, as, after saying goodbye, she flew down the stairs after him like a flapping raven after a piece of meat.

It took about ten minutes for the news to percolate throughout the court.

TWENTY-TWO

''Ave a Good Cry. It'll Cheer You Up No End'

1965

Early one chilly, overcast morning, just after break-fast, feeling hopelessly overworked and very frus-trated herself, Angie addressed her favourite patient rather irritably when she found her crying.

A weeping patient was not that unusual, and Angie asked mechanically, 'Now, what's up, Martha?'

She set down a basin of warm water on the commode by Martha's bed, preparatory to helping her wash herself.

'I was thinking,' replied Martha with a huge sobbing sigh. 'Just thinking.'

'Well, there's nothing wrong with thinking, is there? Here's the flannel. Come on now, wash your face and maybe you'll feel better.'

Martha sat up and reluctantly folded back the

bedclothes. She rolled her tiny body to the edge of the bed, so that her spindly legs dangled over the side. She took the wet flannel and slowly ran it round her face and neck.

'I was wishing I could read and write. Then I could write a letter – if I had paper and a pencil and a stamp.'

'You mean you can't write?' Angie took the face flannel away and handed a piece of soap to Martha. 'Hands next.'

'No. Lots of women like me can't read nor write.'

She obediently soaped her hands, rinsed them in the bowl of water, and dried them on a towel. Slow, hopeless tears ran down her cheeks and she hardly saw how tired the black face before her was.

'Well, bless me, I didn't know that. Put your towel under you, now,' Angie instructed her, as she vigorously soaped the flannel again; she was obviously not very interested in Martha's lack of basic education. 'Let's do your underneaths.'

Though Martha had all her life accepted being humiliated by others, nothing made her feel worse than opening her legs in front of various carers, even a doctor.

She sometimes complained that, 'Even me hubby never seen me in me skin.'

She did her best, however, to wipe herself clean without soaking the undersheet on the bed. Then, as she dabbed herself dry, she tried to stop weeping. She wiped her runny nose on the towel, before handing it back to Angie.

'Could you write a letter for me, to my Jamie, Angie? He's in Manchester.'

'I don't have time nor money even to write to me own friends, dear. Ask Matron.'

If Angie dared to do anything extra for a patient, she envisioned, an enraged Matron might dismiss her for wasting time. In addition, if she found out about a letter, she might not like whatever message or complaint was escaping from her domain, and blame the aide for any subsequent trouble. It was safer to refuse.

A little more awake after her wash, Martha was smart enough to realise Angie's fear of her own Them. A black immigrant would have to watch what she did.

'It's OK, Angie. I just wondered,' she said.

She nearly laughed. Ask Matron? Matron rarely came upstairs, and she never gave you a chance to open your mouth, except to make you take a pill.

She noted that the curtains round the bed next to hers had been drawn back. The bed itself had been stripped and a new pile of neatly folded bed linen was sitting on its mattress. Must've done it in the night, she decided.

'Where's Pat?' she inquired.

'In the hospital morgue, I suppose.' Angie's voice was flat, disinterested. 'There's got to be a coroner's inquest.'

Martha was shocked. 'Poor Pat. She's dead? I thought the doctor had, maybe, sent her to hospital. I didn't realise she was dying.'

'For some reason, yesterday, he come upstairs ahead of Matron, and, soon as he seen Pat, he ran down to the office to phone for an ambulance.' Angie grinned wryly. 'And did he ever give Matron hell, Martha. You could hear him in her office shouting at her – he didn't even bother to shut the door.'

'Holy Mother! Why?'

'He reckoned Pat were dying, and, of course, she was, poor thing, and Matron didn't even seem to care about it – and she's supposed to be a registered nurse. This last few days I've been warning her the woman wasn't right.'

There was scorn in Angie's voice and a hint of fear: she dreaded that Matron might push the blame for neglect onto the nursing aides. She paused to collect the towel from under Martha.

Then she went on, 'Doctor said she should have sent for him days ago.'

Martha suddenly burst into tears again. Poor helpless Pat. Would the same thing happen to herself? she wondered in sudden terror.

A beleaguered Angie forgot that she should have washed her patient's feet. Instead, she said a little conciliatorily, 'Now, don't take on so, love. She's with God.'

She quickly lifted Martha's skinny legs with their map of varicose veins back into bed, and pulled the bedding roughly over them.

She draped the wet towels over one arm and picked up the basin of water, with the soap and flannel floating in it. Slopping water on the floor en route, she scurried over to the patient by the door. This woman was paralysed and could not talk beyond a few monosyllables: she could not, therefore, complain to anyone about being washed in the same water and using the same towels and flannel as Martha.

Martha herself was immersed in her own frightening predicament. No wonder the doctor had not returned to visit her.

She had been only vaguely aware that something was wrong with Pat, to whom he always went first. In the general murmur of voices, she had heard the word hospital; she had not thought of her as actually dying.

It was the first death in the home that she had heard of during her residence there, and it scared her.

The cause of her weeping, before the arrival of Angie, had been the remembrance of Mary Margaret's death just before the war had begun. What sparked the memory she could not quite say, except that, in her general misery, she had longed to be visited by a friend, someone she could really talk to. But what few friends she had had in recent years seemed to have forgotten her.

Now, though her mind was beginning to work a little more coherently, her weeping increased. It was not only because she would never again see Mary Margaret, but now, added to her mourning for her friend, was a stark fear for herself.

She heaved the bedclothes over her head to muffle the noise of her moans, and wept on.

'The best friend I ever had,' she passionately told the bed sheets. 'And now I haven't got nobody, not even Number Nine, and I can't even write to him.'

TWENTY-THREE

'It Broke Me 'Eart, It Did'

1965

The following evening, Angie's relief aide, Freda, was late in arriving for her shift, and, while she waited for her, weary Angie sat down on the end of Martha's bed. She was already dressed in her macintosh and clutched her handbag on her knee.

'And me wanting to get home to me dad,' she remarked fretfully to Martha. 'He isn't too well.'

'Aye, you have to watch them at his age,' Martha agreed. From scraps of information that Angie had let fall from time to time, she understood that the aide's father with whom she lived was very elderly. Old people could die unexpectedly, she ruminated, like when you didn't think they were that ill.

This led to her confiding to Angie the details of

Mary Margaret's death when quite young, and its dreadful consequences for her children.

The choice of subject did not cheer Angie up much. But she was resigned to Martha's stories, so she only half-listened as she waited for the sound of Freda's key in the front door.

'You know, Angie, I should have seen the signs of it coming, and I should have been right at her bedside to comfort her. It broke me 'eart, it did, that I failed her when she needed her best friend most. I didn't even get to say goodbye to her.

'At that time, I were so grateful that Patrick had got his fireman's job, it took me mind off her, temporary, like.'

Angie opened her bag to take out her bus fare, as Martha went on slowly, 'I didn't notice that she hadn't done much sewing for a couple of days – only afterwards I realised it. When Dollie come running and said her mam wouldn't wake up, I whipped upstairs in me bare feet.

'At least Theresa was with her at the last. But she was so shocked at its coming when she were just sitting in a chair, she looked like she would follow her any minute.

'You won't know, love, 'cos you're too young, but in them days there wasn't time to cry or even think much. Once the men was called up, nobody cried for fear of setting off everybody else into hysterics. You just held it in, and got on with what you had to do.

'And with me sister, Maria, moved out to Norris Green, we was short of women in the courts to turn to.

'So I sent Dollie to her Auntie Ellen; and one of her sons ran like hell to Nurse MacPherson's house. She had a phone and rang the hospital – in case Mary Margaret wasn't really dead, she told us.'

Angie nodded understandingly.

'Alice Flynn and Kitty Callaghan took Mary Margaret's youngsters and my kids into Kitty's room, and gave them breakfast. It was the day the autumn term began, so they told Kathleen to take them all to school, except for Number Nine who was too little, of course – Kitty took care of him.

'Because she would be late for work, Kathleen was that resentful at being landed with having to go out of her way to the school.

'"Why can't Bridie take them?" she shrieked.

'I told her flat, "I can't trust Bridie – you know *her*."'

Angie nodded absently, and wondered if Freda would ever turn up for her shift.

'But once Kathleen and Bridie really understood what had happened to Mary Margaret, they was ashen, poor lambs. And they was very good.'

She went on to describe how she boiled water on Mary Margaret's primus stove to wash the body, so that by the time the ambulance found the court she and Alice had Mary Margaret all laid out.

'We told them we needed an undertaker, not an ambulance,' she said acidly.

'What I always wonder, Angie, is who told Them. Maybe it was Nurse MacPherson. They descended like a cloud of flies on horse shit, they did.

'Poor Theresa was told by Them that, because she didn't have no doctor, there would have to be an inquest, so they had her body took away.

'These ladies decided that Theresa herself was too poor and too frail to manage her three grand-daughters. You see, there was a problem with Thomas's allotment to his wife. Theresa couldn't draw it for his daughters' keep until he gave the shipping company his permission for them to pay it to her. Without the allotment, she wouldn't have enough housekeeping.

'So, in spite of Auntie Ellen saying she could help Theresa with them, the kids were took into care. They was sent to Olive Mount the minute they come home from school for their dinner.

They cried their eyes out they did; they was so scared.

'These know-alls did go, first, across the court to poke around in Ellen's house.'

Martha sighed gustily, as she remembered the result.

'What with two idle young sons hanging around, not to speak of so much dirty washing, they decided that it was no place for three girls.

'Believe me, Ellen's boys were so mad that They should think they would abuse the children. Jaysus Mary, how they swore. It was so unfair. And Peter drowneded in the war.'

Martha pinched her lips in long-held indignation. 'To Them Theys, the court was a den of sin, proper wicked. Didn't it have two known prostitutes in it? Poor Helen and Ann, two of the kindest friends you could wish for. The ladies must have forgotten that Our Lord was good to Mary Magdalene.'

'Must have been rotten for all of you,' muttered Angie. Would Freda never come? It was an iron rule of Matron's that an aide could not leave the building until her successor arrived. If Freda did not come soon, she herself would have to work a second shift; Matron would insist upon it.

'It was real hard. Neither Ellen nor me ever saw

those girls again, though, God knows, we looked hard enough for them.'

This mention of the total disappearance of three children caught Angie's attention.

'Really?' she exclaimed.

'Well, it were like this. We dealt with Mary Margaret and the coroner, and then a pauper's funeral for her. Then Ellen and Theresa went to the shipping company about getting Thomas's allotment. The shipping company promised to get in touch with the Australian owners of Thomas's ship, to get his permission.

'Theresa was fair wore out, and a few days later she was in hospital with a heart attack, and she died within a week. Another pauper's funeral, though I doubt if Thomas would have paid for his mother-in-law's burial!

'Inside a day or two, because the war had broken out, the girls were evacuated to the country with the other kids from Olive Mount.

'In the awful haste the kids were sent – there was a panic that the cities would be bombed to hell straight away – maybe there wasn't time to make a record or summat to say exactly where each kid went, with them having two moves so close together.

'Neither Ellen nor I could find anyone to tell us

exactly where they were. Each evacuated child was supposed to be given a postcard to send home with her address. But they never come.

'You'll have no idea how difficult it was hunting for those kids when you can't read or write, and Ellen and her family was not much better than me.

'Her hubby, Desi, could do both. But he wasn't very helpful – I don't think he wanted children thrust on him.'

She interrupted her story to remark, 'One thing we learned in the war was that nobody cared a tinker's cuss about women like Ellen and me – we was barely listened to at all.'

Then, after a few moments' thought, she continued, 'It was weeks before more distant relations even heard of Mary Margaret's death. And they didn't want motherless kids in their homes. Their own lives was already all upset with the war starting and their men being called up.

'So we waited and we waited, hoping that Dollie, being eldest, knew her home address and would send the postcard. But she never did.

'Pretty quick, They made a clean sweep of Mary Margaret's room. It was boarded up as unfit for human habitation: Thomas's few possessions were given to Auntie Ellen for safekeeping. You see, that made Thomas another nobody: he was then a single seaman, who could find somewhere to live without Their help. All they wanted, once they could contact him, was that he pay for his kids' keep – if they could be traced.

'Then the war really got going, and that changed everything – for ever. Who would've guessed I'd end up here all by meself and trembling at the very thought of what They might do to me?'

As her voice trailed away, Angie heard Matron speaking in the hall. She got up and tiptoed to the top of the stairs to peep down.

Matron had let Freda in, and, as the aide struggled out of her coat, was scolding her for her tardiness. 'And where is Angie?' Matron asked. 'She should still be here.'

Angie promptly called down, 'I'm here, ma'am. Just checking the patients on this floor before I leave.'

She turned and called goodbye to Martha, and ran quickly down the stairs.

Martha was loath to see her go – at least she was a bit of company, which kept your mind occupied so you weren't quite so scared. Now, she glanced at the empty bed beside her and began to shake uncontrollably.

TWENTY-FOUR

'Praying Never Did Any Harm'

1965

Half-smothered in grubby bedclothes, Martha barely heard the front door slam after Angie's hasty exit. Yet the distant thud seemed to her to have the finality of the weighty closure of some ancient dungeon door. No escape.

No escape from being left to die unattended like poor Pat, quavered a truly terrified Martha. To be kept in bed by a matron who never spoke to you, until you got so weak that you could not move and eventually died of nothing in particular.

For something comforting to clutch against the powers of Them, she instinctively pulled her rosary from under her pillow.

Dying, and no relations called to fight for you against a ruthless Them. No one tendering precious bits of food to give you strength. No one rubbing your hands and feet to keep the circulation going. No one holding you in their arms while they gave you sips of water. Worst of all, no one to write to dear Jamie, beloved Number Nine, to tell him where you were.

She swallowed a particularly big sob, and wondered if any of Them had thought to let him know that she was in hospital, never mind this present hellhole. When she had been found at the bottom of the stairs of her house, she had been so faint from pain and hunger that she had barely understood what was happening to her: she had simply let Them take over. There had been the cops and the rent man, she remembered vaguely. Then the ambulance men? The Casualty Department? As she slowly realised through her fright that nobody had asked whether she had any family, it occurred to her that each link might simply have told the next one that she lived alone.

So nobody asked her?

Most of her life Martha had lived in a small world where the neighbours knew more about you than you did yourself. No move went unnoticed. She would often say that information went mouth to mouth quicker than talking on one of them telephones.

She had found herself very lonely since Jamie left home, first to do his two years' national service in the army, then to study for the priesthood and, finally, to serve, in a very minor capacity, the Church in Manchester. But the idea that nobody nearby cared what could have happened to her was entirely new. She still did not realise that the upheavals of population which had occurred during the war, the bombing and rebuilding, the extension of the suburbs, had slowly changed irrevocably the Liverpool she had known. The tight little communities along the waterfront had been scattered, consigned to history.

It was true, she remembered as she thought about it in a fog of terror, that each day she spoke to a smaller and smaller number of people. It seemed as if there were always strange faces around, and, come to think of it, even her next-door neighbour was new to the district. Come in a week before she fell, he had.

She began to sweat. Did nobody know where she was? If not, how did you let anybody know if you couldn't read and write? Had Jamie not written to her? And if he had where were his letters, which, usually, the tobacconist up in Park Road kindly read to her.

The sweat which soaked her nightgown cooled, and her teeth began to chatter.

As these wild ideas penetrated, she thought she would go mad with fear for her life. Her eyes widened in terror; her heart pounded like a remorselessly swung mallet.

'Holy Mother, help me,' she gasped instinctively, and pressed her rosary to her mouth. 'Oh, Mother, help me. I don't want to die – I want to get better, and take care of Jamie when he come home.' She had not the slightest doubt that, in this crisis, her desperate appeal would be heard.

Her cry to the Beloved Virgin reminded her of the delicately painted, plaster Madonna in her church, before a bomb hit it. Prayers to Her had been part of her life, a frequent reminder that the Mother of the Lord Jesus was always there, able to walk in the world to listen and to hear, particularly, the prayers of women. A gentle friend, who gave you strength to bear what you had to bear. A pink-tipped hand stretched out to bless you, if you'd done something good, someone who could intercede between a sinner and God Himself.

She lay for a moment paralysed, exhausted, without hope of help from human beings. Then she forced herself to be calm, clenching her hands in an effort to stop her panic. It's true, remember there is someone to ask, there is. Our Lady!

She took several big, shaky breaths.

Her voice worn out and very humble, though still with a dreadful agitation in it, she begged, 'Dearest Lady, help me. I haven't got nobody but you and your Beloved Son. I've even lost dear Number Nine, who serves your Son most faithfully. I can't write to him and I don't know how you could tell him where I am. But could you? Could you put it in his heart how to find me?'

She paused. She felt so very tired, too weary even to cry any more, with a heart that still pounded unmercifully.

When she had gathered a little more strength, she continued, at first formally, 'I beg you to intercede for me in my sinfulness that I may be forgiven for all the stupid things I done wrong in my life, especially with me kids; I never seen some of the warning signs that must have been with them.

'But please, please, Dear Mother of Our Blessed Lord, be merciful. Let me be forgiven. Let me get well and get out of this awful place.'

She heaved a mighty sigh, said Amen and kissed her rosary.

Without any true hope that her sins would be

forgiven, particularly her many thefts from Lewis's and Blackler's Stores, she turned to lay her head on a dry piece of pillow. 'Lord, be merciful to me, a sinner,' she whimpered.

Strangely, it seemed, for a moment, that she had laid her head against the knee of an understanding mother who would, at least try for her. She sobbed helplessly and half-dreamed that the Holy Mother spoke to her, though she did not understand the words.

A little comforted, she slowly calmed. She knew she could do no more. Fatigue overwhelmed her, and she slept.

Holy peace does not last long.

She was roused by Angie, who put a tray on top of the commode. She pulled back the bedclothes and shouted into her ear, 'Breakfast!'

Martha rolled over and slowly sat up. Angie had shot across the room and was tying a bib round the neck of one of the dementia patients, who had to be fed by hand.

Goodness, it really was morning. She blinked at the sight of the sun coming through the windows. How she must have slept! And did she really see the Dear Lady? Was she here?

She came sharply back to earthly necessities.

'I got to pee first,' she told Angie urgently.

Not wanting another wet bed, Angie abandoned the dementia patient, and came to help Martha out of bed. She whipped the tray off the commode and put it on the floor. Then she opened the lid of the commode.

'Come on,' she said impatiently.

Martha stared at her. She felt a little lost, as if she was a long way away from the aide. Though weariness dragged at every limb, as she threw off her bedclothes and turned until her legs dangled over the side of the bed, she felt curiously at peace. It was strange. And she had been so scared last night, she remembered.

Without thinking, she said to Angie, 'You go back to Lena. I can manage.'

To her faint surprise, Angie obeyed.

By moving carefully, she succeeded. She even closed the commode lid and lifted the tray back onto it, without reeling.

'Humph, there's nothing like a good cry to set you up,' she thought with a rueful grin as she heaved herself back into bed. 'It cheers you up no end.' But in her heart, she cherished an inner understanding that help would come from the Holy Mother herself.

She leaned over and took up the plate of food; it felt cold. As she viewed the white mass on a white plate, she muttered, 'Jaysus Mary, give me patience. Macaroni cheese again – and for breakfast? Yuk! What I wouldn't give for a good pile of bacon and fried bread!'

TWENTY-FIVE

'Moaning Minnies'

August 1939 to March 1940

Browbeaten by a ruthless Martha, Patrick joined the fire brigade. Her final, irrefutable argument was that, if he did so, they could then find a better place to live: it would no longer be necessary for him to be close to the docks and live with nine other people in one room.

With a motley crew of new recruits to train, the regular firemen found themselves grossly overworked. Though they themselves were, like most other City employees, very underpaid, they were a tight, almost military brotherhood, held together by the sharing of particular dangers.

They looked with scorn upon the recruits thrust upon them, particularly people like Patrick, who was regarded as brainless scum from the docks.

Patrick had, also, an inbuilt dumb insolence, when other people tried to order him around more than usual, and this did not endear him to his impatient teachers.

The regulars made the training as hard as they could. They were themselves big men, used to carrying heavy loads of hoses, axes and other equipment upstairs at a run. They knew just how to keep a wriggling, deadweight hose, belching out water, focused on a particular target: they became irate when their pupils, trying to emulate them, succeeded in soaking everyone in sight. Each hapless pupil had to learn how to set up a ladder safely, run up it like a squirrel and bring down a supposedly helpless victim of smoke inhalation, a feat that novices found very hazardous, as ladders swayed and teachers swore at them.

Finally, they had to learn the art of keeping themselves alive when coping with a tumbling, flaming building, a sight which truly terrified most of them.

It seemed to a gloomy Patrick that he would never learn all the finer points of firemanship and would himself end up a cinder.

He might have given up, were it not that his new life, though it had its problems, was basically less arduous. It was also more interesting.

For the first time in his life, his narrow world had been opened up. He met men from other parts of Liverpool and, willy-nilly, learned to communicate with fellow sufferers unconnected with docks or shipping.

After a few weeks of doubtful close association, he became quite defensive of them when they were criticised as conscientious objectors, trying to avoid army service or being sent down the coal mines. 'Some of them have failed the army medical on a small point,' he said, 'but a lot are like me, too old for call-up.'

He was secretly envious that many of his fellow recruits could easily read the written instructions which fluttered down from distant bureaucrats, who had rarely ever seen a fire. Though many of his weedy-looking associates seemed to belong to the world of Them, he began grudgingly to respect them. They were quite kindly about explaining anything he did not understand, and did not flinch when faced with dangerous situations.

As he got used to them, they occasionally said they had joined the fire brigade because they wanted to help their country's war effort. They seemed to have very high ideals: they did not believe in killing, even in war, some of them told him.

Ideals were something preached about by the

church; as far as Patrick was concerned they had nothing to do with him. All his life, he had worked at very heavy jobs to keep himself alive, help his ever-increasing family and, maybe, have a bit of fun and warmth in the nearest pub or have a swim or a race or a game of marbles, on which to bet.

It dawned on him only slowly that these pansies, as he privately called them, had some reciprocal regard for him, for his physical strength and his silent, fairly friendly willingness to show them how to shift heavy weights quickly. Though a man of only average height and very thin, Patrick had muscles like iron.

Thanks to exercise in much fresher air than warehouses provided, and to more food, he soon acquired greater energy. He lost some of his diffidence, and he began to add his modest opinions to the general conversation.

The much-despised recruits from all levels of society, thrown together by the war, eventually founded their own brotherhood. It finally became enormous, as auxiliary firemen slowly outnumbered by ten to one the original brigades who were their teachers.

In the first year of the war the civilian population, outside London, was not heavily bombed; and, to their thankful surprise, there was no invasion by the Germans. So the auxiliary firemen were soon regarded by their neighbours as lazy good-for-nothings, like the air-raid wardens, who drew three pounds a week each as if it were a retirement pension.

Collectively the brotherhood endured this contempt, and some of them quietly worked at a second job as well. A poet working with him solemnly assured Patrick that their time would come, which did not reassure Patrick about his own safety.

He cheered up, however, when Martha reminded him that accidents in the docks and in ships were legion, and he had survived them: the fire brigade could not be much worse.

As recruitment into both the Forces and civil defence intensified, the number of young men hanging around in the streets decreased markedly. Auntie Ellen's two sons were called up for the Navy. She was not too sorry to see them go.

'They've been hanging around the house long enough,' she said shortly. 'It'll be a change to get a bit of an allotment from them.'

Brave words. But when the *Athenia*, on its way to America with numerous evacuated children, was sunk in Liverpool Bay by a German submarine, she became sick with fear.

Very soon afterwards, there were sad signs in the

district that British ships were going down in record numbers.

Helen O'Brien expressed her feelings succinctly. 'It tries me nairves something awful,' she said, aware of regular young clients who were dead or had vanished into the call-up.

For those who could not read, or read only poorly, and did not own a radio, word of mouth was the main source of news.

After 3rd September when war was declared, word of losses came like shards of flying glass to pierce the hearts of women. The high number of Liverpool seamen lost was further exaggerated by rumours, and the back streets were filled with numbed, whey-faced wives and mothers.

Mike, in his attic, received a lot of humbly polite visitors asking if they might listen with him to the nine o'clock news.

At first, Martha reckoned that all the beginning of the war did for her was to put neighbours into uniform so that they could boss her around.

In the middle of the continuing general distress over the loss of Mary Margaret and Grandma Theresa, not to speak of her missing daughters, a man wearing a tin hat and blue overalls was noticed in the street outside the court.

He carried a gas mask, a large, hard-cover note-book and a fancy black fountain pen. It took a few moments for his friends to recognise Desi O'Hara, Auntie Ellen's husband, gleefully laughing at them from under his tin hat. He was, however, according to all the women, including his wife, no joke; on the contrary, he was another cross.

A sandwich-board man had suddenly become an official, the air-raid warden. Behind him, they discovered, lay real authority from Them.

He immediately lost much of his original popu-larity, particularly when, in a narrow side road, an air-raid wardens' post was erected. It was complete with cups and saucers and an electric kettle – and plenty of tea and tinned milk! There was also a telephone and switchboard, with a pretty girl in uniform to run it. The local women were really shocked and annoyed at such luxury for men who hung around all day doing nothing.

Undeterred by the false accusations of laziness, Desi went from door to door down the main street and in and out of the few remaining courts. He checked exactly who lived in which house.

'You see, if you're bombed flat, we got to know where to find you,' he explained with a knowing look. He tried to keep his inquiries light-hearted, though it had been explained to him that the aid of a local man who knew where everybody lived would be a priceless help to the Heavy Rescue Units in their burrowing through rubble to find victims.

Then there was the blackout. He insisted that, before lighting so much as a candle, those who had a window had to have black curtains to cover it at night.

Kitty Callaghan, whose husband was in gaol, Sheila Latimer and Phoebe Ferguson, the oakum pickers, and Martha, all of whom had windows, were really miffed at this, and did not hesitate to tell him so.

Martha discovered, however, that she had new clients wherever she went, anxious to buy discarded cloth, preferably black or thick material like worn bedspreads, or leftover pieces of velveteen. A pair of heavy curtains, long discarded, proved unexpectedly valuable. She ceased to tear up worn sheets, and increased her prices for these bigger pieces of material.

As she shared a cup of tea with Tara, her friend of the samovar in the market, she said happily, 'I might as well make a buck while I can.'

Tara reluctantly agreed. Her problem, as the war progressed, was that tea and sugar were becoming hard to buy. The phrase 'under the counter' became common currency, as retailers held back goods in short supply for favoured customers.

Cigarettes became very hard to find, even under counters.

Desi gave up his sermons on the need to carry a gas mask. Women left the mask at home and used the box as a convenient hold-all.

Older men, with jobs for the first time in years, ignored his instructions altogether, despite Desi's depressing reminders of gas casualties in the First World War.

'Too much lumber,' they would grumble, and, if they had time, would wander off on more urgent business, like trying to buy some cigarettes, or finding a pub that was open, with a notice on the door saying that they had beer for sale.

Without Mary Margaret to read for her, Martha turned in desperation to Kathleen. She was astonished to learn that, though she stumbled on some words, the girl could read quite well, thanks to Sister Elizabeth's constant supervision at school.

Though Kathleen complained bitterly at the boring things her mother bullied her into reading, she was herself surprised at the amount of respect and praise she subsequently received from the other women in the court.

'Only Alice can read that well,' she was told.

The praise certainly improved her self-respect.

She read showers of instructions which came through the meagre letter boxes and appeared on posters on every notice board. Home Guard, civil defence, firewatching, fire watchers, Women's Voluntary Services, the urgent need to keep silent about one's daily work; they caused a nightmare of confusion.

'Even a pack of busybodies called the Women's Institute want to teach you how to make jam or put fruit in bottles, for Christ's sake,' muttered these women of the waterfront.

'And them ration books. Don't even say how much you can have. We'll be cheated, we will.'

The court accidentally received pamphlets about building an Anderson air raid shelter in the garden.

'I've had it up to here,' snapped Martha sourly, when Kathleen explained this to her. 'What bleeding garden?'

They ended up having a good laugh at that one: they knew then that the government in London was plumb crazy.

How to use a stirrup pump to put out a fire was another instruction which caused a good deal of ribaldry.

When Desi demonstrated one, they had a great

game spraying each other, while their children, wearing their gas masks, whooped it up playing cops and robbers in and out of the deluge.

The shelter planned for the street outside the court was built, and was inspected, from start to finish, by elderly males who had worked in construction.

'It'll fall down at the first shake,' they decided gloomily. 'Too much lime.'

Just what the latter remark really indicated, none of the women was clear about, but it did sound ominous. Even when air raids became a reality, the shelter was rarely use as anything but a convenient latrine.

For the most part, the tenants opened up the condemned basements of their houses, and, during the raids, took refuge there. Later in the war, they trekked out of the city every night, bedding in prams, children trailing behind them, to seek greater safety in a park or in the countryside.

'What bothers me most,' muttered usually silent Patrick, with a loud curse, 'is the blackout.'

He peeled up a leg of his trousers to exhibit a badly grazed knee to an already fearful Martha. 'Fell over a pile of sandbags. They've got them all round the fire hall – and you can't see a bloody thing in the dark.'

'Aye, I tripped over a paving stone meself yesterday. Want me to wrap up the graze?' There was real sadness in her voice: her world was rapidly becoming a madhouse, as she tried vainly to keep up with the demands made on her.

'What nearly give me a heart attack was way back in June. The first time I heard the air-raid warning go off, when They was trying it out,' Martha remarked to Alice, as they waited in a queue to buy some tins of beans at the corner shop. 'Did it for you?'

Alice agreed that it was the most awful sound in the world. 'And the all-clear don't sound much better,' she added.

'It's a proper Moaning Minnie!' interjected the woman in front of them, her mouth twisted up grimly.

Everybody within hearing laughed at this likening of it to a constantly complaining woman.

The awful noise was, for the duration of the war, promptly named Moaning Minnie: under that name it didn't seem quite so scary.

Desi found it easier to explain to male smokers and, through them, to their smoking wives that the flame of a match could be seen from afar. 'And the Jerries can see you,' he would explain, pointing skywards.

He did not need to say any more to the menfolk; they all knew the saying from the trenches of the First World War, 'Never share a match. By the time you've lit the third man's cigarette, you'll be dead.'

He did not mention flashlights or car lights or bicycle lamps. He himself had been provided with a flashlight, but nobody else in his little area owned such luxuries.

Martha reckoned her heart was broken when Brian, in late September of 1939, was suddenly imbued with a desire for adventure. At seventeen and a half, he lied to the recruiting officer that he was eighteen and applied to join the army.

The recruiting sergeant loved men from the courts, and immediately snapped him up.

'They make the best troops in the world. They've already endured everything,' he would say over a pint of ale. 'Anything they face in the army comes easy to them after living in a court.'

Martha wept on the boy's shoulder. 'How could you leave me like this? I need you. And you've got a decent job with Mr Beamish.'

'Somebody's got to fight the war, Mam. I'll get seven shillings a week – and out of it I can make a bit of an allotment. And you won't have to feed me.'

This practical information comforted Martha a

little. She wiped her nose on the end of her apron, and said, with a half sob, 'If you get killed, I'll mairder yez.'

The threat, often made in his childhood when he ran out into the street, made Brian laugh, and it was a cheerful young man who went off to war.

His mother wept, and not only for his lost wages; he had given her a lot of moral support. 'Even Bridie listened to him,' she sobbed to Alice Flynn, who, for once, fervently thanked heavens she had no sons.

Martha was almost immediately upset again when she received a postcard from Warwickshire to say that Lizzie, her eldest girl in service, had found herself a lovely job in a Naafi canteen. 'I got a nice room in the village,' she wrote, 'with another girl from Liverpool.'

When Martha heard from Alice what the post-card said, she exclaimed, 'Mother of God! What's happening to me family? And me nearly on me knees when I first had to get her ready for a job, with new clothes and all.'

'What did you do?' asked Alice.

'Ach! Spent a whole day going from one place to another, begging clothes for her. They was nice about it, but They get fed up with you, don't they?'

Martha stared glumly at the postcard, while she chewed a piece of nail off her thumb.

'Well, you won't miss her wages, like you will Brian's.'

'She were a good girl; she sent me a bit from time to time.'

Alice tried to cheer her up by suggesting, 'She might meet a nice lad in the Naafi.'

'She could.'

Alice's suggestion proved correct. Lizzie had a hasty wartime marriage in Warwickshire during a soldier's forty-eight-hour leave.

'There wasn't no time, Mam,' she wrote on a postcard, 'to bring him home nor nothing. Maybe later on.'

The postcards dwindled in number until by the end of the war, Martha had lost track of Lizzie and, indeed, had almost forgotten her. When Lizzie saw her husband's parents' pleasant, clean house and ordered life, she could not bring herself to take him to Liverpool. 'Me mam and dad died in the war,' she said, and thus divested herself of court life.

Soon after Brian left home, sister Elizabeth from the children's school came to visit Martha, about the evacuation of her other children to the country.

She was met with an immediate refusal.

'Our Kathleen's working in a canteen,' she told

the Sister. 'And Bridie'll start work soon. And Tommy helps me quite a bit with what he brings in.' Her voice rose in anger. 'And if you think I'm going to send little Joey, Ellie and James to a foreign place, you should have another think.'

'But you don't want them to be killed, do you? You can go with them, you know,' protested the teacher.

'Of course I don't want them killed, Sister! But who do you think is going to look after me hubby and the kids here if I go away?' Nuns really didn't know anything.

The Sister knew Martha of old, and she gave up: her children would soon be working, and the wages they would bring in were something all mothers in the poverty-stricken district looked forward to, to be enjoyed until the offspring married and left home.

She felt sorry for Kathleen, who, being a girl, would be expected to give up all her earnings. She knew the child was, when in school, already a boiling volcano of suppressed rage, a rage which sometimes came out in the playground when she could be quite a bully: and, like many others, she occasionally came to school with an obvious bruise on her face or arms or legs

It was a pity, she thought. Kathleen had potential

to do better for herself, if only her mother would give her a little help – cut her hair and make her clean and neat. She did not inquire more precisely what kind of job the girl had found: her mind was filled with the problems of evacuation.

Though she had assured the child that inward and spiritual graces were more important than outward show, she had, towards the end of her last school term, talked gently to her about grooming in preparation for going to work.

She would have been delighted to know of the sound advice the child had subsequently received, though she would certainly not have approved of the woman who gave it to her.

TWENTY-SIX

'Kathleen Was So Uppity'

July 1938

Not all Sister's advice to Kathleen had been lost upon her; every girl wanted to look like Jeanette MacDonald or some other queen of the films; the trouble was how to do it when you had nothing. It was even more difficult when your address was a court. She had turned down a job cleaning the floors of a greengrocery which, not without difficulty, Martha had found for her.

'No,' was the immediate, forceful response. 'I want to be a shop girl, a clean job, not a scrub woman. Or go into a factory if I can't go into a shop.'

Her mother was very angry. 'Well, find a job yourself – but don't be long about it.' She turned to pick up her basket of rags, and then she snarled, 'Look in your dad's paper. And, meantime, be thankful you've got a mother who'll give you something to eat.'

She swung her basket onto her head, and stomped out of the house.

Kathleen was shocked. Though her mother had often appeared heartless, it seemed as if now she did not care what happened to her, as long as she brought in some money immediately.

Kathleen knew that she was verminous, so she supposed that some employers would find her unacceptable. But surely Mam would help her as much as she could to reduce that unacceptability, wouldn't she? Like she had done for Lizzie.

Yet, she had not; she had simply found her a third-rate job, for which she would need nothing but the clothes she stood up in. The hurt sank into her, to join the sense of humiliation she had endured in school. That misery, though shared by other children from the courts, had been almost intolerable. Had it not been for sharp-eyed Sister Elizabeth and her encouragement, Kathleen would have run away. At home, she had accepted the conditions in which she lived; she had no other experience; in a way, she was afraid of the world outside it: and there had always been Mam, sharp-voiced, heavy-handed, but at least there, the centre of her small universe.

A number of visits to the Wesleyan Central Hall with her mother and Mary Margaret, where, for twopence, they could watch an old film, had told her that there was, indeed, a strange world out there. But it was so different that she could not imagine becoming a part of it.

Why should Kathleen do anything different from her mother? Martha would ask anyone who would listen. They had to learn that there were some things which even a miracle-working mam could not alter; she had tried with Lizzie, and Lizzie hated her life as a domestic servant.

In Martha's estimation, it was a certainty that her world would never change for the better: her children had to be aware of that and learn to manage in it.

Ann O'Brien had heard many heated exchanges between Martha and her children. Living in a room next to them, she knew all the family and most of their woes, and, as consolation, she gave them little gifts, when she had had a good night's work and had anything to give.

Martha was being too hard, she felt; Kathleen would be on the streets in no time, if she did not watch it; and, being no beauty, she'd never get off them. She wouldn't wish her own grim life on any kid. Somebody ought to help her.

Soon after the girl had left school in July 1938, Ann was not surprised, one wet summer day, to find Kathleen snivelling in the archway leading into the court. She put down the bottle of milk she had been carrying, and put her arms around the inadequately clad girl.

'What's up, love?' she asked, and then joked, 'Your mam thrown you out?'

'Not yet,' Kathleen admitted. Then she added cynically, 'She wants me wages too much.'

As the rain pattered on the pavement outside the archway, she looked up at the concerned, raddled face bent over hers. Here was an old friend.

She poured out her desire for a nice clean job. 'A decent factory job or something. I tried Bibby's, but I didn't get past the door. I don't know why.' She leaned against Ann's thin chest. 'What I really want, Ann, is to be a shop girl – like the girls in Boots the Chemists. Sometimes I look at them through the shop windows and they look loovely!'

'Well, love there's nothing like aiming high.'

Ann smiled and then glanced round her. Child-less herself, she envied Martha her girls. She looked hastily around the court. She could not take Kathleen into her own room behind Martha's room: Martha had never encouraged that.

She said kindly, 'Let's go and get a cup of tea in

the cocoa room across the road. Have a little talk, eh? Put your jacket up over your head against the rain, now.'

Kathleen nodded agreement, and they scuttled across the road and into the café. Now that the war was looming, dockers and seagoing men did not have much time to idle in cocoa rooms; they had found work, so the café was almost empty. At the back, two elderly men sat playing a game of draughts, while they sipped their cocoa; when the door slammed behind Ann, they did not even look up.

With a steaming hot mug of tea in front of her and kind Ann looking on, Kathleen gazed at her old friend with hope shining from her black-ringed eyes.

Ann truly did not want Kathleen walking the streets like herself, though a virgin was always welcome: men would pay a good price for a first go at her.

After thoughtfully sipping her own tea, she said, 'Well, I'm going to talk to you straight, aye?'

Kathleen nodded eagerly.

'First off, have you got a reference from the school?'

'Oh, aye. Sister wrote me a real nice one.'

'Good. Next thing is, you've got to look all bright

and clean yourself; you got to have nice neat hair and clean hands.

Kathleen sighed hopelessly and shrugged.

'Don't take on, love. You go to the bathhouse and wash your hair and yourself real well; and we've got scissors, so our Helen, she could cut your hair real nice.'

'I've got lice in it,' replied Kathleen. 'They keep coming back.'

Mobile dandruff! Ann smiled grimly. They always will come back until you get out of the court, she thought.

She said, 'Your mam knows to rub paraffin in your hair every week, I'd think. Then wash it.' She glanced at Kathleen's begrimed fingers clutching the end of the table. 'And cut your nails: you got to have clean nails for a clean job.'

To Kathleen, getting herself clean seemed a hopeless task. Her only acquaintance with a bath was what she had seen in films, where women sat amid a pile of soapsuds which always covered them modestly. She remembered that they sang soulful love songs, as they lifted one leg up above the suds to admire its pearly whiteness, clearly shown in the black and white picture. Martha had condemned the latter, saying roundly, 'It ain't decent to show off your legs!'

Despite her doubts about baths, Kathleen wanted to follow Ann's advice. Her face fell, however.

'I haven't got sixpence for the bathhouse.'

'We'll find it from somewhere, don't worry. What you do need is a decent frock, stockings and shoes – and a coat or mac. And, somehow, to keep the lice out of them.

'You know, Alice Flynn's got an iron. Maybe she'd lend it to you. A hot iron down the seams of everything every few days would keep the vermin down.'

Kathleen nodded. What hope?

Ann looked with distaste at Kathleen's jacket, which hung dripping from the back of her chair. 'You gotta be respectable-looking, somehow. If you look nice, an employer might train you in something to start you. Then you can work up – and one day you might get into Boots.'

The latter remark made Kathleen smile shyly. Ann was wonderful; at least she understood.

'If you like, I'll have a talk with your mam. She was getting impatient with you, that's all, because she's got too much to do; the threat of the war's got us all het up.'

Kathleen did not have much hope about this suggestion; she was still feeling the pain of rejection. But she had faith in Ann.

She agreed.

When Ann brought up the problem of equipping Kathleen to go out into the world of work, Martha was very defensive. 'She could learn to be a fent woman, like me. Just 'cos she can read she's got too stuck-up.'

But Ann was patient, and she finally pursuaded Martha that the girl could be as good as a bank if she had a decent job. Helen was recruited to help in the transformation, and thought it would be a proper lark.

After combing her hair for lice with the comb which had belonged originally to Mary Margaret, Kathleen submitted to her impatient mother's rubbing paraffin into her hair. The next morning, a sleepy Helen combed out the dead lice and cut it for her. She then bustled her off to the bathhouse, where she paid the sixpenny entrance fee.

Kathleen was so scared of the bossy attendant and of the huge white bath full of water, steaming like a witch's cauldron, that she threatened to bolt. But Helen held her hand firmly, made her strip and almost forced her into the bath. She then washed her hair and instructed her on how to wash her body and face.

'Got to do it thorough,' she ordered. 'Every week! Clean job – clean girl.'

For years, Helen had not taken a bath herself or bothered to wash her head. Older than Ann, she had as a child been bathed in the Mersey River, before the docks and warehouses closed it off altogether, and she had remarked laughingly to Ann when approached about Kathleen, 'It was a lot easier to be clean in them days; not like it is now.'

She, too, knew the Connolly children well and she agreed that, with a little cooperation, Kathleen could be given a better chance than either of them had had.

What emerged from the bath was a little maid with a peerless white skin and shiny black hair which floated softly round her face, and a skinny little body with tiny breasts, not yet fully formed.

'Aye, you look like a real little love,' Helen told the child, as she dried her off on the clean towel provided by the bathhouse.

The problem of clothes had been partly solved by Martha's talking to Tara, her market friend. She had told her about Ann's interference regarding Kathleen.

She said, 'Of course, I don't want her on the street. I only want her to have an ordinary job until she's a couple of years older. Then, maybe, she'll be big enough and strong enough to get a factory job, if she's lucky. And she said herself that a factory job would be OK.'

'Did you get any clothes for her?'

'Nah. Where would I get clothes for her? No charity's going to help me much.

'God's truth! You know, I'm afraid to ask anybody for help. Last time I did, it were for Mary Margaret's kids – and They took them away. When I think of that, I worry about Them taking me own little ones.'

Tara nodded agreement. 'What about trying for a cheque?'

Cheques were issued by loan companies, usually to be spent in certain stores which charged inflated prices. The sum was paid back by weekly instalments. Tara herself was able to obtain such cheques because her husband was known to have regular work as a tram driver and was likely, therefore, to pay off the loans which they represented. Tara used them all the time because the clothes she bought had often worn out before the loan was paid off. So immediately she had finished paying off one cheque, she applied for another.

Now she said, 'I think you might just manage to get one. You work regular in the market, don't you? That's a job. Why not have a try? You could be lucky.'

Two companies snubbed Martha and turned her down. A third company said that they would consider her application if she could provide written confirmation that she had a regular business in the market.

Defeated because she had no pedlar's licence to show them, she consulted Tara again.

Tara suggested shrewdly that this third company might be more lenient, because they wanted clients who were not likely to be called up and be reduced to a soldier's pay with their debts frozen, if war began.

'That may be,' responded a glum Martha. 'But how do I convince them about me?'

Tara's reply was unexpected. 'Who's your favourite butcher in the market?' she inquired.

Martha cheered up immediately and looked positively roguish. 'They all are!' she declared. 'They're forever teasing me.'

'Ask any two of them to write a little note on their billheads to say they buy regular from you and know that you have a steady business in rags,' she ordered.

Quite shyly, Martha did this. Once it was clear to the butchers that they were not being asked to guarantee her loan, two of them did as she asked. They both wished her luck.

Martha got a cheque to the value of one pound, the company's smallest issue. Like Tara, she became hooked on the system and was launched on a merry-go-round of debt which seemed eternal.

So, when Kathleen walked out of the baths, she had on, for the first time, a petticoat and panties, lisle stockings, held up by a pair of elastic garters contributed by Ann, a navy-blue skirt, a pink-striped blouse and a navy-blue waterproof jacket with a zip fastener. She also had on a pair of second-hand lace-up shoes too big for her, bought by Martha herself, with much grumbling, from a second-hand shop; the one-pound cheque she had obtained had proved insufficient to cover new shoes.

On their way back from the bathhouse, Helen and she stopped in front of a tobacconist's shop. The door had a mirror as its middle panel. Despite a tobacco advertisement on it which announced 'THREE NUNS, None Nicer', Kathleen could see a perfect stranger looking back at her.

'Now, don't you look nice?' said Helen, turning her round a little so that she could see the whole effect.

Kathleen giggled. 'None nicer!'

Three days later, she got a job washing dishes in the canteen of a nearby factory.

Ann advised her anxiously, 'It's a start, and it's

313

a clean job. Stick with it, love. I asked Alice and she'll lend you the iron. And never be late for work, remember. Smile, smile, smile, be nice to whoever's telling you what to do, and learn their job: it'll work wonders for yez.'

Advice given to her by her own mother, thought Ann bitterly, and she had not taken it.

Kathleen washed dishes and smiled. Without a clock, she was dependent on the knocker-up, who was a bit early for her. As a result, she was never late getting to work. She enjoyed the midday meal which came with the job, and dreamed of the lovely perfume smell that wafted out of the door of Boots Cash Chemists.

As part of her weekly battle with her mother over handing over her wages, she insisted on keeping a sixpenny piece so that she could have a bath each week.

When, miraculously, she was put in charge of the canteen's china cupboard and received a shilling a week increase in pay, she did not tell Martha. The shilling meant that she could afford to go to the cinema sometimes with the other girls at work, or buy replacement pairs of lisle stockings. Shortly after the war broke out, when stockings were rationed and any spare ones vanished under the counter, she saved assiduously for a few weeks and covered her bare legs with a pair of trousers.

Martha disapproved so much of the trousers that she forgot to ask where Kathleen had got the money to pay for them.

'It's shocking!' she shouted. 'Go, take them off afore your father sees you.'

'All the girls at work is wearing them,' replied Kathleen woodenly, which was true.

Patrick did not care what she wore; he was too engrossed in the map of Liverpool he was studying preparatory to being taught to drive fire brigade vehicles. He simply shrugged, and said, 'I seen lots of women in them in town.'

Meanwhile, his determined little daughter dreamed of earning enough to leave home.

In the middle of the war, like Brian, the day she was eighteen she lied to the military that she was aged nineteen and joined the army, the ATS. In the course of the war, she travelled all over Europe as a cook, and never went back home; she never made it to Boots either.

She never forgot, however, that it was two despised prostitutes who helped her to escape from the court – and from her mother – and throughout her life she was more respectful than most to members of the oldest profession.

The original transformation of Kathleen had not gone unnoticed by Bridie, who hoped for much the same help: she became suddenly more attentive towards Helen and Ann.

TWENTY-SEVEN

'Fresh Tea on the Hob'

1939

'Where's Mam? The door's boarded up. And me sisters? And I can't find Martha.'

Already worried, because he had not received a letter from his mother during a very long voyage down the coasts of Brazil and Argentina, then up the Pacific coasts of Chile and Peru – and back again, Daniel Flanagan stood on Ellen's doorstep, a fine-looking young man, aged almost eighteen, in blue jeans and a shabby pullover. He was tense and scared.

'Are they with you?'

At the sound of the male voice, a shocked Ellen rushed to the door. 'Danny!' she exclaimed.

In all the uproar caused by Mary Margaret's death; the inability to trace her three daughters, whom Ellen imagined were still being sought by harassed billeting officers; the death of Theresa, followed by the upheavals caused by the preparation for war, everyone had forgotten Mary Margaret's son, a merchant seaman: he had, after all, been very rarely home since he first went to sea as a boy of fourteen.

Guilt-stricken, Ellen drew the lad through the lines of washing hung out to air in her room.

'Come and sit down, love. I'll get you a cuppa tea and tell you all about it; I've fresh tea on the hob.' She was ashamed of her neglect and nearly in tears.

The sight of welling tears scared and puzzled Danny even more. He sat slowly down on her bed, the only area over which no bed linen flapped.

He watched her while, with shaking hands, she hastily filled a mug with tea, added tinned milk and passed it to him. 'Help yourself to sugar,' she urged.

When he had helped himself from the tiny blue packet and she had laid it down at the end of the bed, she sat down beside him and put her arm round him.

He did not cry when she explained what had happened.

When he had been paid off by his ship, he

had been told that the small allotment he had made to his mother had not been collected. It was, therefore, being returned to him. Sick at heart, he had suspected that his gentle, sick mother had died.

Now, hearing of the loss of his grandmother, whom he had always regarded as a source of acidly honest wisdom and support, and of his as yet untraced little sisters, his mind would barely function.

'What happened to the postcards I sent to Mam?'

Ellen was puzzled. 'I haven't seen none since she died. Where did you post them?'

'Um? Recife, and – er – one from Rio, and one from a wee place in Argentina where we took on water – forgotten the name.'

Like most women in seagoing communities, Ellen knew all about slow arrivals from post offices in distant places. She said comfortingly, 'Ach, they'll probably turn up in a week or two. Postcards is always the slowest to come. You probably heard your mam complain, sometimes, that your father got home before his postcards did.'

He barely took in what she had said. He was stunned that he had apparently been entirely forgotten by his aunt and uncle; surely they cared that he existed, didn't they?

'Why didn't you write and tell me?' he managed to ask.

Ellen cleared her throat. At first she did not know how to answer. Then she said carefully, 'Well, we thought the right person to get hold of would be your dad, and, of course, we wrote to him – twice. We reckoned that he would tell you. But now you're saying he didn't?'

'No. Never had no letter from him.'

'That's queer, love. And we haven't heard a word out of him up to now, either.' She paused to consider the implications of the lack of mail. Then she said, 'Desi and me has been thinking that the letters haven't yet caught up with him – after all, he's on a tramp.'

She sighed. 'You know how it is, every day you hope for a letter, but it doesn't come, and the days go by.' Her voice became imploring. How can you tell a kid that, because he was rarely at home, his very existence had indeed been forgotten?

He drank the tea and put the mug down on the floor. Hands hanging between his knees, he asked dully, 'What ship is Dad in?'

'He's in an Australian tramp. Your Uncle Desi went to the shipping company office and told them about your mam and give them a letter to be sent out to your dad – the people here are agents for

320

the Australian owners. Desi said they were nice enough and they promised to send our letter to his next port of call.' She paused, mystified, and then said doubtfully, 'And, you know, it is rather odd. Usually, he sends postcards to your mam from most ports what he touches, and we did have a couple – but we haven't had any lately – and His Nibs knows to give them to me.'

Daniel stared dumbly through the open door at the line of wet bedding stretched across the court. He had no idea what to do. Nearly eighteen years of age and signed off from his ship, he believed himself to be naked to the call-up for the Navy, which he was not looking forward to. And now this: it was as if his whole family had been swept down the drain.

Auntie Ellen was speaking again. 'You come stay with us for a bit. Maybe we'll get news soon.'

He nodded. 'Ta,' he said dully. 'I'll go down to the agents tomorrow. See what they say.' He stirred restlessly and then stood up. He wanted to escape from the house; he did not know what else to do, beyond trying to contact his father.

Now, a slow-boiling anger at his aunt's lack of thought for him rose inside him; he did not want to let it boil over.

Through the open door, he had caught a glimpse

of Martha through the flapping washing, as she returned home, so he said, 'I guess I'd better go and say hello to the Connollys; Martha and Mam was always great friends.'

'You do that, love. See if they're in. Desi'll be home soon, and I'll make the tea. So don't be too long.'

Martha greeted him tenderly and told him immediately how much she missed his mother. He heard all over again details of the loss of his family and a further litany of complaints of the misery of being a woman in wartime.

'Your whole life is that upset, what with trying to keep going with your work, and the everlasting queues to buy anything' she said earnestly, as she put the tin teapot over the fire to warm it up. 'You've no idea how bad it is.'

He did not bother to tell her that being a merchant seaman, with a stack of German U-boats on your tail, was not exactly paradise. He simply sat on her solitary chair by her fire, which was comfortingly warm, while she plied him with yet another mug of tea.

He was surprised out of his inertia when Patrick, in his fireman's uniform, wandered in.

Daniel did not get up, but Patrick leaned down to shake the boy's hand and clap him on the shoulder. 'Sorry about your mam and your granny,' he said.

'Ta.' The boy looked up at his old neighbour. 'You know, Pat, I'm real worried about Dollie and Connie and Minnie.' Fear of the unknown was clear upon his young face.

Patrick peeled off his jacket. Determined to be optimistic, he said, 'Not to worry, lad. There's thousands of kids as has been evacuated: they'll be safe with somebody or other. The billeting officers is maybe behind with their lists and reports. The scrum was pretty bad, you know, because the kids went in such a hurry.'

Daniel accepted this suggestion with a nod, and then asked Patrick about his uniform.

He immediately heard a tirade about the problems of being a rookie fireman. In his shattered state, however, he could not concentrate on what was being said and he failed to understand most of it.

Remembering Ellen's warning not to be too long away, he finally rose. 'Like to come out for a drink after tea?' he asked Patrick.

The invitation was accepted with alacrity.

In deep contrition, Ellen fed him half the potato and leek pie she had made for tea, and Desi looked askance at his consequently small portion. Ellen cleared her throat warningly and glanced at Daniel. Desi understood and took an extra piece of bread and margarine to fill up.

When Patrick drifted in, Desi was asked to come for a drink, too.

They went down to the busy Coburg and, though he was so young, helped Daniel to drown his distress in several pints and the noisy chatter of the pub.

Despite getting quite drunk, Daniel still felt alienated from the civilian life swirling around him. Though the lack of information about his sisters and the apparent silence of his father troubled him deeply, he knew he would be thankful to get back to sea, just as his father had always been; a boat was its own world, enclosed, separate, with a boundless ever-changing ocean to look out on and soothe you. It effectively put behind you most family worries, because you could not, at a distance, do much about them.

Seamen are used to being strangers in their own home. But that night Ellen heard Daniel weeping helplessly as he curled up on her sagging settee, and she stirred uneasily. Poor kid, pity he didn't have a wife to comfort him. She hoped a good cry would help him, like it did herself when she felt down.

TWENTY-EIGHT

The Consumption

February 1940 to February 1941

A bereft Daniel went back to sea a couple of months later, still no wiser about his father's and sisters' whereabouts. A trip to the orphanage to which Dollie, Connie and Minnie had been transferred yielded nothing: the vacated building had been taken over by an army unit; nobody knew anything about evacuated children.

He went to the town hall, and was redirected and redirected until he did not know who he was questioning.

Having very efficiently seen the children, accompanied by their teachers and in some cases by their mothers, onto innumerable trains to the countryside, the City obviously thought that their responsibility was over. Now the children were in the reception areas and were the billeting officers' headache.

He was told that each unaccompanied child had a card to post to their parents to say where they were.

'I don't think me sisters can write properly yet,' protested Daniel.

'Then their teacher would surely write for them,' snapped a harried bureaucrat.

'Only Dollie and Connie was in school,' the boy persisted. 'Our auntie says they was took into care with little Minnie and they wouldn't likely be in school for the next few days. In that time they was evacuated with an orphanage.'

The bureaucrat smiled in relief at this information. 'In that case, I am sure that you don't need to worry. The orphanage will take good care of them wherever they are. All you need to find out is which area the orphanage was evacuated to.'

Easier said than done, particularly during air raids. On inquiry, he found that he was still, mercifully, a little too young for the Navy and thankfully, after a daily search for nearly two months, found himself another merchant vessel, a tramp, where he would be better paid: he reasoned that he might need real money to help his sisters, if he couldn't communicate with his father quite soon.

'I got to earn,' he told Ellen. 'Maybe something bad has happened to me dad. Then there's only me left; and I'll need money for the kids. Next time I'm in port, I'll do another round of trying to find out. Meantime, see what you can do, please, Auntie. I don't know when I'm going to be back – you know what it's like on a tramp – I could be gone six months or more.'

In feeding and housing him while he was home, a careworn Ellen decided that she had made enough effort. It was up to Thomas Flanagan to get his children together. There was no doubt in her mind that, somewhere, her three little nieces were being well cared for, either by the orphanage or by billeting officers: they would be better fed and better looked after than they had ever been in the court with a sick mam. She decided that she need not be too worried about them, and she tried to reassure Daniel on this point.

She would, she decided, give a piece of her mind to their father, Thomas, next time he surfaced. He could write well enough to reply to her letters, blast him.

She turned her attention to the pressing need of buying soap powder, which seemed to have vanished from the local shops, and to her urgent need of coal to heat the hot water in her wash boiler.

She found that if she wanted coal, she would have to fetch it herself from the coal yard: delivering coalmen suddenly had better jobs or had been called up.

Desi, too, had a better job, which he was enjoying very much; he did not want to borrow Martha's old pram to go to fetch coal for his wife, nor did he want to collect or deliver the laundry any longer.

The resultant row between Ellen and Desi was an epic listened to with fascination by the entire court: it was as well that their boys were at sea, the court agreed; they would certainly have become embroiled on one side or the other.

In addition, two of Ellen's best clients, wives of skilled craftsmen with their own businesses, had cancelled their laundering because their husbands had been called up: their incomes were suddenly reduced to miniscule army allowances. One of them told her tearfully that she was also besieged by her husband's creditors, because she could no longer keep up the monthly payments for the wireless set and the front-room furniture which they had bought.

Prompted by Daniel's arrival and by her forgetfulness of him, Martha became slowly conscience-smitten about Colleen, who was still in Leasowe

Hospital being treated for consumption. She could not remember when she had last been out to see the child, though Kathleen had reminded her to send a birthday card, and had bought one, written a greeting and posted it on her behalf.

'I never seem to 'ave a calendar, and I'm that befuddled with all of it,' Martha wailed to Kitty Callaghan from the second floor; Kitty had a sister and a sister-in-law from nearby visiting with her on the front step. Martha joined them.

The three other women agreed with her remarks. Forced to find new jobs as older employment vanished for the duration of the war, they were all hampered by near illiteracy.

Martha continued to complain. 'Now I got to find stuff for blackout curtains, 'cos everybody's hanging onto their old linen: consequence, I got no decent fents.' She stared glumly at a rat peeping out from under the steps opposite her. 'And now I got to take time off to go out to Leasowe.' She explained about Colleen.

'Aye, you better go,' responded Kitty. 'She mayn't have much time.'

At this mention of human mortality, the three ladies round Martha immediately assumed expressions of deep, polite sympathy: everybody knew that consumption was a death sentence.

In an effort to find a more cheerful subject, the visiting sister volunteered. 'Me cousin's got a job as a street sweeper. She's taking the place of a man. Getting near a man's wage,' she finished proudly.

Though this did give Martha the idea that she might herself get a man's job, it did not ease her conscience about Colleen. She determined to make the journey to Leasowe the following afternoon. Meanwhile, she agreed with the Greek chorus on the step. She sighed. 'I were caught napping with poor Mary Margaret afore the war. It come sudden, like.'

Tears rose to her eyes, and Kitty hastily interjected to remind her visitors that Mary Margaret had been a much loved neighbour.

Martha rose and said she must go down to the market: she had managed to put together a last basket of rags for sale; she needed money for food.

The other women bid her, 'Ta-ra, well,' and then turned to discuss their own problems. Kitty's sister-in-law, a street flower seller, pointed out that the supply of fades was falling rapidly.

'The market men is selling faded flowers as well as fresh ones, now,' she said with a worried frown. 'It cuts off me supply, like. And, you know, it's very strange, there's a bigger market these days for flowers.'

'Now, why would that be?'

'Don't know.'

'For graves?'

'Could be. But, today, a real smart lady bought me last four bunches – to decorate a church for a wedding, she said. That's why I got time to come over to see you.'

Her companion smiled knowingly. 'Oh, aye,' she said slowly. 'Youngsters is getting married 'cos the lad's called up, and they don't know when they'll see each other again. With them U-boats, there's lots of decent lads what won't come home again.'

When Patrick came home at teatime, Martha's sourness at his refusal to give her the fares to Leasowe sent him out for a gill immediately after he had eaten.

'Colleen is for you to deal with. Children is your job,' he had said primly; he could not even remember what the girl looked like.

Tommy had witnessed the exchange between his irate parents, and shyly offered his mother a shilling for her fares. She gratefully accepted and gave him a big hug. 'My, we are rich today. What did you do to get that?'

'Cleaned out a big stable,' he replied with a grin. 'Lovely horses in it – real gentle Belgians.'

His sister Kathleen regarded him silently over the box on which tea had been served.

You bloody liar, she thought. You always say that.

Then she felt sick: he was her kid brother, yet she felt sure that he was doing something like Ann did for a living; what the nuns at school were always hinting at and warning you against. You could be condemned by God to burn in hell everlasting. Worse still, you could even have a baby. The latter fate, she knew, was unlikely where Tommy was concerned.

That night, in real fear, she prayed for the souls of kindly Ann and Helen – and of sweet, generous Tommy.

The following morning, in order to look respectable for the hospital, Martha borrowed the clean white apron of one of Ellen's clients: Ellen starched it specially for her. 'Let me have it back tonight,' she warned. 'I got to redo it for tomorrow, so Mrs Williams gets it back with her regular wash.'

Martha promised.

She enjoyed the train journey out to Leasowe, grateful that the train was running despite last night's air raids: the Jerries seemed to love hitting railway lines.

Nobody sat by her, because she wore a shawl and

was, therefore, probably verminous. This shunning did not worry her; she was used to it and regarded, with cynical amusement, other passengers shuffling past the vacant seat next to her.

At the station, set in peaceful countryside, she had to ask directions, because it was so long since she had visited that she had forgotten the way. She was directed politely by the porter on the platform; he was used to parents visiting the hospital.

The wind, carrying the beginning of rain, blew her black skirts, her white apron and her untidy hair into disarray, and she was breathless when, at last, she reached the hospital's inquiry desk.

'Don't you know that Thursday is not a visiting day?' she was asked testily by a nurse.

'No.'

'You'll have to come tomorrow.'

Martha's temper began to rise. She stood her ground. 'I come all the way from Liverpool, and I don't have the money to come again,' she replied baldly.

'Tush. The children have to rest, you should know that. They can't be disturbed by anybody who turns up whenever they feel like it.'

Martha took in a big breath, prepared to go into the attack. Her small frame seemed to expand before the seated woman.

'She's my kid and I want to see her now.' She closed a bony fist and thumped on the table, so that the inkpot began to slide off it.

The nurse caught the pot.

She snapped back. 'You'll have to see Sister, then. That's her door over there.' She looked poor Martha scornfully up and down, and added, 'Knock, and wait for her to answer before you go in.'

Martha vented her scorn, by sticking her nose in the air and saying, 'Ta, ever so. I know me manners.' She swept over to the door indicated.

Sister was a more thoughtful lady than the nurse at the desk. Since Martha had come such a long distance, she could pay a short visit. But she must be very quiet, so as not to disturb the other patients.

She looked reprovingly at Martha and then went on, ' Colleen has not had a visitor for a long time. I'm sure she will love to see you.'

Engulfed by guilt, Martha bobbed a small, old-fashioned curtsey as she thanked her. The nurse took her outside the building itself, down to the end of the open verandah. She leaned over the small bundle in the last bed, and whispered, 'Your mother's come to see you, Colleen.' She then hurried back to her desk.

With an effort the child turned her head. Sleepy

blue eyes regarded Martha, and a thin voice inquired doubtfully, 'Mam?'

Martha forced herself to be cheerful, though her heart sank: she had seen that grey look, lightened only by pink on each cheek, on too many other faces in the courts: and, come to that, didn't her own daughter know her?

'Of course, it's your mam, love. How are you?' She put out a grubby hand from under her shawl and touched the child's cheek playfully. 'Don't you know your old mam?'

She got a faint smile in response, and, emboldened, she now dug into her skirt and disinterred a small, fairly clean stuffed rabbit, which she had bought in a second-hand shop. 'See what I brought you.'

Colleen struggled to get a hand out from under her bedclothes, but she was tucked in so tightly against the cold wind that she was unable to do so.

Martha hauled the bedding loose, regardless of the keen sea breeze, and put the toy into the curve of Colleen's flannel-covered arm. She then quickly covered her up again. She was shivering herself, and a little unnerved by the steady beat of the incoming tide on the sandy shore; the noise seemed to go on and on.

Fresh air was supposed to be good for tubercular patients, but she decided that it was hard on ill-clad visitors.

With the rabbit tucked into her arm, Colleen's pinched little face with its deadly red rose on each cheek wrinkled up into a tiny beatific smile.

'Like him?' inquired Martha in order to fill the silence between them.

'Yeah.'

'His name's – er – Charley,' she invented.

Colleen smiled again and closed her eyes.

Martha laid an arm over her and began to pat her gently. She sat there for what seemed like ages, keeping up a slow pat, pat, pat, in unison with the waves, with no idea what to say.

Finally, the nurse descended upon her and told her that her time was up.

Martha quietly removed her arm, rose, and looked down at her sleeping child. She did not, for fear of the disease, dare to kiss her.

Almost in tears, she said, 'God's blessin's on yez, love,' and moved out of the way of the nurse, who impatiently retucked in the disturbed bedclothes.

Back at the desk, the nurse said, 'Before you go, Sister wants me to check your address and telephone number.' She paused for a second, and then added with a sneer, 'If you have one.'

With an effort Martha refrained from slapping her. She carefully gave her address. 'I don't have no telephone.'

She cried all the way back on the train, whilst a sudden squall beat in sympathy upon the window-pane. Crouched in her seat, she kept her shawl up over her head so that her red eyes would not show.

In the dreadful, snowy January of 1941, Colleen died. Since Martha had no burial insurance, she was given a pauper's burial.

Freezing, as she pushed her pram down to the coal yard, Martha mourned the child with sniffy whimpers. At the same time, she worried that Joseph, now a skinny ten-year-old, slow-poke Ellie, aged seven, and her darling Number Nine, who was just five, would die of cold, if they did not first get picked up for delinquency of some kind.

Despite being underclad, they ran wild in and out of the courts. Thank goodness, they all had boots, thought Martha.

Though Patrick was mean enough, the regular money he was bringing in, her own efforts to keep her business going, and Kathleen's and Bridie's wages were having their effect. Cold-blooded Bridie had hunted for employment which would give her the most money for the least work, and had opted for a job as a cleaner in a munitions factory. There, as she slowly swept floors all day, she hoped she would be exempt from any call-up of women.

With Bridie working, however, Martha did not have a girl to watch the youngsters, while she herself coped with the avalanche of unexpected problems brought on by the war.

'You can't even count on being able to catch a tram,' she would grumble, 'never mind find a mouse trap in the shops.' And all her weary friends would agree heartily. More money was coming in to some families, but there was little to buy.

In addition, though she and Patrick had discussed it, she had not had time to look for a better house for the family, never mind considering what rent they could now afford to pay.

Martha had become so wedded to the idea of buying goods through the system of cheques that the cheque man coming to collect the consequent weekly repayments became another dreaded Satan Hisself, like the rent man.

As she sadly considered the extra debt she was in and endured the icy cold of her sodden feet, while haunted by the ghostly thought of Colleen being thrown into a public grave, she turned into the coal yard.

Apart from coal, she wanted desperately, a good

338

cry, a cup of tea and an aspirin. But there was no tea or aspirin in her home. And, while in the crowded coal yard, she dared not even cry: on seeing her weep, most of the other women would have burst into tears: sure as fate, they would have lost somebody and be mourning them, she decided grimly.

TWENTY-NINE

'He Give Me a Good Idea'

February 1940 to May 1941

During his next voyage, a worried Daniel Flanagan did not receive a single letter from home. For company, he finally joined a couple of orphaned ordinary seamen, Peter and Ethan, who never bothered to inquire if there was any mail for them when the eagerly awaited letters were brought by the pilot boats to their ship.

'Don't you even have a girlfriend?' Peter asked Daniel, as, from a distance, they watched the pilot climb aboard.

'Can't afford one,' replied Daniel with a wry grin. 'Do you?'

'Nope,' replied the others. They laughed sheepishly.

Then Peter said with a hint of defiance in his

voice, 'Got a girl in every port. No commitments then.'

They laughed, this time with knowing winks. Then they were suddenly sobered by the sound of the bosun's whistle.

Back home in the court, it did not occur to his uncle, Desi, that he should write to his already bereft nephew, since his wife could not.

During an air raid Auntie Ellen had been hit by a piece of shrapnel. She was in Walton Hospital and was not expected to live.

As an air-raid warden, Desi was himself too exhausted amid the nights of bombing and their aftermath to think of anything other than his wife and how to remain on his feet.

He also found himself more grief-stricken than he had expected. He had always referred to her as the Old Tartar. Now he was surprised to realise that he loved her very much. Amid the jungle of the ruins around him, he prayed almost incoherently that she would live. He was tender with love when, at the end of March 1941, she returned home, frail and very dependent upon him.

On the same February evening that she was hit during the pounding of Liverpool, Daniel was guarding the gangway of his boat while docked in New Orleans. During a quiet moment, while boxes of fruit, intended for his ship, were being unloaded from a train, the bosun exchanged a casual word or two with him on the need for vigilance.

He cussed the slowness of the railway porters, and walked uneasily up and down the deck. Then he stopped near Daniel, and drew an opened letter out of his pocket. He peered at it, but evidently decided that it could not be read in the fading light. He put it back in his pocket.

He noticed Daniel watching him with interest, and said with sudden cheerfulness, 'Letter from the wife. Just got our first boy.'

Though the bosun's voice was normally like a foghorn, he made this announcement with quiet pride.

'Congratulations, sir.'

The bosun smiled and nodded. According to most of the deckies, the bosun was known to be human – occasionally. In the temporary quiet on the deck, the thought encouraged Daniel to say, 'I've not had a letter from home since we left Liverpool – and I'm proper worried.' He immediately followed this with a roar at a small boy sidling up the gangway, probably bent on petty theft.

'You get down there, afore I throw you down.'

The child promptly turned and bolted down the

steps, evaded an annoyed official on the dock and vanished into the gloom.

The bosun laughed. Then he said more soberly, his Liverpool accent broader than usual, 'Something wrong at home?'

It seemed to Daniel that this was a kindly question put to a fellow Scouser, not Authority talking to the bottom of the pile.

'Yes, sir,' he replied, and poured out, as briefly as he could, while watching the gangway, the loss of his immediate family.

At this, the bosun blew like a surfacing whale.

'Phew! That's quite a story,' he said, as he glanced over the rail to check on the pandemonium below.

He cleared his throat. It was not his job to be father confessor to an ordinary seaman, he thought. On the other hand, he was only a lad – a kid from Liverpool on his own. He rubbed his hand over his face, and suggested, 'Have you thought of telling Dale Street about your sisters being missing? The police keep a list of missing persons – and, what's more, they can demand answers where you can't. They may even have picked them up, and, if they did not know their surname, shoved them into temporary care, some place.'

His stance suddenly changed, as trolleys began to

move on the dock. He blew his whistle and began to shout orders.

As the loading progressed, Daniel decided that not only had the bosun been very decent, he had been brilliant. None of the family had thought of asking for police help – largely because they were scared of them, he supposed.

Sick tired as he was at the end of his watch, he went down to eat and, while he was eating, scribbled a letter to the Chief Constable of Liverpool, enthroned in Dale Street. He gave Auntie Ellen's name and address, as his nearest relative in Liverpool.

The Chief Constable was bedevilled by looters, traffic blocked by ruins, and a huge influx of strangers into Liverpool. The latter had brought not only further crime, but an increase in prostitution, drug-trafficking and general lawlessness.

Nevertheless, because it was unusual to receive a letter from New Orleans, and, further, because children were vulnerable to abduction, his secretary laid the letter on his desk, separately from the main pile.

The usual comforting remark from the police, regarding missing children, was often, 'They're just runaways: they'll turn up when they're hungry.'

So it was a couple of days before a surprised Desi

was asked by the local constable if his nieces were still missing.

Startled by the unexpected inquiry, he replied that they were, had been since September 1939.

On hearing the date the police seemed more worried about the girls than Desi was. Desi was nervous that he might be accused of not doing enough to trace the children, so he hastened to add that his wife, who was their aunt, had continued to make inquiries without success until she was hurt in a recent air raid.

He informed them that their father, who was at sea, had been notified through his ship's owners that the children were missing, and Desi presumed that he was actively pursuing the search as best he could while at sea, though they had not heard from him.

Fearing the worst, the police immediately put the youngsters on the Missing List, while inquiries were made of billeting officers and police in Shropshire where the girls had been evacuated.

THIRTY

'There's Jaspers in 'Ere'

March to May 1941

All through that fierce winter and later air raids, though Martha swore that times were worse than they had ever been, the family was, in fact, living better. As food became rationed, they bought and ate the rations, and then, thanks to Patrick's steady work, added to them by arduous queuing for unrationed delights, like sausages or offal.

The spongey pre-war white bread gave way to a weird but nourishing standard loaf, the contents of which varied according to what grains or potatoes the Authorities could obtain. Martha's jaws ached as, without teeth, she learned to chew the heavy, solid slices. During time spent in endless queues for the right-sized boots for her children, she complained bitterly of 'pain on either side of me face'.

Her happy Saturday evenings at the Coburg or other local pubs, her one consolation in a hard life, almost came to an end, as the supply of beer was sharply reduced by demands from the Forces or for lack of ingredients.

Instead, she spent many a sixpence at the cinema, a real cinema, she boasted, not a chapel one like Central Hall. Sometimes she went with Tara and delicate Auntie Ellen, and sometimes with Kathleen and Bridie. Both her girls would have preferred to go dancing, but they could not yet afford the necessary dress and high-heeled shoes, even if they could find them in the shops.

Martha was glad to have at least two of her children – in her opinion, the two more vulnerable ones – corralled with her in the cinema. Girls that went dancing often became pregnant – and the last thing Martha wanted was any more mouths to feed. A lifetime's observation of errant young seamen, who haunted the area of the docks and who could become the likely fathers of such offspring, had taught her, she said.

She made Tara laugh by telling her, 'At the hint of a baby, they take off, like rats into the river.'

As the snow melted and a slow spring crept in, clothing Princes Park in faintest green, Martha decided that it was time to go house-hunting. She had not yet been able to pin Patrick down as to the amount of rent he would pay. But she guessed that, now he was experienced, he was earning more.

Strangely, in a time of general shortages, there were quite a number of houses with the To Let sign in their windows. When men were called up and, as a result, incomes shrank, young wives gave up their homes and went back to live with their mothers 'for the duration', as they put it.

She put on a decent flowered pinafore, wrapped her black shawl around her, and went to see the agent whose address was on most of the signs.

He was not particularly keen to show her any of the houses available until she mentioned that her husband was a city fireman. Then he immediately produced keys to two of them, for which she signed with a cross.

After living in a court, the streets of Toxteth seemed almost frighteningly wide. Some had shade trees in bud, and each house had a well-swept front step abutting the pavement. The street to which the agent had directed her was empty, except for one or two passers-by and three little girls playing hopscotch.

She found the house she was seeking, and hesitantly unlocked the door. She stepped into a narrow hall, and was faced with a steep staircase to the upper floor. To her right was a closed door.

She cautiously opened it and peeped into a room fairly well lit by a bow window. It had a fireplace littered with ashes; the bare wooden floor looked as if it had not been swept for months. She tiptoed through to a further door, as if she might disturb someone. Behind it, she found a living room with a large kitchen range and a kitchen sink, equally littered with the debris of months.

Through the window of this room, she could see a small yard enclosed by a high brick wall. At the end of the yard was a little shed. She wondered if the shed was a lavatory.

She stood in the doorway, her fingers on the brass knob, ready to retreat. It was so silent, so empty.

She reckoned that upstairs there must be the same space. She took in a big breath – it was silly to be so nervous.

She immediately became aware of an all-too-familiar smell.

Jaspers!

She stepped hastily back into the hall, lest a bug drop on her from the lintel. Bugs go to bed in the daytime, she knew that, but they did not take their odour with them. Her room in the court had been permanently bug-ridden and she was very keen that she might get rid of the pests by obtaining a decent house: most of her family had been bitten by them so often that they were practically immune to the great red welts they produced, but the children would be glad enough not to have to endure any more.

She turned and scuttled out of the house with such speed that she forgot to lock the front door.

She walked over to the second house and found the same problem.

Indignantly, she marched back to the agent, slammed the keys onto the counter, and said sharply, 'They both got jaspers.'

The agent sighed. He had taken for granted that a woman in a black shawl would be bug-ridden already and would not be bothered by the presence of vermin.

'And what rent would you be asking for a house – with bugs?'

'The rent's controlled – seven shillings a week.'

'Holy Mother! All that!'

'That's a low rent for a through house. We can get the house fumigated for you.'

Martha was shocked at the rent, and ignored the offer of fumigation. 'Haven't you got nothing smaller – with no bugs?'

'Not in this district. We do usually get the houses

stoved before each tenant goes in; then keeping them vermin-free depends on the tenant.'

That would get rid of the vermin, thought Martha – but not the rent.

'Ta,' she responded, and walked out. She joined a nearby queue in front of a grocer's, and was cheered by finding that it was for sausages.

At teatime, so tired that she hardly knew how to stand, she shoved a plate of sausage and potatoes under Patrick's nose, and then sat down. He was late and the children were out at play, despite the blackout. She told him crossly about the houses.

'Try down by the Dingle – it's real nice down there, by the petrol installation.'

'What about you doing something about it?'

'What with learning the city, I'm finished,' he grumbled. 'I been driving all over the place so I can find anywhere in the dark.'

'What about me? I'm never off me feet. How do you think I got them sausages? And then I been to see the houses and I come home and cooked and fed the kids.'

'Ach! Stop it. You don't know you're born. All you got to do is find a place not too far from where any of us works – and let them stove it.'

'And pay seven bob a week in rent?' she retorted. 'It's only one and sixpence here.'

'Get yourself a regular job like everybody else is doing, and we'll manage it.'

She swallowed. She felt like murdering him, but she was too tired.

He finished his tea, belched and got up. He slowly put on his uniform jacket again and buttoned it up.

'Going down to the Coburg?' she sneered.

He ignored the gibe, opened the door of the room and swung out, only to collide with old Joseph, the pickpocket from the second floor. He was about to ascend the stairs to his room.

For a moment, they were so close that old Joseph had to restrain himself from neatly taking the change out of his neighbour's pocket. Never a good idea to rob the neighbours, however; he had always held to this precept and never had stolen anything in the house; the result was that, despite his occupation, he was regarded as reasonably trustworthy.

Patrick grinned at him, and continued down the front steps.

To old Joseph, the blackout was a godsend. In the dead dark, quietly and unhurriedly shuffling the length of a cinema queue, making the most of the dim outline of his aged bentness, he could pick several pockets or open a handbag, before vanishing, unsuspected, into the blackness of the street itself.

Unbeknown to Martha or Patrick, he was enjoying himself teaching young Joe, their son, the techniques of his craft. Joe regarded this as a great game; he had enlisted his younger sister, Ellie, into aiding him by begging from a woman to distract her attention, while he neatly took change from her pocket or, preferably, something edible out of her shopping bag.

A few days later, it was Brendan, the seaman son of Kitty Callaghan, his neighbour on the second floor, who, while on leave, alerted Patrick to what was happening.

Young Joe had made the worst of mistakes by trying to take Brendan's wallet out of his back pocket.

He caught the child by the wrist, held him down against his thigh, pulled down his shorts and gave him a thorough spanking. Then, holding him by his guernsey, he shook him hard.

'You ever try that again,' he hissed, 'and I'll belt you till you bleed.' He flung the howling boy away from him and ran down the stairs to meet his girlfriend outside the court.

Martha came to the bottom of the stairs to see what the noise was about, and Brendan smiled at her as he passed her: he had no doubt that Martha would sort out her son in short order.

She met Joe hitching up his trousers, as he descended. He was still crying.

Faced with the need for an immediate explanation, he reduced his wails to a whimper, and said, 'Brendan pulled me pants down and tried to do something to me.'

Number Nine was sorting his precious cigarette card collection on the floor. He now glanced up nervously at his brother; his mother had warned him not to let anybody touch him or pull his shorts down.

Pat was reading the football news. He looked up, as Martha dragged the boy into their room.

'Tell your dad,' she ordered, only half believing the accusation, because Brendan had smiled at her.

The paper was put down. Gimlet eyes glared at the boy. Faltering, Joe repeated the accusation.

There was silence in the room. Patrick knew he must be careful. Someone upstairs would have heard the rumpus and news of the accusation might flow through the court. Honour would demand that he face Brendan with it, and, likely, he would have to fight him. But he had known the lad since he was a kid; he was a nice enough lad, despite his rogue of a father, and he had more girls floating round him than most young men.

He again looked hard at the squirming ten-year-old, still held in his mother's firm grip.

He took a chance, and ordered, 'Now tell me what really happened.'

'Like I said.' Joe was scared, and he wriggled harder in hope of escape.

His father stood up, and said, 'I don't believe it. Brendan isn't like that.'

There was no answer.

Patrick suddenly hit him across the face, and Joe yelped and clapped a hand to his stinging cheek, while Number Nine ducked instinctively.

'You don't have to do that,' interrupted Martha. 'The kid's scared.'

'I'll make him scared. Come on, let's have it.'

No reply.

He slapped the other side of his son's face.

'Want any more?' he asked.

Joe turned his face into his mother's ample skirts and howled. Martha hastily slammed the door into the hall, to contain the noise.

Then she put her arm round the boy. 'Come on, love. You can tell your dad anything. He'll take care of it.' She looked warningly up at her husband.

'He said I was trying to pinch his wallet, and I wasn't,' Joe blurted out.

Ellie had been curled up in a corner, trying to keep warm under an old coat while her dress, soaked by rain, dried in front of the fire. Now she unwisely put in a word which she imagined might exonerate her brother. She said, 'He isn't good enough to try wallets yet.'

Her father spun round. 'What?' he roared. 'What're you saying?'

It all came out. Ellie thought it was a game and said so. Joe admitted the truth of it.

Pat strode to the door and, as he ran up the stairs, Martha shouted up to him, 'Now, don't hit him – he's old.'

No, thought Patrick. But I'll tell him. And when the startled old man opened his door cautiously, Patrick kicked it wide – and told him succinctly what he thought of such a creep.

Expert at looking old and helpless, Joseph cringed. He said he had done it just to amuse the children. He never thought of them putting it into practice. For sure, he didn't – not with a neighbour, that was certain.

Defeated, Patrick shouted at him not to dare to do it again, and clumped downstairs. He wasn't past stealing from the docks himself; he had done it many a time. But docks, ships and big stores were fair game and belonged to Them, as Martha often said. Neighbours were different – they were, well, neighbours – and you had to live with them, and simply watch that they did not steal from you.

Downstairs, he threatened both children with a real belting if they tried anything like that again.

White-faced at the thought of what a leather belt with a brass buckle could wreak on their respective behinds, they weepily agreed to instant reformation.

Martha sighed, and pulled the mattress down from the wall.

'Get to bed,' she ordered. She turned to Number Nine. 'And you,' she added sharply. The child knocked his pack of cards together and hastily scrambled to his feet.

As the mattress flopped to the floor, the air-raid siren began its frantic warning whoop.

THIRTY-ONE

'It Were a Landmine'

1965

'That was the worst air raid I ever knowed,' confided Martha to the long-suffering Angie. 'It were called the May Blitz.'

She was seated on a hard-backed chair by the window of the ward, her bare feet on the chilly linoleum floor, while Angie changed the sheets on her bed and then emptied the contents of the commode into a slop bucket.

'Really?' she replied.

'Yes. We had seven solid nights of bombing, and that last night they nearly done us in.'

Only half listening, Angie turned to glance at the two dementia cases in the far corner of the room. One of them was becoming restive and was pulling at the rope which tethered her securely to the end of her bed. The other one, her folded hands on her lap, was sitting on the side of the bed, her rope drooping onto the floor.

Angie clicked her tongue irritably. Better have them both back in bed and tie them down, as soon as she had finished with Martha.

Undeterred by Angie's apparent lack of interest, Martha continued.

'We was in the cellar, as usual, and I were that worried about Kathleen and Bridie. They was going to the pictures – or that's what they told me they was going to do.' She laughed. 'A pair of minxes, they was; chasing the lads was more likely, I reckon.

'When they tried to get home, the street had been closed off by the police and we had been moved to a rest centre in the basement of a school and they was sent to join us there.'

She paused to clear her throat, and then went on reflectively, 'There was over a hundred people crammed in with us; some of them had been there for days, bombed out and nowhere to go. And there was only one lavatory: you can imagine the mess; even the court was better than that.

'Pat told me later that They refused to put in more lavatories, or some mattresses to sleep on – nothing to make it comfortable – because they wanted the bombed-out to be forced to go and find new homes by themselves; They didn't want them to settle in and live in the shelter.'

She snorted, as she added, 'I think we would have starved, if it hadn't been for the WVS, coming in with soup and sandwiches regardless of the bombing. Wonderful volunteer ladies, they was. Real brave.'

Angie had given Martha's pillow a final pat and had slammed the lid on the slop bucket. She paused, however, before getting her patient back into bed, not quite believing that she had heard aright.

'Only one loo, Martha. It couldn't be?'

Martha shook a finger at her. 'It was deliberate, as I just told you. To drive people out; that means women with young kids – and no transport – to find a place for themselves. Imagine a city with miles and miles of ruins, if you can. Near hopeless, it had become.'

'Good Lord!'

Martha rose slowly, but steadily, ready to get into bed again, and then she asked, out of curiosity, 'Do you know what a landmine's like? 'Cos that's what we got in the middle of the court. It was a dud and it didn't explode, praise be.'

'No, what is it like?' replied Angie, her interest now aroused.

360

'It's like a big red pillar box – except it isn't red. The police got everyone tiptoeing out of the court, fearing it would explode before they got us all past it – it had gone halfway through the paving stones.'

The new occupier of Pat's bed said slowly, almost sleepily, 'I know what a landmine's like, my God.'

Martha was startled. They were the first words the woman had spoken since she had been brought in a couple of days before. According to Angie, she had been transferred from the hospital because she, like Martha, had no home to go to.

Martha turned towards her, amazed that, unlike the other patients in the room, she could speak. Oh, blessed relief! Talk!

'You do, Missus?' Martha asked gently.

'Oh, aye. They're as big as a pillar box, like you said. One fell on our house.' The woman stopped, and then said in a faltering voice. 'Blew out three houses. Killed me hubby and me four kids. They said I were lucky – because I were visiting me cousin down the road at the time.'

She paused again, and then added bitterly, 'I don't think I was lucky.'

Holding Martha's arm ready to help her into bed, Angie gazed compassionately down on the new patient.

'Don't say that, Missus,' she pleaded. 'It must've been awful. But you're here still.'

'I don't want to be.' Though vehement, the woman still sounded a little sleepy, as she went on, 'And the pills you keep stuffing into me don't help, I can tell you. I can barely put two words together.'

At the latter remark, Martha gave a little laugh. Then she said in the most consoling tone she could muster, 'None of us wants to be here, love. I'm real sorry about your hubby and the kids. I know how terrible it is to have nobody left – and I'm real glad to have you next door to me to talk to.' She smiled her most winning smile at her fellow sufferer.

The woman nodded. 'That's proper nice of you to say so,' she replied politely, and sighed. She lifted her head slightly from her pillow, and asked, 'Nurse, could you give me a glass of water – I'm fair parched.'

Full of pity, Angie left Martha standing, while she went to a little centre table, where there was a jug of water and a glass, to be shared by all five occupants of the room. She poured the water and handed it to the woman. The glass was drained and handed back to her.

'Ta ever so.'

For the moment, Martha could not think of

anything more to say, so she stared longingly out of the window, where a ray of sunshine was lighting up a broken statue of Cupid in the middle of a weed-ridden lawn. She dreamed of being allowed to sit outside in the sun and breathe real fresh air, but, according to Angie, Matron disapproved of the idea.

When Angie had suggested that a few of the patients were, perhaps, well enough to be allowed into the garden, she had been promptly crushed.

'We don't have time to go out with them, and they cannot be left alone – they might fall or wander off. Don't put any ideas in their heads about that.'

In other words, Angie had thought, she can't be bothered. They're much less trouble if they are confined to bed.

While Angie returned the glass to the table, Martha slowly climbed into bed by herself. She gave a huge smile of triumph, and Angie grinned back as she tucked her in.

As Martha watched, the sheets of the new patient were changed without taking her out of bed: Angie had to lift and roll her over to get a sheet under her, as she did for total invalids. Though the bulky woman did not appear disabled, she did not do much to help Angie in this difficult task.

Since the Home lacked a lift, on her arrival in the

ward she had been brought in on a stretcher carried up the stairs by the gardener and his grown son. She was wrapped in a blanket and they simply lifted her, blanket and all, onto the bed. As the blanket was removed, the bedding had been quickly whipped over her.

In an absent-minded way, Martha was puzzled.

'Oh, my God!' she gasped under her breath.

In a quick glimpse, Martha understood and was filled with pity.

The woman had no legs! No wonder she did not use the commode, but had a bedpan instead. No wonder that, in an effort to give her a scrap of privacy, kind Angie kept most of her covered with a bath towel when washing her. Poor thing!

After Angie had scuttled across the room to tend the restive dementia patient, leaving Martha's new companion propped up on either side by extra pillows, Martha said to the grey-haired woman, 'Me name is Martha Connolly. What's yours?'

'Sheila McNally,' she replied dully. She did not turn to look at Martha, but lay back with her eyes closed.

Martha gazed at her with some anxiety. Where did one begin with a woman so incapacitated that she would never get out of bed alone, even though her mind seemed all right?

With no one to visit her, no one with whom to communicate, except the hard-pressed aides, Martha longed to talk with her new neighbour. She was not sure, however, how to begin. She stared disconsolately out of the window at the top of a tree, all she could see of the garden from her bed. A raven flew into the branches cawing its arrival. Lucky bird – to be free.

She was relieved of her dilemma by Sheila's asking, 'How long you been here?'

'About eight or ten weeks.' Martha was not really sure: no calendar brightened the blank walls; every day was the same; they came, they went, and you endured as best you could from meal to meal. At least in the court, you'd usually known what day it was. Saturday: Patrick was usually around, because one of his shifts was on Sunday. Sunday: what was left of the family was home. Monday: wash day, and work all week.

'Blessed Virgin! exclaimed Sheila. 'I hope I don't last that long.'

So she was Catholic? That was something.

'Aye, don't say that, love. Maybe you'll get better and be let out,' Martha lied comfortably.

'Not me. They cut me legs off in the hospital. I'm in here 'cos they can't do nothing more for me.'

''Tis a terrible thing to happen to yez,' Martha

365

agreed as gently as she could. 'But you could do a lot if you had a wheelchair.'

Sheila snorted. 'Me? Who's going to pay hundreds of pounds for that?'

'National Health might.' Martha thought for a minute, and then she chuckled, 'You could zip around this floor in one, and frighten the living daylights out of the Matron. She always shouts at you if you get out of bed and dare to look down the stairs. She'd have palpitations, right off.'

Sheila carefully turned her head, and actually grinned at Martha. 'You don't like her, do you?'

'I don't think she's human. Doctor give her bloody hell the other day, when Pat, what had your bed, died. Said it were her fault.'

'Humph. I don't like her neither – first minute I seen her, I says to meself, you won't get no help here, you won't.'

'Have you got anybody who'd ask the doctor for you?'

'Does he come here?'

'Yes.' There was unease in Martha's voice, as she added, 'It's hard to get to talk to him, though, 'cos Matron does the talking, if you know what I mean.'

'Oh, aye, I do. They was a bit like that in the hospital. They was always talking over your head, like.'

'What was you in for?'

'I got clots in me veins. Doctor said they would cause gangrene, so they took me legs off.' She stopped, and then said unhappily, 'I agreed to it: everybody knows how terrible gangrene is: I couldn't face it.'

They had a very satisfactory afternoon together, first tearing Them apart, and then sharing their wartime experiences. They particularly discussed the night that the deadly landmines were dropped and Sheila lost her family and her neighbours on either side of her.

When you've had a bad time, it's good to talk it out with your friends, thought Martha wistfully. It's been a long time. I don't know what I would have done without Angie.

She wished she could have offered Sheila a cup of tea and an aspirin to ease the pain she said she had in the legs that were no longer there, a pain which Martha told her she had heard soldiers from the First World War complain about.

Sheila looked at her doubtfully. 'So you understand about it? That goddamned Matron didn't, when I tried to explain it to her. Said it was me imagination.'

'For sure, I understand. Heard more than one old soldier complain the same, in me time.'

They beamed at each other. As Martha looked into a pain-lined face and saw a sudden twinkle in bloodshot hazel eyes, she knew she could do something for this woman. She could be useful to her by simply being a friend.

You had to work at easing a friend's sorrow: it took time. She knew that from experience. She stretched out her hand towards the other bed, and Sheila thankfully grasped it.

In the comfortable silence which ensued, Martha remembered to quietly thank the Dear Virgin Mother for sending her a friend.

''Ave you got a rosary, Sheila?' she asked.

'Oh, aye, it's about all I have got.'

Martha chuckled. 'Same with me.' And, for no reason that they could think of, they both began to laugh at their penniless predicament.

THIRTY-TWO

'The Oldest Profession'

May to June 1941

The landmine in the court was delicately disassembled by two extraordinarily young, light-footed soldiers. It was then carefully carted away, and the Connolly family and their neighbours returned home. They spent some time staring into the hole left in the paving, until the City sent an elderly man to shovel the bits of broken stone into the hole and roughly patch it over.

Though pressed by Martha, Patrick had refused to do this temporary repair. He was the only physically strong man left in the court, other than the harried Desi, who also refused.

'I've had enough,' Pat said flatly. 'I'm run to death and you know it.

Martha reluctantly agreed. Often he was home

only long enough to snatch a few hours' sleep between raids. He sometimes fell onto the mattress without eating his dinner and slept immediately.

As the year progressed, air raids became more frequent, impatiently accepted as inevitable. Overworked women, without the support of their menfolk, grew grim-faced and more careworn.

While Patrick drove his fire engine through streets illuminated only by blue flares dropped by enemy planes, his family, desperately seeking sleep, went down to James Street underground station at night. There, they curled up wherever they could find a corner of platform or stairs, and slept.

In order to catch the trains which would carry them under the river to the relative safety of the Wirral Peninsula, passengers edged carefully amongst them to reach the one-foot wide space of platform along the edge of the railway line. The railway employees insisted on this area being kept clear so that they could board their trains.

The frightened refugees shared fleas, lice, influenza, coughs and colds with hundreds of others.

Only when dysentery became common and the railway company disgusted with human waste on the lines, did the local government put portable lavatories into the underground stations; as with the rest centres, it was argued that lavatories would encourage the frightened Liverpudlians to stay longer: they might even live in the stations.

They also irritably pointed out that the refugees from the bombing were already at fault for trespassing on railway property and certainly should not be there at all. Their presence had to be discouraged: they could be prosecuted.

In London, the government finally realised that Liverpool, as the headquarters of Western Command, had to be better protected from air raids.

Barrage balloons appeared in the sky, and Martha became fascinated by their floating silently overhead; she would stand in the street and watch them dancing slowly above her like friendly, airborne elephants.

Tommy explained to her that they stopped the Jerries from dive-bombing or machine-gunning the streets by keeping the enemy planes at a higher altitude.

'It makes it harder for them to machine-gun vehicles like Dad's fire engine,' he told her.

'Well, that's nice to know,' she said. But she wondered if it made much difference whether you were killed by a bomb dropped from a height, or a closer bullet.

He also told her that the Spitfires, which eventually went up to challenge the German planes, were piloted by Polish airmen, who were allies.

'They come over when Poland was taken by the Jerries.'

'Oh, aye, I know that,' said Martha. 'Seen lots of Poles around.'

Though she had spent little time in school and could not read, Martha knew of the existence of Poland and most other countries. Liverpool was a great port. In the pubs and in the narrow streets, she often met and talked with seamen or their wives. When anything momentous happened in the world, it always seemed to Martha that she met a sailor who had been there at the time and had witnessed the occurrence. It was a great way of getting news.

To the regular swarms of seamen were soon added serving men, like the Poles, in a variety of uniforms from all over Europe. In addition, came skilled British craftsmen transferred from the south or the Midlands to work in new factories in Speke or to serve the ships crowding into the Mersey.

They were joined by a ragtag of bewildered refugees from Europe, including Germans who had been trade unionists or Communists in their native land and were, in consequence, targets of the Nazis.

Finally, dispossessed and terrified, came Jews from a dozen countries with stories of horrors which were almost unbelievable.

They were soon joined by hordes of youngish, single British women, called up to work in factories far from their homes. These women had never earned so much in their lives and were out to enjoy what they earned. They bought clothes and food on the black market, to the irritation of local women old enough to be their mothers who could not afford to do this; and Tommy, in his early teens, learned the pleasure of having female partners, who paid well.

Finally, came the American soldiers, pouring into Burtonwood, the largest military camp in the world. They had more money, more chocolates and more of the new nylon stockings than anyone in the back streets of Liverpool had ever dreamed of.

'They're like Cadbury's in uniform,' remarked Martha, 'and they got more nice stockings than George Henry Lee's.'

The call-up or transfer of their menfolk and their single daughters, with the consequent disintegration of the support system of long-established neighbourhoods, played havoc with families. Absolutely carelessly, the government mixed up the population of the country in a way that it had never been since Viking raids a thousand years before.

They failed to predict a fast increase in illegitimate births and an alarming growth in sexual diseases, particularly syphilis which, even before the war, had been considered endemic in Liverpool.

Painfully aware of the danger to her girls, Martha scolded Kathleen and Bridie when they were out late.

'How you going to get a good husband,' she screamed at them, 'if you don't have a good name?'

Before the war, girls knew very well that they must guard their reputation with considerable care. It did not do to be too flirtatious or to walk the streets in the dark with a boy, until you were being seriously courted by a young man, and were walking arm in arm together: it would be presumed that, after showing his intentions publicly, he would take the girl home to be inspected by his mother, after which a very long engagement, complete with ring, would usually ensue.

Now, both Kathleen and Bridie laughed good-naturedly at Martha's warnings.

'Ach, don't be so old-fashioned,' they said; and as soon as they had earned enough to pay for suitable attire, they went dancing and met young men that they would never have even seen before the war.

It did not take Kathleen and Bridie long to learn the finer points of sex.

Tommy knew all too well. He found himself unexpectedly worried at what his sisters might be doing, when he was himself stricken by pain from a hard sore on his penis.

Afraid to tell anyone, he endured as best he could.

He relaxed, however, when the sore appeared to heal. He decided that he had been mistaken, and went back to looking each evening for pretty, willing young women.

During the day, he worked for Brian's late employer, Mr Beamish, the butcher, which pleased Martha very much.

Mr Beamish had welcomed him. He had already lost his two assistants to the army, and had been battling the problems that meat rationing had imposed upon him, aided only by a very elderly retired butcher.

Soon after Tommy had begun to learn how to reduce an animal to a myriad of small, edible rations, he came home with a throat so sore that he could hardly speak, a rash and a bad headache. Dosed with hot tea and a lot of aspirin, he continued to drag himself to the butcher's shop: at least it took him out of the fetid atmosphere of the Connollys' room; even a butcher's shop was better than that.

Then, one busy Friday, while dealing with a long queue of women waiting hopefully for some unrationed liver or kidneys, the lad crashed to the sawdust-besprinkled floor in what appeared to be a faint. Shocked women crowded round him, recommending a glass of water, which did not help.

A nearby doctor was called, and the lad was shipped off to hospital.

A couple of hours later, when Mr Beamish had sold all his stock, he closed his shop and fled to the court to tell Tommy's parents what had happened.

Directed to the correct door by Helen O'Brien, who was sitting on the step, he found Martha napping on the mattress, while Kathleen made herself some tea. He blurted out what had occurred, and retreated from the stinking room as fast as he could.

As she snatched up her shawl, a very distressed Martha ordered Kathleen to watch the children, and made all haste to the hospital. Hospitals meant death. But not, O Lord, for Tommy, she prayed frantically; he's too young.

At the hospital, she was coldly informed by a

supercilious clerk that Tommy would remain in hospital 'under observation'. She could visit him any afternoon. Mystified, she was allowed to her son's bedside in a huge ward to visit him. She could not wake him from his drugged sleep.

She went slowly home and duly reported what had happened to Patrick.

'Well, if he's that dead asleep, he won't feel any pain,' remarked Patrick, trying to be comforting. 'They'll know in a day or two what's the matter and then they'll do something about it.'

'Oh, aye,' Martha agreed with a sigh. 'I can't be huntin' for rags to sell and going to the market with them, and then drag meself down here to visit him every afternoon. I'm getting real good prices nowadays – and we'd know it if I stopped earning. What am I going to do?'

'If they've got him that sound asleep, he won't know if he's got a visitor or not.'

Martha agreed. Though she worried about him, she went to the hospital very infrequently, and the answer was always the same. 'He's under observation.' She never questioned the studied vagueness of the replies she got from the nursing staff, and he always seemed to be deeply asleep. But Martha cheered herself up by noting that he was still breathing.

She would not have felt so concerned if it had been either Kathleen or Bridie lying there. She had always found both of them awkward to deal with, a constant worry as they grew older and more wayward. In fact, she would be thankful if both of them got called up, except that she would miss their wages.

She took it as an insult, however, when, the following year, Kathleen unexpectedly volunteered the day she was eighteen.

As for Bridie, she proved to be a shocker. 'I was that ashamed,' Martha later confided to Ann O'Brien. 'At first, I couldn't believe it.'

Ann thought sadly, Well, I saved Kathleen for you.

Soon after the May Blitz, hard-headed Bridie realised that, properly handled, prostitution could be lucrative. She was sixteen.

Small, plain, but prettily dressed, she discovered her own abilities. She continued to live with her parents and to work in the daytime as a cleaner in a munitions factory because this made her exempt from call-up. Late in the evening she would dress as if she were going to a dance, and make rather more money by quietly standing near the entrance to Lime Street Station watching the uniforms swarming by.

378

Still blithely unaware of exactly what Tommy's illness was, Martha and Patrick accidentally discovered Bridie's part-time occupation.

One raidless evening, when the Coburg had no beer and was shut, the couple had ventured out to a cinema in Lime Street. On coming out after the film was over, they saw her, in the dim light of a passing car, accost an airman.

They had imagined her dancing in one of the fairly respectable clubs in their own neighbourhood, and, at first doubted that it was her.

'It can't be her,' whispered Martha. 'She wouldn't dare.'

'It's her all right,' muttered her weary husband, as anger surged in him.

An outraged Martha wanted to go straight up to her and haul her away.

Patrick restrained her. 'Wait till she comes home,' he advised. 'She's over sixteen now and she could very well tell a cop that you assaulted her.'

Martha spluttered. 'But we can't let her go off with him.'

'She's probably done it before,' Patrick replied bitterly.

They had to wait up until four in the morning.

She came almost silently up the steps and into

379

the hall. She carefully turned the knob of their door and entered like a ghost. She paused when she saw that a candle was still burning and that her father was standing accusingly to one side of the mattress, upon which Joseph, Ellie and Number Nine lay sleeping.

Her mother gazed at her apprehensively from their only chair.

'Where you been?' Patrick snarled, his belt twitching in his hand like a lion's tail just before it springs.

She slowly took off her hat and kicked off her high-heeled shoes before answering.

'To a dance,' she finally replied. Her sulky expression dared him to ask more.

'Not you,' he replied tightly. 'We saw you pick up an airman in Lime Street.'

'So what? We went to a dance together.'

He took two steps closer to her, and she cringed. All he did was inhale deeply.

He could smell the maleness on her.

'Give me your purse,' he demanded.

Surprised, she handed her handbag to him.

He took out her purse, opened it, and poured the contents into his calloused hand. There was almost two pounds in it – in change.

'That's almost what you earn in a week at the

factory,' he said accusingly, as he threw the change back into the handbag. 'Where did you get it?'

'I can save,' she told him without much hope.

'Not you – you're always buying clothes and suchlike. You got a whole boxful of stuff, right here. And you give your mam the same as Kathleen does, I know that.' His voice rose. 'You're on the street, aren't you, you dirty bitch? You are, aren't you?'

Martha watched the inquisition, her mouth half open. She had always believed that the Catholic school and its nuns, backed by her own Catholic efforts at keeping her girls 'good', would save them from the streets. She had hoped that they would marry respectably, in spite of living in an overpacked court.

As it dawned on her that she had failed, she burst into loud laments.

Without turning to look at her, Patrick said sharply, 'Shut up or the neighbours will hear.'

The noise came down a decibel or two.

Patrick tossed the handbag at Bridie. It fell at her feet. As she bent to pick it up, he swung his belt and brought it down hard across her shoulders. As she staggered under the heavy blow, the buckle caught the side of her neck and cut her quite deeply. She gasped with pain and clutched her throat. Then she ducked a second blow, turned, opened the door and fled down the steps.

They never saw her again. Cold, calculating, with a strange scar on her neck, she became an excellent businesswoman in her chosen profession.

She was careful to keep her job in the munitions factory, because then she was unlikely to be called up. Because of her fatigue, however, she soon gave up walking the streets herself. With an elderly lover of suitably large proportions to act as bouncer, she rented a house in Hill Street and, with four older women working for her, she became known as Madame La Belle.

She taught her women birth control, learned from a chemist who stocked the necessary materials, and she watched their health carefully. Over the years, a surprising number of her women managed to find husbands and left her for a more respectable world.

She never lacked replacements, and, after the war, was able to employ out-of-work younger women, released from their wartime occupations.

She once served a term in prison for keeping a common bawdy house. At the age of forty, however, she still managed to retire with her lover to comfortable obscurity in Birmingham.

Martha wept at her daughter's fall from grace, though she never knew the half of it. To account for the girl's sudden departure, she told the neighbours that she had got a safer job in Preston. 'Munitions factories is dangerous,' she said.

Unlike her mother, some of the neighbours had caught glimpses of the girl with various men in the town, and they conjectured that she might be pregnant and had been sent away to secretly give birth somewhere else. They sniggered behind their hands.

After a while, Martha's usual optimism returned, and she talked again about going house-hunting. 'To get a decent place for when the kids come home at the end of the war, and our Tommy's out of hospital,' she explained to Auntie Ellen.

Nowadays, rather than sit on the step with the other women, Ellen tended to sit indoors in a rocking chair bought for her by Desi at a sale. 'It eases me back something wonderful,' she would sometimes tell Martha.

Seated outside on the step whenever it was warm enough, Helen and Ann hoped that the hospital would soon decide what ailed young Tommy, so that, like Auntie Ellen, he could come home.

Because, unlike his mother, they wandered in areas of the city which he also haunted, they had

seen him quite frequently in compromising circumstances, and they suspected more about Tommy's illness than his mother did. They heartily
agreed with her that all her children deserved a
better home.

THIRTY-THREE

'Don't Know if I'm Coming or Going'

May to September 1941

Quite unaware that she would never see Lizzie or Bridie again, Martha comforted herself with the thought that, one day, the war would come to an end. Then Brian would be discharged from the army and would come home.

She hoped, too, that, in time, Bridie would be smart enough to give up what she was doing, and come creeping home to be comforted by her mam.

As for Lizzie, letters had stopped coming from her some time back, because the girl knew her mam couldn't read them or reply to them, she told herself.

Anyway, who, in civvy street, had time to find someone with leisure enough to write a reply on her behalf, a harassed Martha wanted to know.

After the war Lizzie would surely want to come home to work near her old mam, wouldn't she? Together with Tommy, who would surely recover, Martha would have five sets of children's wages to look forward to, until they all got married. The family would be temporarily rich.

Comforted by these optimistic thoughts, she had a very private cry over Bridie's precipitate departure.

In September, Number Nine went cheerfully off to school. 'Because I'm five,' he said proudly.

Martha found herself with a little more time to spare, so, in the hope that the war would end soon, she decided to try again to find a house.

She took Patrick's advice and walked south, down to the Dingle, where the loss of homes from bombing had been less severe.

It was a longer walk than she remembered. When she and Patrick were courting, they had walked once or twice down to the Cassie shore by the river, beyond Dingle itself, and had never found the distance a problem – because we was young and in love, she supposed.

Who'd have thought, she ruminated, that it would result in eleven pregnancies, nine of which had survived, though she had lost little Colleen to the dreaded consumption; and that, twenty years later, she would have only two children at home who were bringing in wages, Kathleen and, normally, Tommy; and three of them still in school.

Even Tommy was not earning for the moment: he had not been well for some time now, but she had put it down to the stress of the bombing. Last time she went to visit him in the hospital, he hadn't talked much and he looked proper sick, she thought. The weary nurse in charge of the ward had been real nice to her, though, and had said that he was still under observation. She suggested that Martha should visit him again in two days' time when the doctor might have a chance to talk to her.

Reluctant to break it to her that her child would be dead in a week or two from the shameful disease of syphilis, the nurse hoped the doctor would tell her.

Martha ignored a house to let in Mill Street, though it looked straight out at the street and was not enclosed in a court: Mill Street didn't have a very good name.

She ambled on, her feet dragging. But there was nowhere to sit to rest for a while, so she continued until she came to Dingle Lane. She hesitated, and then decided to walk down it towards the river and then double back along Cockburn Street which was close to the riverside; there were rows and rows of respectable-looking little houses in the streets leading off it.

She suddenly found herself facing a high locked gate: she had forgotten the huge petrol installation which lay next to the Herculaneum Dock.

To her left was another narrower gate leading into the installation, and outside it stood a police constable. Despite his uniform and his tall helmet, he looked quite amiable, so, curious, she edged a little closer.

The constable saw a tidy-looking shawl woman in a clean apron hesitating in front of the big gate, and asked her if she had come in reply to the advertisement.

Puzzled, she answered, 'No. What advertisement?'

With a nod of his head towards what looked like a small office behind him, he replied, 'They're advertising for women labourers, Missus. It's to clean oil barrels. The men is all called up.'

Martha forgot about house-hunting and remembered only that the fent business was nearing zero. 'Is it very heavy work?' she inquired.

'Not really, Missus. They've got some new stuff to clean the barrels with, like a special soap. It's called detergent. I'm told it cleans up oil like you'd never believe.'

Martha smiled her sweetest smile. 'Could I try for a job, do you think?'

'Sure. All you have to do is come in here, and go knock on that door there. Say I let you in.'

Her smile became conspiratorial, her eyes twinkling. 'OK,' she said, 'let me in.'

A Petroleum Board desperately short of men willing to do a dirty job at the minimum wage ensured that the elderly clerk behind the door was pleased to see her, despite the unpleasant odour surrounding her. He did not, however, invite her to sit down when she told him her errand.

He confirmed that the job was an outdoor one, and asked what experience she had had.

'I'm a fent woman in the market, but it's hard to find rags to sell now the war is on,' she told him. 'I'm real strong, though.'

He surveyed her four foot ten inches, and wondered if she could even reach inside a barrel. Then he decided that their need was so urgent that he should give her a chance.

He said he would give her a week on trial. If she was satisfactory, she would work forty hours a week, cleaning up oil barrels for reuse, at a wage which seemed to her to be excellent.

After taking down details of her address, age and state of health, he told her, 'You should wear wellington boots to keep your feet dry. We will provide you with a leather apron to protect your skirts.'

'Yes, sir.'

'You'll need a warm jacket, not a shawl – and something to cover your head.'

Martha had no idea where she was going to get the garments, but she said, 'Yes, sir. When shall I start?'

'Monday. Come into this office at seven thirty AM, and I'll give you an identity card, which you must carry at all times. Then, the foreman will tell you what to do.'

He did not tell her how chapped her hands and arms would get in the winter time, how the detergent would strip the skin of her hands of its natural oils; nor did he mention that the residual oil in the barrels would, despite the apron, probably penetrate her clothes and cause a rash on her body. In a war such miseries were secondary, and women like this were pretty tough, anyway.

Martha was staggered at her good luck. She paused by the constable at the gate and thanked him for letting her in.

He returned her grin. 'You're welcome,' he said. And, as she walked home, Martha tried to remember if she had ever been told before that she was welcome. She came to the conclusion that she had not.

To think it were a cop what said it to me, she reflected with honest surprise, and she giggled like a young girl.

Her mind busy with how to get to the installation at such an early hour in the morning, after making breakfast for Patrick and the children, she temporarily forgot about house-hunting.

Her room in the court was empty, and the court itself almost deserted, because everybody had work. Only Helen and Ann sleepily gazed up at her from the doorstep: their evening employment never changed. They each held a hunk of bread and a mug of tea. They guessed that, eventually, because they were unmarried, they would be sent to a factory somewhere to work at a full-time job, but it hadn't happened yet. They were thankful.

'Where you been?' Helen asked.

An excited Martha told them, and then asked, 'Did the kids come home for dinner?'

'Oh, aye,' said Helen. 'They was running round the court with their bread in their hands. What with Bridie being away and Kathleen working, you must miss your girls being here to keep an eye on them.'

'Oh, aye, I do. But Joe's eleven now, plenty

big enough to take care of Ellie and Number Nine.'

The other women agreed. Then Ann said, 'It's getting in the food and coal and not being able to queue, if you're at work all day, what is going to bother you most.'

Martha had not given much thought to the problems of shopping when all the shops closed at five o'clock. She shrugged and said, 'The kids is going to have to do a lot more for themselves, and they got to help me, too. But I'll be bringing in good money, and it won't hurt Patrick to do a bit of queuing. He's like all the men; he ducks out of everything.'

At this last remark, all three women burst into laughter, because it was so true; they rarely saw any man, except the very old, in queues for food or doing battle with the rationing officials.

They commented that, though she had returned from the hospital some months before, poor Ellen still seemed in pain.

'She's moving round a bit better since she got a rocking chair – nothing like a rocking chair for exercising your back,' said Ann. 'But I don't think she'll ever have much use in her right arm again.'

'Poor dear,' responded Martha with feeling.

'How will she ever do her laundering when the war's finished? When Desi won't have a job as air-raid warden?'

Nobody knew.

THIRTY-FOUR

'Never Known Meself Go to Bits Afore'

September 1941 to 1942

After her interview with the Petroleum Board at Dingle, Martha had a very busy weekend. She found an old peaked cap of Patrick's to wear at work. When she cheerfully popped it on her head, Number Nine laughed, and insisted on trying it on his own head.

Before going to the pawnbroker to try to buy herself some sort of a short coat, she decided to go through Bridie's box of clothes to see if something of hers might be suitable.

Of latter years, she had often 'borrowed' garments from Kathleen's box to pawn when she was short of money. Kathleen usually raged uselessly: she then consoled herself with the thought that soon she would leave home and strike out for herself. She always demanded that they be retrieved before the end of the week, which did not invariably happen.

Bridie was different and, as she grew up, Martha had become very wary of her. She was small but she was also vicious and ruthless.

Kathleen had once 'borrowed' a blouse from her and had been unmercifully beaten up by her smaller sister. While Martha screamed at them both to stop, Bridie had even snatched down Patrick's docker's hook from its resting place on the mantel-piece and threatened to tear her sister's face with it.

Kathleen had fled to the comparative safety of the next court.

Now that Bridie was gone, at least temporarily in her mother's view, she felt free to rummage in her big cardboard box, the top of which had always been kept firmly closed by its owner, with KEEP OUT scrawled on it. Even if it did not hold a suitable jacket, there might be something pawnable in it, which would save her using housekeeping money to buy herself a heavy work coat.

On the top of the pile of clothing was a bright-red dance dress, princess style, which Martha had, once or twice, seen the girl wear when she said she was going to a dance.

Underneath it lay a pair of patent leather high-heeled shoes. There was also a very nice blue macintosh, a couple of blouses with wickedly low V necks and, lastly, a tweed skirt with matching jacket.

Martha tried on the jacket. It felt nice and she was sad that she had no mirror to see what she looked like in it. It also went onto the pawnbroker's pile because it was certainly not thick enough for the outdoors in winter. She sighed as she put it down: she had never in her adult life worn anything but a thick serge skirt and a series of black blouses under her shawl.

There was also a small box which held a couple of pairs of glittering diamanté earrings.

'Strewth, she didn't half have money to spend!' muttered an amazed Martha, as she destined these also for pawning.

When she undid the fent in which she had wrapped the clothes, the pawnbroker looked doubt-fully at the collection of new-looking garments. Martha Connolly rarely brought in hard-to-obtain clothing like this: the garments might be stolen.

Martha noted his reaction and lied quickly, 'Me daughter's bin called up – and everything'll be too small for her afore she comes home. She looks proper nice in her uniform.'

The pawnbroker made a face: he could imagine the family row when the daughter returned on her first leave.

He opened the little box of earrings, picked one out and peered at it. He then put it back into its box and dumped it in front of Martha. He said disparagingly, 'Woolworths. They're not worth nothing to me.'

Martha was very disappointed. She had had a sudden hope that the jewellery might be a valuable gift from one of Bridie's admirers. She reluctantly stuffed the box into her pocket.

She was agreeably surprised, however, when the pawnbroker gave her ten shillings for the clothing.

She said, 'Now I want to buy a working jacket for meself. I got meself a job, working outside.'

She went joyfully home with a man's heavy tweed jacket with a generous collar. She wore it until the end of the war when men came home to reclaim their jobs, and, as Martha succinctly put it, women were back on the rubbish dump.

Most of the mixed crew of working-class women amongst whom she found herself were wives or sweethearts of skilled men, and the finer grades of snobbery were already established. Martha ranked as the very bottom. She was to all of them a dirty, uncouth Roman Catholic from the docks. It was said that she could not even read or write. She stank and was probably verminous. As far as possible, they shunned her. Even in the company canteen, she ate by herself, unless the café was so crowded that sharing a table became a necessity. Surrounded, as she had been, by neighbours similar to herself, she did not care about her fellow workers, except for odd spurts of carefully suppressed indignation, because they, too, could be quite foul-mouthed. 'They don't know nothing,' she muttered to herself.

In fact, despite them, she always said that her years of scrubbing oil barrels were some of the best of her life, because, for once, she had steady money to buy what food was available.

At first, she rode to work on the overhead railway. Then, when she found a house in Dingle at a controlled rent, she was able to walk to work.

Patrick was irritated to death that he then had to take the overhead railway, in reverse, to get to his fire station near the Pier Head. He grumbled even more when the line was damaged a number of times by the heavy bombing, and he had to switch to buses, which charged higher fares.

The new house, which led straight off the street, had a parlour with a small fireplace and a kitchen-living room with a large kitchen range. There were three little bedrooms upstairs, and Ellie was amazed when Martha told her, on the Sunday they moved in, that the smallest room would be for her alone.

'Soon as we can get a little mattress for yez,' she promised.

At first, Ellie was silent at the idea. Then she began to whine. 'I don't want to be by meself. Why can't I be with you?'

'You're going to be a big girl soon – and you'll like to have your own place.'

'No, I won't. I want to go home.'

'Ach, don't be stupid. This is your home, today – now!' Martha had had a bad day and was growing irritable. 'Shut up, afore I give you something to cry about.'

Ellie backed away, then turned and clattered down the bare staircase. In the tiny hall, she hesitated and then ran through the open front door into the street to find her brothers.

The street was unfamiliar and strangers turned to stare at the child's sudden exit.

Joe found her silent and miserable, squatting by the side of the tiny doorstep, the front door slammed shut behind her by Martha.

'Come on, and explore with Number Nine and me,' he said cheerfully.

Behind the house was a small, brick-lined back yard. At the end of it in a shed was a flush lavatory, which Joe demonstrated to her. She was scared by the noise of the flush.

On the Sunday night of their removal, the vast empty space of their new dwelling hit Martha, Patrick and the children so forcibly that they all huddled together, without complaint, on their solitary mattress which had been temporarily dragged into the parlour. Martha saw an immediate problem in that she had no blackout curtain big enough for the little bow window.

She felt herself suddenly bereft of the support of Auntie Ellen, Kitty, Sheila, Helen and Ann, and Alice, on all of whom she had relied to keep an eye on her children: the reality hit her like an icy draught, and she shivered.

And I'm the one what will be blamed by Patrick for anything what goes wrong, she decided dismally. And I don't have nobody to turn to.

When Patrick and Joe went together back to the court to return the borrowed handcart on which they had moved their scant belongings, and the younger children had gone out on their own exploration, she sat on the bottom step of the staircase and cried.

She cried not only for her old friends, but also for Brian, Tommy, Kathleen, Lizzie, Colleen and even for naughty Bridie. For all the communication she had with them, they might as well be dead, like Colleen, she sobbed.

Despite the triumphs of a better house and a better-paying job, for the moment she lost completely her usual sturdy optimism.

Without the sense of being enclosed safely in a tight group of friends and family, she felt naked in a cruel world.

'Jaysus! I don't know how I'll fill all the emptiness,' she whimpered to herself, as she remembered with longing the cosy living room of the O'Reillys and their many kindnesses to her. 'It must have taken them all their life to get together a home like that; I'll never manage it. And, dear Holy Mother, I'm so tired. I wish this bloody war were over.'

She dragged herself to her feet, meaning to go to make herself a cup of tea. Then she remembered that she had used up all her tea, and would not get a fresh ration until Monday.

'Blast them Jerries!' she muttered, as she heated a cup of hot water on the kitchen's ancient gas stove.

She was quite glad to scuttle off to work the next morning, just to be amongst people, even if nobody spoke to her, except to give an order. You could always get a mug of tea from the canteen.

THIRTY-FIVE

'Too Tired to Tip a Bloody Wall Bin'

1965

A week after Sheila's arrival at the home, Martha and she were sitting up in their respective beds, still gossiping, while they drank their illicit cups of tea: Martha had prevailed on Angie to bring an additional mug for Sheila.

'A cuppa tea is a real comfort,' she had pleaded, and Angie agreed. She hoped that she would not be dismissed for breaking rules before she found another job: Matron was, every day, becoming more dogmatic and bad-tempered.

'The evening aide – Freda, isn't it? She said last night, when you was dozing, as Angie's going to leave us,' reported Sheila, after draining her cup.

Martha clapped her cup down on top of the commode. 'Oh, Mother of God, say it isn't so.

What will we do? Sheila, if we're left to Dorothy and that Freda – and that awful Mrs Kelly woman wot sleeps all night and never hears you call – you could die and they wouldn't care.'

Sheila nodded agreement. 'I feel sick about it meself,' she said.

Martha's voice quivered, as she went on, 'I can't blame her, though. Angie is too tired to even tip a bloody wall bin, poor kid.'

Sheila sighed and hummed tunelessly, as she considered this. 'Dunno that we can do anything,' she replied finally. 'Maybe they'll find another Angie.'

'Humph. I doubt it. Angie is real smart – and she feels for yez. I wish I could give her a nice goodbye present, if she's really leaving.'

'Well, couldn't we?'

'Sheila, we don't have no money. And if we had it, how would we buy her anything? We're stuck here – in bed.'

'What you mean? No money? We got pocket money.'

Martha slowly turned herself in order to see Sheila better. 'Pocket money?' she queried, absolutely amazed.

'Yeah. They take your old age pension to pay this Home. But you're supposed to get a bit every week out of it for "insensuals" – you know, what I mean. Buy yourself a new nightie or a newspaper or some sweeties.

'In all the time I was in hospital, I got me full pension; me friend saw to it for me. Hospital was under National Health – didn't have to pay a penny for that. Used to buy meself magazines to read, from a woman who came round with a pushcart to sell them – and she'd get you books from the library.'

She paused to rescue one of her supporting pillows which was about to fall off her bed. She wobbled perilously for a moment as she shoved it close to her side. 'I was expecting to be paid me bit yesterday, but nobody bring it or tell me it was there for me.'

Martha was dumbfounded. She slowly got out of bed and went to her friend, to tuck the pillow in more firmly: without extra support, Sheila found it difficult to balance herself when sitting upright. She finally said, 'I got a widow's pension, and, of course, I were working – cleaned a school after the men returned from the war and wanted their jobs back in the petrol installation.

'I don't know what happened about the pension after I were took into hospital. I thought I'd collect the arrears when I come out of here: never dreamed I'd never get better and be stuck here in bed for ever.' She paused to consider this, and then continued, 'I never thought about me pension being used to pay for me to be here. I weren't never told anything about it being paid to Matron. I suppose it must have been written down in all the papers that They made me sign – with a cross, of course.

'You see I can't read or write, so I had to trust the ladies who arranged to put me in here.'

'You can't read or write? Hmm. Well, I can. I'll ask Matron,' promised Sheila. 'She'll know.'

'She's never been up here to see us since Pat died. And you'd better be careful what you say. Make even a small nuisance of yourself and you'll be made to take pills to keep you quiet; Angie told me once.' Martha nodded knowingly.

'I've heard that about other places,' Sheila responded slowly. 'To think of it! Me sister come all the way from London to find a place for me, and she chose this one 'cos it's got a name for being well run, and, what's more important, they had a vacant bed. I'm sure she never thought about me being drugged for speaking up.'

Martha snorted. 'Well, she's right in a way. They clean the place regular and the meals come OK. But that's it.' Martha's idea of cleanliness was not very great. She went on to say, 'But the staff is on the go all the time. Only Angie tries to find time to talk to yez.

'What drives me mad, Sheila, is that there's nothing to do. You can't even walk around for a bit to get yourself strong without being ticked off and brought back to bed.'

Sheila ignored Martha's last remark: without legs, you were in no shape to walk.

'Do you ever get any visitors?' she inquired. 'One of them could buy whatever we said for Angie. We could ask one of them to talk to Matron about our pocket money to pay for it.'

'Sheila, I don't have no visitors. Me sister and her family I were in touch with was moved out to Norris Green. Last time I saw her was when I visited her once, during the war, and I've never heard a word since then.

'The ladies who come to the hospital arranged for me to come in here: they needed the hospital bed for someone real sick, and I didn't have nobody to take care of me if I was sent home.' Her lips trembled. 'I just signed with a cross anything They asked me to sign.'

She sighed, as she remembered the secret dread she had suffered while signing. 'When you can't read, you just do what They ask and hope it's all right. They always say it's OK and for your own good and tell you not to worry!'

She sighed again, and went on, 'By the time I come out of hospital I wouldn't have had no home, anyway, because I didn't pay the rent while I was in hospital.

'You know, Sheila, I never thought about the rent, to be truthful: I only thought about the pain in me leg. The landlord – his agent, that is – would've put the bailiffs in and they'd have sold up every stick I owned in there, to cover the rent I owed. They'd think I'd just done a flit to get out of paying. Then they'd put in a new tenant.'

She did not rant about this. Bailiffs were a fact of life, and you did your best to evade their invasions. Bad luck, if you didn't move your furniture out quickly, before they got to you.

Anyway, she was stuck in this Home for ever, as far as she knew. She shifted restlessly, as she returned to the subjects of their conversation, visitors and getting Angie a gift. 'Are you expectin' your sister or anyone to visit, Sheila?' she asked.

'No. I'll be lucky if she writes me for Christmas; she lives in London. She's working and she's got kids still. I had one friend who come to see me in the hospital. But she's not young and it's a long ride out here.'

'People soon forget you, don't they?'

'Not really. But life's not easy for anybody since the war – and after the war things didn't change much for years, did they? Still rationing and shortages of everything. And so many people was moved around, while the war was on, and never come back home!'

Martha agreed heartily. England had been left a shabby, hard-pressed wreck, with a population transplanted hither and yon, who tended to settle where they had been planted.

'You still had kids at home at the end of the war – you was telling me,' continued Sheila. 'What happened to them? They should be here.' Sheila was very downright.

'Well, I told you how Patrick died in January 1951. We both had the flu so bad: it were a big epidemic. And there isn't much you can do about flu, except stay in bed and wait to get better. I got better and so did Number Nine.

'Patrick just died one night – give me the shock of me life. But truth to tell, he were worn out by the war – and real cut up when the auxiliary fire service finished up. He worked on reconstruction sites for a while, but he were out of work when he died.' She stopped, and then said, 'He weren't a bad husband – he did his best, God rest him.'

'And the kids?'

'Scattered, like you'd never believe.' She hesitated, and then said, 'Our Tommy died during the war. He got fits. He was in hospital for a little while. But there was nothing they could do for him.' Her voice broke. 'Aye, he were a lovely-looking kid, and, you know, I been told that if they had had the medicines they got now a few years earlier, the doctors could have saved him.'

'Aye, that must hurt.'

'It did, Sheila. It did.' She sat quietly for a while: she had never quite understood Tommy, as she had her other sons. He had always been very secretive – never outgoing. Even if he told you something, you were never quite certain if it was true.

Both she and Patrick had been terribly shocked when they learned the cause of death. Syphilis.

Observing their fraught expressions, the doctor had told them gently, 'You know, the lad needed only one girlfriend to give it to him.'

Patrick had accepted this as reasonable. Martha had nodded agreement; but many odd memories of Tommy were suddenly making sense. She closed her eyes to hide her distress, as she reproached herself bitterly. 'To think I only watched me girls!'

Sheila, respectful of the loss her new friend had endured, did not disturb her.

After a while, Martha sniffed and cleared her throat, and went on with her litany.

'Joseph were called up to do his national service after the war, and they sent him to Africa – to Bulawayo. When he'd done it, he could stay there if he wanted – their government was looking for white settlers – and he did; and he married out there. I don't never hear from him – I doubt if he knows where I am. Anyway, men aren't letter writers, are they?' Then she said sadly, 'And me big boy, Brian, were killed in Normandy.'

'Oh, Martha, how dreadful.' Sheila's voice was full of pity. Then she asked, 'Who else was there?'

'There was Ellie and Number Nine.'

'I do love the way you called your baby Number Nine.'

Martha smiled. 'His proper name was James, after Father James, our priest, dear man. He were our gift to the Church.

'I don't think families do it much now. But when we was living in the courts, it were usual to give one kid to be a nun or a priest. Was it like that with you?'

'We had in mind to give our second girl . . .'

'Aye, you poor dear. It must be terrible to lose her.'

'Martha, it finished my real life to lose everybody

410

in one go. I haven't never really been alive since.' For once, Sheila sounded defeated, and she shook helplessly.

To steady her, Martha stretched out towards the other bed and rested her hand on her arm. 'Well, I'm proper grateful that you're here now,' she said earnestly. 'You're a real comfort to me.'

Sheila allowed her eyes to fill with tears. Then she said, 'Likewise, love.'

They remained quiet while the ghosts of their past visited them, and then Sheila made an effort at being more cheerful. She said, 'You mentioned another little girl, Ellie, I think it was.'

'Oh, aye, Ellie. That was real queer. You know, after the war, we thought all the foreign soldiers would go home – or at least stop being soldiers and settle down with us, like a lot of Poles did.'

'Sure, I remember.'

'But they didn't. The Americans stayed for years and years in camp; they're still there, some of them. Most people didn't even know they were there for a long time, 'cos they wore civvies when they was out of the camp.

'Well, our Ellie met one at a dance and married him. Even after she were married, she was still in England, but not always in the same place. Then he took her to Pittsburgh, in the USA, where his parents were. Last I heard of her was that he were working in an iron foundry. No kids.'

'And she doesn't write?' asked Sheila.

'Nope. You know, Sheila, when you got so many kids holding onto your skirts, like I had, and you don't know where the next meal's coming from, it's hard to give them all the attention they deserve. Especially the middle ones in the family: they're just hungry faces waiting to be fed or bare feet that you got to find boots for. And they resent it. Working full time through the war didn't help me much to give time to them, either.

'Kids like that is happy when they're big enough to get out from under you and have a life of their own. They don't think what you've done for them, do they?'

Sheila did not know. Her children had, in her mind, grown up as dream children, who earned good wages while they were home, and then, when they married, had brought pretty, playful grand-children to visit her. She often thought what a lovely life might have been hers. Now, in a week of hearing stories of Martha's children, running loose, always hungry, in a crowded court, disillusionment had set in. Children thought only of themselves and how soon they could leave you – and get lost.

That sounded hard on harried mothers.

'And what about Number Nine?'

Martha's face softened. 'Oh, aye. He were a bright little boy. He did well, he did. He finished secondary modern school and then he did his national service – he didn't get sent abroad like Joe did. And all the time, Father James keep in touch with him, 'cos he was named after him.

'When he finally come home his dad were gone, of course. Just Ellie and me was home at the time; and Father James reminded me of me promise to the Church.

'Quite honestly, I thought Jamie wouldn't want to go – but he did. So I'd no sooner got him back from national service than he was off again to a seminary, and now he's in Manchester helping in a parish. He's a priest, of course.'

She giggled. 'It's funny to have a learned scholar for a son, seeing as I can't even read!'

'Good luck – bad luck?' suggested Sheila.

'Well, it would've been nice to have a man around the house; and he were a real man by the time he'd done his two years in the army. It would've been less lonely,' she finished wistfully. Then she said more cheerfully, 'It was a great day when he was ordained. I was that proud of him.'

'Don't he ever come to see you?'

'He's been home a few times to see me, and

413

he does write home. But, you see, he's probably written, and I'm not there. There'll be a new tenant in the house who doesn't know me.'

'That's a proper difficulty. You must have his address, though?'

'Oh, aye. I know his address off by heart.'

'Why don't you get somebody to write to him for you?'

Martha stared at her incredulously. 'In this place? Here, you're lucky if anybody'll come to help you pee. I doubt if Matron would stand me a stamp to post it either, she's that mean. I wouldn't dare ask her.'

'I can write for you, if I can get me hands on me pocket money.'

Martha frankly did not believe that Sheila could get a letter smuggled out of the building, unless she could persuade one of the aides to carry it out, which she doubted.

In any place money not in your skirt pocket was liable to vanish. You'd fight that bitch downstairs for it and lucky you would be if you got it; you'd fight for pen and ink; for a stamp, and then you couldn't be sure of getting the letter to a pillar box. And the thought of an irate Matron standing over you with pills to be taken so that you were too dazed to bother her again made Martha crawl with fear.

414

So great was her desperate confusion at the loss of all she had known, she decided that, like Angie, she hadn't the strength even to tip a bloody wall bin, never mind fight Matron.

THIRTY-SIX

'Sometimes I Feels Like
'Arry Carry'

June 1941

In June 1941, Daniel Flanagan finally sailed into his home port of Liverpool after a voyage lasting over a year, as his ship crept from port to port, backwards and forwards, round the coast of Africa, picking up and putting down freight. Amongst the crew's mail brought aboard by the pilot boat were two letters for him, one from the police.

He tore open the latter, anxious to get at the contents. The police were looking into the disappearance of his sisters and hoped to have news for him shortly. The letter was a few months old. During the rambles of his tramp freighter, it had followed him to Cape Town, only to be returned and retained in the company's office to await him, because his ship had already left for Port Elizabeth

416

– with further ports of call as yet uncertain, to quote a pencilled scribble on the envelope.

He smiled. There would probably be more recent news by now. He failed to appreciate that, in the midst of the chaos with which the police were dealing, some kind soul had thought to write him a letter of reassurance.

The second letter was more recent and was an almost unbelievable shock. It was from the agent which served his father's ship in Liverpool and had been sent to him care of his own ship's agents there.

In reply to his inquiry as to his father's whereabouts, they regretted to have to tell him that Thomas Flanagan, trimmer, had gone on shore leave in Sydney, Australia, and had failed to return to his ship. He was now officially classed as a deserter.

Daniel was horrified. The shame of it! It was too much, enough to make one commit hara-kiri. Added to the shame was a new worry. Even if they found his sisters, how would he manage the kids and go to sea at the same time? He himself simply did not earn enough money.

Desertion, particularly in Australian ports where British immigrants were welcome, was far from unknown, but it was a very serious matter, and he wondered why his father had been mad enough to do such a thing.

He would have broken a legal agreement, lost his kit and his wages. Also lost would be that vital final entry in his discharge book, saying that his completed service in his last ship had been 'Very Good'. This entry would normally ensure his being considered for re-employment in another ship: without it he did not stand a chance.

Since there was a war on and laws fenced one in more tightly every day, Daniel wasn't sure whether or not his father would be liable to a prison sentence if he was caught.

His mind reeled.

He himself would now be paid off and would then be obliged to apply for another ship. He was dead tired, having spent most of the very long voyage wrapped in a life jacket, which was not easy to either work or sleep in. There was also the dreadful tension, night and day, of knowing that the U-boats were waiting like cougars ready to pounce; every seaman knew that an ageing freighter, liable to drag a little behind the rest of a convoy, was an easy prey.

It was late afternoon by the time he had walked past the cynical eyes of the customs officers, who occasionally took a man on one side to check his kitbag or tin suitcase. Jostled by the stream of men behind him, he longed to lie down and sleep. He had no home to go to, however, and had no desire to spend money on a room in a lodging house.

He stood on the dock road, trying to get a grip on himself. Should he go straight to the police station? Or maybe to Auntie Ellen?

He decided on Auntie Ellen. He could at least dump his kitbag with her. It was possible, too, that she might have been in touch with other aunts or relations and have some news of the girls for him.

Perhaps it would be best to be armed with any further information she had before seeing the police: he had all the reluctance of an inhabitant of the courts to being interviewed, face to face, by a constable. Yet he loved his funny little sisters and he was determined to trace them.

Grim-faced for so young a lad with leave to look forward to, he took the overhead railway to the Pier Head and, as the train rattled along, he noted the crowded shipping in the docks and river – nice targets for the Jerries, he thought glumly. Then, to take him close to the court, he caught a tram.

As, with warning clangs of the driver's bell, the tram nosed its way on the short trip through the city, the gaping ruins left by the bombing were swiftly revealed to him. He decided that, wherever his sisters were, they were probably safer than if they were in Liverpool.

Court No. 5 was extraordinarily quiet. The air-raid shelter directly outside the entrance cut off much of the noise of the main street. Within the court itself, no children played on the filthy, litter-strewn cobbles. A thin tabby cat sat on a doorstep leading to a closed door. At his entrance, a seagull took flight from the roof. No washing flapped on the clothes lines stretched across the court. Without the noisy activity of its usual inhabitants, the confined space felt eerie. The smell had not changed much; weeks at sea made him notice the contrast.

Kitbag on shoulder, he stood for a moment before turning to Auntie Ellen's front door, which, like the ones opposite, was shut. He banged on it with his fist, but got no response.

He tried the handle. It was unlocked, so he swung the door open, plonked his kitbag on the step and called, 'Auntie Ellen! Desi!'

No response. Shoving his kitbag further inwards, he stepped over the doorsill.

He had never before seen the O'Hara room undraped with washing. Lack of it, however, did not make it look any tidier. An encrusted saucepan stood on the hob of a cooking range filled only with ashes. The bed was a muddled heap of bedding and men's clothing. A copy of the *Evening Express* lay scattered round a rocking chair – Desi's efforts at housekeeping, as he cared for frail Auntie Ellen, were not very good.

After staring doubtfully at the untidy mess, he decided, 'They must still be here.'

Stepping carefully, to avoid tripping over a couple of boxes used as tables, he knocked at a door in the far wall. Behind it, he remembered, there should be another tenant in a windowless room. Since she had to walk through the O'Haras' room every time she went out, she would know all about their comings and goings.

There was no answer. He cautiously opened the door, but it was so dark that he could see little. It was, however, apparently unoccupied.

Leaving his kitbag where it was, he turned and walked out and across the court to Martha's house. Without much hope, he knocked on her door.

For a moment, he thought that he was again out of luck. But there came a sleepy 'Coming' and the sound of shuffling feet. The door was opened a crack, and tousled Helen O'Brien, her black shawl clutched over a flannel nightgown, peeped out.

She looked at him blankly, and then her lined face split into a welcoming grin.

'Danny!' she exclaimed. 'You looking for Martha? Come in, love. Martha's at the market.'

She clasped him round the waist and eased him into Martha's unlocked room; the place was so cluttered with abandoned boxes, assorted rags and other junk that there was not much room to move.

Helen turned her head away from him, and shouted, 'Annie, put your dressing gown on and come on in here. Danny Flanagan's come. And put the kettle on.'

'Well, that's real nice,' came the reply, and a moment later, there was the sound of the primus stove being pumped up and then a cheerful roar as it caught.

Helen did not feel it was proper to ask such a nice lad into their room; though, had she met him in the street, she would have accosted him in her usual playful way, as a seaman in search of a woman.

She sat him down on a box, and seated herself on another one by the littered hearth of the range.

'Well, now, did you go over to Ellen's house? 'Cos she's been took a little walk by Kitty Callaghan. I seen them go, and Desi's at work, I expect.'

Daniel swallowed, sensing more bad news.

'Yes, I did. Where's she gone? Do you know?'

'Nope. She'll be back soon, though; she's still quite weak.'

Daniel's blank incomprehension suddenly registered with Helen. 'I forgot you been away so long,' she exclaimed. 'Your auntie got hit in the back by a piece of shrapnel in February. Real hurt, she was. In hospital for three weeks.'

Before Danny could express his surprise and concern, she added, 'I expect you know about her boy, Shaun, being in hospital in Halifax, Nova Scotia? His ship was sunk, and he's suffering from exposure: the water must be proper cold up there.'

'Good Lord! I haven't heard nothing about neither of them. How's Auntie Ellen now?' He was shaken not only by the wounding, but also by the fact that his main source of help was out of action. 'And poor old Shaun?'

'Well, Ellen's not been able to really get her strength up again. She says Shaun is getting along, however, which is something.'

He nodded. War was not kind to seamen or their families.

Though he squatted on a box by Helen so politely, he wanted to explode with fear and with frustration.

A smiling Ann, who had taken the time, while the kettle boiled, to comb her hair into its usual neat bun and to tie her dressing gown properly, emerged with a mug of weak tea in each hand. When she had fetched the sugar and another mug for herself, she joined them.

Danny now felt able to ask the question burning on his lips. 'Do you know if anything's been heard of Dollie, Connie and Minnie? I'm really worried about them.'

Helen replied, 'Well, no. There were a copper here a few months ago, end of March, I think. He was actually looking for a gang they believe is picking up kids off the street and selling them for you know what. And since he knows Desi, he remembered the girls and thought he'd just check that they'd either returned home or was safe in Shropshire where they was supposed to be billeted. The billeting people had assured the police that they could certainly find any child which had passed through their hands, and would let Desi know where they were. So the police passed the job to them – the police is up to their necks in work.

'This Constable Phillips was real surprised that Desi and Ellen had had no word about them, and he promised to inquire again for him.'

'God forbid they've been abducted!' exclaimed Daniel. His face blenched.

'Don't take on so, love. Everything'll probably

turn out all right,' soothed Helen. She put out a hand to touch his arm. 'Constable Phillips thinks it is more of a paper muck-up than anything, with your sisters.'

Daniel put his mug down on the floor. 'In a minute or two, I'm going over to Dale Street. Will you tell Desi I'm home – I guess he won't mind if I stay with him. And tell Martha when you see her.'

Helen felt privately that Desi had been very careless in not following up the lack of news about the missing children. But she knew, from a few stray comments from Ellen, that he did not want the responsibility for them foisted on him. Then, with the air raids he had been worked to death, and, of course, he had had to cope with poor Ellen's wounding – and now, maybe, Shaun, if he did not recover enough to be shoved back into the Navy.

'Do you have any news of your dad?' asked Ann, her nose in her mug.

'Yes, in a way.' He hesitated and then decided that he might as well tell them – it would come out in the end. 'He jumped ship at Sydney and vanished. I guess Australia is a big place.' He made a wry face.

There was a shocked silence, and then Helen said slowly, 'Well, I'm glad Mary Margaret's not here. She couldn't have borne it, poor dear. And your Grandma Theresa would have hit the roof!'

At this mention of his mother and grandmother, Daniel wanted to weep for them in his helpless frustration. And he wanted to kick his father. Thomas had, by his very serious action, left him the responsibility of looking after three helpless little sisters.

When I'm only earning peanuts, how can I keep them? It's not fair – and nobody knows where they are, he thought in a wild mix of despair and rage. He must, however, first find them.

He got up from his box, thanked the two women, and said he would be back later on in the evening.

At the police station, the elderly constable was kind; you never knew what the distraught person on the other side of the desk had been through, he always averred, and this lad looked real stricken. He actually had a vague memory of his frantic inquiries just before he sailed.

As a result of the information received from Constable Phillips, he told the boy, they had been in touch by telephone with the police in Shropshire. The police there had reported that the woman they spoke to would not admit that any child in their care could possibly be missing. She was, however, checking: sometimes kids got moved around from one billet to another, because of bad behaviour.

'Give her a day or two more,' advised the constable. 'Like most of us, they're badly short of staff.'

Sifting through the papers relating to the case, the constable inquired, 'Have you heard from their father yet?'

Reluctantly, Daniel said that he had not.

'Do you know where he is? Has he been informed about his children?'

'He's in Australia, but I don't know where.' Daniel's voice was low and resentful.

'Humph. I thought you told me he was a seaman. Was he put ashore – for sickness or something?'

They'll find out quick enough, if they want him, thought Daniel, and decided he had better be honest. 'He's jumped ship in Australia,' he said. 'Failed to report back after shore leave.'

The constable looked up. Poor kid. 'And you're also a seaman.'

Daniel forgot his sisters for a moment. His face glowed with pride. 'Apprentice,' he replied. 'Paid off this afternoon. Another year, and I'll be an ordinary seaman.'

Under his white moustache, the constable smiled at the boy. He knocked the papers into a neat oblong. 'Well, let us know immediately if their father turns up. Meanwhile, we'll hope to have your sisters' address before you sail again. Then we can consult a welfare officer about someone to keep an eye on them, and get you some help if it's needed. Bear in mind that the children are probably comfortably billeted.'

He smiled again at Daniel. 'Before you sail, let us know your ship, and the welfare officer will keep in touch.' Better not to tell him that he was too young to be the children's guardian. Let a social worker tell him that.

He stifled a yawn; he had been on duty for twelve hours.

THIRTY-SEVEN

'She Lost 'Er Rag'

1965

Since Angie had skipped work for a day to go for an interview, Sheila sent a polite verbal request to the Matron, via Dorothy, saying that she would like to see her when she had time.

It was delivered to Matron as, 'That woman on the first floor with no legs wants to talk to you.'

Matron did not look up from her desk. She was filling in a report ordered by the City's Health Department, and did not welcome interruption: she did not want any civil servants snooping round her nursing home because she had not filled in a form correctly.

'She'll have to wait,' she snapped at Dorothy.

Dorothy made a face behind her back. She did not bother to go upstairs to give Matron's reply to Sheila.

Matron came up the next morning, and asked what the trouble was.

'No trouble,' replied Sheila, determined to be pleasant. 'I'd like to have me pocket money, out of me OAP. I don't know why I didn't get it come Friday.'

'A small sum is kept in trust for you. It is not handed to you, in case it is stolen: it is similar to the care taken of your possessions during a stay in hospital.'

Sheila swallowed. 'I want to buy some stationery and some stamps. So may I have last week's, please?'

Martha stared resentfully at the Matron, and wondered what the reply would be.

It came in the form of a question.

'Do you have a relation who will shop for you? You have not had any visitors, so far.'

'No. I thought I might ask Angie.'

Matron's lips compressed. Her chin lifted slightly. She said, 'The staff has its work to do. It can't run messages for every patient.'

Sheila's face flushed. She said, 'Well, not every patient is like Martha and me. Those women opposite don't even know they're here.' She gestured towards the two dementia sufferers, firmly tucked up in bed that morning. 'Nor that poor soul

430

there.' She pointed to the stroke victim, equally neatly imprisoned in bedclothes.

'Well?'

'Martha and me, we're in our right minds. But we don't have no visitors to help us.' She looked imploringly at the woman in front of her. 'Surely one of the staff can do something to help us.'

'You are, according to my records, both Roman Catholics. Arrangements are being made for a priest to come to administer Holy Communion. Ask him to find help for you.'

She turned to leave the room.

'I forgot. I want me radio back,' Sheila added.

Matron put her hand on the doorknob and turned.

She said loftily, 'It is, also, being kept safely for you. It cannot be used in the ward, without earphones, because it will disturb other patients.'

She had reached the hallway when Sheila exploded.

'God damn your eyes! Can't you use your common sense?' an enraged Sheila shouted after her. 'You get me my pocket money, or else. And as for the radio, there's only Martha here what is capable of hearing it – and she'd be thankful to have the music, wouldn't you, Martha?'

Before Martha could open her mouth, the Matron

turned swiftly and snapped, 'Bad language is not allowed here. Please learn to control yourself.'

Martha saw Sheila heave herself more upright with her hands, as she prepared to respond. She hastily hissed, 'Watch it, Sheila. Don't lose your rag!'

Matron swept across the hall and down the stairs. She entered in her patient records that Sheila Mary McNally was showing signs of being out of control: anger and abusive language.

Sheila leaned back into her mass of pillows and burst into tears of frustration.

'Don't take on so, Sheila, love,' begged Martha. 'She's right. A priest could find a volunteer to help us, I bet.'

But Sheila was still crying when lunch was delivered by a harassed Dorothy.

In an effort to feed all the patients on Martha's floor as rapidly as she could, the aide nipped backwards and forwards to the old-fashioned dumbwaiter in the wall of Martha's room. The dumbwaiter rumbled up and down, on its frayed rope and block and tackle, bringing up two trays at a time from the kitchen. Trays were whisked out of the dumbwaiter and plonked onto each patient's lap or bedside chair.

Furious, Sheila looked disgustedly at the mass of

spaghetti and tomato sauce with its thin sprinkling of cheese, and swept it off the bed. Tray and plate fell with a crash to the linoleum floor.

Dorothy was just placing a tray on a small table by the bedside of the stroke victim. She was wondering how long it would take her to shovel the sticky strands of pasta down the throat of someone who could barely swallow.

At the noise, she whirled round, 'God Almighty!' she exclaimed. 'What have you done?'

'It's nothing,' Martha hastily interjected. 'It's an accident. She can't balance stuff very well on her lap, as you should know by now.'

Dorothy ignored Martha's remark. She left the stroke victim and came over to Sheila.

'What a damned mess you've made!' she scolded. 'And I can't get you another one, either. Cook puts out the exact number, and there's never nothing left over.' She turned, and marched towards the dumbwaiter. 'I'll have to get Rosie to come up to clear it.'

Sheila regarded her in sullen silence.

Martha called to Dorothy, 'She can have some of my lunch.'

Still silence. Dorothy had reached the end of her tether. She had done a double shift and was exhausted. Now, she had no real idea what to do.

'Dorothy!' persisted Martha. 'Ask the kitchen for a clean plate. Sheila can have half of mine.'

Dorothy slowly turned back from the dumb-waiter's horn.

Then she said reluctantly, 'OK, I'll get one.'

She looked again at Sheila, and advised, 'You'd better cheer up and hurry up. Doctor's coming to see you this afternoon.'

Sheila abruptly swallowed a sob. 'He is?'

'Yes. There's six patients he's going to do an "altogether" on. Says he's going to do six a week until he's examined everybody in the home.

'You're all going to have a bath as soon as I done the lunches.'

Martha was suddenly very apprehensive. An examination all over? What did the doctor think they were suffering from? She had never been examined since she had arrived from the hospital.

She trembled at the thought of the pills that she might have to take. Was it to find an excuse to sedate her and Sheila?

'It's me nerves,' she told herself almost inaudibly, as she flung her arm across her pattering heart to stop herself shaking. 'Dear Lady, be with me now. Intercede for me!' She knew that the Madonna was not omnipotent, but she could do a bit for you, Martha was certain. 'Hear me now.'

434

She remembered Matron's remark that a priest was also to visit them. This recollection now frightened her even more.

Had some awful disease broken out in the Home, like the flu, which might cause the doctor's visit to be followed by that of a priest, so as to be on hand to give extreme unction?

If it were so, that bitch downstairs would never tell you, never warn you, she felt sure of that.

Cut off from everything, except what happened in the little ward, without hope of any kind, poor Martha's common sense was rapidly seeping away.

Meanwhile, Sheila lay quietly, while Dorothy set down two remaining dinners for the dementias, safely out of their reach. Then she turned and shouted down the horn of the dumbwaiter to the troglodytes toiling in the basement to send up another plate, an empty one, and a clean spoon. 'And ask Rosie to come up to the first floor to clean up a spill.' She pulled the rope to send the dumbwaiter down to them.

With a rumble like a distant earthquake it returned within a minute, with a white dinner plate, shiny, empty, and a spoon of doubtful cleanliness.

'Want me to divide it for you?' Dorothy inquired of Martha.

Sheila turned wearily towards Martha, and said, 'I really don't want any, Martha. Ta, ever so.'

'Ah, come on now. Just a bit.'

'No. I'm not hungry.'

'You will be later, love.'

Sheila managed a smile. 'I'll be all right. I really couldn't eat now.'

Dorothy tapped the iron bed end with the spoon. 'Hurry up. Make up your minds.'

'I guess she won't,' said Martha, and began hurriedly to eat, while a stout complaining maid, carrying a bucket, a mop and a dustpan and brush, arrived to pick up the broken plate, which she threw into a bin. The further unaccustomed noise upset the dementias and they began to whimper.

Sent down again, the dumbwaiter delivered two more trays and, with a tray in each hand, Dorothy fled into the next bedroom.

THIRTY-EIGHT

'The Vet'

1965

Martha had barely emptied her plate before Dorothy left the half-fed stroke patient and told her to come for her bath. She held her firmly by the elbow, and took her to the bathroom. The bath itself had already been filled. She ordered her to get in and wash herself all over.

A scared Martha obeyed. The water was already cool, and she shivered as she carefully lowered herself into it.

'I'll be back,' promised Dorothy and ran back to the stroke victim, to push another mouthful of spaghetti into her, before she gave a quick bed bath to an exhausted, acquiescent Sheila. She then tucked the woman in and ran back to rescue Martha, who had been trying ineffectually to get out of the bath by herself.

With Martha safely reinstalled in her bed, Dorothy was still trying to persuade one of the dementias that the stone-cold meal she proffered was meant to be eaten, when the Matron walked in with the doctor. Dorothy, almost panic-stricken was still three bed baths short of the list given her to do. But it was no good worrying: the doctor would have to accept the stroke patient and the two dementias as they were: she was desperate to go home and sleep.

Matron frowned at Dorothy, but made no comment. A curtain was pulled round Sheila.

Martha swallowed. When you spoke to him, would this doctor be like the Vet, the dreaded Public Assistance doctor, provided by the City to look after the health of the poor? He was called the Vet because of his callousness: nobody went to him unless they were in unbearable pain.

A very apprehensive Martha listened attentively to the subdued conversation between the doctor and Sheila.

Unaware that the doctor was perhaps being prompted by the Holy Mother herself, Matron tried to interrupt him. The eavesdropper in the next bed felt much better when she heard the doctor curtly reprimand her. She don't know what Our Lady can do, Martha thought, remembering her frantic prayers and sensing her beloved presence.

Judging by Sheila's wincing, he was gently probing the healed stumps of her legs. He asked where they hurt and what exercise she was getting.

She heard Sheila laugh and say, 'I don't get none, Doctor.'

'But we have to strengthen your arms and back, Mrs McNally, so that you can help yourself, as the legs become less painful. I will see what can be arranged.

'I can't promise anything, but if your arms and upper back are strong, you should be able to do all kinds of things for yourself from a wheelchair. We'll have you breaking the speed limit yet!'

Martha heard Sheila chuckle. He sounded very kind, as he teased her into a better frame of mind and continued to give her hope that she might yet have a reasonable life.

'Dear Holy Mother, thank you,' breathed Martha with profound relief. No Vet ever talked to you like that.

She was so impressed by his voice that she took her artificial teeth out of their glass, where they had lain unused for a week in the same few inches of water. She stuffed them into her mouth. They tasted foul.

When the curtain was pulled around her bed, she sat up, however, and welcomed the physician with her best toothy grin.

He put his clipboard down on the bed, and said, 'Mrs Martha Connolly, I believe?' As he sat down on the commode, he held out his hand to be shaken.

She shook his hand heartily and let it go only reluctantly: she was so flattered to be addressed as Mrs Connolly. For once, she felt that she was a real person. He asked her questions similar to those he had asked Sheila, and her replies were the same.

'You see, I'm not really sick, Doctor, any more than Sheila is.' She glanced defiantly up at the Matron's stony face, and then back to the doctor.

'Me problem is that I don't have no home to go to. Nobody to help me if I leave here.' She did not bother him with the detail of how she came to be homeless; Liverpool always had plenty of waifs and strays.

He asked, 'What drugs are you taking?'

It was a leading question, because Matron had no record of her taking any medicines.

In response, Martha gaped at him. 'I has to take what Matron gives me,' she said.

'Were the pills prescribed by your general practitioner?'

'I don't know, Doctor.'

'Humph.' Many of the patients seemed to be on sedation of some kind. He must check the origins of their prescriptions: he knew that it was not uncommon for nursing homes to drug their patients 'to calm them, while they got used to their new surroundings'. He did not approve of the practice.

He stood up and turned to the Matron, who seemed unusually tense.

'I would like to examine Mrs Connolly's hip. Also, check her heart and lungs.'

Martha gulped, but allowed herself to be stripped of her backless nightgown by a silent, angry Matron.

After his examination, Martha modestly gathered up her nightgown to hide her flaccid breasts and bulging tummy.

'Do you have a next of kin, Mrs Connolly?' the doctor inquired. 'Nobody is named on your chart.'

'You mean a relation?'

'Yes. Somebody with whom you are usually in contact?'

'I got squads of kids; one of them's in Manchester,' she told him with a grin. 'But I don't hear from them, except for Number Nine.' As the doctor opened his mouth to say something, she hastily added, 'You see, Doctor, I can't read nor write. And you lose touch with people when they is scattered all over the earth.'

He understood. 'And who or what is Number Nine?' he inquired, his eyes twinkling.

Martha laughed. 'Oh, him? That's me youngest, James. Number Nine is his nickname.'

'And where is he? Do you know his address?'

With considerable pride, she told him that she certainly knew his address: he was in Manchester, doing a stint as assistant priest. 'But he don't know where I am. There was nobody here to write to him for me. And I don't have no money for a stamp.'

The doctor looked dumbfounded. 'Nobody could write for you?'

'No, sir.'

The Matron fidgeted uncomfortably: the doctor's examination of his patients was going much further than she had expected. She realised, too, that in this case, the next of kin had, somehow, been omitted from her meticulously kept records. As far as she could see, it was the first technical error that Dr Williams had found in his inquiries about her patients.

'Surely, Mrs Connolly, anybody would have done that for you,' the doctor protested.

'There was nobody who come to speak to me, except Angie – she's the aide – and she don't have

442

time to breathe, with sixty patients.' She paused, and then went on, her voice trembling at the recollection, 'For ages, nobody but me in this ward could even speak or do anything: they was paralysed, or like them over there.' She pointed towards the dementias. 'Not until Pat died; and Sheila, who you just seen next door, come in.'

The doctor decided that from somewhere he would have to get help: his practice had become so heavy that he could not take on much more. But to whom could he turn?

It can be safely assumed that the Holy Lady took note of the need for assistance from someone on earth who could be inspired to aid him and also give the Matron some guidance.

The doctor carefully lifted the bedclothes over Martha's naked legs, and promised to arrange exercise for her.

Dr Williams was a conscientious, well-respected man, but now he berated himself for having taken for granted Matron's goodwill towards her patients.

It was often said that there were two places in which you most needed a friend outside – when in hospital or when in gaol. Add to that a nursing home, particularly a privately owned one, he decided angrily.

It was certain that there had been neglect, and, in

some cases, malpractice, that the patients were too poor, too alone, too lacking in physical strength, often too ignorant, to defend themselves. They lacked someone to speak up for them.

The Matron had originally approached him to look after the medical needs of her patients, because, otherwise, the insurance company would have been chary about covering her.

The place was too neat, too quiet. It was not a hospital, so one would imagine that there would be some signs of normal residency. But no books or newspapers lay around, no picture postcards were pinned on walls adjacent to beds, such as he had seen in the homes of seagoing men. Nothing to suggest mental stimulus. He had not even seen a radio or a piano.

He had asked her if there was a sitting room where mobile patients might fraternise, but she had assured him that they were far too disabled to make use of such a place.

And there was no lift, so patients could not, without difficulty, walk very far – even if they could walk.

Some of the patients might be quite gifted, and, if given encouragement, might be able to play the piano for the other residents or get them together for a singsong or a game of cards. Something to lighten their lives should have been a priority of the home owner.

It had not occurred to him, at first, that she was the owner, that it was in her financial interest to keep her staff minimal and beds full at all times, preferably with patients who would have little opportunity to complain. He had imagined her as managing the Home for a corporate owner.

Now, as he encouraged them to speak out, the patients had been carefully polite, though pointed, in their remarks.

He was amazed that these pathetic women – and most of them were women – who still had their mental faculties, had not had complete mental breakdowns.

It would not cost much to make them happier. If they had a home to go to, one or two could certainly be discharged.

He wondered what further discoveries he might make if Matron were not present. Getting rid of her was impossible, however, because he was supposed to be chaperoned. He could not very well even demand the help of a nursing aide instead of her, while she was available.

An ordinary visitor would, however, not be chaperoned.

It was this latter thought which, on his return

home, made him pick up his phone to talk to the pastor of the nearest church: he remembered from the records that over half of the patients were Protestants of one denomination or another; a minority were Roman Catholics.

The pastor was shocked at his descripton of the sterility of life in the home, and at the lack of physical therapy or mental stimulus.

'And they are united in saying that the food is awful.'

'I must say that I have never visited it,' admitted the pastor. 'It is privately owned, you say? I do not usually go to such places unless invited.'

'It's like a human warehouse,' the doctor told him passionately. 'Some of those patients could be sent home. But it is obvious that they are afraid to speak up, and ask for what they need.

'The six I have examined thoroughly had no bruises, thank God. But most of them are anaemic and some of them are, I believe, being forced to take sedatives.

'I'm going to talk to the Ministry of Health; and I'll examine every single one of them within the next week or two, to see what can be done to help the poor souls in there.'

'More strength to your arm,' responded the minister.

'But they need someone to talk to freely, without the Matron listening in. Could you chance a snub from the owner, and go to see them?'

With some amusement at being asked to conspire with the doctor to get more information out of his patients, the pastor was at the same time a little worried about the breaking of the usual confidentiality between himself and his fellow believers.

He promised, however, that he would try to visit each one as a private person. 'Many of them have probably got relations keeping an eye on them,' he warned.

'As far as I can see, very, very few. But nobody minds a pastor visiting in a hospital, do they? Or a priest?'

'No. I visit public hospitals regularly and talk with each patient. They seem to enjoy a visitor, and the nursing staff are very cooperative. Quite often they need spiritual help.'

'Well, go for this, too. At worst, you could tell the Matron that I had asked you to visit all the Protestants. The woman can't very well object to a pastor being concerned with the spiritual welfare of her charges, can she? Keep a note for me of anything that you think I could help them with.'

'OK. Would you like me to talk to Father Thomas for you? You said there were some Catholics there.'

447

'Rather! I need all the help I can get. There's an old dear there called Connolly – I'm sure she would welcome a priest. She was so tense that she was clutching her rosary all the time Matron and I were seeing her.'

The doctor rang off. He leaned back in his chair to rest for a few minutes, before his evening surgery began.

While he sat looking at his loaded desk, he considered the Matron of the warehouse. She wasn't a wicked woman, he felt: she simply lacked any real warmth or compassion. She looked on her home as a business, say a boarding house, to be run efficiently and make money. She had probably imagined, when she began it, that visitors and relations would fill the emotional and social gaps.

When his wife brought him a cup of tea, he asked, 'Where, in the name of God, could I get at least two wheelchairs, preferably electric, free?'

'For free? Who for?' She sounded incredulous. She put the cup down in front of him.

'Yes. And probably a piano, some radios, a television set, some packs of cards, some board games – and, most of all, friendly volunteer visitors – and good therapists. Maybe the National Health would provide a physiotherapist, though the patients are supposed to be beyond help.'

His wife looked at him aghast. 'Gosh! Is it that place you called the warehouse, which you've been so worried about lately?'

'Yes, I'm doing a very careful survey, and it's pitiful.'

'Sounds as if you need Father Christmas.'

The doctor's wife saw the earnest appeal in her husband's tired eyes, the prematurely lined face, and she appreciated the tangle he was in.

Something had to be done. But say the wrong thing and he could be sued for libel: from what he had told her about the Matron, she sounded both shrewd and ruthless. He should never have agreed to take the job in the first place, dear fool.

Simply to cheer him up, she grinned mischievously, and promised, 'I'll find out. There are hordes of charities in the city I can ask.'

'Could you, love? It would be so worthwhile. There are probably other places, equally bad.'

'Well, to be honest, now that Josh and Emelda are married, I really need something to do. It will give me an interest.'

'It could be a lot of work,' he warned.

'Let's talk about it in detail tomorrow, when you may not be quite so busy. I would need to know more about the place and to visit it myself.'

And so it was agreed.

And thus the word went round; she knew her Liverpool.

A small advertisement for a wheelchair for a woman who could not afford one produced five within a few days, most of their owners having departed for the cemetery.

In no time the doctor's wife had formed a small committee, consisting of a physiotherapist, Lavinia; a speech therapist, Edwina, and several other friends who had kindly volunteered. It was agreed that Lavinia and Edwina would visit the care Home and report back.

'At least, we two can go as private visitors and take a look,' Edwina said, unaware that this willingness had drawn an approving smile from a Dear Lady.

THIRTY-NINE

'Rubbish'

1965

'Well, I'm buggered!' exclaimed Martha to Sheila, after the pastor had called on them two days after the doctor's visit. She cackled with laughter. 'Never in me life did I imagine I'd be talking to a Prottie sin-shifter!'

A dozing Sheila smiled vaguely. 'He were nice, though,' she said with an effort. 'And he can't help being a Prottie: he were probably born one.'

'Oh, aye. Nice, he is. You saw how I told him I got out of bed after Angie finished with us last evening, and went for a little walk down the passage, though me poor knees creaked something awful. And I said how much I wished I had a walking stick.

'And he said he got a spare and would bring it in if the doctor said I could walk. I can't get over it.'

'Right.' Sheila made an effort to rouse herself. She felt so lethargic after the pills she was being forced to swallow each night that even Martha could not get any further response from her. She closed her eyes and was soon asleep again.

Two days later, for the same reason, she missed two ladies who tiptoed into the ward.

Downstairs, they had told Rosie, the cleaning lady, who had answered the door bell and had let them in, that they were visitors to see Mrs Connolly, first floor.

She had directed them up the fine mahogany staircase to Martha's room, and had then continued mopping the tiled floor of the entrance hall. After a moment, though, she stopped work. Should she have let them in? she worried: it was not her job and Matron might not like strangers coming in.

She hesitated. She knew that Matron was in the basement kitchen, talking to the cook.

She decided that she would do nothing: the ladies would probably leave within half an hour. Matron would never know about them. She resumed her mopping.

Matron, therefore, had no idea that her domain was being inspected.

Since they had never seen Martha, Edwina, speech

452

therapist, and Lavinia, physiotherapist, stopped by the first bed they came to, which smelled like a latrine. The person in it opened her eyes, stared bewilderedly at them and muttered inarticulately.

'She said she's Florence,' explained the speech therapist. She smiled at the patient and nodded at her understandingly.

'Mrs C can talk properly,' whispered the physio. They both smiled again at the incapacitated patient and then passed to the dementia victims tied by short ropes to their beds. On seeing strangers, they retreated to the length of their ropes and gibbered threats at the strangers.

Slowly, softly and distinctly the speech therapist replied gently to them. Nobody ever spoke to them like that, and, after looking at each other like frightened monkeys, they relapsed into surprised acceptance of their presence.

'Who you wanting?' asked a harsh voice from the other side of the room.

They both jumped and turned. 'Mrs Connolly?'

'Oh aye, that's me. Come on over. Who are you?'

They approached a little shrimp in an untidy bed, the only untidy bed in the room.

No doubt about this one being able to talk. She was already saying, 'One of you can sit on the commode, and you bring that chair from the other side of Sheila's bed.' The shrimp pointed to a chair on the far side of the next bed. 'It's nice to see yez.' She then inquired again, 'Who are you?'

They explained that Dr Williams had said that she might like a visitor, so they had come.

The physiotherapist sat on the commode and hoped that she would not smell too badly when she left. She leaned over and put a small parcel in Martha's lap. 'I'm Lavinia,' she said, 'and this is Edwina.'

Martha bobbed her head in acknowledgement. This was proving to be quite an entertaining day, she decided. She looked down at the parcel.

'It's for you,' Edwina assured her. 'We thought you might enjoy a few chocolates.'

The pinched little face, surrounded by a loose mass of white hair, was turned slowly upon the two women. The light-blue, bloodshot eyes were filled with tears.

'Well, I never! That's real nice of you.' Then Martha burst out with sudden confidence, 'I haven't never had a present since I been here – nor a visitor till a few days back. A priest come – a Prottie. It were a real surprise.'

She paused to look down at the pretty box in her lap, and then said, 'Can I open them?'

The parcel was unwrapped, the little box opened and, upon Martha's insistence, the visitors had a chocolate each pressed upon them. Martha felt that they were now her guests, and she beamed at them, as she popped a chocolate into her own toothless mouth, and slowly savoured the first one she had tasted for years.

She then put two chocolates down on the clean sheet beside her pillow. 'Them's for Sheila when she wakes up,' she explained, and gestured towards the next bed.

'That's very thoughtful of you,' praised Lavinia.

Both ladies were then inundated with an almost unbelievable story of how Sheila in the next bed had been given a pill each evening for the past four days. 'Just because she spoke up and asked for her pocket money and then swore at the Matron when she didn't get it. She's sleepin' most of the time, poor dear.'

Feeling a little smug at being able to tell the tale to an outsider, Martha leaned back and folded her hands on her stomach. She said indignantly, 'You can't hardly believe it, can you? She done no harm and she tried not to take the pills, but she were held down. And her with no legs, poor soul!'

'No legs!' Lavinia winced, and glanced round towards the sleeping woman.

'That's right.'

'Perhaps Dr Williams prescribed a painkiller?' suggested Edwina.

'Rubbish! Not him. He were talking about a wheelchair for her.'

Martha looked righteously outraged, as she unclasped her hands and shook a knobbly finger at Edwina. 'If Matron don't want to be bothered with you, you get a pill – so, believe you me, you mind what you do and what you say.'

Martha picked up the box of chocolates and again proffered it to each lady in turn. They both politely refused, but suggested that Martha herself have another one.

Martha did – on the theory that you never knew what Matron might get up to if she found contraband chocolates in the place: best to eat them now, before she heard about them.

After hearing the story of how she had broken her hip and lost her home, Martha's visitors took their leave.

Martha's expressions of thanks for their visit were almost pitiful. As she clung to their hands, they promised to come again.

They then tiptoed in and out of the other rooms on the floor, staying a few minutes with any patient who seemed able to communicate with them. They were made politely welcome. They did the same in the wards on the top floor.

Feeling completely depressed after looking into the faces of so many old, obviously fairly helpless patients, they slowly descended the stairs. Nowhere did they find anyone attending to the residents: and, in two cases, they themselves poured glasses of water for patients who asked for them.

Lavinia swallowed. Then she said slowly, 'It's the silence that gets me. And their awful look of patient resignation. I've always found that old people love to talk their heads off.'

Edwina smiled in response. 'It's true,' she agreed.

Finally, down in the hall, the indifferent Rosie, who was now cleaning the glass doors, unlocked them and ushered the ladies out.

At the bottom of the front steps, Lavinia took in a great breath of fresh air. In the trees birds sang, and in a nearby flowerbed early pansies bloomed.

'Poor devils!' she ejaculated. 'They should be out here, enjoying the sunshine.'

Edwina slowly pulled on her gloves, as she nodded agreement. 'I wonder how many places there are like this?'

'Too many, I suspect,' replied Lavinia soberly.

As they walked slowly back to her car, she said,

with considerably more spirit, 'But we can see what we can do for this one.

'You know, we should make our committee as strong as we can,' she continued. Her voice lightened. 'Get a VIP to be president, at least a duchess. What do you say?'

Not to be outdone, Edwina replied, 'What about our MP? He's a member of the Opposition. He could ask questions in Parliament about the care of the elderly, couldn't he?'

Lavinia cheered up considerably. 'Brilliant! That would draw attention to other similar Homes, wouldn't it?'

'It would.' Edwina sighed a sigh as gusty as any that Martha could produce. 'I don't know how either of us is going to find the time for all this – both with kids and full-time jobs.'

They were, of course, unaware that a far more important lady than any duchess was taking an interest in two humble elderly women from the waterfront, who represented so many others. She thought a local Roman Catholic duchess, whose humble prayers she received from time to time, would be an excellent choice, and could perhaps be motivated to become a patron. She was a very capable woman.

To Edwina and Lavinia that afternoon it seemed

that they suddenly received a huge infusion of physical and mental energy. They both felt imbued by a sense of power for which they could not account.

As Lavinia unlocked the car door, she said thoughtfully, 'You know, one day . . .'

Edwina smiled at her, as she immediately interjected, 'One day, we'll be old, too.'

Their laughter was rueful, as they acknowledged this fact.

FORTY

Dreams of a Plate a' Ribs and Cabbage

1965

A few days after Edwina's and Lavinia's visit, Martha emptied the box of chocolates, except for one, which she had determined to save for Angie.

To fill in the time and with an unfocused sense of gratitude for small wonders which seemed to be occurring, wonders like the promise of a walking stick, three nice visitors and a box of chocolates, she decided to say a full decade on her rosary. She was still at it, with eyes closed, when Angie came in with a tea tray for her.

'Bread and margarine and jam and a slice of plain cake!'

Martha put down her rosary and looked disconsolately at the tray. It was what she would have eaten herself at home, provided she had had a main meal at lunchtime. But a small portion of liver and boiled potatoes, followed by inadequately cooked rice pudding, had not felt particularly filling.

'What I wouldn't give for a good plate of ribs and cabbage cooked meself,' she sighed. Then, as she picked up her knife, she remembered Angie's unexplained day off the previous week. Out of curiosity, she asked, 'Where were you, Angie? I missed you the other day.'

Angie was shaking a lethargic Sheila into wakefulness. 'Just took a day off,' she replied absently. 'Come on, Sheila, girl.'

As Sheila slowly sat up, Angie turned back to Martha, and added with an elfish grin, 'Said I was sick to me stummick.'

'Holy Mary! Matron'll fire you if you do that very often.'

'I don't care. I went and got another job.'

'You never!'

'I did. Start in a month's time.'

Martha felt like someone about to be bereaved.

'Where?' she asked dully, through a mouthful of bread and margarine.

Angie's face lit up.

'Oh, Martha,' she whispered, 'it's real nice. It's to look after an invalid lady. There's a little cottage by the gate where me and Star and Dad can live.

And he's going to be the gardener – he's that set up about it. It's near a village.'

'Humph!' grunted Martha. 'You'll be run off your feet with two houses to keep.'

'No, I won't. She's got a housekeeper, too. All I got to do is look after Mrs Bowen herself, personal attendant – like I have to do for you and the others here. And look after Dad and Star, what I do now.'

Even sleepy Sheila, struggling to make her eyes focus, turned her head towards the aide, as Angie stood between the beds, and went on.

'When I answered the ad, it were for a husband and wife; I thought I'd better tell her we was father and daughter. And I said we was black, 'cos some folks can't stand us.' She shrugged at her last remark, as if she accepted that it was a fact of life. 'I really didn't think she'd answer. But she did – and we liked each other on sight.'

'What about Star? She's got to get some learning,' said Martha, aware of her own great lack of it.

'Mrs Bowen says she can go to the village school – and she'll ask the school teachers to watch her, so she don't get bullied.'

Martha was quiet, as she chewed. Then she said, 'We'll really miss you, love, won't we, Sheila?

Don't know what we'll do without you.' Then she remembered the chocolate and took the little box out from under her pillow. She held it out shyly to the girl, and said, 'I kept this for you. You was so busy this past day or two, I forgot to give it to you.'

A surprised Angie opened the box.

'It's all I've got to give you, after I shared them with Sheila and the ladies,' Martha said with real regret. 'Those two strange ladies who come to visit me give me a box of them.'

Angie came round the side of the bed to lean over the little woman. She put her arms round her and hugged her closely. She said, 'I'll miss you, too. Tell you what, though, I'll write to yez – and maybe Sheila will read it for you.'

Sheila put down her mug of tea. Her head was clearing. 'For sure, I will. Don't I get a hug, too?'

She was duly hugged.

Angie said, 'I were talking to the cook downstairs, and there's a rumour that this place is to get a real overhaul. Department of Public Health, and all. Sounds as if things will be better for you.'

'Oh, I hope you're right,' said Sheila fervently.

'They might close it down if Matron don't pull her socks up,' warned Angie.

Martha looked shocked. Fear swept through her

of what those terrifying people, the Theys, could do once they got started. 'Where would we go?' she asked apprehensively.

'Right,' replied Sheila. 'Where could they put us?'

It had not been Angie's intention to scare her two patients, and she said quickly, 'Matron's nothing but a bloody bean-counter, for all she claims to be a registered nurse. But if They put enough pressure on her and watched her, this place could be quite good. One thing, if they put in a lift, then folk like you could move around.'

Sheila's grunt was dismissive.

'Why not, Sheila? You could learn to lift yourself out of bed and into a wheelchair and away you go; with a few alterations in a kitchen, you could keep house in a flat. And I've caught Martha here walking not so badly.' Angie smiled down at her favourite patient.

Without much real hope, Sheila and Martha awaited events. They both noted with relief that no more nightly pills were pressed upon Sheila: a shaken Lavinia had told Dr Williams about it, and the outraged doctor had, over the telephone, reduced the Matron to tears, a phenomenal victory.

A week later, a sturdy walking stick was delivered

to the nursing home, with instructions from Dr Williams that it was for the use of Mrs Connolly, who was to be encouraged to walk. It was taken in by Rosie, who brought it upstairs to Martha.

Since the Matron rarely visited the first floor, it was some time before this dereliction of duty on Rosie's part was discovered: a jubilant Martha was already walking quite steadily on the day she bumped into Matron escorting Dr Williams upstairs to the second floor, where lay two more patients whom the doctor felt should, like Martha, be able to walk.

Dr Williams expressed his pleasure at seeing an upright Martha. The Matron said nothing. Looking at her face, Martha began to fear a pill.

She managed to get herself back into bed, and, after a moment's thought, lifted the stick in with her. 'With that bitch, you never know: she might take it away.'

She leaned back on her pillow and spent the next several hours, including teatime, filled with foreboding, until Freda, the evening aide, shook her out of a doze.

'Come on,' she said sharply. 'Time for bed. Get out and do a pee before I put the lights out.'

Sheila was already perilously poised on a bedpan, and she giggled, as Freda went over to persuade the dementias to do similarly. 'No pills!' she whispered gleefully.

'You're right,' responded Martha. 'Thanks be!'

Martha said her prayers, her face alight.

Like a pair of Sleeping Beauties, they slept soundly and naturally, as hope lifted their spirits.

They awoke to the usual sounds of Angie's heavy tread across the wooden floor, and her cry, 'Time for up, girls,' and then the nervous whimpers of the dementias, as they struggled up in their beds in alarm. A basin, with a ewer of warm water beside it, was plonked on a table beside the stroke victim, and she was swiftly wiped down.

Martha, who had for much of her life managed with little water, did not complain when her hands and face were washed in the same water. Sheila, however, refused to use it. An irritated Angie, who knew she was in the wrong, but was, as usual, hard-pressed, snatched up the basin, took it to the bathroom and threw the water away.

Without a further word, the basin was refilled from the ewer and presented to Sheila.

Looking as upright and determined as she must have done before she was disabled, a tight-lipped Sheila triumphantly washed her hands and wiped her face.

Though she was fond of Angie, Martha watched

the scene in awe. Sheila had actually corrected an aide! Long since drained from Martha was the determined optimism and physical strength which had got her through her earlier years, when she had fought to keep her family fed. Her later isolation in a respectable Protestant neighbourhood had also taught her to keep her mouth shut. Our Sheila was being real brave, she decided.

Angie had barely given the faces of the dementias a quick wipe, when the dumbwaiter rumbled up to their floor from the kitchen. She opened the tiny lift's wooden door and took out the ward's breakfast trays. Breathing hard, she carried the five trays, balanced on top of each other, to Martha's commode and dumped them down.

As a tray of porridge and slopped tea was handed to Sheila, which she was expected to balance precariously on her thighs as best she could, the invalid continued to be her usual acerbic self.

'I feel I come from Glasgow,' she remarked to Martha, as she dipped her spoon into the milkless porridge. 'With so much of this stuff, I'll be wearing a kilt next.'

Martha suddenly choked with laughter. Here was Sheila as she ought to be. She hoped frantically that pills could, for ever, be crossed off their list of nightmares.

They spent most of the morning discussing whether one really could arrange a scullery so that an invalid in a wheelchair might be able to cook.

'I gave up me home,' confided Sheila. 'It were a little house. I reckoned I was stuck for life in this place – and I may be yet. Me next-door neighbour what used to come to visit me in the hospital put some of my stuff in her attic, but most of it were sold.'

Martha nodded, her expression dismal. 'Same with me,' she said. 'I don't own nothing. And I lost touch with most of me friends when I moved to the Dingle.'

When they were supposed to be taking an afternoon nap, they were, instead, still enjoying a great game, as they explored ways to arrange a scullery for a wheelchair, and what fun they could have together cooking their favourite meals.

'Tripe and onions!' cried Sheila.

'Ribs and cabbage!' Martha almost shrieked.

They were still laughing at their wild bursts of imagination when the muffled sound of male voices arguing in the hall below drifted up to them.

They paused in their discussion, suddenly fearful that they had made too much noise.

Martha queried, 'Doctor giving Matron what for?'

More than one pair of boots could be heard trudging up the long staircase.

FORTY-ONE

'Kids Is the World's Worst Liars'

1965

Both women looked up as, through the open door, two men almost burst into the room.

A dumbfounded Martha was engulfed in two sets of arms, as the men chorused, 'Mam, Martha, thank God we've found you!'

As Martha looked into Number Nine's wide, innocent blue eyes, she burst into tears.

'Oh, Jamie, love, I never thought to see you again.' She turned to the other young man, 'Danny, me love. Oh, Danny!'

An amazed Sheila was spellbound. Then she noticed Number Nine's cassock, and, as Daniel produced a pocket handkerchief to mop up Martha's tears, she ventured to ask, 'Are you Martha's boys?'

'He is,' replied Daniel, giving Number Nine a

friendly poke with his elbow. 'I'm just a friend.'

'Not just a friend,' replied Martha through her sniffs. 'He's Mary Margaret's boy, what I told you about.' A scrawny arm came out from the confining sheets, to wrap round Daniel.

'Aye, how you've grown. You're a real man! Haven't seen you since the war. Whatever happened to you?'

Sheila gulped. She was determined not to spoil the reunion for Martha by crying. But such an arrow of pure loneliness shot through her that she badly wanted to scream to high heaven with the pain of it.

Martha gathered her wits, while a very handsome man sat down on either side of her bed. Each of them held a tiny gnarled hand.

'How did you find me?' she demanded. 'I couldn't even find somebody to write to tell you where I was.'

'Somebody here would have done it, Mam. Surely they would?'

'Not this place,' spat Martha.

James decided to leave that issue to another time. He said, 'All the letters I had written to you for weeks past, at home, came back in a bunch, last week. They were marked "Gone away". It scared me to death, because they were so old.

'Usually, you'd get Tara to read them to you,

and occasionally she'd write a line back for you. So I asked for a week's leave, and was given it.

'I went to our house, and a perfect stranger answered the door. I was really amazed.'

Martha gave him a special squeeze. 'Poor lad!'

Number Nine smiled at her. 'The man said that he had returned all the letters in one go. He had kept them on the mantelpiece, because he didn't know what to do with them. Finally, he asked the rent collector for advice, and had been told how to return them, and he did so.'

Martha interjected, 'And Tara went to Ireland, to Cork, to live with her married daughter, a couple of weeks before I fell down the stairs – I miss her. She wouldn't know where I was neither.'

James paused, and nodded, and then went on, 'I wasn't too sure what to do next. So I tried next door.'

He grinned mischievously, and Martha saw again her beloved little boy. 'The woman there was obviously very surprised to have what looked like a Catholic priest on her doorstep. She nearly slammed the door on me. I told her quickly that I was trying to trace my mother, and she then said that you had been taken to hospital weeks and weeks ago – didn't know which hospital. Didn't know you, only of you. Not very helpful.

'She had seen the bailiffs take over – and had bought one of our chairs at the sale which they held.'

'Blasted Prottie,' muttered Martha angrily. 'Would hardly speak to me because I'm Catholic. Wall-to-wall Protties, it is, down there. All through the war, as you may remember, they made us feel small.'

Once they had moved from the court, James had been very short of playmates, other than his brother and sister. He ignored his mother's bitterness, however, and smiled at her.

He continued, 'I tried all the hospitals. Nobody answering to your description was on their lists. I was beside myself. And I didn't have much money for tram fares, and so on.'

Daniel spoke up. 'So he went to see old Auntie Ellen – she lives with Shaun – she's never been well since she was wounded in the war. You'll remember what a bad time she had – and Shaun himself?'

'Oh, aye, I do.'

'Well, Number Nine stayed the night with her. And, by chance, I docked the next morning. Signed off and came up to see her. I were proper surprised to find Jamie visiting her too,' he finished irrelevantly. Then he said with pride, 'We done all the hospitals again, together.'

James smiled gently. 'We got the bursars to check

ex-patients' files – you'd be surprised how many Martha Connollys there are who've been treated in hospitals over the years!

'Once they understood more precisely what had happened, they were very good and it didn't take long. The lady who found you said I had been notified, as I was your next of kin. But they had our home address not the seminary's – an empty house – so the letter was returned.'

He sighed and glanced at silent, sad-looking Sheila. Then he said, 'And that's how you were handed over to a social worker, Mam. Somebody had to take care of you.'

His mother nodded reluctant agreement. 'I remember the woman. She said to sign this, sign that. So I make me cross; and all I knew was that I would be sent here to be looked after till I was better.'

She looked at her son and then kissed him again. 'Jaysus, I'm so thankful you come.'

A startled, but delighted, Angie performed a minor miracle by squeezing four cups of tea out of the kitchen.

As she thankfully sipped her tea, Martha asked in curiosity, 'What happened to Dollie and Connie and little Minnie? Were they found and do you still see them?'

Daniel grinned. 'Oh, aye, I see them from time to time.'

Martha's face lit up. 'Tell us,' she urged.

Sprawled on the end of her bed, he paused to gather his memories, and began.

'Well, you know, in the war, some of the civilian population, folk like us, was much less looked after than They would like you to believe. It was simply because of the pure muddle of fighting a war and feeding people and everything: nothing worked quite perfectly, specially for bunches of nobodies like us what often didn't know what we was supposed to be doing.

'Remember our Dollie? Now, she was tough, you know that, and she were eleven years old by then, quite capable of looking after other kids. And she was scared stiff, after Mam died. And, of course, Dad and me, we were at sea.

'The three girls were bundled off into care, and within two days they was evacuated with the other children to Shropshire. It seems that in the general rush to get the children out of the city, no paperwork was done on them – I guess They thought They would catch up on it once they was safe from being bombed.

'Dollie told me the three of them was absolutely terrified, because they didn't understand what was

475

happening to them, except that their mam was dead and their dad was at sea, and none of Them seemed to like Auntie Ellen or Grandma Theresa. They didn't seem to have a single familiar person to cling to. She said they were bundled about in all kinds of strange places by women who didn't even know their names and fed food they didn't like by these strangers.

'They ended up with a crowd of other kids they'd never seen before outside a railway station, and more strangers came to look at them. They were even more scared when the strangers picked out a child or children and took them away. It was clear, she said, that nobody wanted three dirty little girls, even if they were evacuees fleeing from the expected raids on Liverpool.

'So they slid behind a parked car and then run like hell down a back lane of what must've been a village in Shropshire.

'That night, a farmer found them curled up together, sleeping in his stable. They were cold and hungry, and Dollie had told Connie and Minnie not to say a word to anyone. When the farmer tried to get them to say who they were, none of them answered, so he persuaded them to come in to see his wife. She bathed them, to warm them up, she said, and then gave them some breakfast and soon they were out collecting eggs with her. She got their first names out of them. But they all lied that they did not know their surnames or their address – and, of course, they really didn't know the address of the Home they'd been taken to. But the farmer knew from their voices that they come from Liverpool.

'Dollie said she thought he wanted them to stay and work for him, because his daughter and his labourer were both called up. Because, you know, they wasn't helpless. Dollie was over eleven, Connie was about eight and even Minnie was over six. Many a farmer's kids are helping by that age.

'When he went to market, he inquired if They had any children that they still wanted to billet. He was told that they had all gone.

'So he must have simply chanced keeping them without saying any more. Who would notice, anyway? Within a few weeks, they would be regarded as the farmer's three evacuees from Liverpool.

'And Dollie kept them there until the war ended. It wasn't all beer and pickles, and Connie said that at first Minnie cried a lot. But the farmer's wife grew very fond of them and fed them reasonable.

'Dollie never thought of trying to write to me, care of Auntie Ellen. She reckoned, anyways, that, once they connected with Liverpool again, they would be put back in an orphanage, and their life on the farm was much better than any orphanage would be.

'Each morning they went to school, and Dollie gave their full names. But she said they were orphans and had no family left in Liverpool. She said she was deliberately vague about how they had come to be evacuated. The school was quite disorganised, because another evacuated school was foisted on it in the afternoons. Our Dollie was always a good liar, and her story was accepted without query.

'When I was trying to find them, the people I talked to wasn't much help, and even the police accepted the billeting officer's word that they could be easily traced and that their brother would be informed of where they were.

'Connie told me that they heard on the farm's radio about the bombing of Liverpool, and that scared the three of them even more.'

Martha smiled lovingly into Number Nine's neatly shaven face, and then turned to ask Danny, 'So where are they now, poor little lambs?'

Danny laughed. 'Our Dollie was never a poor little lamb. They're all married and with kids of their own now. Before the end of the war, when Dollie was fourteen, she had had enough and demanded that the three of them go back to Liverpool – 'cos most evacuees had returned. By that time, the police had finally traced them anyway They ended up in foster homes for a bit, in Liverpool. Later on, we all lived together for a while in a little flat, with a social worker keeping an eye on us. The girls, as they left school got jobs.

'And who did they marry?' Sheila ventured to ask.

'Dollie's married to a bus conductor, Connie's hubby is a motor mechanic, and Minnie did quite well for herself. In 1953, she was an usher in a cinema, and there she met our George, a crane driver. He was a great picture-goer; even now, you can't unglue him from the telly when there's a good film on.' He laughed at his recollection of his kindly brother-in-law.

'And what about you?' Sheila's eyes twinkled as she surveyed the fine-looking, middle-aged man.

'Me?' He reddened, and then said shyly, 'Well, I'm courting. I'm a bosun now, earning well; but I wanted to be free of any domestic responsibility for a while . . .'

Sheila nodded. 'But having nobody of your own is lonely, isn't it?'

'Aye, it is. I've finally realised it!' He grinned.

This exchange between Danny and Sheila alerted

479

Martha to her friend's inner desolation, in comparison with her own joy. She broke in, 'Aye, Sheila, love, you must be feeling lonely, like nothing on earth. But you don't have to worry. You've got me. And Number Nine will keep an eye on both of us, won't you, Jamie?'

'Of course,' he replied without hesitation and with a gentle smile towards Sheila. 'I've already asked if I can be moved to a Liverpool parish.'

He had not yet realised that in addition to finding his mother, for which he was truly thankful, he had acquired an adopted Auntie Sheila.

Still less did he realise that a certain Great Lady, to whom he frequently addressed his prayers, was enlisting mortals to arrange that mother and aunt would, for years, look after him, and, often, his fellow priests, as they ministered to a Liverpool flock.

To be free to do his job properly, the Great Lady had argued to herself, even the holiest, most humble of priests needs a housekeeper. In a presbytery, with their pensions restored to them, so that they were not wholly dependent upon Number Nine, these two elderly ladies, between them, would do very well; over the years they would probably look after a number of priests.

And she would make sure that she motivated a

handyman in their parish who could and would adapt a kitchen to a wheelchair.

Satisfied, that she had done her best as an interceder, she quietly blessed the little group around the bed in the care home, and equally quietly withdrew.

Martha and Sheila never forgot her. Regularly in their prayers, they thanked the Dear Lady and her Beloved Son for their extraordinary good luck, as they felt it must be, to have such a nice presbytery in which to live and such good men to care for.

Twopence to Cross the Mersey

Helen Forrester

Helen Forrester's poignant story of her poverty-stricken childhood in Liverpool during the 1930s has become a bestselling modern classic.

When Helen Forrester's father went bankrupt in 1930, she and her six siblings were forced from comfortable middle-class life in southern England to utmost poverty in the Depression-ridden North. The running of the household, in slum surroundings and with little food, and the care of the younger children all fell on twelve-year-old Helen. She writes about her experiences without self-pity but rather with a rich sense of humour which makes her touching account of these grim days before the Welfare State funny as well as painful.

'Records, with remarkable steadiness and freedom from self-pity, the story of a childhood that . . . most people would have set down in rage and despair'
EDWARD BLISHEN, *Books and Bookmen*

'Her restraint and humour in describing this stark history makes it all the more moving' *Daily Telegraph*

ISBN 0 00 636168 4

Lime Street at Two

Helen Forrester

'An extraordinary autobiographical document'   *Observer*

Helen Forrester continues the moving story of her early poverty-stricken life with an account of the war years in blitz-torn Liverpool, and the happiness which she so nearly captured but which was to elude her twice.

In 1940 Helen, now twenty, reeling from the news that her fiancé Harry has been killed on an Atlantic convoy, is working long hours at a welfare centre in Bootle, five miles from home. Her wages are pitifully low, and her mother claims the whole of them for the housekeeping. Then early in 1941 she gets a new job, and begins to enjoy herself a little. But in May the bombing starts again and another move brings more trouble to Helen, trouble which will be faced, as ever, with courage and determination.

'Remarkable that from so bleak and unloving a background came a writer of such affectionate understanding and unsettling honesty'   *Sunday Telegraph*

'What makes this writer's self-told tale so memorable? . . . An absolute recall, a genius for the unforgettable detail, the rare chance of subject'   *The Good Book Guide*

ISBN 0 00 637000 4